PRAISE FOR FRANK
PORTOFINO

"Great insight and unselfconscious humor."   —*Publishers Weekly*

"Calvin's observations reveal the ironies of a family that speaks in biblical phrases but faces all-too-human foibles . . . Under Mr. Schaeffer's graceful rendering, this is a story of sympathetic characters, a deft feat considering some of their narrow views." —*Washington Times*

"Delightful . . . a wickedly funny story."   —*Chattanooga Times*

"Wonderfully lucid and witty . . . *Portofino* walks a beautifully balanced line between the serious and the humorous, poking gentle fun at the foibles of religious zealotry without disparaging the deep dedication behind it. Hilariously funny at times." —*Anniston Star*

"A wry coming-of-age tale . . . splendid laugh-out-loud moments."
—*Kirkus Reviews*

"Charming."   —*Boston Sunday Globe*

"Richly ironic and satirical. At times it borders on hilarious . . . wickedly charming."   —*Milwaukee Journal*

"Schaeffer, by turns, is sentimental, celebratory, evocative and very funny, but we are never far from a sense that harshness and violence are real; we are never entirely sure how things will turn out . . . A rich brew of cross-cultural comedy . . . enlivened by discoveries and misapprehensions, family squabbles and healings and the dizzy sensibility of a boy whose world opens up in all kinds of poignant and hilarious ways . . . Shaeffer makes this utterly unpredictable family—besides the parents, there are Calvin's two sharply drawn older sisters—both painful and appealing." —*Los Angeles Times Book Review*

"[A] sweet-natured, comic tale."

—*Kirkus Reviews*

"Funny . . . poignant . . . Shaeffer manages to be both irreverent and sympathetic toward the foibles of this hilarious holier-than-thou family . . . What's wonderful about this loopy coming-of-age story is Schaeffer's sensitivity in showing Calvin's need to break from a family he both despises and loves."

—*St. Paul Pioneer Press*

"Clever, humorous, and satisfying."

—*Booklist*

"Schaeffer's greatest feat is transforming Calvin from a rotten little kid into a character so compelling that I felt as if he were pulling me through the pages . . . On a par with Calvin's metamorphosis is Schaeffer's near-perfect touch with the details of religion. Somehow he manages to integrate the most serious issues of religious practice, even explaining their relevance to a less-informed reader, without losing the flow of the novel."

—*St. Petersburg Times*

"Irreverent, amusing . . . Schaeffer's slapstick jokes and often tender evocations of youth make for an uneasy but entertaining cross between *Portnoy's Complaint* and TV's *The Wonder Years*."

—*Publishers Weekly*

Also by Frank Schaeffer

THE CALVIN BECKER TRILOGY

Portofino

Zermatt

Saving Grandma

NON-FICTION

Keeping Faith
A Father–Son Story About Love
and the United States Marine Corps

Faith of Our Sons
A Father's Wartime Diary

Saving Grandma

FRANK SCHAEFFER

CARROLL & GRAF PUBLISHERS
NEW YORK

SAVING GRANDMA

Carroll & Graf Publishers
An Imprint of Avalon Publishing Group Inc.
245 West 17th Street
New York, NY 10011

Library of Congress Cataloging-in-Publication Data is available.

ISBN: 0-7867-1391-7

Printed in the United States of America
Distributed by Publishers Group West

For my children Jessica, Francis, and John

Saving
Grandma

Chapter 1

MASTER CALVIN BECKER   JENNIFER BAZLINTON

L'ARCHE   1 HARROW COURT

CHALET LES TULIPES   LONDON W1

TROIS-TORRENTS-SUR-MONTHEY   ENGLAND

VALAIS

SWITZERLAND

April 1, 1967

Dear Twit,

How are you? This is just a friendly little reminder to return my mask and snorkel that you walked off with! If you don't want your neck twisted, deliver them safe and sound when you come out at the holls!

Love, J

PS. I presume you *will* put in an appearance as per usual? If not please inform.

PPS. No amount of prayer meetings will deliver you from my unholy wrath if you fail me!!!

Mom handed me the postcard.

"I wish she'd be less flippant. Maybe this year the Lord will open the door to your sharing the Gospel with her."

I tried to avoid Mom's glance.

1

"Uh-huh."

Once again I wished that I could read well enough to decipher Jennifer's handwriting and that Mom had not chosen to read Jennifer's card out loud in front of my sisters.

Rachael always wanted to pry information out of me about the state of Jennifer's soul and Janet made fun of me about how Jennifer was my girlfriend. But Jennifer was a lot more than a girlfriend, she was my best friend.

I never talked about Jennifer if I could help it. I had known her since we were three years old. Our birthdays were only a month apart. I watched her grow more beautiful each year we met on the beach at Paraggi, near Portofino, Italy, where our families had been vacationing for twelve years.

Rachael must have seen me staring at my feet, trying not to look at Janet, who was smirking about the postcard. Rachael was curious but not mean, so she changed the subject before Janet could make one of her nasty remarks about English girls being stuck-up, or warn me about getting too attached to an unsaved, worldly girl.

"God has blessed us with a wonderful family," said Rachael.

"You mean Grandmother?" muttered Janet.

Mom fixed Janet with her brightest reproving smile.

"The Lord has been good to us in spite of your father's unfortunate mother!"

Dad didn't say anything about how good God was even though Mom turned to him expectantly. She was probably wishing he would say something like, "And the thing I am most thankful for is the wonderful wife the Lord has given me!"

If Dad had said that, then our rare family day off and stroll down the Montreux quay would have been perfect, complete, the sort of time Mom called a special gift. Dad was not in one of his Moods, or anything like that. It was just that since Grandmother arrived in 1965, two years before, Dad hardly ever joined Mom and my sisters in times of praise and thanksgiving anymore. He seemed to get less joyful in the Lord with every day that passed. Not that Dad had ever been as close to the Lord as Mom. Rachael once said that Dad was a much less mature Christian than Mom.

In the spring of 1967, my father wasn't a happy man. He was forty-seven years old. He looked his age. He had had no regular exercise since he was in college, where he was an alternate on the hurdles team. Dad never won anything. Mom said he was too short even by the athletic standards of the late 1930s. Now he had a potbelly and a sour expression. The only time he seemed happy was when he was preaching. He'd smile for dramatic effect. Mom said that his working-class background had a long reach, that since he became born-again Dad had changed some, but that his perfection would only be achieved in heaven. Dad wore khaki pants and plaid shirts except for Sundays when he preached; then he wore his black suit.

Mom was forty-five and beautiful. My oldest sister, Janet, who was nineteen, said how it was amazing that Dad managed to talk Mom into marrying him, that Mom could have had just about anyone. Janet looked more like Dad than Mom. I don't think she ever forgave Dad for her thick forearms and wide, flat nose. Dad and Janet both had too much upper-body strength. I was fifteen and taller than her, but Janet could still get me to do just about anything she wanted by threatening to punch me or giving me an Indian wrist burn.

Rachael was also older than me. She was seventeen. But she was a petite replica of my mom. She had fine-boned features, a tiny waist, and slim delicate wrists and anklebones that looked as if you could snap them with two fingers. But no one did. Not even Janet would lay a finger on Rachael. She cried easily. Mom said she had never once had to do more than give Rachael a stern look in order to get her to obey. Dad had to strap me often. He strapped Janet, too. Our hearts were a lot harder than Rachael's. Rachael was so good she often seemed to be the only Christian in our family. Her heart was so tender for the things of the Lord that she'd tear up when she listened to even the most boring missionary story. Every Easter she cried when we sang "Low in the Grave He Lay."

Mom wasn't always happy but she was our spiritual leader. She always had been. For one thing she was raised in a godly, educated family, so she knew how Christians were supposed to act. Her father had been the son of a wealthy banker from Rhode Island. While Dad's relatives were swearing, drinking, and sorting coal in Pennsylvania, Mom's dad was getting a Ph.D. in Greek and New Testament studies at Princeton University. Besides having high cheekbones and a tiny waist, Mom enjoyed the benefit of perfect teeth. Dad's teeth were bad. Mom said it was because of his working-class diet, that Dad's mom neglected the bare-minimum duties of sensible nutrition.

Dad still didn't use his fork right. Mom led him to the Lord but had more success with Dad's soul than his table manners. That's why Mom worked so hard to get me, her only son, to be more like her refined father than like my dad. She never came right out and said anything, but I knew what she meant when she'd look away from Dad when he chewed with his mouth open. Mom tried hard to educate me. She'd say, "This is how a gentleman cuts a piece of meat. Oh, how I wish you could have seen your dear grandfather's hands!" Mom maintained that you could tell everything you needed to know about a man's breeding by how he held a knife and fork.

To please Mom I tried to have gentlemanly hands, to hold my knife and fork the right way, like an Englishman. But I'm afraid that I was a disappointment to her. I looked too much like my dad. I was taller and had upper-class teeth, but I also had some bad habits, some unbecoming, working-class desires.

My vacation friend, Jennifer, lived near London. She was Church of England, so she didn't have to worry about the things of the Lord like my family did. We were fundamentalist Presbyterian missionaries. Jennifer was more beautiful than anyone in my family and a lot nicer. I knew how Dad must have felt when he got Mom to marry him. I was grateful Jennifer paid any attention to me.

I did not enjoy growing in the Word as much as Mom or Rachael. My mind wandered when I prayed. I spent a lot more time thinking about Jennifer than reading my Bible. I guess that in the spring of 1967 I was still pretty sure that I was one of the elect, that I would get to heaven and all, but I knew I would not be getting any crowns. I would just be fortunate to get my name in the Book of Life. Rachael and Mom would get the crowns in our family. They never imagined anyone with their clothes off, had Moods like Dad, or sulked like Janet.

I don't know if Janet was spiritual or not. She enjoyed the idea of getting killed for Jesus but she wasn't nice to anybody. Janet reminded me at least once a week that we would face persecution soon. She said the Russians had the name and address of every Protestant, born-again missionary in Europe so that when they invaded they could round us up right away. Janet loved to read missionary stories about martyrdom, the worse the massacre the better. She said we needed to face our predestined fate squarely.

On this particular day off no one was getting martyred. We were rambling around the Swiss lakeside resort of Montreux. We ate lunch at the Zürcher Tearoom *(eminé de veau au riz)* then strolled, talked, fed the ducks and swans, and watched retired Swiss and English tourists doing the same things. Dad was being quiet. He didn't fight with Mom that day, so we had a pretty good time.

Dad, Mom, Janet, Rachael, and I, Calvin Becker, were the fortunate missionary few. We had been called by God to serve him in a part of the world that Mom said most people only dreamed of visiting. The Lord could have called us to be missionaries anywhere. We could have already been shot dead in Russia, or languishing in Africa, or rotting in Borneo, where there were no tearooms, or polite Swiss people, who glanced up as you passed and said, *"Bonjour, messieurs et mesdames, bonjour, mes enfants."*

We were walking along the shore, enjoying our freedom from persecution, when one of the paddle-wheel lake boats that plied the waters of Lake Geneva, the *Helvetia,* lumbered to a water-churning stop at the Territet dock. The swans, who were aimlessly puttering around in the murky water, swam expectantly out of the narrow mouth of the harbor to meet the boat. The huge white birds struggled as they bobbed over the foaming wake, stirred up by the enormous, side-mounted, orange paddle wheels that drove the hundred-foot steamer. The swans bounced up and down in the backwash as they maneuvered for scraps of bread. Rachael pointed to one whose feathers were a mottled brown. "Daddy, *look*! There's a young one."

Dad nodded. "That's right, it was born last year. It won't be white till late summer, if it lives. Young birds have a high mortality rate."

Rachael clapped her hands. "The ugly duckling!"

A family of ducks drifted too near to the swans. One swan craned its sinuous neck menacingly toward the intruders. It hissed angrily and beat immense wings, stirring the water. The startled ducks quacked raucously and fled.

Mom pointed at the swan chasing the ducks. "See how the mother protects her young."

Rachael clasped her hands. "Just like the good shepherd."

Mom nodded and smiled. "What a beautiful picture of Christ and His Church!"

Just then the "beautiful picture" flapped her wings and pecked viciously at her own offspring. The young swan had just snapped up the crust of a sandwich flung by one of the passengers from the boat's deck. The mother seized her young one's food, swallowed it in a gulp, then furiously chased her baby away.

Janet grinned. "What's *that* a 'picture' of, Mom, a church split?"

"Janet, we don't *ever* joke about the Things of The Lord!"

Dad laughed for the first time that afternoon. "That's pretty clever, Janet."

"Really, Ralph!"

Mom frowned but didn't argue. There was no point getting Dad into a Mood over Janet's rebellious levity.

"Dad, can we ride on the boat?" I asked.

"It's awfully expensive, dear," said Mom. "Besides, it's headed the wrong way. It's going back toward Vevey. We want to catch the train home from Villeneuve."

"*Please,* Mother!" begged Rachael.

"What do you think, Ralph?"

"Please, Daddy!" Rachael said again.

Dad was still smiling about Janet's remark. I guess that's why he said, "Okay, but hurry."

As soon as we were on board, the man unhooked two thick hawsers from the dock's pilings, threw them to a sailor, and signaled the all clear to the captain, who was standing, regal, aloof, and bedecked in gold braid, on the flying bridge high above the water.

Inside the main passenger cabin, smelling of chocolate, stale beer, and perfume, there was a polished mahogany rail that ran around a cavernous open space, a cutout to the deck below. You could lean over the rail and look right down into the heart of the engine room.

Two huge pistons, each at least twelve feet long and a foot thick, made of solid steel, began to move. The smell of hot oil wafted up on the vapor cloud that hissed from polished brass valves, one at the base of each piston. The pistons, valves, oil containers, crankshafts, and massive revolving axle, that went out either side of the ship and drove the paddle wheels, all began to churn in unison, slowly at first, then with increasing speed. Above the engine was a gilded iron plate displaying the date and place of the massive engine's construction, WINTERTHUR—1920.

Dad glanced at the plaque. "Built the same year I was and doing a lot better than me by the looks of it."

The two other times we had ridden on the *Helvetia* Dad said the same thing. He had a way of repeating his few humorous remarks.

Standing on the back deck, behind the second-class nonsmoking lounge, I felt the power of the pistons churning under my feet. The noise from the paddle wheels filled the air with a deafening, wet, rushing roar.

When everyone was looking over the rail I took Jennifer's card out. Jennifer had signed it *Love, J.* At least I could read that. I ran the tips of my fingers lightly over her handwriting. "I love you, too," I whispered. "I love you, Jennifer."

Stretching to the horizon, we left a wake which turned from white to green effervescent foam, as it endlessly receded into a twilit infinity behind us. The passing landscape was inverted by the placid water into a mirror image that rippled, then broke into a pastel abstraction as we swept across the lake's silken surface. Staring at the water made me think of what happened the year before on our vacation. Jennifer had been perched on a rock above the turquoise Mediterranean, her sandy-blond hair tied back in a neat ponytail. She stood on tiptoes preparing to dive, her tall, slender figure swaying in silhouette against the pale blue sky above me. I had my mask and snorkel on and was treading water. I ducked my head under the water as she dove, and watched a cascade of silver bubbles stream from her sun-bleached hair as it fanned out in the limpid water. Jennifer plunged all the way to the rippled sandy bottom, twenty feet below. She turned and pushed off, leaving a puff of sand hanging in the water. She shot up with such force that the top of her bathing suit slipped. There, in front of me, not more than two feet away, were Jennifer's breasts. They were pale below the sharp line of her tan.

Jennifer knew I had seen her. When she surfaced she adjusted her bathing suit, shook the water out of her ponytail, and laughed. Nothing ever embarrassed Jennifer.

Rachael nudged me. "Look at how beautiful the vineyards are at this time of year."

"Uh-huh."

Mom pursed her lips. "They are outwardly beautiful, but isn't it a shame to think that what is so outwardly beautiful has been planted to produce wine."

Janet nodded solemnly. "Whited sepulchers, white on the outside, bones and vile worms on the inside."

Mom didn't seem to notice the sarcastic note in Janet's voice.

"That's right, darling. It's hard to appreciate the external beauty of the vineyards when we know what all that alcohol will do to people's lives!"

Janet rolled her eyes. "Isn't it just *too* awful!"

Rachael, as immune to sarcasm as Mom, nodded. She surveyed the coastline and vineyards above the medieval town of St. Saphorin. Rachael shivered at the thought of the sinful harvest of alcoholic ruin that would be produced from the picturesque rows of vines enclosed by ancient, rock-walled terraces. Mom and Rachael grimaced in unison. It was a burden to be of the elect, the few who understood the truth about how deceptive our pleasant-looking world really was.

Chapter 2

WHEN THE BOAT DOCKED at Vevey, Dad said, "I hope no one minds walking all the way back to Villeneuve to catch our train?" Villeneuve was a good four-hour walk south of Vevey. We all looked at Dad to see if he was serious. We had already walked our feet off.

Mom smiled sweetly. "Ralph, do you really think . . . ?"

Dad barked out a mirthless laugh and looked around at us. "I had you all worried there for a minute, didn't I?"

"Oh *Daddy!*" squealed Rachael. She pretended to pound on Dad's arm as if she was a little girl. It was so rare these days for Dad to make any kind of joke that I wanted to get in on the fun. I pushed forward and gave him a good-humored shove. This was a mistake. It made Dad take a step back into the street. A car had to jam on its brakes to avoid running him over.

The driver rolled down his window. *"Mais il faut faire attention!"*

Mom shouted, *"Calvin!* You nearly had your father *killed!*"

"Idiot!" yelled Janet.

"Calvin, be more careful, will you?" shrieked Rachael.

But Dad didn't get mad. "Okay, okay, that's enough. Calvin didn't mean to."

Dad waved the car on. Everyone was so relieved that the near miss hadn't put Dad in a Mood that they forgave me and said no more about it.

We crossed the street and began to trudge up the narrow byways of old Vevey toward the railroad station. It was starting to get dark.

Yellow light and smoky alcohol-laden air poured out of the many restaurants and cafés we passed as we walked up the cobbled sidewalk. Sales ladies were taking in baskets of dried flowers, galvanized buckets full of red and pink roses and carnations, and boxes of fruit. A butcher we passed used a long wooden pole, with an evil-looking hook on the end, to reach up into his shop window, unhook the heavy carcass of a lamb, and transfer it to the giant refrigerator at the back of his establishment. Rabbits dangled by their hind legs in pairs lower down in the window, their heads skinned and macabre looking.

I pointed at the row of pink carcasses. "How come they leave on one whole unskinned foot, Dad?"

"That way people know it's rabbit, not cat."

"Dad, they *wouldn't* sell cat meat, *would they?*"

"Maybe not in Switzerland, Rachael. But they still leave one foot on because a rabbit's foot is different than a cat's. That way no one can get cheated."

"It's *so gruesome!*" exclaimed Janet. "The Europeans are *so* morbid!"

"Well, dear," Mom murmured as we walked past the butcher's and averted our eyes from an unseemly display of women's underwear in the next store window, "the European mentality is a little more primitive than ours. They don't have deodorant, or supermarkets, or pasteurized milk—because their founders weren't Protestants like America's founders. Until the Reformation they were living in the dark. Centuries of pagan Catholic superstition have taken their toll."

"But Vevey's in the Protestant part, isn't it?"

"Yes, Janet, but it wasn't that long ago that all of Switzerland was in the grip of Rome. Besides, most of the churches are liberal now, so they're pretty much back where they started. Europe's a dark continent. The Reformed Faith has practically been extinguished here, hasn't it, Ralph?"

"That's right."

Mom nodded. "When you live your life based on a lie, then it's easy to lie about everything."

Rachael wailed, "You mean when we're on vacation in Italy, we might be eating *cat* at the Hotel Nazionale in Portofino?"

"I don't think so, dear. The Nazionale's a nice place. But I'm sure it happens at some hotels. Italy is *a very dark* country. Worse than most."

"But I like Italy."

Janet gave me a sideways glance and laughed. "You mean you like Jennifer!"

"He has every right to befriend her. How else can he witness to her?" said Rachael.

"That's likely! I hope that's all he does!"

Mom frowned. "Children, children, please, we all like Italy, but that's not the point. It's a wonderful place on the *outside* but it's what's on the *inside* that counts."

The train was crowded. We got stuck in the smoking compartment. There were no seats anywhere else in second class. Every time someone lit a cigarette Mom's lips tightened. I could see she was trying not to breathe and at the same time to be Christ-like and be a good witness.

The one good thing about people who smoked was that you knew for sure they weren't saved. You could get to work right away witnessing to them without having to inquire if they had already asked Jesus into their hearts as their personal savior. A person who defiled his bodily temple with tobacco might as well have been wearing a badge that said LOST.

While Mom smiled evangelistically at the stolid, stone-faced Swiss, I looked out the train window as we doubled back along the lake and passed Clarens and Montreux. We were on a stretch of railroad that hugged the shore just beyond Territet, the place where we caught the boat a few hours before. We hurtled through a short tunnel behind Castle Chillon, then down the lake on a long graceful curve of track.

The bend in the rail gave me the opportunity to look back at the castle and, on the opposite side of the lake, the French Alps rising in sheer cliffs out of the water. Ahead of us the Dents du Midi, the tallest mountain in our part of Switzerland, stood soft and gauzy above the Rhône valley. Patches of snow, below the Dents' seven jagged peaks, that gave Les Dents du Midi, the Teeth of the South, their name, were shaded a delicate pink. The "Alpine Rouge" matched the pastel glimmer of light fading from the darkening sky.

The ride from Vevey to Aigle, where we would catch the local, narrow-gauge tram up to our village, Trois-Torrents (Three Streams), was only about twenty-five minutes long. As the brakes squealed and we slowed to a stop, Mom began to hand our fellow passengers gospel tracts. The Lord had not opened up any doors to witness to anyone. Everyone had refused to answer Mom when she asked them if they knew Jesus as their personal savior. So the least Mom could do was to hand them literature about the way of salvation.

Riding the two-car tram, an ancient, red, boxy cog railway, from Aigle to Trois-Torrents was almost like an airplane ride, except no airplane could fly so excruciatingly slowly. We left Aigle, trundled across the Rhône valley floor, rode through acres of orchards, stopped at Monthey, then began our ascent up the mountainside. That was the part like the plane ride: the valley floor fell dramatically away as if we were in a steep climb.

As the tram lurched up the line the view of the valley opened up in a wide panorama. Towns, orchards, rail lines, and roads, a bright toyland framed by impossibly high mountains, so high as to seem unconnected to the valley, spread out below, around, and above us.

The landscape next to the rail line was dotted with geranium-bedecked chalets and barns, some leaning at crazy angles in their ancient decrepitude. The chalets had dates carved under their wide overhanging eaves: 1642, 1733, 1821. Dad once preached a whole sermon on the fact that it was tragically ironic that the seeds of Christianity had lain dormant for so long in this ancient land and how it was sad that the Swiss had so forgotten their Reformation heritage that American missionaries, like us, had to come to replant John Calvin's Reformed seed in the barren, apostate Swiss.

Our chalet was not as old as most in our village. Chalet Tulipes had been built in 1921. The date was carved deep into one of the beams under the apex of the steep roof. Along with the chalet next door, Chalet Tulipes was home not only to our family but to our ministry—L'Arche (the Ark).

When the tram creaked to a stop, in front of the Trois-Torrents post office, we got out and walked the rest of the way home in the dark. We could have ridden right up to the stop in front of our chalet, about a five-minute walk further up the road, but Dad, who was in no hurry to get home to Grandmother and the young people who lived with us, said, "Let's spend a couple more minutes alone before we rejoin the battle."

There was no traffic at that time of night. We were able to walk hand in hand across the road the whole way home. As we sauntered up our tiny village's main street, Mom led us in a Bible chorus, "I Will Make You Fishers of Men."

One villager looked out of her chalet as we passed. She shook her head in a disgusted sort of way, reached out, grabbed the handle of the wooden shutter, and slammed it shut with such force that a geranium in her window box got decapitated.

Dad glanced up as the shutter slammed.

Mom sighed. "It's so tragic. How I long for the day when they open up a little." Mom shook her head wistfully, then began to sing another chorus, "The B-I-B-L-E, Yes, That's the Book for Me!" twice as loud as she had been singing before.

I looked away so Mom wouldn't see that I was not singing. I kept hold of Jennifer's postcard and tried to remember how many days there were in June. I was trying to calculate how long it would be between our day off, April 6, and August 20, when we always left for our vacation.

Chapter 3

WHEN THEY ARRIVED AT L'ARCHE, the young people would be assigned a dormitory in our house or next door. In our chalet the girls would sleep in the girls' four-bed bedroom and boys in either the boys' three-bed bedroom or, in the summer, on the big, geranium-fringed, second-floor balcony that ran under wide, dark eaves, along the whole length of the front of our chalet. When the boys slept on the balcony, it was in dingy, green, army-surplus sleeping bags that had been donated to our ministry by a born-again sergeant stationed at the U.S. Army base in Frankfurt, Germany.

In the spring of 1967, God, as if compensating Mom and Dad for their trial by fire—in other words, Grandmother—was blessing our ministry with a rich harvest. Young people were sleeping all over our house, filling the bedrooms as well as our balcony and the living room, singing hymns, being counseled, guided, and discipled, and using up all our hot water. L'Arche was full of youth seeking God. They were sent to our mission for spiritual refreshment by Reformed Protestant missionaries and pastors from all over Europe. They sent young people to us hoping that they would return home converted, or at least deepened in their walk with the Lord.

We worked on our young people night and day to help them grow in the Lord. At least everyone did but me.

The day began with devotions at breakfast. Then Mom, Dad, or Dick Keegan, our fellow worker in the vineyard of the Lord, along with Jane, Dick's wife (they were the "houseparents" of the chalet next door), gave a talk or a Bible study. After that the young people helped around the house and garden until lunch. In the afternoon Mom, Dad, Dick, or Jane saw young people for individual sessions of spiritual counseling.

On Sundays church was held in our living room. During the week the living room got used for times of prayer, discussion, Bible study, singing, pastoral counseling, and countless sessions of sharing, when Mom would gather the young people around her and talk to them for hours about what God was doing in her life, and what he could do in theirs if they would only trust him.

If the young people were already saved, but not yet spiritually kindred, we strove to correct their theology, to bring them to the light of the Reformed Faith. If they were unsaved we strove to convert our young people to Born-Again, Reformed, Protestant, Calvinist, Fundamentalist, Bible-Believing Christianity, to get them to invite Jesus into their hearts by praying the Sinner's Prayer: "Dear Jesus, I know I'm a sinner and I ask for Your forgiveness for my sins and I just thank You for dying on the cross on Calvary for me, please come into my heart and dwell in me. Amen." It went something like that.

Because we didn't believe in dead ritual, tradition, or liturgy, the young people could change around their prayers if they wanted to, even the Sinner's Prayer. If they chose to only say "I accept You into my heart," that was good enough as long as they were thinking about Jesus at the time. If the young people understood more about the Things of The Lord, then they might be able to pray a prayer that had more theological discernment in it. Maybe they would even include some Reformed theology about the sovereignty of God: "Dear Heavenly Father, we just come before You and thank You that You are sovereign and that You have numbered the hairs of my head and that You have chosen me as a brand from the burning, Your own from before the beginning of time, to be Your bride, and that You have promised to bring Your elect to Yourself and to dwell with them. Thank You for having seen fit to count me, in my utter depravity, amongst the elect and for having drawn me to Yourself through Your irresistible Grace out from among those Vessels of Wrath predestined by Your perfect will, from before the dawn of time, to perish for eternity."

Not everyone understood Calvinist, Reformed theology well enough to pray a really theologically discerning Sinner's Prayer. But with sufficient training, our converts from Catholicism, Liberal Protestantism, or just plain backsliddenness could grow in the Lord, and as time went by, when Dad, Mom, Dick, Jane, Janet, and Rachael had trained the newly saved up in the Lord, they got better at praying correctly. With enough effort they might even become spiritually kindred, as thoroughly Reformed as us.

The day after our family day off by the lake, two young people, a shy-looking boy and girl, about eighteen years old, got off the tram and knocked at our front door. They were from Belgium, but like most of our young people, they spoke some English.

"I hope they're only traveling together and not involved," Mom whispered to me as the boy and girl crossed the road and walked up the path.

As they stepped into our chalet Mom glanced apprehensively at them. The boy was holding the girl's hand. Europeans had a different attitude toward the Physical Things, Mom often remarked.

"Calvin, show dear Robert to the *boys'* bedroom while I show Elise where the *girls* sleep," Mom said after they had introduced themselves.

Mom didn't want there to be any unpleasant misunderstanding, like the year before, when two French young people had *said* they were a brother and sister and, regrettably, Mom believed them and had let them sleep in sleeping bags, side by side, on the balcony.

At two A.M., Rachael heard a suspicious noise. She looked out her window and saw the French young people doing something, "even worse if they really were a brother and sister!" as Janet said later.

Rachael ran down the hall and pounded on Mom and Dad's door. But it was too late. By the time Mom rushed downstairs to intervene, the boy was lying on top of the girl.

I was woken up by the ruckus, by Rachael running down our hall calling, "Help! Help! Fornication!" I looked over the rail of the balcony and saw the boy's naked bottom energetically pumping up and down, framed by the geraniums, in the moonlight. I knew what he was doing. Mom had often explained the Physical Things to me in our talks together. It was a subject she never seemed to tire of.

Mom used a variety of euphemisms for anything biological. "Touching yourself," for doing the "unnatural thing boys are tempted to do." Women "fell off the roof" once a month, and a whole range of other delicate and fascinating topics came under the heading of "female troubles."

Years before I saw the French boy's pale bottom in the moonlight, Mom had explained all about how the male uses his Little Thing to ejaculate the Amazing Seeds God makes so they can find the Wonderful Egg, how the Amazing Seed and the Wonderful Egg are already predestined to be saved or lost, how the fertilized egg is predestined to receive the Gospel or to reject it and harden its heart.

When Mom burst onto the balcony, through the dining-room door, the boy rolled off the French girl. She screamed and pulled her sleeping bag over herself to cover her nakedness, like Eve had when she sewed fig leaves together to cover hers years before.

I momentarily saw one of the French girl's Precious Milk Glands and I think I saw the Wonderful Place Babies Come From, but I'm not sure if it was that or if it was the French boy's kneesock. It was too dark to tell.

The next day the "tragic French couple," as Mom called them, were gone by the time I woke up. Dad made them pack their bags and wait out on the road until the 6:36 A.M. tram to Aigle arrived. Dad didn't let them stay in the house in case their presence would corrupt the others. Dad wrote to their pastor, who was a Protestant, but only a Baptist, and told the French Baptist pastor what two of his flock had done to our balcony.

At family prayers after lunch, the day after the incident, Dad told us as how this disastrous occurrence was a good example of the terrible consequences of wrong theology. "It just goes to show," said Dad, "what happens when you start flirting with Anabaptistic Arminian conceptions of free will!"

As I sat at lunch that day I wondered if the French Baptist boy's Amazing Seeds were still swimming around or if they had found the French Baptist girl's Wonderful Egg and if the egg would receive the Good News gladly or depart sorrowfully, like the rich young ruler in the Bible story, and reject Calvinism and be lost; an Egg of Wrath.

So after the French Baptists' defilement of our balcony we always made sure that the boys and girls understood the rules about where they were to sleep. That's why I explained to the newly arrived Belgian guests that the boys had to stay in the boys' room at night except if they needed to use the toilet.

After I escorted the Belgian boy to his room, and while Mom was getting the Belgian girl settled, I went upstairs to our bathroom to get some bleach to punish Grandmother for hitting me with the Parcheesi game board earlier in the day.

Grandmother was away at Dr. Zwingli's office getting an X ray at the time. She tolerated our local doctor because he spoke English fairly well. But she didn't like him. She said maybe he wasn't as half-brained as most foreigners, but she said that his stringy goatee made him look like "some damned commie from New York come ta organize the niggers."

I took the bleach over to the glass tank. It held the goldfish I had given Grandmother the year before, as a welcome-to-our-home present. I poured. The water turned opaque. The powerful smell of bleach filled the room.

I put the bleach bottle back in the bathroom cupboard. When I returned to Grandmother's sitting room the bleach smell was gone and the water clear. The fish were floating. This surprised me. I thought the bleach, diluted in so much water, would take longer to kill them.

I worried that the bleach had sucked out their color. But it turned out the reason the fish looked colorless was because they were upside down. Their stomachs were white. When I poked one with a pencil it rolled over. I saw its sides and back were still bright orange. This relieved me. If the fish lost their color then someone might have guessed that they had been bleached to death. Naturally I would be blamed.

When Grandmother returned from Dr. Zwingli's office she demanded to know where Louie, Dewy, and George were. I said they had died of parasites and that Dad had flushed them. The last part was true enough.

"I bet they did, ya li'l shit, I bet they did! How'd ya kill 'em, ya brat?"

I got indignant and pretended I was filled with righteous anger at her false accusations. I walked down the hall to Dad's bedroom. A moment later he stalked into Grandmother's sitting room.

"Mother, I will not have you bearing false witness against my son!"

"If he was mine I'd know what to do!"

"Well, he's *not* yours! I thank the Lord you only got *one* life to ruin!"

Dad stormed out.

"Son-of-a-bitch."

Dad spun around. *"What did you say!"*

Grandmother got sulky and pretended to cry about her goldfish, which was a lie. She had never liked them. The very first day I gave them to her, she said they smelled "like some Spick from Cleveland gone bad."

Dad yelled, "Cut it out! I heard what you called me, and as a matter of fact, I agree with you!"

Grandmother stopped pretending to cry and cackled with laughter.

I didn't understand what Dad meant, or why Grandmother laughed, until Rachael explained how clever Dad was.

"If Dad's a 'son-of-a-b' then who's the 'b'?"

Grandma was not so easily deceived as Dad. Weeks after the bleach incident, whenever I went into her room, she was still saying, "How'd ya do it, ya li'l shit? How?"

Chapter 4

IT WAS IN THE SPRING OF 1965, at Christmastime, that Grandmother had befallen us. Dad held that the only reason Christmas was celebrated by most people in December was because of the custom of the winter solstice. Mom said that the Catholics had begun this worldly compromise with paganism. Nevertheless, Dad said, he did not want to deprive us of the joy of Christ's birth. So we celebrated Christmas on March 25. By celebrating Christmas in March we demonstrated that we were not compromising with the world's spirit.

In the spring of 1965, besides Grandmother arriving, another momentous event had occurred. A home had opened for cerebral-palsy children, what people call spastics, next door to our chalet. This was great for me since a boy my own age came to live right next door.

Jean-Pierre had cerebral palsy but not a really bad case. He could walk pretty well, and unless he was too excited, he spoke fairly clearly. We were both thirteen years old when he moved in. Jean-Pierre was tall, a good six inches taller than me. But he was thin. He had a long, horsey face, a wide thick nose and thick lips. Janet said he was homely. Everyone agreed he was friendly.

The reason Jean-Pierre and the other spastics moved to Chalet Beau-Rivage was because three middle-aged, Born-Again, Bible-Believing American physical therapists, who we called The Ladies, Mary Lou, Mardie, and Margaret, from Lynchburg, Virginia, felt led to take advantage of the spiritual resources we had. Dad taught the spastics about the Lord while Mary Lou, Mardie, and Margaret ministered to their bodies.

The Ladies were Reformed Presbyterians like us, that's why they knew about our ministry. They had been reading all about L'Arche in the P.C.C.C.C.U.S.A. (Presbyterian Church of Calvinist. Confirmed, Confession United States of America) newsletter, *The Harvest News*. Years before God called them to Switzerland, The Ladies were part of our praying family. They sent monthly love offerings long before the Lord brought them to work side by side with us in his vineyard.

After The Ladies and their spastics arrived, Mom said it was now like a real American neighborhood, that God had provided new friends for all of us. Mom said, "Now you have boys and girls to play with who love the Lord right next door." She said they wouldn't pollute my mind, or lead me astray, like the French-speaking, Catholic, peasant children in our village tried to do with their coarse papist behavior and foul language. Rachael said that now, on Sunday, we really were like the early church since we had "the halt and the lame in our midst."

The only bad thing about having so many spastics in church was that they ruined the singing. They slurred their words when they sang "The Old Rugged Cross," "Just As I Am," "Trust and Obey," or "Abide with Me." And they sang real loud.

The more the spastics liked a hymn the louder they bellowed. Mom and Rachael would exchange understanding and pitying glances, about how sweet they thought it was that these, dear, precious, handicapped little ones loved the Lord so deeply and sang so fervently. But a couple of months after they arrived, Janet said she was tired of their bellowing, shrieking, and twitching in church. Even Rachael had to admit that it was hard to worship with a spastic next to you gurgling "Amazing Grace" to a different tune than everyone else.

Except for the hymns, the spastics were a great success. Dad got more members of his "permanent congregation," as opposed to our "guests," the young people who came and went. Mom had more people to share her spiritual insights with, and Rachael and Janet had a houseful of patients to learn nursing on, and to inspire spiritually by sharing the hope of the Gospel with, explaining to the spastics that they were only trapped in their handicapped bodies in this life because in heaven they'd get new bodies when they died, maybe even sooner since Jesus might come back any day.

Jean-Pierre, my new friend, didn't demand much of me. He was just grateful I didn't hit him with a stick, or make him sleep in a cupboard, the way his mom had before the Swiss authorities took him away from his parents and put him in the home. Even though he was thirteen when he moved into Chalet Beau Rivage, Jean-Pierre didn't know how to read. Janet said that unlike me he had an excuse for not reading; his mom had fractured his skull. He was not stupid, though. Jean-Pierre could speak English quite well. The fact that he couldn't read was okay with me.

A few weeks after Jean-Pierre arrived, in late May of 1965, I was sitting up in the blue spruce tree in our front yard, getting ready to drop a big rock on a cat that was eating a sardine I had put at the base of the tree for bait. I heard a howl like somebody had slammed his finger in a door. I wouldn't have paid much attention to the howl except that it made the cat bolt. I'd spent the better part of the morning getting the twenty-pound rock high into the tree, so I was annoyed.

The howl had unmistakably been Jean-Pierre's. After I was sure the cat was gone for good, I yelled, *"Jean-Pierre, qu'est-ce que tu fais?"* He didn't answer. I dropped the rock, climbed down, and ran to the spot in the hedge where the yell had come from.

The hedge trees formed a low tunnel of branches that ran along the perimeter of our garden. It was a perfect place to hide in. That's where I found him. Jean-Pierre was sitting crouched down between the double row of pine trunks. I was about to scold him for scaring the cat when I saw him. Then I forgot about the cat.

Jean-Pierre was half sitting, half lying in the thicket of the pine boughs. He was trying to pull up his pants. His trousers were stuck on twigs that poked in from the sides, so he couldn't cover himself. His face was bright red. He was twitching and breathing hard. The more he struggled the more he began to convulse until finally he burst into tears and sobbed, *"Je m'excuse! Je m'excuse!"* He covered his face as best as he could with his twitching hands, as if he thought I was going to hit him. He lay crying, pants down, with his Little Thing being very naughty, as my mom would have said.

At first I thought I'd better run away. But I knew Jean-Pierre would get in trouble if someone else found him like this, which they would in a minute. Spastics don't cry quietly. I ducked into the cool evergreen tunnel and helped him pull up his pants. Jean-Pierre wouldn't look at me.

"Jean-Pierre, what were you doing?"

"Calvin, please do not tell."

"Tell what?"

"Tell 'ow you find me."

"Jean-Pierre, were you touching yourself?"

He didn't understand, so I motioned with my hand. He hesitated, then nodded sheepishly.

"Is that what made you shout?"

Jean-Pierre blushed but wouldn't answer.

"Jean-Pierre, Mom says the normal thing for a Christian boy to do, when he's tragically tempted to touch himself, is to pray for wet dreams. Mom says they're God's gift to boys to help them to relieve their animal desires."

"Ees that what you are doing?"

"Yes, I did pray for a wet dream for a whole week once, but I never got one to relieve my tragic animal desires, so I started touching myself again."

"Et puis?"

"It was fine."

"Your *maman* . . . ?"

"When she asks me if I've been touching myself I tell her I never do. I say God sends wet dreams whenever my Little Thing has animal needs, gets naughty, and stands up."

"Ow many times you . . . ?"

"Three, four times a week. How about you?"

"I trying *tous les jours,* but I cannot fineeshing, I think too much they will finding me because I making *le bruit,* the noise."

"I'll keep a lookout for you."

"*Vraiment?* You are to doing *these?*"

"*Oui. Vraiment.*"

"*Merci!*"

I don't know what Jean-Pierre thought about, if he had a picture or story in his mind when he relieved his animal needs. I never asked. I knew if I asked he would inquire about me. I didn't ever talk about Jennifer to anyone if I could help it.

I had a story I told myself. In my story I ran away to meet Jennifer in Italy. I stayed with my friend Gino, an artist who lived in Portofino. Sometimes I touched myself and sometimes I just day-dreamed about meeting Jennifer in Italy. I had been telling myself the same story for years.

After I helped Jean-Pierre, he went back to Chalet Beau Rivage. I decided to stay right where I was, decided to tell the story.

I closed my eyes.

No one locked their doors at the Pensione Biea in Paraggi. When I stepped out of the bright, sunny hall into the cool, dark bedroom, I knew right away that Jennifer was staying in this room as usual. I knew this before my eyes adjusted to the dim light filtering through the closed shutters. I knew by the smell of Pears soap and talcum powder. It was the same smell I recalled from when I kissed Jennifer the first time. Whenever I kissed her I always breathed in to try and fill my mouth and lungs with her fragrance.

I could see Jennifer's few belongings neatly arranged on top of the plain pine dresser that stood against the whitewashed plaster wall. Jennifer had practically no toilet articles and wore no makeup. Her blue-and-gray pleated plaid skirt hung over the back of a chair. This was part of her boarding-school uniform. She only brought a few clothes on vacation. Most of the time she wore her bathing suit, a pair of shorts, and a T-shirt or a light cotton print dress.

Jennifer's hairbrush and comb were the only things on top of the dresser. Next to them was the bottle of Nivea suntan lotion she never used. (Probably her mother had put it there.) Next to that were two ribbons and a rubber band: her ponytail equipment.

I looked down at the floor. Sitting by the door I saw Jennifer's thong sandals. They were made out of leather. They had dark, shiny imprints of Jennifer's feet in them from several years of wear. Next to them were a pair of brown oxford shoes. Jennifer kept them polished, probably had to at her girls' school. That was all there was of her visible in the room. But it was enough. Each object vividly recalled some detail or other about her. The sandals made me think of Jennifer's fine-boned, slender feet; beautiful and brown, ending in narrow ankles below long, graceful legs.

The time passed so slowly I was tempted to go out and wait in the hall, even to creep up the stairs to the dining terrace, to see if Jennifer and her parents had finished eating.

I decided not to for fear Lucrezia might see me. She'd shout *"Calvino!"* and hug me. Her mother would come out of the *pensione* kitchen, wiping off her plump hands on her apron, and make a fuss. Jennifer and her parents would hear the commotion. My surprise would be ruined. Besides, they'd all ask where the rest of the family was.

Someone was bouncing a ball in the alley below Jennifer's window. I heard shouts and squeals from the beach. The bus pulled up, then pulled out again. I could tell it was heading toward Portofino because the driver sounded the horn. (The first big curve came up right away.) A speedboat revved its engine as it accelerated out of the bay. I wondered if a water-skier was being pulled behind it.

Then the door opened and Jennifer walked in from the bright sunlit hall. She closed the door behind her.

Before her eyes adjusted to the shade of the room, I said, "Hi, Jennifer."

She gave a start. *"You bloody little swine!"* she shouted.

"Sorry, did I make you jump?"

"Yes, you bloody well did!"

"Are you glad to see me?"

"Not particularly."

"How long have you been here?"

"About ten seconds, I should say."

"You know what I mean."

"We arrived the week before last. Where have you been?"

"Something came up."

"Got carried away at an all-night prayer meeting and began to cut yourselves with knives I expect."

"Something like that."

"Well, how are all the loony little Becker tribe and the rest of the praying idiots this year?"

"Fine."

"Converted the raging heathen of Switzerland yet?"

"I guess so."

"Been having a jolly time singing hymns and being a general nuisance?"

"That's about it."

"And your dear old dad, has he been locked up yet?"

"Jennifer, there are a couple of things I need to tell you and that I can't let you tell your mom and dad."

"Calvin, did he kill someone?"

"No."

"You know, Calvin, even for you this is a bit thick."

"It's a pretty long story."

"Wovwey! Jennifer wike her bedtime stowy."

"Don't talk like a baby!"

"Why not? Jennifer wike her big stwong fwend. Tell Jennifer stowy, pwease, pwease!"

I couldn't endure standing there talking nonsense with Jennifer, all the while smelling her hair and skin so close in the shadows. I reached out and pulled Jennifer toward me by her shoulders and I kissed her. She lifted her face to mine and kissed me back, hard. Then she surprised me. She pushed me backward onto her narrow bed. I fell on the plain gray wool blanket and Jennifer fell on top of me and pressed her long slender body down on mine. I breathed her in and she kissed me and I put my arms around her as she pushed against me.

We lay kissing and rubbing our bodies against each other, and instead of Jennifer ending it all by jumping back and laughing at me, the way she always had before, she kissed me harder and harder and pushed her narrow, sharp hips against mine!

When my hands found her breasts she didn't brush them away but arched her back up a little so I could touch her more easily. I realized if she kept pushing her hips onto mine that in another second or two, it would make my Precious Seeds begin their exciting journey.

I noticed how Jennifer was breathing as hard as I was, how she was rubbing herself on me, how wet her mouth was. I saw that she had her eyes closed. It dawned on me that she was *enjoying this,* was about to do the same thing I was! This amazed me. I had no idea girls did this sort of thing, I had always thought that animal desire was a boy's problem, that girls only had eggs, babies, and Bible studies, not that hot shooting twisting feeling between their legs that rockets up into your stomach and fills your mind with thoughts that are red and dark until there are sparks.

So I was very surprised that Jennifer seemed to have forgotten all about me and was off in her own world, concentrating on what she was doing, and moving her hips up and down on mine faster and faster and breathing in deeper and deeper, almost gasping. I started to get the picture of her I always had in my mind when I touched myself. Suddenly I remembered that Jennifer was *really there,* that I didn't need a picture! I only had to open my eyes and sure enough there were her real breasts in front of me!

Jennifer's back was arched, she was supporting her weight on her arms, planted one on each side of my shoulders. The straps of her dress were slipping. Only one button separated me from my story. I undid the button; her white-and-blue flower-print dress opened. Her breasts were right in front of me. I felt like I was drowning.

I fainted, died, exploded, and Jennifer did, too. I heard her gasp.

As soon as she was done she jumped off me and stood in the shadows looking at me. Then she laughed.

"You look so surprised! You should see your face!"

I didn't know what to say, so I stared at the sunlight reflected off the water, flickering on the cracked plaster ceiling. I noticed how wet and clammy my swimming trunks were. I sat up and glanced down at the spreading stain. Jennifer followed my gaze and laughed again.

"Are we having little troubles?"

I sat up. There was no use pretending things were normal. There was a big sticky patch that made the dark blue material of my bathing suit practically black. I got off the bed, walked to Jennifer's shower, took off my T-shirt, stepped in with my trunks on, turned the hot tap, and let the lukewarm water play over me. I pulled out the waistband of my trunks until they filled with water and all the Precious Seeds washed away; made their way down the drain and out into the Mediterranean sea.

Jennifer stood in the doorway and watched. When I looked up, she smiled. It was like the smile she had given me the first time I kissed her. There was no mocking laughter in her eyes. She looked sweet and serious.

I stepped out of the shower. Jennifer handed me her towel.

"Calvin, I missed you."

She kissed me again but this time it was gentle.

"I missed you, too. I missed you horribly."

"Now," said Jennifer, "we've got that out of the way. Why don't you tell me what you were mumbling about, tell me your story. What are you doing here alone?"

Chapter 5

MOM'S MOM, OUR GOOD GRANDMOTHER, had been a godly missionary with the China Inland Mission, before China was lost to communism. But she had gone to be with the Lord and her gentlemanly, educated husband in heaven.

Before she invaded our house, Dad's mother lived in Philadelphia. She was our vile foulmouthed grandmother. She was not even a nominal Christian, let alone born-again.

Before Grandmother Becker moved in, Mom and Dad almost never talked about her. Dad never did. Mom only mentioned her when she was explaining to us children about how Dad had had an underprivileged background, about how that excused his un-Christlike behavior, how when he got in one of his Moods, or his dark days, when he was furthest from the Lord, that it was not all his fault.

Grandma was a regular cause of Dad's backsliding. Even before she arrived in our house she was like a sort of plague. When Dad got letters from his mother he got depressed. Nothing plunged him into one of his Moods faster. Dad's father had not been born-again but, Mom said, he was in his own rough-and-ready, working-class way a decent enough man. Grandmother Becker, however, was a different matter. I once heard Mom tell Janet that "it's tragically ironic that that woman should have outlived Pop Becker, not to mention my own precious parents."

The nightmare began when Dad received a letter from Grandmother in February of 1965. She said she was having dizzy spells. This letter was an evil omen. I remember the day it arrived because it happened to be when Mom, Rachael, Janet, and I were opening a box of Calvert School correspondence-course books and work sheets that had come in the post along with Grandmother's portent of doom.

In 1965 I was being homeschooled again. I was back from the boarding school in England that I had gone to after I got too old to stay at the school I had been tricked into attending. I was tricked when Reverend Bahre, Ph.D., the chairman of our mission board, was visiting our ministry in 1963. I happened to be sick in bed at the time. That's why I wasn't able to avoid him and got sent away.

The moment I saw how thin Reverend Bahre's lips were, how close his eyes were together, below his crew cut, how big and oily his forehead was, I got a deep sinking feeling in my stomach.

Reverend Bahre had joined Mom and Dad and the young people for lunch, devotions, prayer, and Bible study. Then he was shown around our chalet and the rest of the mission. About two minutes before he barged into my room Rachael raced up the stairs to warn me that he was on his way. I grabbed my Bible and opened it. I thought it would be a good idea to seem spiritual. Dad said we all needed to work hard to give the chairman a good impression. I should have left that Bible well enough alone.

Reverend Bahre glanced down at my Bible. "Am I disturbing your quiet time?"

"No, I've just finished my daily time with the Lord."

"Well, if I'm disturbing you, I can come back later."

"No, that's fine."

"I missed my own quiet time this morning, and boy, do I need my spiritual breakfast! Mind if I just sit right down here and have my daily devotions with you?" Reverend Bahre gave me a big smile and patted my shoulder.

"That would be great."

I tried to smile in a way that would show him that the joy of the

Lord also shone forth from me, that I was looking forward to sharing his spiritual breakfast or brunch or whatever.

He settled comfortably on the edge of my bed. "Does it bother you to have me sit here?"

"No, that's fine."

"Praise the Lord!"

Reverend Bahre bowed his head. "Dear Heavenly Father, we just come to Thee on this gladsome day of Thy redemption, surrounded by the splendors of Thine Alpine handiwork, to thank Thee for all the great things Thou wilt do in our lives today! In J-e-e-z-u-s-s' precious, powerful, righteous, and sovereign name, and in thanksgiving for the sweet bondage of Thine Irresistible Grace, we bow before Thee, in the name of J-e-e-z-u-s-s, we pray. Amen."

He looked up, smiled, and said, "This is great!"

I nodded and tried to feel holy.

"Now, how about you turn to Habakkuk, chapter three, verse twelve, and read from there to the end of the passage. That's my portion for the day, brother."

The sinking feeling in my stomach got worse. I turned to the Old Testament and started to flip the pages, hoping I would find Habakkuk fast enough so that it would look like I lived in the Word, knew my Bible as well as Mom, or at least Rachael.

I could have found Habakkuk if only I had paid better attention to Janet when she tried to get me to memorize the books of the Bible. But not being able to read limited how much I could memorize. And Janet punching me every time I got a book wrong sort of put me off the subject. By Second Kings I was usually too bruised to concentrate.

"I love the Word," I said as I fumbled with the pages.

"Great! The Word is the Rock upon which we build."

"Yes, it's a great rock."

I kept leafing, looking for an *H*. I saw *P* and figured it was for

Psalms or Proverbs, I saw an *E* and I knew it was Exodus, because of the *X,* but I didn't see *H* for Habakkuk.

"I read Habakkuk just the other day," I said. "I love Habakkuk."

"Great, so do I."

I leafed some more.

He watched me closely, "Are we having trouble finding the passage?"

"No, it's just I never can remember which comes first, Psalms or Habakkuk." I tried to laugh.

"Oh, *that's* easy, Psalms comes first!" Reverend Bahre had no trouble laughing heartily. He seemed to be in an excellent mood.

I leafed some more but it was no use. "I don't think this Bible has Habakkuk in it."

Reverend Bahre laughed even harder. "Well, well, well, let's take a look, brother!" He took the Bible out of my hands and turned right to the place. He didn't even have to flip any pages, just opened it right up to Habakkuk as if he were a magician doing a trick.

"So *that's* where it is!"

"Yes, right here. Praise the Lord!"

"Oh."

"Okay, now read the passage."

"What was that again?"

"Chapter three, verse twelve to the end of the chapter."

"Oh?"

I turned the page. I saw a big "3."

"There ya are!" Reverend Bahre bellowed.

I stared at the verses below the chapter heading till I found a "12." I put my finger next to the spot.

"Right here?"

"That's it, brother!"

"You know . . ."

"Yes?"

"What with having the flu and all, my eyes seem to be a little tired. Would you mind reading?"

"Sure, you just read verse twelve and I'll read the rest."

I waited for a second.

"You know, my medicine has made my eyes go fuzzy."

"When did you take your pills?"

"Before breakfast."

"That's strange, you were meditating upon the Word just a couple of minutes ago when I came in."

"I was praying."

Reverend Bahre stopped smiling.

"But your Bible was open. Don't you read the Word *before* you fellowship with the Lord, brother?"

"*Of course,* I always do! But today, with my flu and all, I was just praying."

"I see."

He sat looking at me for a moment then smiled again. "It must be tough to be missing school because you're sick."

"Yes, but I'll catch up."

"Friend, tell me about your school, won't you?"

"Mom and Janet teach me. Mom when Janet's away at boarding school, and Janet when she's home."

"Oh?"

He didn't say anything else. The silence got kind of heavy. I felt I should say something.

"It works out great. Praise the Lord!"

"Friend, how is it that a boy of eleven can't read?"

"I can read!"

"Then let's read the daily passage."

"But my eyes are—"

He took my Bible out of my hands and read the verse in a loud, slow preaching sort of voice. " 'You marched through the land in indignation; You trampled the nations in anger.' Habakkuk 3:12. One of my favorite verses. Praise J-e-e-z-u-s-s-s!"

Reverend Bahre slowly closed the Bible and stood up and smiled.

"It was *good* fellowshipping with you, brother!"

I had waited in my bed wondering what to do. I didn't wait long. About five minutes after Reverend Bahre left, the door opened. Mom and Dad came in.

"Calvin," said Dad, "why in *heaven's name* did you tell Reverend Bahre that you weren't getting an education?"

"Oh Calvin!" sobbed Mom. "You know you don't want to be taught by n . . . nu . . . nuns!"

"Will you keep quiet, Elsa!"

"Dad, I never said anything like that to Reverend Bahre!"

"Don't lie to me! How else did he find out?"

"He tricked me."

"It's your fault, Elsa!"

"Ralph, be reasonable. What did you expect me to do?"

"He can't even read and you know it!"

Suddenly Dad stopped yelling and turned to me. "I'm sorry, Calvin. It's all been too much for me!" He sat down on my bed and put his head in his hands.

We sat quietly for a while. I glanced at Mom. She was staring out the window. A tear formed, swelled, then dripped off the tip of her nose.

Dad stopped rocking back and forth and roused himself. "He says they'll pay for his education."

"Who?" asked Mom.

"The P.C.C.C.C.U.S.A. Missionary Aid Society."

Dad and Mom stared at each other.

"Oh, *Ralph!*"

"It's the only way. We don't have any alternative unless you'll let him go to the village school!"

Mom started to cry. Dad put his arm around her and looked at me. "Your mother's upset because she'll miss you. I will, too."

Mom began to sob.

"What do you mean, Dad?"

"You're going to have to go to the mission school, to Great Dunstable."

I felt like the floor of my bedroom was sinking.

"It's a wonderful place," said Dad. "You'll love it."

I spent two happy years in Sussex, England, at Great Dunstable Preparatory Boarding School for the sons of missionaries. Then I got too old for GD and got sent home.

So I was back where I started and Mom was teaching me again. On the weekends, when Janet and Rachael were back from the Presbyterian, American-English boarding school they attended in Lausanne, the John Knox School, for the daughters of English-speaking, Presbyterian, Reformed missionaries, they would try to help Mom teach me out of a sense of obligation. But no one enjoyed my education, least of all me.

The good side to being homeschooled was that most of the time the Lord's work kept Mom and my sisters occupied. The bad part was that I still couldn't read very well; boarding school hadn't made up for six years of Mom's "homeschooling."

I guess my inability to read was a sign of how God blessed our ministry. If Mom hadn't been so occupied with her spiritual children she would have had more time to teach me. Mom maintained that even though I was a "little behind" in reading, the Lord had marvelously provided for me to have the wonderful education of living in a foreign land, of learning to speak French, and going to Italy and Zermatt every year on vacations that usually only the very wealthy might be expected to enjoy.

My not being able to read was sort of a family secret. After the

Reverend Bahre fiasco, we didn't mention it in front of the young people or visitors, just like we didn't mention Dad's Moods or when my mom and sisters were having female troubles or were off the roof. There were some things you just didn't talk about.

Anyway, on the day we were unpacking the correspondence-course books, and Grandmother's letter arrived, I was idly looking at the pictures in one of the new schoolbooks. I turned a page and saw a photograph of a nude woman. She was only a statue. She had no arms, or head, and one of her breasts was chipped, but the rest of her was all there.

"Mother!" hissed Janet in an urgent whisper.

"Yes, dear?"

Mom glanced up. She froze. Then Mom unfroze very quickly, snatched the book out of my hands, and said, *"Oh dear!"*

Mom snapped the book shut and glared at the cover.

"Greek Mythology! I don't think!"

Janet, Rachael, and Mom exchanged unhappy, pious, womanly glances. Mom sighed.

"I will write to the Calvert School. Janet, put all these so-called schoolbooks back in the box until I've had a chance to look them over *very carefully.*"

"But, Mom . . ."

Janet rounded on me furiously.

"Calvin!"

"No, it's all right, Janet. He should have these things explained. The photograph of that distasteful statue would be unsuitable in *any* child's textbook but it's doubly tragic because it's being used to glamorize, make titillating and falsely attractive, that which is actually *tragic sin!* There are still millions of people who worship gods of wood and stone. There's a lost world out there and it's our call to reach that world but not to be defiled by it. Do you understand, darling?"

"Yes, Mom."

"Good!"

Mom stood up and beamed at us.

"Now! Let's not think that because there are *some things* we can't do that Christians can't have fun! Godly activities are twice the fun of sin anyway! Sin soon loses its attraction and gets boring! What do you say to putting all these books away and baking a big batch of chocolate-chip cookies with the chocolate chips that came in the Missionary Alliance Mercy Box last week?"

When the cookies were done, and cool enough to handle, Mom put a dozen or so in a paper bag and sent Rachael, Janet, and me out for a walk. The day was one of those spectacular, postcard-perfect winter days you get in the Swiss Alps. The sky was a dark violet blue, the sun was hot, the air cool and dry. The Rhône valley was filled with a bluish haze that made the mountains seem to float between earth and sky. Across the valley, larch, beech, and pine trees created a patchwork of grays out of which the massive crags, boulders, and snowfields of the Dents du Midi rose to a cresting, jagged wave.

Janet, Rachael, and I took off up the "back road," a dirt track that ran behind our chalet to the logging path that cut up the steep mountain slope that our house nestled against.

I glanced at Janet. She wasn't looking too mean that day, so I ventured a question.

"Can I have a cookie?"

"Not until we get to the goat pasture above the spring. Then you can. If you eat now you won't be able to walk as fast. Calvin, for someone who says he wants to be a doctor, I'm surprised you don't know that when we digest, the blood from our limbs goes to our stomach and deprives our muscles of oxygen. It's not good for you. Besides, you need a goal to aim for, a treat to spur you on so you won't fuss about how far we're going."

Rachael was panting. "How far *are* we going to go?"

"If you wouldn't talk so much we would get there a lot sooner!"

Rachael stopped and took a breath. "Ah, c'mon, Janet, don't be stingy. This is supposed to be fun. Mom said so."

"Just because something is 'fun' doesn't mean you don't have to work at it."

I spoke up. "This isn't school. Mom gave the cookies to all of us. I can have one when I want! Who put *you* in charge?"

"I did!" Janet grabbed my arm and expertly twisted it behind my back.

"Ow!"

Rachael stamped her foot. *"Let him go right now or I'll tell Mother!"*

Janet stamped her foot in mockery of Rachael. *"Dad doesn't like tattletales!"*

"I mean it!" yelled Rachael. She started to cry.

"Oh, all right! *Here!*" Janet released me, then threw the cookies over a hazelnut bush.

"Janet!" shrieked Rachael as the cookies sailed into the air.

Janet laughed and strolled effortlessly up the almost vertical slope. She made it look easy. She was not even out of breath. Rachael stood panting and staring after her. She shook her head sadly over Janet's wickedness and terrible strength.

I scrambled up the steep, frozen, moss-covered bank to where the brown bag lay split, cookies tumbled out on last year's soft gray pine needles.

"It's okay. The cookies are fine!" I called to Rachael.

I ate a cookie.

A few minutes later I caught up to Janet.

"You were right. My legs *are* too tired to walk! Can't we cut through to the field and just sit and watch the cows?"

"You're a lazy bum!" said Janet, but she smiled. I had asked her the right way, giving her scientific knowledge its due.

Janet led the way into the field and sat down on a tussock of dry, brown grass protruding from a patch of snow. Our village was directly below us, about a quarter of a mile down. We had a bird's-eye view of the barns and chalets. Most of the chalets' roofs were made of corrugated tin, dull red tile, or lichen-stained slate. They all had round poles laid across them to prevent snow from cascading dangerously onto passersby.

The dark wooden buildings were tightly packed together. They made a solid geometric pattern that was only interrupted where the main road, and the track of our little tram, ran parallel to each other, bisecting the heart of Trois-Torrents.

Huge, placid brown-and-white cows ambled across the fields. The snow had melted on the steep, sun-drenched bank of the hillside above the village, so the cows were let out to browse on last year's stubble. As we sat munching cookies the music of cowbells drifted up to us from the herd. Even from where we were sitting we could see a puff of steam each time a cow took a breath, then exhaled.

Chapter 6

MASTER CALVIN BECKER   JENNIFER BAZLINTON

L'ARCHE   1 HARROW COURT

CHALET LES TULIPES   LONDON W1

TROIS-TORRENTS-SUR-MONTHEY   ENGLAND

VALAIS

SWITZERLAND

March 12, 1967

Dear Twit,

Curiouser and curiouser, said Alice. Must I really wish you and your tribe a "Merry Christmas" in March each year?!

Dear silly old imbecile! Merry Christmas to you! Miss you—

J.

PS. When do you celebrate New Year's? April 1st?!!! Ha! Ha!

Rachael handed me the card. She was sitting on the edge of my bed. She looked wounded.

"I wish she wouldn't mock our faith all the time."

I didn't answer. I never argued about Jennifer with my family. Even back when I was thirteen I didn't like to hear them talk about her. It was bad enough that when I wrote to her I had to dictate to Mom or Rachael.

I was embarrassed that Jennifer had found out about our March 25

44

"Christmas." Janet told her one day on the beach. But I still enjoyed getting Jennifer's card. Any word from her was better than none.

I changed the subject.

"Rachael, I wish we could have a Christmas tree this year. Plenty of Christians have a tree. Even some people in our denomination do."

"Calvin! You know perfectly well that even in the P.C.C.C.C.U.S.A. there are some people who have a weak view of Scripture!"

"What do Christmas trees have to do with that? I heard Dick Keegan tell Jane he thought we were silly."

"Dad says Christmas trees are an evil Norse custom, not Christian at all." Rachael shook her head sadly. "Calvin, sometimes I think you don't care about the Things of The Lord very much. Besides, if Dick really said that you should have told Dad. When did he say it?"

"Never mind."

Rachael turned and walked out of my room. As she closed the door she said, "You didn't even thank me for reading her distasteful card to you."

That year's Christmas season began in earnest when the missionary box, sent with a letter signed by all eighteen members of the P.C.C.C.C.U.S.A.'s mission board, arrived. The box was full of stale gingersnap cookies, used, redried tea bags, socks, and a Bible storybook for each of us children. Once, when I was six, they put in candy corn. But in 1965 there wasn't any candy. Nothing seemed to go right that year.

Even though pine boughs might have been used by pagans for wicked purposes, Dad said that we need not be as separated from the world as the Closed Brethren or Amish. So it was all right for us to decorate with evergreens, Dad said, so long as we never forgot what the real purpose of Christmas was, and didn't go so far as actually having a tree.

Sober decorations notwithstanding, our Christmas celebration was not too worldly. We didn't sing profane songs like "Rudolph the

Red-Nosed Reindeer" or "Frosty the Snowman," let alone, "I'm Dreaming of a White Christmas."

The only reason I even knew about those songs was because of Billy Graham's compromise with the world's spirit. He had let George Beverly Shea sing worldly songs, even "I'm Dreaming of a White Christmas," on a Christmas record that was put out by the Billy Graham Evangelistic Association.

Billy Graham's record was given to us by a well-meaning, but confused Methodist missionary who visited us in March the year before. We had played it once, to be polite, while the missionary, who was not a kindred spirit, and who admitted she celebrated Christmas in December, was staying with us.

When the theologically misguided missionary left, Mom hid the offending record on the top shelf of the Sunday-school materials cupboard in our living room. Mom didn't throw it away, the way Dad did with a bottle of wine some Swedish Lutherans gave us one year. That's because the record was just proof of poor spiritual discernment, not a real sin like wine. And besides, the misguided missionary had given us a large gift designated for the chapel Dad hoped to build someday. So Mom kept the record in case the missionary visited again and asked about it.

"Dad," I said one day, when I went to his room before that fateful Christmas, "please ask Mom not to give me too many clothes this year."

"Why?" Dad looked up from his Bible and sermon notes. "Do you want toys? Aren't you a little old for that? Wouldn't you rather have *useful things* like shirts and socks?"

"C'mon, Dad, ask her, will you?"

Dad smiled. "I'll see what I can do, boy."

Dad started to work again.

"Dad?"

"Mm . . . ?"

"What do you want for Christmas?"

Dad looked up from his Bible.

"Just be a good boy. That'll be enough."

"No, seriously, Dad. What can I get you?"

Dad put down his pen and leaned back in the rickety rush-bottom chair.

"How about a Rolls-Royce?"

"Okay, Pop, which bank should I rob?"

"How about the Crédit Suisse? That's where they keep the gold bars. How about you just get me a gold bar?"

"Okay, Pop. You got a deal. What will you spend it on?"

"A house where there are no young people asking questions, no prayer meetings, no Swiss authorities giving us a hard time over renewing our residency permits, and no fellow workers who I have theological differences with!" Dad laughed and picked up his pen.

"What would you rather be doing, Pop?"

"How about lying on the beach at Paraggi or skiing in Zermatt?"

"Don't you like it here?"

"I was only kidding, Calvin. Of course I wouldn't want to be any-where else than the place of the Lord's choosing."

"Dad?"

"Yes?"

"Dad, what do you think God will lead me to do?"

"I can't say, Calvin. He leads us all individually."

"Mom says she's praying that I follow your footsteps into the min-istry."

"Well, that would be fine, but you'll have to wait and see what door the Lord opens."

"Mom says her dad got his call when he was only eight years old, that he knew from then on that God was calling him to China's lost millions. How did you get your call, Dad?"

"The Lord spoke to me through your mother." Dad started to work again.

"Do you think he'll speak to me through her, too?"

"I hope not!" Dad teetered precariously on the back legs of his chair before he managed to right himself. Gripping the edge of his small rolltop desk, he pulled upright and laughed. "Just kidding. Your mom's a wonderful woman and has a special heart for the Things of The Lord."

Dad looked back down at his papers and Bible concordance. "Go on, boy, I have a lot of work to do on this sermon."

"Okay, Dad."

I walked down the hall to my room and closed the door. I sat down on the bed and stared at Jennifer's Christmas card. I started to get glimpses of my story. Then I lay down and closed my eyes.

"Oh, you unspeakably silly boy! You imbecile!" said Jennifer after I told her about running away. *"How pathetically feeble!* Really, I don't know what we shall do with you!"

"What about sneaking me some food every day, for a start?!"

"Look here, boyso! Don't think you can get bossy with *me,* you beastly twit! And don't think you can expect me to steal food for you from the *pension!*"

"I didn't ask you to 'steal,' just to get me some food. You know, rolls, bread sticks, whatever you can."

"I see, you want me to starve myself and bring you *my dinner!*"

"Jennifer! One minute you're kissing me and, well, you know, then you're yelling at me for running away and won't even feed me! What kind of friend is that?"

"I never said I wouldn't feed you. I just don't know how you plan to work things out without getting yourself into dreadful trouble, even worse than now. What will you do, you gormless twit?"

Jennifer stood looking at me, then suddenly burst into tears and threw her arms around my neck and said in a rush, "Oh Calvin, I'm so bloody sorry for you! It must be rotten having such a balmy family!"

She held on to me. I felt her tears wet on my neck. I felt her breasts pressing softly on my chest. I felt her hips against mine.

After a couple of minutes she stopped crying and wiped her eyes. "I'm as silly as you are. Why I should cry I don't know."

"I think you're wonderful."

"You silly, silly boy!" Jennifer blew her nose. "*Of course* I'll get food for you and anything else you need. I've got some money, you know. I'll give you that as well."

"You don't need to. Gino's taking care of me."

"You'll need more money when you want to go home after the holls. You'll need to buy a ticket."

"I can hide in the train's toilet."

Jennifer laughed.

"Calvin, you shall do *exactly* as I say. I've got ten pounds my aunt gave me when I passed my O-levels. I've saved it and you shall have it."

"Jennifer—"

"If you say one word about it, I shall turf you out and never speak to you again!"

"But—"

"Not one word!"

Jennifer went over to her dresser, opened a drawer, lifted up a pile of neatly folded panties, and took out an envelope with a card in it. From the card she removed a crisp, new ten-pound note and handed it to me.

"Calvin, I love you and I always shall. I will do anything I can to help you and if you wish I shall even tell Mum and Dad that you are to live with us and that if they don't let you I shall kill myself!"

Jennifer looked fierce. Her cheeks flushed. Her blue-green eyes sparkled. I felt as if my heart would burst.

There was a knock at Jennifer's door. Mrs. Bazlinton said in her rich, fluffy voice, "Jennifer darling, are you in there, my pet?"

I leapt across the marble floor to the bathroom and into Jennifer's shower cubicle. I pulled the shower curtain behind me and held my breath as Jennifer said, "Yes, Mum."

Mrs. Bazlinton opened the door. "What on earth are you doing, darling? We went out to the beach after siesta and you were nowhere about."

"I had a bit of a rest myself, Mum."

"Are you feeling well, my pet?"

"Oh yes, Mum. I suppose I must've slept a bit longer than usual."

"Well, that's all right, then. Shall we go out to the beach now?"

"That would be lovely. You toddle along, I'll be there in half a sec."

"I'll just have a tinkle before I go."

Mrs. Bazlinton opened the bathroom door.

I breathed as quietly as I could and hoped that when she said she'd have a tinkle Mrs. Bazlinton had meant she'd go to the toilet, not take a shower! You never knew what the English might do next.

I heard her clothes rustle. The old wooden toilet seat creaked as she sat down. I tried not to breathe. When she started to go I heard a silvery sound, not a steady stream like mine, with a beginning, middle, and end, but an intermittent splish-splashing. Then I heard her take a piece of toilet paper, use it, and flush. Loud sucking and gurgling sounds, from the old-fashioned wall-mounted toilet tank, covered up the noise of her retreat and allowed me to take a couple of deep, long-overdue breaths.

I didn't know for sure if Mrs. Bazlinton had left until a moment later when the door opened and Jennifer said, "Are you going to stay in there all day, you nasty child, watching people's mums having a tinkle?"

"I didn't mean to be in here when she did that! Besides, I didn't watch!"

"I bet you didn't, you Peeping Tom!"

"Jennifer!"

"Never mind the protestations of innocence! We'd best make a bit of a plan. What do I tell Mum and Dad for starters?"

"Tell them that I'm staying in Portofino with friends of my family and that Mom and Dad will be coming down next week after you all leave. They'll believe that."

"I hope you're not as good a liar with me as you seem to be with everyone else!"

"Jennifer!'

"You have a criminal streak a mile wide, my lad. Good thing for you they've abolished hanging!"

"*You* always tell the truth, I guess!"

"That's beside the point, laddie. At any rate, there's no time to discuss your sadly deficient character. Mum will expect me on the beach in a minute or two."

"My plan will work fine. Tell them what I told you. Then I can be with you all I want without having to sneak around."

"I suppose that will have to do. But you can hardly come with me now. Wait here for a bit. I'll go and tell them I just ran into you. Follow me in ten minutes or so."

"Sounds good to me."

Chapter 7

I ALWAYS WOKE UP BEFORE IT WAS LIGHT on March 25, usually at about four A.M. Christmas morning of 1965 was no different.

The first thing I did was to lie still in the dark trying to remember why I felt excited. Then it hit me. I shoved my feet to the bottom of my bed. Sure enough, I felt a magical weight pressing down on my ankles as I slid my feet between the cool sheets. The Christmas stocking, a heavy, overstuffed, three and a half feet of lumpy, gray wool, bulging with presents, was the source of the delicious weight. I savored the moment, gently kicking up and down to feel the stocking and to hear the crisp wrapping paper crackle.

We had very fixed Christmas traditions. Any change in the routine would have been unthinkable. Our Christmas traditions were so absolute, so holy, that Mom even used them to illustrate a theological truth: the Physical Things were to be kept for marriage, just like our Christmas presents were to be kept, unopened, until the appointed time.

There were time-honored stages of foreplay with my Christmas stocking. Several hours had to be endured in which everything but the actual opening could take place.

I lay in the dark relishing the feeling of the stocking's weight on my legs. After I squeezed the last drop of pleasure out of the feel and sound of it, I reached up to my bedside lamp, switched it on, and slowly turned around, sat up, and looked.

My stocking was so bulky, stretched, and packed that every gray wool fiber was near breaking point. I felt each package in turn but removed nothing. To do so would spoil everything. When enough time had gone by to warrant the next step I got out of bed, carefully gathered up my stocking, and supporting it tenderly in my arms, tiptoed down our low-ceilinged hallway.

I observed a sliver of light under Janet's door. I knocked softly.

"Come in," whispered Janet.

"Merry Christmas!" Rachael blurted out excitedly.

"*Shhh!*" hissed Janet. "You'll wake them too early and put Dad in a Mood."

Janet and Rachel were sitting side by side, buried deep under the huge shapeless eiderdown on Janet's bed. Both had their stockings propped up in front of them. As I opened the door they slid to the edge to make room for me.

We waited as the hands of Janet's alarm clock moved with excruciating slowness, to the appointed hour eight A.M. Then we trooped into Mom and Dad's bedroom, clambered up on their double bed, and prepared to open our stockings as they bid us a Merry Christmas, rubbed sleep out of their eyes, and smoothed back their hair.

After the stockings had been opened, we sat surrounded by mounds of torn colored paper, eating the tangerines that had been in the toe. Dad wiped his mouth on the back of his hand.

"Hand me my Bible, will you, Janet?"

Janet, who was seated next to Dad's bedside table, a small wooden nightstand with a drawer and locked cupboard, wrapped a handful of tangerine peel in a scrap of tissue paper, reached over, picked up Dad's heavy Scofield Bible, and handed it to him.

I knew the overfamiliar passages by heart. But listening patiently to the Christmas story was the price of admission to the gifts piled in the living room.

When Dad read the part where Mary says, "Behold the maidservant of the Lord! Let it be to me according to your word," his voice choked up. He paused to collect himself. Every year his show of emotion embarrassed me. But Mom and Rachael exchanged an appreciative glance.

When Dad finished reading, he asked Mom to close in prayer.

"Dear Heavenly Father, we just come before Thee in thanksgiving for the most precious big present of all. . . ."

As Mom's voice rose and fell my mind began to wander. It always wandered when Mom prayed; besides, I had heard her Christmas prayer many times. As Mom went on and on I cast a gloating eye over the pile of stocking presents littering the yellow bedspread. A stapler, a box of staples, a roll of Scotch tape, a package of heavy brown rubber bands, a box of paper clips, a book, *Medicine for Young Minds* (Rachael said she would read it to me later), two Dinky Toy cars, a Ferrari and a yellow Swiss postal bus, and a pair of socks.

". . . And Lord, we just ask that You will make Yourself known to us that You will be especially close to each of us today in a special way—" Mom's prayer was interrupted by the phone ringing in the downstairs hall.

Rachael quietly slipped from the bed, her head still reverently bowed. I heard her bare feet patter lightly on the linoleum to the head of the stairs, then the creak of the worn treads as she leapt down the steps three at a time.

Mom finished her prayer as Rachael answered the phone.

Mom looked around at us. "Oh dear, I do hope some young person isn't at the Aigle station and on their way to us on *Christmas Day!*"

"No one would do that. Everyone knows we celebrate Christmas at this time of year," said Janet.

Dad frowned. "I wouldn't be so sure. People do funny things. They have no idea that even pastors need a little privacy once in a while!"

Rachael yelled up the stairs, *"Dad! Come quick, it's for you!"*

Dad muttered, "This had better be important. I hope Rachael has the sense to not bother me on Christmas day with some fool nonsense!"

Dad slid out of his side of the bed. Some of his presents fell to the floor. He walked out of the room without bothering to put on his bathrobe or slippers. I saw Janet avert her eyes. Dad's pajamas kind of gaped at the front. Mom noticed Dad's immodesty and frowned. Then she sighed. "Oh dear, I do hope this doesn't put Ralph in a Mood. He seemed *so relaxed* this morning."

Janet scowled. "Some people would disturb a funeral!"

Two minutes later we heard Dad's footsteps stamping back up the stairs. The door burst open. Dad stood glaring at us. His face was flushed. A vein pulsed in the side of his neck.

"Oh, Ralph! What's happening? What's wrong?" shrieked Mom.

Janet leapt up.

"Is it the Russians? Have they attacked?"

Dad remained silent for a long thirty seconds, during which time Rachael moaned to herself, "Oh no, oh no, oh no," until finally Janet gave her a shake.

Dad spoke. "Mother had a dizzy spell. She has fallen and broken her hip. They think she may have had a stroke. They're not sure. They've done surgery. That was Uncle George. He called to say that Mother is insisting I fly home . . . *today!*"

"Oh no!" Mom said in a long-drawn-out wail.

"Oh yes!" Dad glared at us as if it was our fault.

"Oh, but, *Ralph* . . ."

"There's no use talking about it! Uncle George says that she may be dying, that if I want to see her alive I have to leave, *now!* He also says there are some questions concerning her will. . . . I need to see if I can make a train to Geneva and fly out."

"But . . ." Mom tried to speak, then her mouth bunched up and started to quiver along with her chin.

Dad spoke again in his most solemn voice. "Christmas is over! I'm sorry, children, but sometimes in life things happen which change *everything!*"

Chapter 8

AFTER DAD INTONED "sometimes in life things happen which change everything," the day turned into a nightmare. Our family began to hemorrhage money. Mom commented, to no one in particular, that it seemed typical that Grandmother had chosen Christmas day, of all days, on which to unleash a "monumentally tragic crisis."

There was a flight from Geneva to London that would get Dad on a connecting flight for Philadelphia. If Dad took a taxi, all the way from our house to the Geneva airport, a two-and-a-half-hour ride that would cost over one hundred Swiss francs, he could just make it.

Mom counted the money from our various funds and piled it in a heap on her basement office table. She opened the vacation drawer and took out the Portofino-Zermatt vacation box; three hundred and twenty francs. The girls'-school fee envelope yielded one hundred and eighty francs. Dad had seven hundred francs in the mortgage box. There was a hundred-franc note a wealthy American businessman had given to us. Dad had been saving it to buy new hymnbooks so that our young people would be able to have real books, and not have to sing from mimeographed sheets that smelled like lighter fluid and rubbed off on their hands.

Combined, our funds, including eight francs and fifty centimes I had saved to spend on a new mask and snorkel, were just enough to pay for the cab fare to Geneva and the round-trip Geneva–London–Philadelphia airfare.

Usually when we had just enough of anything Mom said as how it was a clear sign of God's sufficiency, especially if the money was miraculously the exact amount needed to purchase whatever our ministry lacked at the time. But on this occasion, no one was saying anything good about how the funds we had saved covered the price of Dad's cab fare and airline ticket.

It was ten o'clock in the morning when the taxi pulled up. Dad gave Mom a long hug before he got into the old black Peugeot station wagon. Before Dad slammed the door he turned to us and, in a loud trembling voice, said, *"Pray for me!"* Then the taxi headed down the long, steep stretch of road, rounded the first hairpin bend, and disappeared.

Mom put her arm around Janet's shoulder, took me by the hand, and nodded to Rachael. "Come, children. We will take this to the Lord right away."

Mom led us into the living room. Even though it was March 25 and the presents and candles were all there, it didn't feel like Christmas. Mom was changing our tradition, having a prayer meeting when we should have been opening presents.

"Dear Heavenly Father, we just come before Thee with our hearts full of doubts and fears. We just claim Your precious promises that 'where two or three' are gathered in Your precious Name, 'there I will be in the midst of them . . .' "

Mom prayed even longer than usual. I began to try and spot the different name tags on the presents that I could see from where I was sitting, *C* for Calvin, *R* for Rachael, *J* for Janet. I picked out a large square box, just the right size for a chemistry set, with a *C* visible on the tag. Even though it didn't feel like Christmas, my heart leapt a little at the sight of that promising box.

No one had served ginger ale, the candles weren't lit, there were no cookies, and Dad was somewhere over the Atlantic in a record Mood. Nevertheless, I realized, something would have to be done with the presents. No matter how long they prayed, eventually the women would disengage from this bout of spiritual warfare and we would get to open our gifts. My spirits began to rise.

Rachael, Janet, and Mom were licking up every drop of spiritual gravy. Their voices shook with pious emotion. Mom's head was bowed so low it touched her knees. Rachael cried as she wrestled with principalities on Dad's and Grandmother's behalf. She punctuated Mom's requests with heartfelt mutterings: "Yes, Lord!" "Thank You, Lord," "We just praise You, Jesus!"

After about twenty minutes of fervent intercession, Janet's hand was so warm and wet that when she reached out to hold mine, to forcibly draw me into the circle of prayer, my fingers popped out of her grasp the way a bar of soap does when you squeeze it in the bath.

It was a long while before I had the opportunity to redirect the women's attention away from spiritual warfare and back to the presents, but eventually Rachael, Janet, and Mom resurfaced, blinked their eyes, and smiled tearfully at each other, murmured a last "Praise You, Jesus," then fell silent.

I took a deep breath. "What about the presents?"

"Oh, how *can you!*" said Janet, her voice full of quivering, indignant anger at my worldliness.

"At a time like *this!*" Rachael remonstrated.

Mom wiped her eyes on the hanky she was clutching.

"It does seem a little strange to open gifts now."

Janet gave me a murderously bright smile. "We'll just put them away for next year."

"*WHAT!*"

I jumped up so fast I knocked over the coffee table. It had a life-sized set of praying hands on it made out of solid brass. The inspirational sculpture, a prize Dad had won in a preaching contest at seminary, clanged dully on the wooden floor as it rolled under the couch. The women stared at me with shocked faces.

"*Darling!* What on *earth's* gotten into you?"

"Sorry, Mom, it's just, well, I wanted to see how you'd like my present for you."

"Oh, I see. Well that's different. I thought that—"

"He wants his big present. Don't let him fool you!"

Rachael gave Janet a reproachful look.

"That's not very nice, Janet."

"Don't you go taking his side!"

"Children, children, *please*." Mom hesitated. "Well, it is Christmas day, and we can't help your father by not giving the gifts. So, however inappropriate it seems, I don't think it's actually wrong. I suppose we might as well."

Janet shook her head darkly and gave me a smoldering look. Mom sighed and slipped a package out from under the others and handed it to me. Still, whether Mom sighed or not, the important thing was that she did hand it over.

After we each opened a gift, Mom relented further and lit the candles. A few items later Mom sent Rachael to go and get the ginger ale.

The wood-paneled walls of our living room began to glow with candlelight. The delicious incense of Christmas—ginger ale, wrapping paper, and chocolate—was restored to its proper place. Eventually, even Janet loosened up and stopped pretending she was too grown up to be interested in our festive proceedings. When Mom gave her a large squishy package and said, "Janet, this is your big present. I hope it fits!" Janet squealed and shrieked.

None of us admitted it, but soon we were having just as good a time as we would have had if Dad had been with us.

Chapter 9

IT WAS NOT A HEALTH BUT A HYGIENE PROBLEM. Mom said that she was not surprised to learn that "that filthy old woman doesn't even clean her ears!" Mom said this at the end of the first week of April 1965 after Dad called from Philadelphia. He instructed Mom to pray for the Lord's leading concerning Grandmother, concerning what to do with her. It turned out she was not dying. The dizzy spell that made her fall had not been caused by a stroke, but by wax buildup in her right inner ear.

Dad was an only child. Because he had no brothers or sisters, there was no one else to help with Grandmother. Mom explained this to us after she hung up the phone, called Grandmother a filthy old woman, then gathered us together for prayer.

"Oh dear Lord," Mom prayed as we sat around her in a circle in the living room, along with two French young people, "Thou knowest that Grandmother Becker hath been a trial and tribulation to us these many years. Thou knowest that we have prayed and longed, even weeping before Thy precious face, for her salvation. And, Lord, Thou knowest that Ralph and I hath wrestled before Thee as to what Thy will is for us to do with Grandmother now she is bedridden and needs constant care. Thou knowest that the cost of a nursing home is beyond our means since we have sacrificed all our worldly goods in order to serve Thee. But, *oh Lord!* We just fall down before Thee to beg Thee that Thou *wouldst remove this cup from us!*"

God's answer was, "No." He didn't remove Grandmother Becker from us. The next afternoon Dad called Mom to tell her that the

P.C.C.C.C.U.S.A. mission board would not help with funds to put Grandmother in a nursing home. Since there did not seem to be any other alternative, Mom and Dad decided that the Lord was leading them, for His own very mysterious purposes, to bring Grandmother to Switzerland to live with us.

After the phone call Mom hung up and burst into tears.

"This is going to be a time of severe testing, children! Your Grandmother has always been a thorn in your father's side. *You may never see him in a good mood again!*"

Mom raced up the stairs. We heard her run down the hall and slam the bedroom door. Then we heard an explosion of muffled sobbing.

A few moments of awkward silence followed.

Janet said, "I'll go up and see her. You stay here."

Rachael's lips were moving in prayer. I didn't pray but I was wondering what it would be like to live in our house if Dad was going to be in a perpetual Mood, sulking, shouting, and throwing things day and night, day in and day out, for years and years.

Janet came to the head of the stairs.

"Rachael! Calvin! Mom wants you to come up!"

Rachael gave my hand a squeeze, turned, and led the way. When we got to Mom and Dad's bedroom we found Mom sitting on the edge of the couch, nervously twisting and untwisting her handkerchief. Mom looked up and smiled sweetly. She delicately dabbed a last smear of tears from under her red eyes.

"Children, the Lord has just spoken to me. I am now willing to accept His will for our lives."

Mom smiled. She looked pretty even with her face flushed and a little swollen.

Rachael rushed over and hugged her.

"That's *wonderful,* Mom!"

"You are *dear* children!"

Mom blew her nose.

"Children, I have been *silly*! We are living by faith as a demonstration of God's existence. The Lord has always shown Himself to be *faithful*, providing for our needs year after year, and now, in the matter of Grandmother Becker, I haven't trusted Him!"

Rachael began to cry and kiss Mom's neck.

"Oh Mom, it's so beautiful . . ."

Mom hugged Rachael, then pushed her away so she could continue sharing God's revelation with us.

"The Lord has brought me to my senses! He has given me a new heart for Grandmother! What an *opportunity* to show forth Christ's love! What an *answer to prayer*! *Why*, now we can *really* witness to Grandmother! I wouldn't be surprised if the reason these events were ordained was for the *very purpose* of saving Grandma! The wax buildup, her dizziness, and her tragic fall is probably the *one way* the Lord could bring her into contact with the Gospel! Isn't it *wonderful*, children? *Let's thank Him now*!"

Rachael sobbed. Even Janet sniffed once or twice. Mom's cheeks were flushed vivid scarlet, her voice was about an octave higher than normal, her smile looked a little trembly, and her breath smelled strong. Yet she prayed in a firm, vibrant voice as we bowed our heads.

"Oh Lord, we ask for Your forgiveness for our lack of faith! *Thank You* for answering our prayers for Grandmother! *We thank Thee* for this opportunity to be a *light unto her*! We just *claim* Your promises! *Thank You* for using the humble wax in her ears and her frail bones as an instrument of Your Grace. *Thank You* that in Your sovereignty You have given us a chance to be used by You to bring dear Grandmother into Thy kingdom! Amen, and amen!"

After Mom finished, it was as if a bright bubble of happiness burst upon us. Each of us tried to outdo the others in our newfound good feeling.

Rachael said she would move into Janet's room so Grandmother could have a bedroom *and* a dayroom to sit in. Mom said she would sew Grandmother new curtains and a matching bedspread. Rachael and Janet planned to make a huge "Welcome Home, Grandma" sign and hang it over the balcony the day Grandmother arrived.

Rachael offered to read Bible stories to Grandmother. Janet's idea was to spend time praying with her; she would ask Grandmother to become her prayer partner on our weekly days of prayer.

Mom said that Grandmother had probably mellowed with age and would not be as difficult as she used to be. I suggested that we buy Grandmother a pet to keep her company. Mom agreed that that was a good idea.

"Perhaps a dog or a cat would be too much, dear, but a bowl of goldfish would be perfect!"

Chapter 10

IN LATE MAY OF 1965, a week after Grandmother came to live with us, I almost dropped her as I felt her hot, evil-smelling urine soaking into my pants. I knew if I dropped her, I would get into terrible trouble, so even though she was urinating on me through her nightgown, I grimly held on as we staggered toward the toilet in a close, damp embrace.

Instead of saying she was sorry, Grandmother pretended nothing unusual had happened. After I got her settled on the toilet all she said was, "Get out, ya brat! Don't come back till I finish. *Ya hear?*"

I ran down the hall to my room, changed, then went downstairs. There were some young people standing in the kitchen, helping Mom fix a tuna-fish casserole for our lunch, and singing "In the Sweet Bye and Bye" in broken English.

"Mom, could you come here a minute?"

"In a second, darling."

"It's pretty serious, Mom."

Mom stopped stirring her pot of noodles, cheese, and tuna and dried off her hands. She stepped into the hall.

"Mom, Grandmother went on me."

"Oh dear, I am sorry!"

"Mom, I'm not taking her to the bathroom anymore. She's Dad's mother, let him take her!"

Mom looked sorrowful.

"You know your father can't risk putting his back out again after what happened at the airport when he tried to lift her into the taxi.

He still can hardly walk. With Rachael and Janet back in school, who else can help? You know I'm not strong enough. Besides she's the only grandmother you have!"

"That's a good thing; a few more like her and I'd get drowned!"

Mom didn't like my attitude. She marched me upstairs.

"That's not the tone to take with your mother." Dad didn't say it as if he was very angry with me. He was having even more trouble getting used to Grandmother's invasion than me.

"Dad, she didn't even apologize."

Mom and Dad exchanged grim glances.

Dad sighed deeply. "I'm sorry, Calvin. I'm sorry you have to share this burden with us."

"She sets a poor example, I must say. How I wish you had had the privilege of knowing *my* mother, Calvin."

Dad turned angrily on Mom.

"Let's just call it a day, all right, Elsa?"

Grandmother, who had been sitting on the toilet the whole time, screamed, *"Am I gonna sit on the can all day? How long do you think it takes a body to wipe her butt!"*

"Really!" exclaimed Mom. She glared at Dad and trembled all over, as if she had suddenly been caught in an icy draft. Then Mom stalked down the hall to the bathroom, shouting, *"Mother, I wish you wouldn't speak in that foul manner in my home!"*

After we got Grandmother back to her sitting room, Mom went down to the kitchen, Dad went back to work on his sermon, and I retreated to my room. I lay down on my bed. I could hear the young people start to sing "This Little Light of Mine" as I closed my eyes.

The late-afternoon sun slanted in hazy rays from above the rim of the hills that surrounded the Paraggi bay. The umbrellas cast long shadows, making dark oval patches that stretched down to the water's edge. Naked babies played in the tiny waves that rippled along the shore. Tired grown-ups, their energy spent from a day of doing nothing in the hot sun, lounged on their deck chairs or towels.

A few people were swimming, but at the lazy end of the day, most of the morning's energetic activity had ceased. By now the rowboats for hire were pulled up on sand. The Banini was methodically moving up the beach collecting oars and seat cushions.

As I stepped from under the huge blue umbrellas which shaded the snack bar patio, the Banini glanced up from where he was gathering an armful of boat cushions. He waved a sinewy brown arm and broke into a wide grin. His missing teeth made a black gap between his nicotine-stained incisors.

"*Calvino!* 'Ow are you?"

"Fine."

"And you mama and papa and *sorellas,* 'ow are they?"

"Fine."

"You stay in Portofino or 'ere?"

"Portofino."

"*Bene! Bene! Domani mattina* you coming to 'elp *mia* weeth the boats, yes?"

"Sure, I'll be here like always."

"*Bene, bene.* I looking for you."

The Banini pressed the enormous stack of boat cushions to his faded blue T-shirt and padded off, his deformed, yellow toenails clicking on the concrete walk.

I looked beyond the terrace, down the row of deck chairs, until I spotted Jennifer standing with her back to me, one hip thrown out with abandon, her plain black bathing suit turning her slender figure into a graceful silhouette against the glare. She was standing, looking down at her parents, who were sitting in their deck chairs. I could see her mother's profile as she lifted a cup of tea to her lips, sipped, then said something to Jennifer that made her toss back her head, laugh, and shift her weight from one foot to the other.

I envied Jennifer her normal parents. Her dad was reading a pale pink copy of the *Financial Times,* not some newsletter about the latest theological split in the P.C.C.C.C.U.S.A. Her mother was knitting, instead of preparing Sunday-school lessons, or witnessing aids, like the Heart of Salvation or the Gospel Walnut, or writing prayer letters to raise money.

I stepped off the cracked concrete slab that formed the snack-bar terrace, and began to walk up the beach, past the Italian family who always occupied that particular stretch of sand. They had so many children, aunts, nieces, grandparents, fathers, and mothers, I could never figure out exactly who everyone was. They generally invited me to share their lunch.

"Calvino!" said one mother. *"Benvenuto! Come vai?"*

"Bene."

"E tua Madre?"

"Bene."

"E tuo Padre?"

"Bene."

"E le tue sorelle?"

"Bene."

"Molto bene bravissimo!" She acted as if the fact that my family were all well was a great accomplishment.

By the way she stood, hands folded in front of her, slightly leaning back, I could see she was pregnant again. Even though she wasn't showing very much yet, her belly button was already distended. This mother had been pregnant most summers. Babies tumbled out of her one after another in a happy profusion. Each summer last year's baby was a brown toddler, playing naked at the water's edge, the only white flesh on its tanned body the creases behind its dimpled knees.

The mother patted me on my shoulder and mentioned that she was about to buy *gelato,* ice cream, for everyone. She asked if she should get one for me. I said, "No, *grazie,* I have to see someone."

"Maka sure and coma back and play weeth Alfredo."

I moved down the beach nodding or saying hello to all the regulars until I arrived at the Bazlintons' encampment.

Mr. Bazlinton looked up from his newspaper.

"How splendid to see you, old chap!"

Mrs. Bazlinton put down her cup of tea and beamed at me. "We were worried you weren't going to come on holiday this year!"

"Jennifer tells us that you've come ahead of the tribe," said Mr. Bazlinton.

"Yes, that's right, they'll be here next week."

"What a pity, we shall just miss them," said Mrs. Bazlinton without much conviction.

"You poor chap, all alone in Portofino for a whole week!" Mr. Bazlinton laughed. "You must spend as much time with us as you like. We'd be delighted to have you join us at lunch if you wish."

"That would be nice. Thank you, Mr. Bazlinton."

"Well, *that's* settled then! *Splendid!* Care for a cup of tea and a biscuit?" Mrs. Bazlinton held out a box of McVitties Digestive Biscuits. She always brought them from England.

"Not now, Mum, there's hardly time left for a bathe before the sun goes down." Jennifer pulled at my arm. "Come on, Calvin, don't just stand there!"

"Off you go, old chap. No sense in keeping the ladies waiting." Mr. Bazlinton winked at me.

We swam past the end of the pier into the open water of the bay. Earlier in the day you had to be careful that you didn't get run over by the speedboats that skimmed across the placid water towing skiers. Now, at the languid end of late afternoon, the powerboats were gone. The cove fell into a silent, limpid green calm, undisturbed, flat, the high white clouds and the gray olive-clad hills reflected on the still surface.

We swam, silent, side by side, in a straight line to the far point below the castle, the place we always went. The point was a place of significance. Once Jennifer had cut her foot on a broken wine bottle there. I had stopped the bleeding with a tourniquet made out of the rubber strap of my diving mask.

The loudest sound we made was when our feet inadvertently broke the surface with a dull *clop*. When we were children we always used to race each other or stop to dive to the silver sand far below, to see who could bring up a handful, streaming out from between clutching fingers, spent breath bursting in a hot, tight, aching chest, to prove we could touch the bottom of the bay. But now we were quiet.

After fifteen minutes of slow, deliberate swimming we climbed out on the big broken pieces of rock that tumbled down to the sea, forming the foundation of the hill the "castle" sat on. I looked up. The huge villa was shut tight, yellow shutters closed, awnings rolled up. There were no open umbrellas on the terrace that surrounded the fieldstone foundation. We were alone. We walked to the only rock you could sit on comfortably. Sharp broken bits of fossilized seashell were embedded in all the other, less eroded boulders.

When we used to snorkel off the point, we climbed down from the road above, left our towels on the smooth rock, then dove in. Now we had no towels with us, but the rock was as familiar and comfortable as ever. It was warm from a day of sun.

"I discovered this rock," said Jennifer.

"I remember. When we swam here for the first time, your dad stood on the pier with his binoculars. He was worried we'd drown."

"It seemed a long way then."

"When you got out in the middle of the bay, remember how deep the water looked?"

"I always thought sharks or something dreadful would come out of the blue depths! Every few strokes I'd put my head under, with my eyes open, to see if anything was below us."

"I liked it better after we got our masks and snorkels. Then I could see, so it didn't scare me anymore."

Jennifer shivered. "Even then I'd think I'd see something moving out of the corner of my eye. You know just on the edge, looming in the abyss, as it were."

"I never knew anything ever scared you. I always thought you were the bravest person I ever met."

"I never knew you were frightened either. I kept quiet because I didn't want you to stop playing with me because I was a girl!"

Jennifer reached out and took my hand. We sat side by side and watched the shadow of the hill creep over the bay, turning it from turquoise to dark green. I glanced back at the beach. Most of the people were gone. I could see the Banini folding up the last of the deck chairs and umbrellas.

As the sun sank below the horizon the rays touched the tops of the cypresses above us. For an instant the crest of the hill seemed to be on fire, tipped with burnished gold. Then the sun was gone.

The air stayed warm. We sat holding hands. I moved closer to Jennifer until our sides were touching. She let go of my hand and draped her arm around my shoulders, tilted her head, and laid her cheek against mine. We watched the light recede across the sea until the water was a seamless sheet of dark cobalt blue all the way to the horizon. A tour boat, headed to Portofino, chugged its way past us. It was the last boat of the day. Only a few tourists lined the rail watching the coast slide by. Jennifer's cheek felt warm against mine.

Chapter 11

GRANDMOTHER CHEATED. Her dishonest gamesmanship drove us crazy, was one of the many reasons no one wanted to visit her unless they were forced to. By April of 1967, two tedious years after Grandmother's arrival, no one wanted to be around her. Dad had to force me to play Parcheesi with her. Mom said that it was like giving Grandmother a cup of cold water, that it was the Lord's will that I should be kind to her and play Parcheesi. I didn't say what I was thinking, how Mom hadn't given Grandmother a cup of Parcheesi for months, God's will notwithstanding.

"Hi, Grandma."

"You're late!"

I sat down on a stool across from Grandmother's easy chair. It had a fold-down tray made of thick, ugly plywood. The visiting nurse had provided this attachment so Grandmother could read, write, and play Parcheesi.

I glanced out the window. I wished I could have been outside. It was a bright spring morning. I could see the first crocuses scattered in mossy hollows on the banks of the back road, bright clusters of yellow, purple, and white.

Grandmother rolled the dice. I sighed and looked down at the board. Right away she moved her piece an extra square, then picked up the dice fast so I couldn't prove she had thrown a five instead of a six.

"Your turn. Hurry up!"

"Grandma, if you're going to cheat I won't play!"

Grandmother clamped her jaw shut with a snap. Every wrinkle of her small, sallow face was illuminated by the bright April sun. She was so shriveled and tiny her feet didn't touch the ground. But small or not, she was venomous.

"You're a liar and a brat! A brazen brat!"

Grandmother took a swing at me across the board with her blue-veined fist.

I ducked and wondered, for the hundredth time, why she smelled so strange, sort of like egg-salad sandwiches.

"Ya gotta play with me! Ya got no choice! Ain't ya ever heard of the Good Samaritan? Ain't ya supposed to be a Christian an' all? Are ya prayin' for me, ya li'l shit?" Grandmother cackled with laughter.

I let Grandmother's cheating go until she picked up one of my pieces and moved it backward. Even after two years, I found it impossible to ignore Grandmother's deviousness when it got that blatant. I told her the red marker in her hand was mine. She smiled and put it five squares back from where it had been. When I picked it up to move it to the correct square, she grabbed my hand.

"That's not where it was! Put that down, d'ya hear!"

We began to wrestle back and forth. Grandmother was surprisingly strong. Her claws dug into my wrist.

"Grandma, you can't move my piece!"

"I'll do what I damn well please!" She swept all the markers onto the floor, picked up the Parcheesi board, and hit me over the head. That's when I vowed revenge. At the very instant I was jumping back so she couldn't hit me again, I saw her goldfish and knew what to do.

"How d'ya like that, ya runty li'l shit!"

I smiled.

"You wait, you'll see."

I marched down the hall to Dad's room. I burst in just as he was getting a skinny, tall Roman Catholic boy from Austria to pray the Sinner's Prayer. Dad had him kneeling next to his bed. The boy was repeating after Dad, "Dear Jesus, I ask You into my heart and accept Your sovereign work on the cross, for the remission of my si—"

"She's cheating."

"You know that's her weakness, boy. Please be patient. Can't you see I'm busy?"

"She called me the S-word and she *hit me!*"

"Please wait here," Dad said in a grim voice to the kneeling Catholic. The boy got confused and started to stand up.

"No, no, we have *not* finished. You're not saved yet. Please wait."

Dad pushed the bewildered boy back onto his knees, then strode up the hall.

"Mother, I won't have it! How many times have I got to tell you that I won't have you striking my boy! And that I won't have the S-word used under my roof!"

Grandma gave Dad a sly, sideways glance.

"Go to hell, Ralph! I'll say shit anytime I want! *Shit! Shit! Shit!*"

"Mother, I'm warning you!"

I chipped in under my breath, "Why'd you ever bring her here in the first place?"

Dad rounded on me with a bellow and gave me a solid slap that resounded loudly off the low wood-paneled ceiling. Then he clutched at his hair and moaned. He dropped his hands limply to his side, walked over to Grandmother, and stood in front of her staring down.

"Now look what you've made me do."

"Serves him right!"

Dad's face flushed and the vein in his neck began to pulse, but he didn't answer Grandmother. He pulled me into the hall.

"I'm sorry, boy. I apologize for losing my temper. She's more than I can bear!"

After Dad went back to finish midwifing the birth of the new, spiritual lamb, like Mom called it when our young people got saved,

I stood in the hall, rubbing the welts on my cheek, contemplating the lethal properties of bleach, and listening to Grandmother laughing in the crazy way she always did when she succeeded in causing Dad to lose his temper.

Chapter 12

BY THE SPRING OF 1967 Jean-Pierre had been in the home next door for two years. By then he didn't care how many lies he needed to tell so long as it meant he didn't have to stay indoors in Chalet Beau Rivage with The Ladies.

Mom let me be with Jean-Pierre all I wanted. I told her that we spoke to each other about spiritual things. I even got her to let me sign him up on the Prayer Warrior Chart, to be my prayer partner.

One Monday, when we were supposed to be praying, I had just finished holding my hand over Jean-Pierre's mouth so he wouldn't bellow. I pulled his pants up then we sat under the hedge talking. I told Jean-Pierre about Grandmother's cheating and my revenge on her goldfish.

Jean-Pierre said that all of this was further proof that you could not trust women. I explained that that was only partly true. I knew a girl I could trust. I hadn't meant to mention Jennifer but it sort of slipped out. Jean-Pierre said I shouldn't even trust her. I told him that he hadn't met Jennifer, and if he had, he wouldn't say bad things about her. Jean-Pierre got upset.

"You have lying to *moi*! You saying I am your only *ami*. Your only friend!"

He wanted me to say he was a better friend than Jennifer, that he was my one true friend. I wouldn't say it, so Jean-Pierre crawled out from under the hedge and went home to Chalet Beau Rivage to sulk.

I stayed under the hedge after he left, closed my eyes, thought about Jennifer, and relieved my animal needs. As I pulled up my pants I got an idea.

My idea pleased Jean-Pierre very much, even though he jumped and bellowed when I punctured his hand with the point of the Masai spear I had been given by some missionaries from Kenya. Since I cut myself first, Jean-Pierre didn't complain. We clasped hands until our blood mingled, ran down, and dripped off our elbows. I wiped our cuts with Kleenex soaked in Mercurochrome and put Band-Aids on the wounds. After the blood-brother ceremony Jean-Pierre called me *"mon frère Calvin"* and promised never to mention Jennifer again.

When we were done with our ritual we walked to the village. Jean-Pierre had heard from the post office lady that Farmer Ruchet was going to kill a pig.

I asked Mom if I could skip homeschool and help Farmer Ruchet. I told her that he had asked Jean-Pierre and me to help him move last year's hay from his barn, above the village, to his farm.

"Of course," Mom answered, "it will be a witness to him."

Everyone in the village liked Farmer Ruchet and his tiny, kind, hardworking wife. They were like old winter apples, wrinkled, dark brown with weather, sweet, and silent. I spent as much time on their farm as I could. Most of the other villagers were resentful of *les Américains,* but the Ruchets were friendly.

Mom handed Jean-Pierre and me a tract, *"Jésus, Mon Ami Eternel,"* to take to the farmer. I dropped it over the hedge at the bottom of the garden, where it fell onto all the others. The dozens I discarded over the years had become a compost heap of wasted good news.

Farmer Ruchet was merciful. He would entice his lumbering pigs out of their pen with a handful of hot, boiled potatoes, laying them on the muddy, rutted cart track that ran past the pigsty. When the pig was contentedly slurping up the tubers, the farmer produced a heavy, square-headed mason's hammer which he had surreptitiously stuck in the back pocket of his sagging wool trousers. He kept the hammer hidden to spare his pig's feelings, so its last thoughts would be of delicious, hot potatoes. He stunned it so fast the pig probably thought a bad potato killed it. When the pig's forelegs buckled, eyelids blinking, the whites of its eyes rolled up, Farmer Ruchet stuck his butcher knife in. Farmer Ruchet said that the taste of pork that died content was better than fearful pig. Besides, he told me, "God doesn't like to see them suffer."

The first time I saw Farmer Ruchet kill a pig was when I was eight. I stood too close. I got washed with warm blood. This made Farmer Ruchet laugh, but Mrs. Ruchet scolded him for allowing me to stand right where I would be sprayed by the high-pressure, crimson jet. His wife made him apologize as she handed me a wet dish towel to wipe the blood off my face. When I walked home, covered in blood, Mom got mad, said that I was to promise never to watch slaughtering again, that my blood-drenched clothes made her sick. It was after that I began to lie about why I was going to the village when I wanted to watch butchering.

Jean-Pierre and I ladled boiling water over the enormous sow with a wooden dipper. We got the water from a huge copper tub Mrs. Ruchet set to boiling over an open fire next to the mouth of the evil-smelling, dark pigsty. When I asked Farmer Ruchet why he was killing this particular pig in the spring, instead of waiting until winter, he explained that the sow had pneumonia. He had given her a huge dose of *pénicilline vétérinaire*, but he had started the treatment too late. The meat would still be good as long as we slaughtered her before she died of the disease.

The boiling water scalded the pig's white skin pink and loosened the bristles. Wreathed in steam, the sweet smell of blood enveloping us, we took butcher knives and used them, razorlike, to scrape the bristles. I was worried Jean-Pierre would cut himself. But the fascinating work seemed to steady his usual spasms.

I wanted to be home by five P.M. I didn't want to miss seeing the visiting nurse change Grandmother's bandage, a protective patch of gauze over the oozing scar on her hip that had never healed completely, even two years after her surgery. Dr. Zwingli told Mom it probably never would mend, but that at Grandmother's age, it didn't matter, as long as the wound was kept clean and free from infection. Grandmother did not want me around when medical things got done to her. I always asked the nurse lots of questions about what she was doing, about how antibiotics, stitches, and the pin in Grandmother's hip worked. Also I liked to listen to Grandmother curse.

The nurse didn't understand what Grandmother meant when she yelled, *"Damn! That hurts, ya clumsy Swiss bitch!"* The nurse would cluck her tongue disapprovingly and say, *"Non, mais!"* when Grandmother acted up. She didn't understand the words Grandma yelled but she certainly understood the tone. Grandmother's tone was mighty strong, especially if you considered that she was a minister's mother.

I let Jean-Pierre walk back to Chalet Beau Rivage alone. He took a lot longer to make his way up the back road than me. He didn't mind. He did not want me to miss anything important on account of him. He liked me to tell him all about the bad things Grandmother did.

The nurse's visit was especially good that day. Grandmother slapped her. I heard the loud *clack* right out in the hall, where I was standing out of sight, listening.

"C'est impossible de soigner cette dame!" shouted the heavyset nurse as she ran out of Grandmother's room. As usual the nurse's body odor preceded her in a malodorous tidal wave. I always wondered why Swiss women looked so clean but smelled so bad. The nurse stormed down the hall, thick-soled shoes squeaking angrily on the linoleum.

After Mom examined the slap marks, she marched into Grandmother's bedroom. I heard Mom's voice quivering with fury.

"Mother, you have to apologize! You know if the visiting nurse won't come to the house you'll have to be taken all the way to Dr. Zwingli's office once a week and we can't afford the taxi fare!"

Grandmother cackled.

"Then why don't ya get a job?"

Mom stormed into the hall and slammed Grandmother's door. Grandmother was still laughing.

Chapter 13

As the month of April 1967 began to wane, Dad seemed more on edge than ever. Grandmother's presence in our home was intolerably permanent. Her noise wound Dad tighter and tighter. One of the many things that drove him into his increasingly frequent rages was how Grandmother would sit and talk to herself all day.

He said it was like living inside a music box, that she had turned the upstairs of our chalet into a madhouse. Dad said that Grandmother's ceaseless noise was as bad as the nightclub music from La Busola that once kept him awake during our vacation and made us change hotels. "It's worse," said Dad. "After La Busola opened I only had to suffer through one vacation in Paraggi before we changed hotels and went to Portofino to the Nazionale. Mother's here day and night, night and day. There is no excape!"

That spring other things were driving Dad nuts, especially his growing disappointment at the unworthiness of his fellow worker Dick Keegan. Dad talked incessantly about how so few people the mission board sent out over the years, to be our collaborators—for instance Dick—had pure enough doctrine, how they were not really kindred spirits, did not share Dad's vision of the Lord's work, how this was sad proof of the doctrinal erosion that was eating away at our denomination.

When Grandmother had been talking to herself for a while, especially if it was after Dad just had a theological "discussion" with Dick Keegan, Dad's door would suddenly fly open and he would charge down the hall to Grandmother's sitting room shouting, *"Mother! You're driving me nuts!"*

Grandmother never said much back. She would glare at Dad through her thick glasses, so thick that they made her eyes look twice as big but no friendlier, and shout, *"What? What?"* as if she couldn't understand him because of her problem with waxy buildup. But she could hear perfectly well; the visiting nurse syringed out her ears once a month.

"Don't talk to yourself, Mother! That's *what!* How can I work if you mutter and carry on all the time?"

"What? What!" Grandmother would yell again as Dad turned around, stamped back to his room, and slammed the door so hard it made his wall shake and the door of the small wood-burning stove in the hall rattle.

Usually if Mom tried to solve Dad's problems she got yelled at, but for once, something Mom did worked. She bought him a record player. The only negative comment Dad made was that it was a shame it had taken Mom two whole years to think of it.

On April 29, the day after his birthday, Dad traveled to Zurich to teach the Reformed men's Bible class. While in Zurich he purchased a dozen opera records. Mom said that she was pleasantly surprised by Dad's choice of music, given his limited background. (Later we found out that they had been on sale in a boxed set.)

When Grandmother would carry on, Dad turned up the volume of the opera he was playing. By mid-May, we could read Dad's music the way African witch doctors cast and read the bones. When the music went so loud that the bells in the grandfather clock in the dining room under Dad's bedroom jingled, Grandmother had been talking more loudly than usual. If no one was singing you knew not to knock on Dad's door, someone was being counseled. That was the only time Dad turned off his record player.

Grandmother knew exactly why Dad played his operas all the time and she resented it. She would say to anyone who would listen to her, "With 'em fool Dagos singin', I can't hear m'self think!"

If you stood out in the hall between Dad's room and Grandmother's sitting room, you would hear *Tosca* or *Turandot* blasting away on one side and Grandmother shouting herself hoarse on the other. It became a kind of competition.

"Ah, Tosca!" the tenor would bellow as Grandmother yelled, *"Smarty-pants Janice, not so smart now, huh!"* about someone she had outlived, whose death she had just read about in the obituary section of her newspaper.

Grandmother's newspaper was another sore point with my father. The only thing that Grandmother enjoyed reading were the obituaries. She loved to gloat over the fact that practically everyone she knew was dead or dying. When Grandmother read the obituary section she always read in a high, cracked voice. Grandmother was spending considerable money, far more than she was contributing to our household expenses, to have the *Philadelphia Inquirer* airmailed to Switzerland. This made Dad especially furious, but there was nothing he could do. The one time he complained, Grandmother yelled, *"I'll spend my stinkin' money any way I damn well please. An' if you piss me off about it, Ralph, I'll change my will an' leave it all ta the Mormons!"*

Grandmother shouted the obituaries in such a way as to annoy Dad as much as possible. She was clever about it. She waited for the pauses between acts, then bellowed something like, *"Ol' Curtis Gruber's dead! Ha! Ha! Ha!"*

When a lull in Dad's music went on long enough to give Grandmother the opportunity to scream a string of obituaries, I would suddenly hear a terrible scratching noise as Dad furiously shoved the needle onto the next act, or to a louder part in the opera, in order to drown out Grandmother's maniacal rantings. Dad's twelve opera records soon got terribly scratched. But he never added to his collection or replaced them. His room resonated with thunderous crackling, as if a forest fire were raging in his bedroom right along with the operas. When I asked Dad if having to play his music so loud bothered him, he answered, "No. It may be noisy but at least it's *my* noise!" The village children who came to deliver milk or fresh vegetables would stare up our chalet's dim, wood-paneled stairwell when they heard the exchanges of booming opera and shrill screaming coming from our troubled top floor. After Mom paid for the produce, they ran off giggling. When I saw them in the village, or stopped by their farms with Jean-Pierre, to visit a baby goat or see a calf being born, they laughed at me and pretended to sing arias, then tapped their heads.

Jean-Pierre never made fun of me for how noisy our house was but I could tell he didn't like it. Spastics do not like loud or sudden noises. After the installation of the record player, Jean-Pierre said he'd rather be out-of-doors or even back at the home. Ladies or no Ladies.

Between Grandmother and the music, Dad got into the habit of yelling all the time to be heard above the racket. After a while he almost never turned off his record player, and even when he was not angry, or "on edge," as he called it, he bellowed. Sometimes Dad's music even drowned him out.

One day after Dad had an argument with Dick Keegan over the theological implications of Dick's Wednesday-night Bible study, Dad yelled down the stairs for more hot water for his tea and no one answered him. Mom and Janet and Rachael were on the terrace behind the kitchen, out of earshot, drying dishes and singing "Blessed Assurance." No one knew whether it was Dad calling for hot water, or if it was one of the places in the opera where the tenor yells accusations at his lover. After Dad shouted for hot water about a dozen times, he lost his temper and pitched the tea tray, with the empty teapot, cup and saucer, and milk and sugar, down the stairs.

I was in my room pursuing my medical studies—dissecting a mouse and trying to get its heart started with electric shocks from a twelve-volt battery—when I heard the crash. I opened the door and peeked out. Dad was so angry he was having trouble breathing. He stormed back to his room and turned up *Tristan und Isolde* so loud that the singer's voice got distorted, like the noise made by humming through a comb and tissue paper. The bells in the grandfather clock started to jingle in the dining room below.

Grandmother heard the crash, too. She screamed out from the other end of the hall, *"He's smashin' the dishes! He's smashin' everythin' in sight! He's goin' crazy as Uncle Harry! I'll be lockin' my door this night. It ain't safe hereabouts!"*

Things were out of hand because of Grandmother. That was why we were all secretly relieved when, one morning in mid-May, she tumbled out of her easy chair, while trying to pick up the obituary section of her paper, and broke her hip again.

With her hip rebroken, Dr. Zwingli said Grandmother would be bedridden for good, that the new break would never heal properly. Now Grandmother had to stay in her bedroom, two doors further away from Dad's room, instead of spending her days in her sitting room next door. This was good news. It meant she was flat on her back and not able to sit up and yell as loud anymore. It meant that we could all stop worrying that she would drive Dad so nuts he might become unhinged the way he did during a ski vacation in Zermatt that ended in a disaster so bad none of us ever mentioned it, except when Mom would say: "We don't want your poor father to be overcome by his doubts the way he did *that* time!"

Chapter 14

THE DAY AFTER GRANDMOTHER REBROKE HER HIP, Jean-Pierre told The Ladies that he was going to my house for a Bible study. I told Mom we were going to the Keegans' to help staple hymn sheets. I already had a chicken in a box behind the back hedge.

We left our clothes under a tall, dark pine. I borrowed Mom's shiniest bloodred lipstick for tribal markings. Jean-Pierre stood as still as his excitement would allow him while I painted stripes on his face, arms, and concave chest.

After I put on my own markings I handed Jean-Pierre Dad's heavy, knotted walking stick. For my weapon I used the spear. Early in the morning I took it to the village, to Farmer Ruchet's barn, where he kept his huge grindstone. The farmer helped me sharpen the two-foot-long oval blade until it cut as well as the knife he used to kill pigs.

"Jean-Pierre, after I let the chicken go, we'll give it one minute to escape. Then chase it. Once I spear it, you club it."

"*Tres bien!*" Jean-Pierre was so excited he barked his answer.

The chicken wouldn't run. She sat where I put her down on the thick carpet of pine needles and old beech leaves and made throaty, clucking noises. I poked at her with the butt end of my spear. Nothing happened.

Jean-Pierre tapped her lightly on the back with Dad's stick. The chicken sat up, ruffled her feathers, then settled down and shut her eyes. I poked harder, used the sharp point. She clucked angrily, flapped her wings, then huddled down again into a servile crouch.

I decided to throw the chicken into the air, see if she would flutter off, start to escape, run—anything. She did flutter, a little, then walked back toward us and started to scratch for bugs in the pine needles at our feet. We watched our exasperatingly domesticated quarry dig past last year's gray-green needles to the older matted dark brown leaves and needles below where the wood lice lived. A pungent stench of mold from the thick, decomposing bed filled the air as soon as she began to scratch.

"Jean-Pierre, chase it!"

Jean-Pierre did his best, gave a war whoop, and ran at the chicken waving his club. She wouldn't move. I figured this was the best she was going to do, so I threw my spear at her as hard as I could and screamed, *"Die!"*

The spear fell short, off to one side. I picked it up and threw it again.

This time I hit her but the glittering blade skipped off her feathers. She didn't even seem to notice.

"The chicken's too light. The spear only makes it bounce. If it was bigger, heavier—"

"I shall holding eet." Jean-Pierre took Dad's stick and used the knob end to press the chicken down. She flapped and squawked.

"Those about to die salute you!"

I put the point of my spear in the middle of the chicken's back and started to push. The point glinted in the sun as it slipped off to the side, tearing out a row of feathers, but not piercing the skin. She struggled, then sat quiet.

Jean-Pierre stamped his foot. *"Merde!"*

"Club it. It has resisted our best spear point! Club the beast!"

Jean-Pierre raised his stick and tried to hit the chicken, but his excitement made him convulse; he staggered to one side. The blow fell harmless, with a dull thud, on the needle carpet.

"Aide-moi! Aide-moi!"

I put my hands over his to guide the stick. She moved at the last minute. We tried a couple more times but Jean-Pierre would kick, twitch, or bellow every time he was about to bring the club down. He could not control his spasms and hunt at the same time. It was even worse than when he relieved his animal desires.

We changed tactics. I held the chicken while Jean-Pierre steadied himself to strike. He hit me on the shoulder pretty hard. It hurt a lot. I yelled at him that he was a fool. He yelled back at me, said that it had been my idea to hunt in the first place when all he wanted to do was hide under the hedge and touch himself.

"Jean-Pierre, you've been touching yourself too much! Once a day should be enough for anyone!"

Jean-Pierre got mad and shoved me. We wrestled on the pine needles and punched at each other.

It's dangerous to fight a spastic. He lashes out, thrashes uncontrollably, and when you're stark naked, bad things happen. I got around behind Jean-Pierre and locked his head in a half nelson, a wrestling hold Dad taught me once when he was in a good mood. Jean-Pierre kicked and scuffed up the pine needles but couldn't shake me. That's when he lashed back in one of his thrashing fits and the calf of his hard, wiry leg caught me between my legs. My Precious Seed Containers got excruciatingly squashed.

I yelled and kicked Jean-Pierre back in *his* Precious Seed Containers to even things up. Jean-Pierre howled, rolled away, picked up his stick, and stood up. He had missed the chicken six or seven times, so it surprised me when he cracked me such an accurate wallop over my head. Then Jean-Pierre got scared. He realized that he had escalated to weapons. I had the spear.

When I picked up the spear and Jean-Pierre saw me tighten my grip, he yelled, *"Mon Dieu!"* and started to run. I dropped my weapon, tackled him, snatched the stick away, stood over him, and raised it above my head to give him a good hit across his shins.

As soon as I brandished the stick I was sorry. Jean-Pierre curled up into a jagged ball and started to whine, high-pitched, like a rabbit when a fox gets it. I looked at his face, at his lumpy nose his mom had broken. That's when I remembered the stories about Jean-Pierre's family. I tossed the stick away, sat down next to him, and helped him uncurl.

As I rubbed Jean-Pierre's taut, sinewy limbs I wished I hadn't started to fight with him in the first place. The chicken clucked. We looked up and laughed. She had finally done what we wanted— flapped up into a tree; escaped like a wild bird.

I climbed up the pine tree, getting sticky resin on my hands and stomach, smearing my tribal markings. The pine sap smelled good.

I clubbed her. My peace offering fell at Jean-Pierre's feet. Jean-Pierre picked up my spear and put the point on the chicken's side, just under her wing. Then, with a yodeling bellow of triumph, he shoved. She was transfixed to the carpet of pine needles. She flapped like mad. This startled Jean-Pierre. He dropped the spear and ran away a few steps.

I scrambled down and retrieved Dad's stick. Since Jean-Pierre got to spear the chicken, I decided it would be fair if I finished her off. I clubbed her and broke her neck.

We smeared chicken blood on our bodies, just like real savages do before the missionaries come to their village. Then Jean-Pierre asked if I would help him.

I kept a lookout and put my hand over his mouth at the right moment. When he was done I collected his clothes, buttoned his shirt, and zipped up his pants.

"Jean-Pierre, I think you'd better go back alone so no one gets suspicious. I'll stay up here awhile by myself."

"*Très bien, mon frère Calvin.*"

Chapter 15

I WAS NAKED FROM THE HUNT.

I lay back on the soft forest floor. I could hear Jean-Pierre's footsteps receding down the forest path.

I closed my eyes.

Jennifer was sitting at the end of the Paraggi pier, moodily dangling her feet in the water.

"What's the bloody use of you being here if you're going to sleep the whole day!"

"Sorry," I said.

"I borrowed a mask and snorkel for you."

"Thanks."

"I had thought we'd go out to the mouth of the bay before all the bloody motor launches began to terrorize the populace. But that was *hours* ago!"

"I had trouble waking up."

"Serves you jolly well right."

"I don't see why."

I sat quietly next to her, waiting to see if she'd get nicer. Jennifer was definitely in a bad mood.

Finally she broke the silence. "Do you want to go for a picnic?" she asked morosely.

"That would be great!"

"I've asked Lucrezia to pack one for us. Mummy said we may go where we like as long as I'm sure to be back by tea."

"You want to walk up to the old road? We could cut down to the water and swim off the big rocks by San Fruttuoso."

"That's quite a good idea coming from a twit like you. Sure you're up to it? Awake enough not to fall and bang your little head?"

There was no point in answering. It wasn't possible to win. Jennifer always had the last word. When we were five years old, we fought over 'who got to keep a crab we caught under the pier. She tried to pull it out of my hand. I foolishly held on. She pulled off its legs when she tugged at it, looked down at them twitching in her hand, then up at me, and said, "See, you've killed it!" Her eyes filled with tears. I spent the rest of that day apologizing, trying to comfort her, and organizing the crab's funeral. The next crab I found I hurriedly handed over before she even asked for it.

Jennifer carried our masks and snorkels. I carried the towels and a brown paper bag, with big grease stains spreading on its sides from our lunch, *panino con mortadella,* that Lucrezia had packed.

"What will we drink?" I asked.

"Lucrezia put in a bottle of Limon Soda."

"Only one?"

"We can share it."

"We'll get pretty thirsty with only one bottle."

"Really! You *are* a wet blanket, Calvin."

"I was just asking. . . ."

"Well, don't!"

When we got to the top of the hill the path forked. If you turned to the right, you could follow the old Roman road along the crest until it wound its way down through the olive groves to the back streets of Santa Margherita. We took the left-hand path, walking on the flat paving stones. Jennifer never stepped on the cracks.

There were farms on the hilltop. Not close together but spread out every mile or so along the ancient road. They were tumbledown places. Most of the farms had fig trees or grapevines hanging over their whitewashed walls. No one was at the first farm we passed, just a dog that barked and strained furiously at his chain.

I absentmindedly picked a fig.

"Don't steal!"

"I'm not stealing! I'd take it even if the farmer was watching. It's hanging over the wall."

"Thief!"

"Jennifer, if I wanted to be bossed around by a girl, I could've stayed home and let Janet do it!"

Jennifer pushed ahead of me. Her waist seemed even narrower than it was because of the way her bathing suit hugged her figure above the top of her khaki shorts. Jennifer's ponytail swung from side to side with each angry step. When she glanced over her shoulder, her flushed face was prettier than ever.

As we walked around a bend in the road, the view changed dramatically. The crest of the mountain narrowed to a slender ridge. The olive groves ended abruptly. There were nothing but pines, cypresses, and big patches of brambles growing on the steep banks that fell away on either side of the dusty track. Behind us, and far below, we could see the harbor of Portofino framed by a semicircle of pastel buildings that formed the town's facade.

The enormous luxury yachts looked small from where we were standing. A bus crawled out of the communal parking lot. The sound of its horn floated up to us on the hot breeze.

When we rounded the next bend and started down the opposite side of the hill, Portofino fell from view. The Mediterranean stretched out in a wide, flat, sparkling sheet to the spotless horizon. Except for our footsteps and the sighing of the wind in the pines, there were no sounds.

We walked about another half an hour. Jennifer stopped and peered down the almost vertical red clay precipice that fell to the water.

"What do you say?"

"Well . . ."

Jennifer ignored my hesitant answer and plunged over the side. She made her descent from tree to tree, clinging to each gnarled pine so she wouldn't tumble headlong. I followed Jennifer over the edge. The smell of pine resin was strong. It reminded me of the chicken hunt. If Jennifer had been in a better mood I would have told her about it. As it was, we proceeded in silence.

When we got to the bottom we stopped at the top of a high dirt bank eroded by waves. It had collapsed, leaving a sheer drop to the huge rocks against which the swells from the open sea surged, broke, and receded.

We started to pick our way along the top of a small cliff, looking for a place to scramble down. Soon we came to a spot where there was a steep, narrow gully, a natural slide that rainwater had eroded. It was filled with powdery sandy dirt and brittle pine needles.

Jennifer reached the bottom, enveloped in a cloud of red dust, stood up, and stepped onto a huge rock as I slid down after her. Gravel got inside my swimming trunks.

There were no people on this part of the coast; there were no beaches, roads, or towns. Once the landslide of pebbles stopped its rattling cascade, only the gurgle of water draining between the enormous boulders, after each swell pushed its glassy green mound of water up and over them, made any sound.

Jennifer took off her shorts, adjusted her bathing suit, then picked up her mask and snorkel.

"Coming?" she asked.

"Sure."

She handed me the old mask and snorkel the Bagnino had lent her, then turned and looked for a safe place to enter the water. I wondered about how we could get back out.

Jennifer found a spot between two rocks to dive from. She stood looking down, measuring the distance she needed to clear the rocks.

"Be careful of sea urchins."

Jennifer gave me a scornful look, by which she meant that she had been doing this sort of thing as long as I had. As soon as she plunged into the sea, she swam out as hard as she could so that the next swell wouldn't carry her back to the rocks. Jennifer treaded water waiting for me.

I timed my dive so that a receding swell sucked me out to where Jennifer was waiting. We lowered our masks, cleared our snorkels of water, adjusted our mouthpieces, and looked down.

The walk, Jennifer's bad mood, the memory of Jean-Pierre and the chicken hunt, Grandmother, Mom, Dad, all faded, overwhelmed by the silent blue falling into infinity below me.

I was startled by how deep the water was. I couldn't see the bottom. The rocks, which formed the shore, were really the top of an underwater cliff that fell vertically down and down into a bottomless, endless, dark blue stillness.

I was nervous. I glanced at Jennifer to see if she was frightened. I felt as if I had stepped out into nothing, into thin air. I swam closer to the shore, but looking straight down the rocky wall was even worse than being a little way from it. I got the same falling sensation I had whenever I looked over the cliff where the big water pipe ran down to the hydroelectric plant in the valley far below our chalet.

Jennifer ignored me, flipped over, and with a trail of bright silver bubbles streaming off her back, she dove. She went down further than I had ever seen her or anyone else go. She went so deep that she began to look dark, small, and blue through the thick layer of water. Elusive shafts of sunlight flickered in long fingers that obscured my view of her.

I got scared. She kept going, swimming straight down the underwater cliff face. I think it was her way of getting back at me for comparing her to Janet, for saying that I might as well have stayed at home instead of running away to be with her.

At last she turned and began to swim back. I could tell by the desperate way she kicked that she was out of oxygen. I knew how she must be feeling, chest tight, a rising sense of panic, as she raced to the surface, trying to reach air before her lungs gasped water.

Jennifer shot to the surface. She spit out the mouthpiece of her snorkel and took deep, shuddering breaths. I swam over and held on to her while she gasped for air and treaded water. She felt cold. I put my arm around her slender waist. She didn't push me away.

It took several minutes before she was able to speak.

"I . . . saw . . . the bottom."

"How far down is it?"

"Twice . . . as far as I dived. It stretches down in a . . . a . . . steep hill from the base of the rock wall. It looks black down there."

"Jennifer, I don't like this. Let's get out."

"Yes, let's."

Before we could get a grip on the slippery rocks, the water began to drag us back, scraping our palms and fingers, sucking us inexorably toward the deep blue water. After each attempt we found ourselves further out than we expected. We would start over again, get into position, wait for a swell, swim in on it, scrabble on the rocks, lose our grip, start again.

After trying three times, I could see Jennifer was getting tired. She started to swim slowly up the shore looking for some easier place to land. She soon turned back, shook her head grimly, and made another attempt. Once again she was pulled off the rock and floated miserably out into deep water.

"Jennifer! You go first. I'll get behind you and push. Then you can help me!"

Jennifer nodded and began to swim to where she could catch the next swell. I swam right behind her. When she got close to the huge boulder, I shoved up against her so that as she kicked and scrabbled, one foot got a good push off my shoulder. I felt her thrust down as hard as she could. She shoved me right underwater. I was carried back out by the retreating wave.

When I resurfaced, Jennifer was hanging on to the rock. As I bobbed in the water, watching, she slowly clambered up to the top of the boulder, then ripped off her mask and snorkel and tossed them out of the way. She turned, lay flat on her stomach, and reached down as far as she could.

"Ready when you are, boyso!"

I rode the next wave in but missed Jennifer and crashed against the boulder at the wrong place.

"*Bloody hell!*"

"*I'll get it next time!*"

I treaded water. I let a few small waves pass me. Then I felt a big swell. I rode it in, making little adjustments so that I stayed in line with Jennifer's outstretched arms.

I was pushed against the rock so hard the wind got knocked out of me. Just as I was about to fall back into the foaming water, I felt Jennifer's strong, slender hand close around my wrist.

She began to pull me up toward her as I scrambled to find a toe-hold.

"C'mon, laddie," she whispered between clenched teeth. "C'mon, laddie, make an effort!"

When, at last I scrambled out, I noticed I had a skinned knee. One of Jennifer's elbows was cut, and we both had torn fingernails.

We stumbled back to the top of the rock where the lichen grew above the high-water mark. We lay side by side under the hot sun, staring up at the cloudless sky through the overhanging pines swaying in the hot breeze. We rested our heads on each other's arms until we were almost dry and our pounding hearts had begun to beat normally.

Jennifer rolled over on her stomach.

Her green eyes looked straight into mine. Her wet ponytail fell to one side of her face. Warm, salty seawater dripped off the tip of it into my mouth. She bent her head down and kissed me. Without saying anything, she moved over me with her body and began to press herself on me.

My heart pounded harder than it had in the water when I thought we were going to drown. I reached up and inched her bathing-suit straps off her brown, slender shoulders. The strap marks were cream white against her dark, sandy tan. As I pushed the straps further down, the strap marks widened out into triangles that ended in her white breasts.

Jennifer was moving up and down on me. I began to move, too.

Slowly I inched my right hand off her delicately freckled shoulder until it lay by my side. Then I plucked up my courage and moved it between our bodies. I waited for Jennifer to sense what I was doing, to spring up shocked and angry, to push my hand away. But instead she did something that amazed me more than anything that had ever happened in my life. She lifted up her body a little so my hand could complete its journey between her legs, upturned, touching her.

What she did next shocked me even more. Her cool fingers pushed past my stomach and slid under my bathing suit. I froze. Jennifer was touching *me*! Not through my bathing suit but actually holding me in her hand, on purpose!

I closed my fingers around the thin strip of bathing-suit material between her legs and worked my hand under the cloth. I felt her warm skin.

She pushed down and breathed in harder and harder, then lay still. We took our trembling hands out of each other's bathing suits. Jennifer smiled. "You make a nasty mess, don't you?" She gave me a kiss on my cheek. Then she got up, walked to the edge of the rock, lay down, and waited for the next glassy swell to surge toward her so she could rinse her hand.

Chapter 16

"IT'S FORTUNATE FOR GRANDMOTHER we're Bible-believing Christians," Mom said a few days after Grandmother rebroke her hip. "If we weren't returning good for evil we would just put her away someplace. We must all take turns being her Good Samaritan."

The Samaritan part I found most repulsive was having to bring Grandmother her teeth. When I picked them out of the glass, slimy and gray looking, I got a queasy feeling. It made me sick to touch her "uppers" and "lowers," food stuck in them, a trail of slime stretching back to the tepid water.

After she became bedridden, most days someone read out loud to Grandmother. When we had young people with us who could speak English well enough, they tried to read to her. But they mispronounced the names in the obituary section. This drove Grandmother wild.

Trudi, a shy, German girl with terrible acne, tried to read out the list of dead people's names in a thick, faltering accent. Grandmother couldn't understand one word Trudi said. She screamed out, *"If I wanted some Kraut moron readin' ta me, I'd ask!"*

After the third mispronounced name, Grandmother gave Trudi such a violent shove that Trudi fell off the edge of her bed. Trudi hit the floor hard, bruised her tailbone, and burst into tears. Then she fled from the room with Grandmother laughing and screaming, *"That's why ya lost the war, ya dumb Nazi!"*

Jean-Pierre and I were doubled up, practically suffocating with laughter in the bathroom. We had hidden there to listen to Trudi trying to read.

It took Jean-Pierre and me all afternoon to find Trudi. (Mom dispatched us on this errand of mercy.) It took Mom the rest of the evening to get her to calm down, to convince her that Jesus loved Germans and so did we.

Mom was afraid that Grandma would do more awful things or say words that might so offend the young people that they would be driven from the things of the Lord. So I was made to spend more time with Grandmother. Mom said that since I was already saved, I couldn't be driven away from the Lord like the young people who might not understand about Grandmother's mental state. From then on I was forced to be with her for several hours a day.

Fortunately, soon after she became bedridden, I figured out a way to minimize Grandmother's impact on my life. Grandmother had a wall clock in her bedroom. Once she had put her glasses on in the morning, she would check it compulsively. She lived by that clock; breakfast at eight A.M., someone to visit her at nine A.M., lunch at twelve noon sharp, nap one P.M., afternoon visit two P.M., sponge bath eight-thirty P.M., lights out nine P.M. Any deviation from this schedule would send her into a screaming fit.

After the first day that I was made to sit with her for three hours straight (Grandmother made me play Parcheesi the whole time and moved her pieces whenever she wanted to, didn't even pretend to keep the rules), I crept into her bedroom and moved the hands of her clock.

The next morning it was nine A.M. before Grandmother thought it was eight A.M. and time for her breakfast. Then, during her nap, I crept in again and moved the hands forward so she lost an hour. This way I could knock two hours off her day.

The first night after my discovery Mom came to my room to say good night and to congratulate me on my brilliant idea. She said that it was a godsend to have a few more hours of blessed relief from "that terrible woman." I took the opportunity to ask Mom about something that had been bothering me more and more.

"Mom, why did God create Jean-Pierre to be a spastic?"

"Sometimes there are things the Lord does that give us an opportunity to show our love for Him in a special way."

"Like Job?"

"That's right. Sometimes it's the only way God can reach out to us."

"Is that how it is with Jean-Pierre?"

"We can't be sure, darling, but it might be. After all, if he weren't a spastic then he would never have come to Chalet Beau Rivage. He might have been normal, but wouldn't have heard the Gospel."

"I see."

Mom paused and sat studying my face for a moment. Then she sighed. "You're not touching yourself, are you?"

"No, Mom, never."

"Good. You know what to do if you get those tragic physical longings?"

"Yes, Mom, take them to the Lord."

"That's right, dear."

"Mom?"

"Yes, dear?"

"I still don't quite understand, how come God couldn't arrange for Jean-Pierre to hear the Gospel in some other way besides making him a spastic?"

"That's a good question, dear. Even some grown-ups ask questions about why certain things happen. But are you sure you're not just changing the subject?"

"No, Mom."

"Because if you *are* touching yourself, you can share your needs with me. We can pray that God will send you a wet dream or heal your animal desires."

"It's okay, Mom. I just want to know about why things happen. I'm not changing the subject."

"Well, dear, hard as it might be to understand, with our fallen, unregenerate minds, we know God is in control, so even if things don't make sense to us, we know they do to Him."

"But, Mom, if our minds are fallen, how can we trust our minds to believe in God?"

My mom patted my hand. "We can't, darling. We can't trust our fallen minds. Only God, through His Grace, comes to us to enlighten our deceitful hearts."

"Then how come we bother to be missionaries, Mom? How come we tell people about Jesus? Why don't we just let God do it all?"

"You see, sweetheart, it's not us who are really doing anything, even witnessing to people. God does it all through us. For instance, I'm not the one talking to you now. God is speaking through me. I'm just His instrument."

"If he's doing it all and we're just instruments, how come he bothers, why doesn't he just save the elect directly?"

"Because, dear, God's working out all things in His own way and His own time."

"That doesn't answer anything, Mom."

"Well, darling, if you need to know more, ask your father."

"I did but he only yelled at me that Dick Keegan's questions were bad enough and he couldn't deal with more than one Doubting Thomas at a time."

"Your father's under a lot of pressure right now, darling."

"So can I ask you?"

Mom sighed and nodded.

"Mom, if God's grace is doing it all, then how come he killed his son?"

"*Darling!* We have to be *careful* not to be *blasphemous!*"

"I'm only asking."

"But, darling, God didn't '*kill*' Jesus, Satan did!"

"Was Satan free to choose?"

"No, darling, his will is fallen, too."

"So Satan is in God's plan?"

"Yes, dear, in a way."

"Then God needed Satan for his plan?"

"In a way, though God has no needs; He's sovereign and doesn't *need* anything."

"But, Mom, if God needed Satan and Satan killed Jesus, then why did God bother to let Jesus die since he had already decided who was going to get saved anyway?"

"*Darling!* What you're saying is sounding as if you've been influenced by Arminian theology! *Who* has been putting such thoughts into your mind? Has someone been telling you these things?"

"No, Mom."

"Well, be careful! Ralph says that Arminianism is the most dangerous of all heresies."

"I don't even know who the Ariminians are, Mom."

"Still you have to be careful of them, dear."

"Why, what do they believe?"

"Never mind! It's easy to slip into error my being overanxious. Let Dick Keegan be an example! Has Dick been talking to you? Tell me the truth now!"

"No, Mom, I never talk to Reverend Keegan about anything at all. Never."

"That's good. Dick's well-meaning, but as you know, tragically, he went to the wrong seminary and has a weakness for free will."

Mom sat chewing her lip.

"Does Jean-Pierre ask these sorts of questions?"

"No, Mom."

"Does he touch himself?"

"No, Mom."

"Then if he's content to accept God's will for his life, why aren't you?"

"Oh, I'm content."

"Good."

"Yes, I'm fine."

"Well, don't speak to Dick if you can help it."

"I won't, Mom. Good night."

"I love you, dear. Don't touch yourself, will you, dear?"

"No, Mom."

"If your Little Thing gets naughty, just take it to the Lord."

"I will, Mom."

"That's good, dear. Sweet dreams."

"You, too, Mom. Good night, Mom."

"Night."

"Night."

"Sleep tight."

"You, too."

"Love you, darling. Don't touch yourself, will you?"

"Never."

"Love you."

"Night, Mom."

"Night."

"And don't talk to Dick."

"I promise, Mom."

Mom gently shut my bedroom door. I closed my eyes. Her green eyes looked straight into mine. Her wet ponytail fell to one side of her face. Warm, salty sea water dripped off the tip of it into my mouth. She bent her head down and kissed me. Without saying anything, she moved over me with her body and began to press herself on me.

Chapter 17

THE NEXT MORNING I GOT UP EARLY. I stood by the hedge between the chicken shed and the Keegan's chalet next door. I was waiting for Dick Keegan to come over and collect his mail. I waited about twenty minutes. When Dick finally walked through the gap in our hedge, I stepped out from behind the blue spruce.

"Dick, can I ask you something?"

Reverend Keegan jumped so hard his glasses flew off.

"Dick, can I ask you about the sovereignty of God?"

"Oh boy. What are you trying to do, get me into all kinds of trouble?" He glanced at the windows of our chalet and laughed nervously.

"I won't tell." I took Reverend Keegan's arm and steered him behind the tree.

"Well, what's your question?"

"About why it's worth doing anything if it's predestined. About free will."

"Oh boy! You sure don't beat around the bush!"

Reverend Keegan sneezed. "These are complex issues. Hay fever. I hate the spring!" He looked over his shoulder. "I should really go get my mail. Maybe we can talk later."

"Mom says the issues are simple if your theology's right."

Dick didn't say anything for a while, just stood and stared out into space. We were standing between the blue spruce tree and the front hedge overlooking the road, field, and forest below. We didn't face each other but stood side by side, our backs to the chalet, gazing out across the Rhône valley, the Dents du Midi, and the other jagged peaks.

The sound of tuneless singing floated over the hedge from the spastics next door. A glider dipped and soared on the thermals that rose invisibly from the checkerboard of sun-drenched fields in the valley. I glanced at the glider, then at Dick.

In spite of the peaceful scene stretching out below and above, Reverend Keegan was trembling. His tall, thin frame was taut. When he swallowed, his Adam's apple bobbed in his scrawny, sinewy throat. He was swallowing a lot right then. His Adam's apple shot up and down a couple of times, making his paper-thin skin and blue veins slide over it.

Dick licked his lips and cleared his throat.

"You know, there are some things that I haven't entirely made up my mind about. Things I'm still thinking through. I can't say that I can really explain all of them right now."

"I won't tell."

"That's not the point. It's just that some issues take a while to work out. Now I really must get my mail!" Reverend Keegan sneezed, blew his nose, looked at the contents of his handkerchief, and sighed.

Reverend Keegan took a step toward the chalet. I grabbed his arm.

"I said I won't tell."

"I don't like being underhanded and my nose is starting to bleed again."

"Dad says you have a weak view of predestination. He says you believe in free will."

Dick's cheeks flushed, "Look, it's not that I disagree with your esteemed father, just I'm . . . I'm as Reformed as the next man, but it's just, ah . . . I'm not as sure as he is about . . . about a lot of things."

Reverend Keegan squeezed the bridge of his nose and held his head back.

"Like what?"

"Oh, about why during the Re . . . Ref . . ." Reverend Keegan sneezed violently. ". . . Reformation so many things that Christians had believed and done, how they worshiped, for instance, were a . . . a . . . abandoned." He sneezed, blew his nose, peered closely at the contents of his handkerchief, and shook his head sadly. Reverend Keegan twisted a corner of his stained handkerchief into a slender spear, inserted it delicately into one of his nostrils, then began to dig deeply.

"Is the sovereignty of God part of all of that stuff that was abandoned?"

"Don't know. I'm just saying that maybe there are some things we take for granted that we ought to reexamine."

Reverend Keegan repeated the pipe-cleaning procedure on his other nostril.

"Like predestination?"

"Well, at least the balance between man and God, free will and God's sovereignty." Reverend Keegan probed deeply until at last he dislodged the offending excrescence. He grunted in satisfaction. "Foreknowledge versus predestination, the mystery of God giving us life. Even the place of liturgy in worship."

"*Liturgy!* No wonder Dad's worried! That sounds *Catholic!*"

"Oh boy!"

"Look, I'm interested. That's all. I've thought about stuff. I just want to know."

"Go to the right seminary!" Reverend Keegan laughed, but not as if he thought anything was very funny. Blood trickled out of his left nostril. He clapped his handkerchief to his nose.

"Don't worry, it always bleeds. It'll stop in a minute." Reverend Keegan tilted his head back, pressed his handkerchief tightly to his face. "Ith you beliethe thath God creathed people thith thee will, the abilithy to choothe, even to choothe bad things, thath are againth Hith will, then you don't hathe tho blame God thor every bad thing that happenth."

Reverend Keegan adjusted his handkerchief.

"I need ithe! I need to take some antihistamine. Ith the Kleenex getting bloody?"

"No, it's okay, it's white."

Reverend Keegan suppressed a last sneeze, walked through the gap in our hedge, past the chicken shed, and back to his chalet. He had forgotten to collect his mail.

I stood awhile longer watching the glider as it spiraled down through thousands of feet of warm air, a silent dot against the vast, immovable alpine panorama. Jean-Pierre's voice was shouting the chorus to "Trust and Obey," especially loud and out of tune. He sang badly on purpose to annoy The Ladies. But what could they do—you can't yell at a spastic for being less than perfect.

Chapter 18

JEAN-PIERRE AND I INVENTED A GAME. Jean-Pierre would go up to our new arrivals and introduce himself as me. The young people did not expect Reverend Becker's son to be handicapped. They tried to hide their surprise by being too friendly. I would announce that I was Calvin's friend Jean-Pierre from the home next door. I acted even more spastic than the real Jean-Pierre. I pretended that I could hardly walk or talk. I slurred my speech, stuttered, and made the newly arrived young people stand patiently trying to understand what I was saying, nervously shifting their weight from one foot to the other, while I staggered from side to side, fell down, got up only to fall again.

Most of our young people were already born-again when they came to L'Arche, so they had to pretend to be patient and long-suffering and not let their Christian smiles, what Grandmother always called their shit-eatin' born-again grins, slide off their faces as they watched me stumble and stutter.

"Wha-a-a-a-a-at's you-you-your n-n-n-n-n-name?" I warbled while I contorted my mouth into a twisted grin, all teeth and slobber.

"I'm Penny," answered a cheerful English girl, with too-short shorts on, who had just gotten off the tram.

Later, I thought to myself, Mom would have a little talk with Penny about not being a stumbling block, a source of worldly temptation, to our male young people. I was sure that by her second day at L'Arche Penny wouldn't be wearing such tight shorts. If she hadn't packed any clothes that were pleasing to the Lord, Mom would lend her some of Janet's.

In the meantime I couldn't help staring at Penny's figure encased in her body-hugging, pale pink shorts.

"I—I—I—I—I—I—I'm, J-J-J-J-J-Jean, Jean, P-P-P-P-P-Pierre," I bellowed. I did a little twitching dance, jerked my head from side to side. "P-p-p-p-p-pra-prai-praise th-th-th-th-th—"

"The Lord!" Jean-Pierre yelled, finishing my sentence for me and making Penny jump. I noticed he was also staring down at what Mom would have called Penny's Special Intimate Gift. Penny's Gift was clearly outlined, a deep V wedged revealingly into her immodest shorts.

"Is your mum in the chalet?" Penny asked Jean-Pierre in a loud, sweet singsong voice, as if he were a tiny child who needed a hearing aid.

Jean-Pierre momentarily tore his gaze away from Penny's Gift.

"Y-y-y-y-yes."

"I think we'll jus-jus-jus-just go and s-s-see her." Penny blushed. Speech impediments tend to be contagious.

"I'm v-v-very much looking forward to meeting your father as well," Penny said to Jean-Pierre.

"Y-y-y-y-ye-yes," answered Jean-Pierre. "H-h-h-h-h-he ha-ha-has a-a-a cl-cl-clo-clos-close w-w-wa-wa-walk w-w-weeth-weeth—"

"The L-L-L-Lo-Lord," I shouted.

"Tha-thank you!" said Penny.

She, and another girl who had arrived on the same tram, a sad, mousy specimen who didn't say a word as she stood staring wildly at us, and who had a nondescript, appropriately spiritual, long gray dress, fled up the path, dragging their backpacks and sleeping bags behind them. Penny's shorts were cut so high that two slivers of her bottom played peekaboo as she walked up the steps to the porch.

At lunch Penny looked startled to see me walk in, sit down, and say grace when Dad asked me to. She didn't shut her eyes but watched me closely while I prayed.

"Dear Heavenly Father, we thank Thee for this food and for the opportunity to serve Thee. Bless each one whom Thou hast led to L'Arche that they may each grow in Thy knowledge. I thank Thee especially for our new arrivals. In Jesus' name, a-a-a-amen."

When I stuttered the amen I squinted at Penny, who was staring at me with her mouth open. I winked. Everyone else still had their heads bowed and their eyes shut like you're supposed to. I made a quick spastic's grimace just before the others looked up. Then I went back to being normal and didn't look at Penny again while I ate my vegetable soup, egg-salad sandwich, and lime Jell-O with slivers of grated carrot in it.

About an hour after lunch, Penny, now wearing one of Janet's modest, knee-length paisley-print dresses, with a high lace collar, long sleeves, and a slip that showed, came up to me. "I don't think what you did was kind at all. It wasn't a charitable thing to do," she said in a sorrowful voice.

"Wh-wh-why n-n-not?"

Penny's face turned bright pink and she spun around and marched off to tell on me.

When Mom caught up with me I was in my room dissecting a sparrow that had crashed into my window and broken its neck.

"*Calvin!* You're never to mock the spastics again!"

"Mom, I wasn't 'mocking the spastics.' It's just a game."

"It's disgraceful to have people think that our son is a CP child!"

"Why? What's wrong with being a spastic?"

"Nothing, but health's a blessing. It's awful of you to make light of it."

"It's Jean-Pierre's game, too, Mom."

"I don't care *whose* game it is. It's not pleasing to the Lord. It's disgraceful and you're *never* to do it again! How can the young people come closer to the Lord when you're doing things like that? It creates altogether the wrong atmosphere."

"B-b-b-but, M-m-m-mom!" I stuttered. I put down the scalpel and tweezers and I bent my arms out at an odd angle and staggered toward her, pretending I wanted to hug her: My mother took a feeble whack at me and tried not to laugh. But she couldn't help it. "You're impossible!" She gave up and laughed out loud.

"You'd better not think that I won't tell your father if you do it again. Just because you made me laugh doesn't mean it's right. I'm warning you!"

"Okay, Mom."

"Do I have your word?"

"Yes, I guess so."

"Very well, then. I'll not tell your father this time."

"Mom?"

"Yes, dear?"

"I was wondering about something."

"Yes, dear?"

"Well, I don't see what's wrong with thinking we have choice, you know, free will, at least a little bit."

Mom's expression changed from one of good humor to intense distress.

"*Calvin!* Why, oh why, do you go on and on about this?"

"It's something I think about. Maybe God doesn't see time the way we do. Maybe it's like the horizon, even though the earth's round, like that, not a straight line at all. Maybe God sees it all at once, so the difference between God knowing stuff, foreknowledge, and predestination and all, is beside the point."

"Foreknowledge! Oh Calvin! Who have you been talking to?"

"It's just an idea, that's all. I haven't been talking to anyone."

"Calvin, I don't believe you! Someone has planted this obsession with free will in your innocent mind! Who? It's Reverend Keegan, isn't it!?"

"No, Mom, I just think about stuff."

"Calvin, don't lie to me. You never thought up a word like *fore-knowledge!* Who said that word to you?"

"I heard Dad say it in a sermon."

"I don't believe you! No one uses that word except people who are undermining the sovereignty of God!"

"But, Mom, if God chooses to allow free will, then freedom is part of God's 'plan,' isn't it?"

"Oh, Calvin! This is horrible! Who has done this thing to you?"

"Aw, c'mon, Mom."

"Don't 'c'mon, Mom' me! I'll need to speak to your father about this."

Mom shook her head and closed my door. I waited until I heard her walk down the hall, then I put a damp cloth over the bird to keep it fresh and tiptoed out of my room, down the stairs, and out the front door.

I lay down under the hedge and closed my eyes. We lay kissing and rubbing our bodies against each other, and instead of Jennifer ending it all by jumping back and laughing at me, she kissed me harder and harder and pushed her narrow, sharp hips against mine! When my hands found her breasts she didn't push them away but arched her back up a little so I could touch her more easily.

Chapter 19

DAD CALLED JANET, RACHAEL, MOM, AND ME into his bedroom. He sat us all down in a row on the couch at the end of the bed, then stood, head bowed, in front of us. When at last he looked up he spoke in a tired, flat voice.

"Something has happened. A spirit of apostasy has been building in our work, an insidious spirit of false doctrine, perhaps even heresy. Calvin, you must speak the truth. The Lord's work is at stake. I've got Mom and the girls here as witnesses, because we have all been called into the Lord's work as a family. It's not my work or Mom's work, it is the *Lord's* work, and you are all—even you, Calvin—covenant partners in the work. I speak to you today not as a father but as a brother in Christ, a fellow colaborer in the Vineyard. Calvin Dort Becker, tell us the truth, who has told you there is a difference, however subtle, however minor, between predestination and foreknowledge? *Who?*"

"No one, Dad."

"If you lie or refuse to answer, I'll have to strap you."

I thought as how if he was speaking to me as a fellow colaborer, it was odd that he'd strap me. But all I said was, "Dad, I swear that no one said anything to me."

Mom gave me a reproving look. "We are not to swear, 'neither by the temple or the gift on the altar.' Let your 'yea be yea and your nay be nay.'"

Janet put up her hand.

"Yes, Janet."

"It's Reverend Keegan, Dad. He's been talking to Calvin. I know!"

I tried to give Janet a steady, honest look. "How do you know he talked to me? It's not true."

Rachael clasped her hands earnestly. "Oh, Calvin! We saw you!"

"When?"

Janet looked triumphant. "We saw you and him standing by the hedge!"

"I was just helping him with one of his nosebleeds. I didn't talk to him."

"And," added Janet, with a lot of meaning in her voice, "I saw something else."

"Oh no! What?" asked Mom.

"Yesterday, when I went into his study to pick up the copy of *Christianity Today,* the copy Dad wanted back, I saw a book by *Karl Barth* on Reverend Keegan's desk!"

"*Karl Barth!*" shouted Dad.

"Yes! Karl Barth. Not only that, he had underlined some passages in red and at one place in the margin he had written the words *I agree!*"

Mom and Dad exchanged a solemn glance. Dad had preached three whole sermons on Barth and his theology—"Barth the Heretic," "Modernity or Truth," and "Choose Ye This Day."

After a long pause Dad said, "That does it. I'm writing to the mission board today. It's him or me. We cannot be unequally yoked with the apostate and expect God's continued blessing of our ministry. It's enough of a trial that Dick's never been a spiritually kindred spirit, that's bad enough. But *this . . .* !"

"Oh, Ralph! Don't you think we'd better at least confront him before going to the board?"

"Elsa, do you expect me to commit the sin of Eli, who overlooked the wickedness of his sons in the temple?"

"No, I guess not, darling."

"I'm going to write to the board *demanding* Dick's removal. That's final!"

Janet looked smug. "*I've* never spoken to him about doctrine!"

"Nor I!" Rachael added tearfully.

They turned to me.

"I never did either!"

"Do you promise?"

"Yes, Dad."

"Oh Calvin!" Mom's eyes filled with tears.

"Take the girls out."

"But, *Dad!*"

The women filed out, heads bowed, except for Janet, who shot me a last, triumphant glance as she closed the door. I heard Rachael sobbing as Mom led her down the hall.

Dad turned to me. "You had your opportunity to tell the truth. What you don't know is that I confronted Dick. He has admitted that he talked to you about free will. I was giving you a chance to come clean. You failed the test."

"Dad!"

"You lied to me. Bend over and pull your pants down."

Dad got out the black, braided belt as I lowered my pants and touched my toes with trembling fingers.

"I want it to be clear, I'm not strapping you because you have been sadly misled—I trust that the Lord will bring you back to Himself from the wasteland of idle speculation and apostasy just as He brought me back to my senses after my doubts got the better of me during our vacation in Zermatt. What I *am* strapping you for is deceit, lying, saying Dick Keegan didn't speak to you when he did. Do you understand?"

"Yes, Dad. But, Dad?"

"Yes?"

"He did have a nosebleed, Dad."

"That's no excuse. You could have put an ice pack at the base of his neck and not asked him about predestination. Bend over."

Chapter 20

"YOUR GRANDFATHER WORKED FOR HITH LIVIN'."

"Here, put in your teeth, you're lisping."

Grandmother slid the awful objects in, snapped them up and down, then continued. "Not like your worthless father. What's he do, I'd like to know? He's a lazy poop, that's what. No good."

I took the bait. I had begun to like her daily tirades. "He spends a lot of time with the young people."

"Is that supposed ta be a job? Talk, talk, talk, pshaw! He's a poop. I'm glad Ralph Senior never lived ta see the day. Your grandfather worked the coal breakers from the time he were eight years old. Pshaw! Your dad's a poop, boy, and you're gonna be a poop, too! I betcha ya are!"

I handed Grandma her cup of coffee. She slurped loudly.

"Why did Grandfather go to work so young?"

" 'Cause he warn't no fancy poop, 'at's why. 'Cause he didn't marry no fancy missionary who gave him notions, 'at's why!"

"Grandfather got married when he was eight?"

"Don't ya get smart with me, ya li'l shit! Your grandfather was too busy to be runnin' aroun' yellin' 'bout Jesus. He was supportin' his mother an' his sisters by the time he were twelve. 'At's your age! He were a *man*!"

"I'm fifteen."

Grandmother finished her coffee and handed back the cup.

"Well, ya look a lot dumber'n 'at! Jesus! This coffee's lousy!"

"You sure are rude. No wonder Grandfather died young—who could stand living with you?"

Grandmother giggled. "Look out the window. Is that plane crashin' or what?"

I should have known better. In the split second I was distracted, Grandmother reached to her bedside table, where Mom had left the metal bedpan after she emptied it, grabbed it in her claw, arched it over her withered chest, and hit me on the head.

"Brazen brat! That'll teach ya!"

After I got up off the floor, I pushed my chair away from her bedside a couple of feet. "How come you never think I might hit you back?"

It took Grandmother a couple of minutes before she could stop laughing long enough to answer me. " 'Cause you're a li'l sucker an' a poop like your dad!"

"He's *your* son, Grandmother!"

"Bad seed."

"So it's Grandfather's fault?"

"Don't ya get started or next time I'll hit ya when it's full of fresh piss!"

Grandmother shut her eyes and pretended to go to sleep. I waited. After about thirty seconds Grandmother opened her eyes and winked.

"If I was God I wouldn't give them nuthin'! I'd let 'em sing till doomsday."

I shifted my weight uneasily from one spot to another.

"Strapped ya pretty good, huh?"

"I guess so."

"I used to strap *him* good!"

"How come?"

"He were no good then an' he's no good now!"

"Why?"

"Since when do people wait around to get what they need? What happened to work? That's what I wanna know. I shoulda strapped him harder. Beaten some sense into him. The lazy bum!"

I couldn't resist. "But Mom and Dad work. Dad works all day. So does Mom. Mom's working right now, leading the Monday-morning prayer meeting."

"That ain't work. Sittin' around readin', singin', an' talkin'. Work? Work's what your grandfather did. He worked! Up at three every mornin'. Rode the first trolley up ta Chestnut Hill. Had the boilers an' the generators all up an' goin' afore the first person arrived at his buildin'. Once a month he'd get into them boilers an' chip out the lime. *'At's work!*"

"Well, different people are called to do different things."

I shifted my weight from one set of throbbing welts to another. Grandmother smiled maliciously.

"Yeah? Since when do they think they hear God talkin' to 'em, personal like, an' go off to some foreign country an' sit around! *Talk, talk, talk!* They don't even get a job but say their prayin' for money instead of doin' somethin' useful. Since *when* I'd like to know?"

Grandmother sat up.

"Give me another goddamn cup a coffee."

I poured and handed her the cup.

"How come you're so mad at Dad all the time?"

Grandmother slurped noisily. "Why ain't you? He strapped ya, didn't he?"

I did my best to imitate Rachael's most pious voice. Doing that always drove Grandmother wild. "Yes, but I still love him. I'm not bitter like you are because I know Jesus."

"If *I* couldn't read, *I'd* keep my mouth *shut!* Not draw attention to myself!" Grandmother snapped. She shoved the cup back at me.

"Maybe I'll just nail your door shut and let you starve!"

"I don't give a damn. The food's not worth eatin' anyways. Suit yourself."

Grandmother paused, licked her thin lips, then brought up her second favorite subject, the first being Dad's stupidity.

"Why ain't ya in school instead of foolin' around playin' waiter? Ya must've been pretty bad ta get tossed outta missionary school." Grandmother laughed. "How come ya don't go to the village school? They afraid you'll try an' play doctor on the other children?"

"No."

"I heard tell that at that Limey joint, ya tried to circumcise one of 'em! Cut off his dick, 'at's what I heard!"

"I did not!"

" 'At's the way I heard it. 'At's all I know."

"You know that's not true."

"Oh, yeah? Then how come no other school will take ya?"

"You know why."

"If she don't like the nuns at the village school, why'd the prayin' bitch move here?"

I imitated Rachael's voice again. "Grandmother, how come you always say such bad things about Mom?"

"Ya know damn well why! She's the tramp 'at got your pop all confused, got him to quit studyin' to be an engineer. Seminary! Pshaw! I ask ya! I bet 'at's why your dear grandfather keeled over when he did—broken heart!"

"Mom says *you're* the one that pushed Grandfather into an early grave."

Grandmother reached out to her bedside table. I ducked but this time she only picked up her glasses, put them on, and rolled over on her side to face me. Her pale gray eyes, huge and furious, magnified to insane proportions by the thick lenses, blinked a couple of times. She measured each word venomously.

"You go down to that prayer meetin' an' tell that lyin' slut to get her little, Goody Two-shoes, born-again ass up here so I can give her a piece a my mind!"

"Grandmother, I can't interrupt a prayer meeting!"

"Then I'll do it."

Grandma smiled wickedly. To my horror she began to scream at the top of her lungs. Between each piercing—and surprisingly loud—yell, she grinned delightedly.

Of late I had perfected the art of winding Grandmother up so as to avoid having to play Parcheesi, but this was too much of a good thing even for me. I tried to stop her by putting my hand over her mouth. She had her uppers and lowers in and gave me a pretty fair bite. I jumped back, holding my thumb. Grandmother kept right on screaming, *"Help! Help! Help!"* in her high, reedy voice.

I stood frozen at the foot of her bed wondering if I should try to beat her to death with the bedpan or smother her or something. But before I could decide what to do, I heard footsteps on the staircase, then pounding feet racing down the hall. Grandmother heard the steps, too. She smiled. "Yup, 'at'll do it. Worked like a voodoo-nigger charm!"

I opened the door. Janet was running toward me.

"What's going on?"

"I tried to stop her!"

"You get that lyin' bitch up here!"

Janet turned to me accusingly.

"What did you do?"

"Nothing, I promise!"

"Rape! Murder! Fire! I seen the Devil hisself a callin' for my soul!"

Janet screamed in horror then shook Grandmother by the shoulders. *"Grandmother, there's a prayer meeting going on!"*

Grandmother slapped Janet's hands away. *"I'll give the tight-assed bitch somethin' to pray about!"*

Janet turned and fled back down the hall. Grandmother shrieked, *"Help! Help me, Jesus! Ralph's the Antichrist!"* then burst into raucous laughter. I stood watching her eyes start to disappear as the lenses of her glasses fogged up with her carryings-on.

A moment later the door was flung open. Mom burst in. *"Mother! What has possessed you to behave in such a way?"*

Grandmother spoke quietly. "Did ya say I pushed Ralph Senior into an early grave?"

Mom looked surprised, turned accusingly to me, then back to Grandmother. "Don't be ridiculous. We're having a prayer meeting!"

"I don't care if you got Jesus down there dancin' a jig, ya lyin' bitch! You're the one who broke his heart by stealin' his son away an' makin' a fool a him. Missionary! *Ha!* No-good snake-oil salesman. 'At's what ya made him into! Ralph Senior worked twenty years to save enough so his son could go to engineerin' school!"

"Well, *you* never helped us any with Ralph's *seminary! I* was the one that worked to put him through!"

"Did ya expect me to let Ralph Senior spend one stinkin' dime on all that crap?" Grandmother screamed so hard her lowers popped out and fell on the floor. Mom let out an inarticulate bark of rage, stamped her foot, grabbed me by the wrist, and yanked me over to the door. As we retreated Grandmother shouted, *"Pick up my goddamned teeth, will ya?"* But Mom didn't break stride, let alone turn around.

Mom pulled me behind her down the stairs and out the front door, to the little covered porch at the side of our chalet. Mom was breathing hard, her cheeks bright red. She stood on the porch shaking for a full minute before she collected herself enough to speak.

"I *forbid* you to listen to her ever again! I will *not* have you hearing such *wicked things!*"

Mom burst into tears and left me standing outside. I could hear her calling, *"Ralph! Ralph!"* as she ran up the stairs.

I stood staring across our yard at the chicken shed. The chickens were gathered in a dusty surging knot, ganging up on one hen, pecking her viciously as she lay in the dirt. Before I could run over to see why they were attacking her, Dad said in a low, ominous voice, "Come up to my room." He had opened the front door so quietly I hadn't heard him.

Mom was sitting on the edge of their bed, blowing her nose. Her eyes were red. Dad closed the door. "This has gone far enough. It's one thing to put up with my mother. It's another to let her deliberately blaspheme and undermine the Lord's work."

Mom nodded. I didn't know what to say.

The vein was pulsing in Dad's neck. "I've spoken to Mother and told her I'll find a way to send her back to America, to the P.C.C.C.C.U.S.A.'s old folks' home in New London, Connecticut, if she ever, *ever* does something like this again."

Mom blew her nose. "We don't want you to talk to her anymore."

"Yes, Mom."

"I will not have my own children exposed to her demonic poison. We have enough trouble right now with the Keegan situation without Mother making things worse! Do you hear?"

"Yes, Dad."

"From now on, when you sit with her, she's not to talk to you. Not about such . . . such awful things."

"How can I stop her, Mom?"

Dad made a fist and smacked it into his hand. "She knows that she'll have to leave L'Arche if she ever does it again. All you have to do is tell her that you'll get one of us if she starts in! Do you understand?"

"Yes, Dad."

Dad kicked the dresser drawers. Mom walked over and gave me a hug. "You're a good boy. We're not blaming you."

"Elsa, what shall we tell the young people?"

"I think I should tell them the truth. It'll be a good thing for them to know we have our problems, too, that we're not perfect. That way we can show them that the Lord is giving us His Grace to cope with adversity. They can learn by our example."

Mom took me by the hand and led me downstairs. Grandmother was still laughing. Mom ignored her. As we walked into the living room I heard Dad start to play *Tristan and Isolde* real loud.

The young people and Dick and Jane Keegan stared at us. Mom met their looks with a nod as she walked up to the front of the living room. I sat at the back and tried not to make eye contact with the young people, who were turning and looking at me.

Mom beamed her most pious smile. "You will all be wondering about this morning's tragic disturbance of our precious quiet time with the Lord. Well, it illustrates something very graphically. We fight not against flesh and blood but against principalities and powers."

"Amen!" said Dick and Jane in unison. Dick sneezed.

I noticed Mom would not look in Dick or Jane's direction. It was as if they weren't in the room. "The Lord allows us to be tested. Today that testing came in the form of His allowing my husband's poor mother to have a demented outburst that disturbed our time of prayer. She's old and spiritually blind." Mother smiled sweetly. The young people smiled back.

Dick said, "Amen!" but Mom wouldn't look at him.

"So, we will pray for her, then get back to the spiritual warfare we were waging for funds to follow God's call for us to expand His work."

The young people bowed their heads. Mom stepped forward, put her chin up, closed her eyes, and prayed in her most vibrant voice. She couldn't have looked more saintly if she had been tied to a stake and engulfed by flames. I knew Mom was going to pray for a long time. I closed my eyes.

Chapter 21

LUCREZIA BROUGHT ME HOT CHOCOLATE. Jennifer had tea. We shared a basket of fresh, crusty, unsalted rolls, with little single-serving-size cups of Yugoslavian apricot jam and tinfoil-wrapped packages of butter.

"In three days I shall be leaving," said Jennifer.

We were sitting alone on the dining terrace of the Pensione Biea. None of the other guests were awake. Even though I wasn't staying at the *pensione*, Lucrezia served me breakfast right along with Jennifer, the way she always had.

I tore up my roll and dipped it in the hot chocolate. Jennifer cut hers in half, buttered it, and ate it in the orderly way she did everything. We could see the Banini on the beach in front of the *pensione*, opening deck chairs.

The sun felt hot. It slanted under the awning and fell on our faces. The silver teapot reflected the light in a blinding glare. The butter began to melt.

When I saw how calm Jennifer was, I got angry. I couldn't have said I was leaving as nonchalantly as she had. I never would have acted as if this was the end of just another vacation, as if I did not have an ache in my chest that made it hard to swallow.

"Jennifer, please don't go."

"Calvin, how on earth do you expect me to stay?"

"We can run away together to some other place."

"You can't possibly think that would work. You can't keep running away all your life."

"I'm willing to try."

"Well, *I'm not!*"

"Then how will we stay together?"

"We shan't. Not now anyway. I'll see you next holls."

"What makes you think I'll be here?"

"Why wouldn't you?"

"I can't hide in Gino's studio forever."

"Calvin, you know perfectly well what will happen in the end. You will go home, or your parents will fetch you. Then things will be back to normal."

"Nothing's normal in my family. You know that."

"Nevertheless, next holls we shall be together. I'm sure of it."

"Mom and Dad will never take me anyplace again."

"Then we shall meet elsewhere, some other time."

"Jennifer, I'm never going back home and that's final! If you don't stay here we won't ever see each other again!"

"What utter rot! In a few years we shall both do what we like. Who's to stop us?"

"A few *years!* How will I live for a few *years* without seeing you? I'd rather be *dead!*"

"Calvin, you are a dreadfully silly boy."

"Jennifer, please don't act like you're somebody else, some grown-up or my mother or something. *Please!*"

"Calvin, I shall miss you horribly but I can't simply give up and cry, or throw myself on the ground and thrash about. We'll have to wait. If you wait I shall as well, until your parents become sensible or you grow up or I do, whichever comes first."

While we talked I had been studying the skin forming over some drops of hot chocolate on my plate. I looked up at Jennifer's face. Her blue-green eyes were swimming with tears. They sparkled, matching the turquoise water in the bay behind her. Her hands tore a roll into tinier and tinier pieces on the tablecloth. Her long slender fingers were white at the knuckles. Her shell-pink mouth was quivering. My eyes filled, then overflowed. We sat looking at each other with tears rolling down our cheeks. I reached out and took Jennifer's hand.

We were looking at each other so hard, loving each other so much, that we didn't notice Lucrezia come over from the terrace doorway with hot milk and boiling water to refill our pots until she said, *"Madonna! che fai? Perché piangi?"*

Jennifer turned to her. Instead of dropping my hand, she held on to it, even though I tried to pull mine away. Jennifer looked at Lucrezia. *"Amore, Lucrezia, amore!"*

We walked down the outside stairs, to the alley that led to the beach. We already had on our bathing suits under our clothes, so we didn't need to go into the *pensione* and change.

The Banini was still unfolding deck chairs in long symmetrical rows. Jennifer asked him how much it would cost to rent a boat. *"Quanto costa noleggiare la barca per tutto il giorno?"*

The Banini smiled and pointed to his old work boat. He answered that he would let us have it for free, as long as we didn't damage it.

"Take me to the lighthouse," Jennifer commanded.

I rowed past the castle point, into the open sea. As I rowed I looked back at the Paraggi cove receding behind us, and into the Portofino harbor to our right, framed by the soft fingers of the cypress tress on the hills.

I steered us across the Portofino bay to the lighthouse. Then I maneuvered into a small inlet between two huge rocks. Jennifer jumped out with the rope in her hand, pulled us close to shore, held out her hand, and helped me onto the warm, wet rock. She tied the rope to an overhanging branch of a crooked pine that jutted over the water, took our towels, spread them on the rock, and sat down.

I put my arm around Jennifer's waist and she draped her arm over my shoulders. We sat facing the sharp line of the horizon for a while without saying anything, watching the gentle waves, feeling the heat of the sun, and smelling the delicious perfume of pine trees and dried seaweed. Jennifer was the first to speak.

"Calvin, if you like I shall promise to marry you."

I had been thinking about how to ask her to marry me the whole time I was rowing. Now that she said she would, I didn't know what to answer. All I managed to say was, "Oh?"

Jennifer looked at me pretty hard when I only answered, "Oh?" I knew I had better tell her how I felt, or she would get mad, maybe take back her offer. Suddenly I knew what to do and say.

I leapt to my feet. "Jennifer, marry me *today!*"

Now it was her turn to look startled.

"What on earth do you mean?"

"I mean I'll row you to the dock at Portofino, then we'll go up to the church and marry each other!"

"Calvin, you can't simply walk into a church and get married!"

"Not with a priest, just you and me. We'll use holy water to make it official."

Jennifer stared at me. Different thoughts were written on her face one after the other. Her eyes changed color from blue-green to darker blue, then almost turquoise.

At last she said, "You are the daftest boy, the oddest person, the biggest gormless twit I've ever met, but I shall always love you, and if creeping about a church, sprinkling holy water on each other, will give you pleasure, then I shall oblige you!"

Jennifer stood up and kissed me so hard my teeth cut the inside of my lower lip.

I rowed us around the point and into Portofino's harbor. We tied up at the old barge that had been made into a floating bar. Chairs were stacked at one end of its deck. A boy was hosing it down. Dirty gray bilge trickled over the edge into the green harbor water, making it muddy around the moss-covered hull. The evidence of the revelries of the night before—cigarette butts, matches, corks, and straws—bobbed around the barge. I helped Jennifer disembark, tied the rope to the leg of a bar table, nodded to the boy, and took Jennifer's hand.

We walked down the quayside toward the piazza, then cut across the square to the wide steps that led up to the church. The building was empty except for the old lady dressed in black who was always there. She was kneeling alone in front of the statue of Mary.

When we entered the church I led the way and showed Jennifer what to do. Even though she was Church of England, she didn't know how to be Roman Catholic as well as I did. Jennifer had never played Catholic, secretly spending hours in the church watching people come and go, pray, confess, and worship, the way I had during my vacations. I dipped my fingers in the stone basin, set into the wall by the church door, took some holy water, and crossed myself. Jennifer watched, then did the same. I turned toward the altar, genuflected, and crossed myself again. Jennifer did, too.

"Where shall we do it?" Jennifer whispered.

"In the side chapel, there, by the statue of Christ."

I took her hand and led her around the back of the dark mahogany pews, through big patches of bright red-and-blue sunlight that fell from the stained-glass windows onto the huge flagstones, over the beautiful mosaic of a sea serpent writhing on the floor, and finally up to a rail that separated the little chapel from the main part of the church.

I dropped Jennifer's hand and went over to the candleholder, where I pulled out a long wax taper, put fifty lire into the money slot, and walked to where a candle in a red glass jar was burning in front of a statue of St. Joseph. I lit my candle and brought it back to the altar. I fastened it to the rail with a wax-encrusted clip, crossed myself, and knelt.

Jennifer did the same.

She looked at me and smiled. "What now?"

"Look up at Jesus and pray for his blessing on our marriage. Also pray to Mary to protect us."

We folded our hands. Jennifer closed her eyes but I studied Jesus' wounds, the cuts from his flogging, each drop of carved blood painted a dark red, the same color as his lips, open in agony.

After I heard Jennifer whisper amen, I took one of her hands, stood up, and asked, "Are you ready?"

"Yes."

"Jennifer, you are gathered here together with me to witness the union of Calvin and you before God."

Jennifer nodded.

"Jennifer Bazlinton, do you know of any reason or impediment that you should not take Calvin to be your lawfully wedded husband?"

"No."

Jennifer squared her shoulders. "Calvin Becker, do you know of any reason or impediment why you should not take Jennifer Bazlinton as your lawful wedded wife?"

I answered, "No."

I started to say, "I declare Jennifer Bazlinton and—"

"Hold on, Calvin, you have to ask about having and holding, don't you?"

"Sorry, I got mixed up. Jennifer, do you take this man to be your wedded husband to have and to hold and to obey as long as you both shall live, so help you God?"

"I do."

"Calvin, do you take me, this woman, to be your wedded wife, till death do you part, to have and to hold and to love?"

"I do."

I turned Jennifer toward me, held both her hands, and said, "Then I pronounce us man and wife."

"So do I," Jennifer whispered. Then she added, "Oh bother, we need rings!"

"I'll get them later."

I pulled Jennifer to me and kissed her on the mouth. Her lips were warm. The old woman turned around and hissed in disapproval. She didn't know it was all right because it was a wedding.

I led Jennifer back to the holy water and sprinkled her. Then she sprinkled me. We kissed again, this time concealed by a huge stone pillar. We kissed for a long time.

When we stepped out of the cool dim interior into the hot bright morning, we stood blinking, dazed. It took a few minutes to get used to the sunlight.

Chapter 22

DAD SAT ON THE STEPS that led from our chalet down to the road. He was waiting for the P.C.C.C.C.U.S.A. board to act on the letter he sent them about Dick Keegan's theology. He was so anxious for their answer that he waited for the post lady every morning for a week. He said he didn't want the letter to fall into the wrong hands.

I was lying on my bed, staring at the familiar faces in the wood grain of my ceiling and wondering how I could stand to wait until August 20. It was May 22. That left three months before I would see Jennifer.

My reverie was interrupted when Dad yelled, *"Oh, no!"* at the top of his lungs.

Dad ran into our chalet calling out, *"Elsa! Elsa!"*

The letter had arrived. The P.C.C.C.C.U.S.A.'s board decided that Dick Keegan had not adopted false doctrine. They said Dick had satisfactorily explained that he was just investigating Arminian theology, in order to better understand it. Dick wrote to the board after he somehow found out Dad was bringing charges against him. Dad accused Mom of having carelessly left his letter out on her desk before sending it. He said one of the young people was probably a "Keegan spy" and had seen the letter to the board and repeated its contents to Dick. Dad said the fact that Dick got in ahead of him went a long way toward explaining why the board had believed Dick's letter.

Dad gathered our family in his bedroom for an emergency meeting. The board was calling for reconciliation, which, Dad said, was a code word for compromise. He said that we could no longer allow things to slide, could no longer compromise with untruth. This meant we could not remain in the P.C.C.C.C.U.S.A.

The board might be calling for reconciliation but, Dad said, he knew apostasy when he saw it. The purity of the visible church was at stake. Dad would not let it be defiled; he would not be forced to work with Dick. Even if Dad turned out to be the last remaining Christian, the final remnant in the world, he was willing to stand alone.

After the emergency meeting, the first thing Dad did was to make the five young people who were staying at the Keegans' move into our chalet. Dad said that as the founder of L'Arche he could no longer, in good conscience, be responsible for the souls of those under Dick's roof.

Dad canceled his speaking trip to the Zurich Reformed men's Bible-study group and to the Reformed pastors' convention in Paris. He said that the greater need was at home, that he dared not go away, "lest the people take unto themselves a golden calf."

Dad went to see Dick and told him that he and Jane were no longer welcome in our chalet, and that the ban on their presence included our church services.

The first Sunday after our "godly separation" from the apostate, Dad preached on apostasy, how the devil subtly infiltrates the church from time to time, to lead people astray. The devil's wiles were, Dad said, self-defeating, because God used these times of testing to purify his true church, to "winnow the sheaves, to separate the truly elect from the pseudo-elect."

When Dad said this, Grandmother, who had been carried down to our church service under protest and who was sitting on the couch, glaring at anyone who looked in her direction, muttered, "Now I've heard everythin', ya screwy nut!" Dad glanced furiously at her but went on preaching.

"It causes me great sorrow to have to tell you that in our midst we have the very situation Paul describes in the book of Romans, chapter sixteen, verse seventeen. Our former colaborer, Dick Keegan, has adopted views that place him outside of the faithful remnant. His ideas are apostate, heretical, and worst of all, antireformational. Because of this I have no choice but *to forbid you all from having any contact whatsoever* with Dick or Jane 'lest ye also be defiled.' "

"Ya ain't tellin' me what ta do!" said Grandmother. No one looked at her.

At Sunday lunch, after Mom served us angel-food cake and cherry Jell-O, Dad announced, "I'm going to post 'No Trespassing' signs on the path between our chalet and the Keegans'. If anyone sees Dick or Jane attempting to enter our property from their yard, you are to call me and I will give them one warning. If they persist in trying to force entry, it will then be my duty to call the police and charge them with trespassing."

Mom, Rachael, Janet, and I exchanged worried glances. Even Mom, who agreed about the seriousness of Dick's apostasy, looked shocked. Dad must have seen our doubtful expressions. He pounded his fist on the tabletop. "*I tell you there's no choice!* Can't you see where all this will lead? We cannot be unequally yoked! We must follow the dictates of Scripture and have *no fellowship* with those who refuse to do the Lord's work in the Lord's way!"

One of the young people, a girl from Holland, started to cry and bolted from the table. Mom hurried after her. We didn't want Dad to shout anymore, so the rest of us all looked straight ahead, ate Jell-O, and kept silent.

After lunch Dad cut up some big pieces of cardboard and wrote, NO TRESPASSING—PRIVATE PROPERTY on them with one of my extra-thick Magic Markers. Then he nailed the signs on our trees so that they faced toward the Keegans' chalet and the chicken shed.

Dad got a ball of string and tied a line across the gap in the hedge that separated our yard from the Keegans'. On the string he hung a sign that faced into our yard which read, NO RESIDENT OF L'ARCHE SHALL PASS THIS LINE—ROMANS 13:1. On the other side, facing the chicken shed, he wrote, NO TRESPASSING—ROMANS 13:4–5.

I watched Dad sealing our borders from where I was standing, on the top-floor balcony outside of Grandmother's bedroom. As Dad stretched the string across the path Dick Keegan came out of his chalet, hesitated, then walked slowly toward him.

"Ralph, what are you doing?" Dick's voice sounded loud and squeaky.

Dad didn't answer. He concentrated on tying the string to one of the hedge trees. Grandmother was in bed behind me. She tried to sit up and craned her neck to look through the open balcony door. "What's goin' on? What's that nut doin' now?"

"He's putting up 'No Trespassing' signs," I whispered.

"Ralph!" Grandmother shouted, "Ralph! You're not playin' with a full deck! You're goin' loopy, boy!" I spun around. "Shhh! Please, Grandmother!" Dad pretended not to have heard her. He kept right on putting up the string barricade. Dick walked up to the barrier.

"Ralph, can't we just talk? Don't you think this is a little silly?"

Dad turned his back and began to tie another piece of string to the tree opposite, across the side path. While I was watching Dad fumble with the knot, I noticed that a chicken was getting pecked in the shed behind him. I decided I'd check up on her later.

Dad finished tying the knot, turned his back, and started to walk toward our chalet. Dick walked along the string, stopped, stood looking at one of the signs for a second, shook his head, picked nervously at his nose, then ducked under the barrier, ran up to Dad, and grabbed his arm.

"What's he doin' now?" hissed Grandmother.

"Shhhh . . . they're talking."

"C'mon, Ralph! We're brothers in Christ. This is no way to behave!"

Grandmother laughed. *"Brothers in Christ, my skinny white butt!"*

Dad wrenched his arm away from Dick's grasp and looked up. I could see the vein in his neck pulsing.

"Calvin! Tell your mother there's a man trespassing in our yard. Tell her to call the police! And tell your ignorant fool of a grandmother to shut up!"

Grandmother smiled and nodded in satisfaction. *"Shut up yourself, ya loopy turd!"* she yelled.

"C'mon, Ralph!" Dick plucked at Dad's sleeve.

I didn't know what to do. I stood frozen, clutching the balcony rail and watching the pecked chicken trying to escape the others.

Grandmother kept on laughing. *"Better'n a three-ring circus,"* she screamed.

"Calvin! Did you hear me? Go get your mother!"

I turned around and bolted inside. As I turned I saw Dad slap Dick's hand away.

I ran to the head of the stairs. I heard the front door slam. Dad must have dashed to the house flat out. He got to Mom before I could even get down the stairs.

"Elsa, did you call the police?"

"What for, darling?"

"I *told* Calvin to tell you to call them. Dick's trespassing."

"Oh Ralph, don't you think—"

"Elsa! Do as I say!"

Dad marched upstairs. I dived across the hall into my room just as Dad strode past. He never even looked at me. A moment later he put on an opera and turned up the volume full blast. I could hear Grandmother's laughter until the tenor drowned her out.

I tiptoed to the head of the stairs. Mom was talking on the hall phone.

A moment later Mom came upstairs to report to Dad. They both shouted to be heard above the opera.

"Well?"

"They're not coming, Ralph!"

"Why not?"

" 'Cause they know you're a nutcase!" Grandmother screamed from her bedroom.

"Shut up, Mother!"

"They say that to drive all the way up from Monthey to Trois-Torrents because a neighbor's in our garden isn't worth the trouble."

"How did they know it was a neighbor?"

"I had to tell them!"

The opera ended with a loud, abrupt scratch. By the sound of it, Dad ripped the record right off the turntable.

"Why didn't you say it was a *stranger!* Then they would've come!"

"How could I lie, Ralph?"

"Don't you lecture me!"

"Don't let him talk to ya that way, Elsa! Kick him in his runty li'l onions till his eyes water!"

I heard a loud smash mixed with Grandmother's cackling laughter. Mom screamed. My parents' bedroom door banged open. Mom ran out. She tore down the stairs with Dad yelling after her at the top of his lungs, *"I have been betrayed!"* There was another splintering, smashing sound. Dad must have thrown something after Mom.

Grandmother yelled, *"I'd'a moved in sooner if I knowed it was gonna be this good! It's better'n This Is Your Life!"*

I sat on my bed for a while until I heard Dad go back to his room. The opera started up again. I locked my door, lay down, and closed my eyes. I pulled Jennifer to me and kissed her on the mouth. Her lips were warm. The old woman turned around and hissed in disapproval.

Chapter 23

I HAD TO SNEAK under the "No Trespassing" string to get to my patient. The pecked chicken was squatting in the dirt. When I opened the wire-mesh door to the run, she shifted uneasily but was too ill to stand. She was helpless. I picked her up, put her in a cardboard box, and carried her away from the Keegans' yard, back to our island of faith.

Our boiler room, which housed the coal-burning hot-water furnace, was always warm. I put the chicken down on the edge of the big, old-fashioned, stone laundry tub, built right into the wall of the furnace room. We kept garden tools in it.

I reached up above the tub and took the box of all-purpose antibiotic powder, *pénicilline vétérinaire*, off the shelf. Then I walked upstairs to the kitchen.

In the cupboard above the sink, Mom kept some glass syringes and needles. The visiting nurse used them when she gave Grandmother shots. I put a syringe and needle in a saucepan to boil. Janet barged in.

"*What* do you think *you're* doing?"

"I'm treating a sick chicken."

Janet peered dubiously into the saucepan. "With the visiting nurse's syringe?"

"I think I should get the penicillin into her bloodstream. She's fading fast."

Janet stuck her head out of the kitchen door.

"*Mom!* He's doing awful medical experiments again! Now he's going to use our syringe to kill some filthy old hen!"

Mom walked in from the dining room. She was laying out Sunday-school flannel-graph materials, gluing the flannel backing onto the paper figures of Joseph and his brothers so they would stick to the flannel-graph board when she taught Sunday school to the spastics. Mom had a new, freshly cut-out Joseph in one hand, a tube of glue and Joseph's coat of many colors in the other.

"Calvin, I really don't think you should. We could catch something. I think we have enough problems right now."

"Aw, Mom, please. I'll boil them up again."

"Well, I suppose that's all right if you boil them for at least twenty minutes."

"*Mother!*" shrieked Janet. "You *must* be joking! How *can* you let him, especially at a time like this?"

"Life must go on, Janet. Calvin's just doing his job. He's supposed to care for the chickens. Our duties can't stop just because of a church split."

It's hard to find a vein on a chicken's leg. First you have to pluck off some feathers, which the chicken objects to. Even if it's sick it pecks your hands and flaps each time you pull out a handful.

I tied a rubber band around her leg to make the veins stand out, rubbed alcohol on the drumstick, then slipped the needle in and pulled back the plunger. No blood. So I tried again, about three or four times. The chicken got mighty restless. When I pulled back the plunger on the fourth try, a crimson stain spread into the milky penicillin solution.

I slowly injected the *pénicilline vétérinaire*. Before I put the chicken back in her box I got an eyedropper and forced her to swallow some sugar water so she would get nourishment and liquid. Farmer Ruchet had shown me how to do this with sickly piglets.

I left the box, with my patient in it, by the furnace and went upstairs. As I climbed the basement steps I heard a commotion. Mom came running down from the top floor. She made a lot of noise on the old wooden boards.

I cautiously peered out of the door at the top of the basement stairs just as Dad yelled, "How *dare* you? You *will* take care of her whether you like it or not! How do you think it is for *me?*"

Dad's door slammed. A moment later his music went way up in volume. Mom came down the last step and saw me before I could duck back. She smiled nervously and smoothed her skirt.

"He's a little upset by the Keegan situation."

"I think the chicken will be fine."

"My father *never once* raised his voice to my dear mother. I had no idea what to do when Ralph yelled at me on our wedding night!"

"I'm keeping her warm."

"Mother told me what I needed to know about the Physical Things, but she never said he'd blame me for . . . for . . . *everything!*" Mom sighed. "He had no idea at all. About . . . anything. Not like you. You've had the privilege of having a mother who's frank and open. Not like poor Ralph, his mother never told him *anything!*"

"I bet she shows an improvement by morn—"

Mom fixed me with a piercing look.

"You know what that terrible woman said on the day of our wedding? She said, 'Don't bring *me* no brats and expect *me* to support 'em 'cause ya won't be able to on some blankety-blank pastor's salary'! *That's* what *she* said! Those were the terrible words I had ringing in my ears on *my wedding night!* I had saved myself for *twenty years* and *that's* all the thanks I got!"

"Please, Mom, I already heard that story."

"Well, you just give thanks that you have benefited from a very different childhood environment than your poor father!"

I was woken up by Dad's shouting. I lay in the dark for a few minutes listening to the rise and fall of his angry voice. I hoped it would be a short fight, one that would be over before my body was vibrating with the adrenaline that always kept me up for hours after Dad's voice dwindled into exhausted silence.

The sound of screaming was followed by a sudden crash.

I sat up and turned on my light. It was three A.M. I tiptoed down the hall. Rachael didn't say anything when I walked in. She slid over so I could sit on the edge of her bed in the dark and wait for Dad to calm down.

"*Are you trying to kill me like Dick is?* . . . *You are!* You and your precious family! You married *me.* . . . I don't care. . . . *I say no!*"

We couldn't hear Mom's rejoinders. She kept her voice low. But we heard Dad all right. "*You're trying to turn them against me! Don't deny it! I know!*"

After about half an hour the fight petered out into a series of growls and murmurs. I heard Rachael breathing deeply next to me. She had fallen asleep.

On the way back to my room I peeked into Grandmother's bedroom. Her head was thrown back, her mouth open. Dad's shouting had not disturbed her in the least.

With her teeth out, Grandmother's cheeks sagged and shuddered with each breath. In the day, her long silver hair was arranged on top of her head in a net. Now it was loose, spread out on her pillow, a tarnished fan around her desiccated, pale face.

Grandmother's night-light cast a pale blue glow on the roof of her mouth. She snored. I watched her sleeping a moment longer, then moved the hands of her clock back an hour and tiptoed out.

Before I went to bed I crept down to check on my patient. The grate of the coal furnace was ajar to provide air for the fire. The lurid orange flicker was enough to see by. I went to the chicken's box and opened it. My patient sat up, flapped her wings, and fluttered to the edge of the stone tub, where she turned around a couple of times, rustled her feathers and clucked softly.

I was pleased. Now Janet would have to admit I had been right about what to do, about how to prescribe for the chicken.

I let the chicken remain perched on the edge of the tub. She could roost there for the night. I watched her settle, preen, then doze. I held my feet, one at a time, toward the coal grate until they were warm. Then I crept back to my room.

It was quiet. I wondered if Mom and Dad were asleep or only too exhausted to fight anymore. I glanced out of my balcony door. The sky over the peaks of the Dents du Midi was beginning to turn pale gray. A crow flapped slowly across the void, settled for a moment on the blue spruce tree, then glided heavily down into our yard and perched, swaying precariously, on the string holding the "No Trespassing" sign.

I felt cold and got back into bed. The crow cawed raucously. I closed my eyes. The fat woman, a loose gray sweater draped over her shoulders, was taking down the rusty steel shutters that kept people from stealing her ice cream.

Jennifer and I strolled across the square hand in hand.

"Would you like an ice cream to celebrate?" I asked.

"That would be lovely!"

We passed the palm-enclosed dining terrace of the Hotel Nazionale, crossed the alley, and stepped up to the *gelateria* counter. The ice-cream lady smiled at us above her generous double chins, folded back the glass freezer top, took her scoop out of a bucket of warm water, and dug up two curls of pale green pistachio and dark, almost black chocolate ice cream. She packed the creamy balls into wafer-thin, honey-colored cones, deftly wrapped tiny paper napkins around them, and handed Jennifer one and me the other.

We crossed the piazza to the low wall, by the slip where the boats got hauled out of the water. We perched there and watched postcard vendors and souvenir merchants trundle two-wheeled carts out of shady alleys into the hazy morning sunlight of the square. They hung up racks of postcards and bundles of fake silk scarves, arranged rows of plastic replicas of Michelangelo's *David* and gondolas made out of seashells with PORTOFINO printed on gold shiny labels stuck to them.

"Jennifer, I wonder why people buy all that junk?"

Jennifer licked her cone pensively. "I expect it's to take back to relatives to show they've been on holiday."

"But why those things? Why not something better?"

"I expect it's cheaper to buy a plastic souvenir than one of Gino's paintings or a Givenchy evening gown!"

Jennifer licked her ice cream.

"Jennifer, when you go back, how will we stay in touch, how will I know what you're doing?"

"We'll write, silly."

"Where will you write to?"

"To wherever you are. To Gino, if you like. If you go back to Switzerland I have your address there."

"If I get taken back to Switzerland, I'll run again!"

"Then let me know where you are."

"Maybe next time I'll run to England, to your boarding school!"

"That would be jolly. I could try and hide you, though I expect you'd be caught in the end."

"You wouldn't mind, though?"

"Calvin, I hope that you don't spend the rest of your life running from one place to the next. There's a word for such behavior. It's called vagrancy!"

"When I'm old enough to not be a missionary then I'll stop running."

Jennifer laughed. "And you'll find your wife and we'll settle down?"

"That's right."

"I hope you learn a useful trade so you can support me in the manner to which I have become accustomed!"

Jennifer's pink tongue encircled a dollop of pistachio that had run down the side of her cone. I watched her lick the ice cream. Her mouth was so pretty and her pink tongue so charming and her eyes so bright that I forgot to lick my cone altogether. I felt a lukewarm, sticky trickle of melted chocolate ice cream slide over the back of my hand. Jennifer leaned over and licked the ice cream off my hand. I pulled my hand away and kissed her. I tasted the chocolate in her warm, creamy mouth.

Chapter 24

AN OLD SEMINARY FRIEND OF DAD'S, who was on the mission board of the P.C.C.C.U.S.A., sent Dad a telegram to let him know exactly what was afoot, that there was a plot against him.

DICK CLAIMS MORE TRUE TO REFORMED TRADITION THAN YOU STOP TOLD SPASTICS LADIES THAT YOU ONLY MAD AT HIM BECAUSE MORE OF YOUNG PEOPLE RELATE BETTER TO HIM MORE OF A KINDRED SPIRIT STOP ACCUSED YOU OF JEALOUSY STOP DICK TOLD LADIES HE THINKS THEY SHOULD HAVE A GREATER VOICE IN THE DIRECTION OF WORK STOP LADIES AGREE SAY GOD CLEARLY SPEAKING TO DICK IN NEW DEEPER WAY THAT MANTLE OF LEADERSHIP HAS PASSED TO DICK STOP LADIES SENT TELEGRAM TO BOARD ASKED THEM TO CONSIDER REMOVING YOU FROM THE LEADERSHIP INSTALL DICK AS LEADER.

Until Dick got The Ladies to change sides, we might have been reconciled. But when Dad got proof of treason he went right over the edge.

Dad tore the telegram into tiny pieces and threw them at Mom. Later he made Janet and Rachael piece it back together like a jigsaw puzzle. Dad said he had acted "hastily, in the heat of righteous indignation," but that he needed the telegram for "evidence."

Dad stormed into the yard and put up more "No Trespassing" signs facing The Ladies' chalet. He strictly forbade us from having any further contact with The Ladies or spastics.

After our garden was secured in all directions with "No Trespassing" signs, Dad made us shut the shutters. After that, the only daylight in our chalet came from Grandmother's balcony door. When Dad attempted to shut her shutters, she picked up her scissors, held them expertly by the points, like a throwing knife, and said, "Ralph, if ya touch 'em, I'll pin your runty li'l ass ta the wall. *I mean it!*" So Dad left her shutters open.

Before the split in our ministry we hardly ever met the young people arriving on the tram. We trusted them to come up the steps to our chalet, register with Mom or Janet, get shown to their rooms, and have the program of study, prayer, work, and fellowship explained to them.

Now Dad met every tram himself, or had one of us do it. He said we could not risk having some innocent young person walk up the wrong set of stairs and wind up next door under the false impression that they had come to the authentic L'Arche ministry when, in fact, they had unwittingly fallen into the clutches of the apostate.

On the morning of June 5, 1967, Dad and I were sitting, bathed in bright sunlight, the scent of field flowers enveloping us, at the bottom of the garden steps. We were waiting for the nine-thirty-eight A.M. tram. Two young people, carrying backpacks and sleeping bags, got off. Dad stood up and hurried across the road.

Dad smiled and held out his hand. "Welcome to L'Arche!"

One of the young people, a short, fat boy with an English accent and a weedy mustache, shook hands with Dad. "Are you Reverend Keegan?"

"No, Reverend Keegan's no longer with us. I'm Reverend Becker."

"Reverend Becker, I wonder if you would be so kind as to direct me to the New L'Arche?"

Dad stood stunned. The vein in his neck began to pulse.

"I don't think I understand you."

"I wonder if you could—"

"I know what you said! I mean I don't know what you're talking about. What do you mean the 'New L'Arche'?"

The boy fingered his thin mustache nervously.

"Why, Reverend Keegan's ministry, sir, the one he wrote my vicar at Oxford about." He held out a letter. Dad snatched it away, turned, and walked back to the chalet.

The young person glanced at me questioningly.

"Excuse me, I don't quite understand. . . ."

"NOT ONE WORD!" Dad didn't even turn around as he yelled this to me. *"DO NOT ANSWER HIM ONE WORD!"*

After the incident at the tram stop, Dad stormed around the chalet locking all the doors. Then he called a special meeting with Mom, Janet, Rachael, and me. He had us come up to his darkened bedroom and sit in a row on the bed. Grandmother was not invited, nor were the four young people we had staying with us. Dad told the young people to wait in their rooms and pray for God to guide him as to what to do next.

Dad clutched the letter so tightly that his knuckles were white. "We are facing a crisis. We can no longer trust *anyone!*"

Dad held out the letter and shook it in our faces. "It's my duty to share this with you," he said. Dad unfolded the crumpled paper and read out loud.

> May 26, 1967
> L'Arche
> Trois-Torrents-sur-Monthey
> Valais
> Switzerland

> Dear Friend in Christ,
>
> I'm writing to you to share an exciting new ministry that the Lord has laid on our hearts. The New L'Arche! (This work will replace the old L'Arche, which is now closing its doors after fourteen years of faithful ministry.) The Lord has led us to continue the

unique faith work of L'Arche while showing us that we must take it in exciting new directions.

Come join with us for spiritual reflection, refreshment and above all, *fellowship*!

One of the *exciting things* we are doing in the ministry right now is to offer a *special rate* to our young people who come to us in the next six months! The old suggested love offering was thirty Swiss francs for a week of fellowship, room and board. Now, in the New L'Arche, we feel led to lower the suggested love offering to fifteen Swiss francs per week!

Won't you join us in our special summer-fall program? Our theme is: "Coming Closer to a Loving God." Dick and Jane are ready to welcome you to the beautiful Swiss Alps!

Greetings in the Name of the Lamb,

The Keegans

As Dad read the letter Mom gasped and turned white.

"Oh Ralph! I can't believe they did *this*!"

"*Now* can you see I've been right all along? *Now* can you see what we have here? *Now* can you see how Satan is working not only to corrupt our ministry but even to set up a counterfeit, an Antichrist ministry, to lead the young people astray?"

"He used our mailing list, didn't he?" whispered Mom.

"He must've snuck in and taken the extra copy we kept in the basement file cupboard before I locked the doors," said Dad.

Dad began to work on correspondence day and night. He said it was his godly duty, as a minister of the Gospel, to inform our donors back home that the board had allowed the Keegans to stay in spite of Dick's trickery and apostasy. Dad worked so hard at performing his godly duty of "sounding the alarm" that he never came down to the dining room. We took him trays of sandwiches and tea. Dad's room began to smell like the men's room at the Milano train station. He had given up bathing.

Dad only came out of his room when he ran out of people to write letters to. Then he would telephone the P.C.C.C.C.U.S.A.'s "faithful pastors," men who had stuck together through four previous church splits, who agreed with Dad that our denomination had gone soft on liberalism again. Dad reported that they were prepared to take their congregations and form a new denomination that would faithfully carry on the living tradition of the old P.C.U.S.A., P.C.C.U.S.A., P.C.C.C.U.S.A., and P.C.C.C.C.U.S.A., undefiled by modernist, liberal, or Anabaptist ideas.

By the end of the second week of June, normally our busiest time of year, fewer and fewer young people were coming to L'Arche. Even though Dad lowered our weekly suggested love offering to five francs, most of the young people who got off the tram were headed to the Keegans' chalet, to the New L'Arche.

Even our church services were empty. On the first Sunday after we discovered their treason, we saw The Ladies march past, pushing wheelchairs, going to the Keegans' chalet by the front road. Naturally they were not allowed to cut through our yard anymore.

The Keegans' church had all the spastics, most of the young people, and the only person who could play a piano, Jane Keegan. Our church had our family, and our four remaining young people. The other side sang a lot louder than we did. Even with our windows and shutters closed we could hear the service next door. They almost drowned us out, but as Dad said, "It only takes *one* Daniel to be faithful to the one true God though a thousand heathens rage!"

Mom said, "We can sing without a piano perfectly well! The early church did. Anyway, God sees the heart!"

That Sunday Dad preached for more than three hours. In his sermon he said that none of these sad events surprised him, that in the last days many would go astray and follow after false teachers. Our job was to remain faithful no matter what.

It was at the conclusion of church that Dad announced that we would have no summer vacation in Portofino. The room seemed to go dark around me. Up until that moment this particular church split was pretty routine. I had lived through two or three others. But when Dad said there would be no vacation I felt like the world was ending.

Janet and Rachael didn't care that we would miss our vacation. They never made friends in Italy; besides, they were enjoying being the "last of the faithful remnant." It meant that they did not have to go back to boarding school. My sisters spent most of their days down in the basement feverishly working on the mimeograph machine, copying letters, addressing envelopes, opening correspondence, keeping track of how many supporters we were getting, updating Mom's map of the world (red pins marked the cities where we had the support of a faithful pastor or missionary; black pins marked the P.C.C.C.C.U.S.A.'s strongholds of falsehood).

While Janet and Rachael worked they sang the Bible chorus "Trust and Obey," over and over again. When I told Janet that I'd rather go to Italy than be the true remnant, she drew herself up, pointed at me, and said, "Get behind me, Satan!"

On a beautiful clear morning, one of those days when the air seemed to magnify the mountains and our hillside was so full of field flowers that it smelled like a florist shop, Dad received an express, registered, notarized letter from the P.C.C.C.C.U.S.A. mission board. The letter ordered him to leave the premises of L'Arche within one month!

The P.C.C.C.C.U.S.A.'s board had learned about Dad writing to, and calling, the P.C.C.C.C.U.S.A.'s pastors and missionaries, how Dad had been urging them to join him in forming a new denomination, how Dad was proclaiming a godly separation from the apostate.

The board accused Dad of subversion. Dad called a Swiss lawyer in Montreux. The lawyer said that because Chalet Tulipes had been purchased in Dad's name, at the beginning of our ministry, under Swiss law, the P.C.C.C.C.U.S.A. would not be able to evict us since they were a U.S. corporation and not registered in Switzerland.

Dad convened a special thanksgiving prayer meeting to rejoice over the resounding victory that God had prepared for us, to praise God for this sign of his enduring faithfulness, to thank him for "delivering the land into our hands."

Mom lifted up her voice. "Dear Heavenly Father, we just come before Thee to thank Thee that Thou hast moved the Swiss authorities to do Thy will, to recognize that this Thy work belongs to *us*, Thy *true* servants. We just praise Thee that Thou hast spoken, that Thou hast crushed the raging kings of this world and hath raised up we who humbly serve Thee. . . ."

When the praying was finally done, we sang "Onward, Christian Soldiers." Mom and Dad both had tears on their cheeks. After the last chorus, Dad wiped his eyes, thrust his clenched fist into the air, and shouted, *"The battle continues! Praise Jesus!"*

"Praise Jesus!" shouted Janet.

"Praise my flabby white ass," Grandmother yelled from her room down the hall. Then she started to laugh. Mom got up and shut the door.

Rachael and Janet went back to mimeographing newsletters and addressing envelopes. I wandered down to the hedge, crawled under it, and looked out between a gap in the branches at the peaks of the Dents du Midi.

"Jennifer, Jennifer, Jennifer," I whispered, "when will I ever see you again?"

I crawled deeper into the pine tunnel, leaned back on a patch of moss, and closed my eyes.

When we finished our ice-cream cones we gingerly walked down the slime-covered slip to the water's edge and rinsed our sticky hands in the sea.

"Jennifer?"

"Yes, my pet?"

"I have an idea. If you don't like it, say so."

"Yes?"

"I know a back way into the Nazionale. There's a room no one ever stays in that I used to play in once in a while and . . ."

Jennifer stood thinking for a minute. She gazed out at the yachts at anchor in the Portofino harbor then back at me. "Did you mean what you said?"

"What about?"

"*Oh!* Don't be so thick, Calvin! What do *you think!* About having and holding! That's what, laddie. Or have you already forgotten your wedding vows, you nasty cad?"

"Of course I haven't forgotten. Of course I meant it!"

"Forever?"

"Forever."

"Very well."

Jennifer turned and started to march toward the hotel. My heart began to beat so hard I had trouble walking. Jennifer never looked back at me the whole way across the square.

As Jennifer approached the Nazionale I walked faster to get ahead so I could lead her to the side of the building, down the narrow alley that smelled of drains and soapy water, to a door that the hotel's guests never used since it led to the laundry.

I took Jennifer's hand as we stepped through the door into a sweet-smelling forest of damp sheets. We pushed through the drying laundry to a dark hall. We took a few steps down the hall, then began to climb a steep, rickety staircase.

At the top of the stairs was a narrow passage. At one end it opened into the main second-floor hall that led to the guest rooms. At the other end were cupboards full of hotel linen, a broom closet, and a dumbwaiter hatch.

I led Jennifer to a narrow door that opened off the hall by the broom closet into a small dark room. The room had one closed and shuttered window. No hotel guests ever slept there. The room had no view; it gave out onto the inner courtyard of the hotel. There was no number on the door.

In the room were two beds. One was pushed against the far wall under the solitary window; the other had been stood on end and shoved, along with three or four dilapidated armchairs, against the cracked plaster wall. There was a tangle of broken bedside lamps and frayed electric cords piled on the bed under the window.

I took the key from the outside of the door and locked it from the inside. Jennifer tiptoed over to the window, opened it, and gently unfastened the hinged lower panel of the louvered shutter. "I can't abide stuffy air," she whispered.

Jennifer swept up an armful of old electric lights and cords off the bed and laid them gently on the floor. When the mattress was clear of the jumble of bedside lamps, she gave it a thump or two. She turned around, sat down on the edge, and looked at me. I was still standing by the door.

Sunlight fell in stripes through the shutter. The surface of the old red-and-brown cracked linoleum was thrown into sharp relief. I could hear nothing but the rush of blood in my ears.

Jennifer smiled and patted the faded gray mattress.

"C'mon, laddie." She spoke so softly I could barely hear her.

I walked across the floor, feeling as if I would fall, and sat down.

She kissed me, then lay back, pulling me down next to her. After a moment Jennifer sat up. Then she stood and, looking straight at me the whole time, slipped off her shorts, unbuttoned her blouse, and pushed the straps of her bathing suit off her shoulders, not slow or fast but normally, as if she had been undressing alone. She pulled down the top of her bathing suit past her sharp clear tan line, past her soft white breasts, and then over her flat stomach, narrow waist, and hips, until her bathing suit fell to the floor.

While she undressed she held my eyes with hers. I could tell that she wanted me to look at her face, not follow her bathing suit with my eyes, not look at her naked body, not stare at her. For her sake I didn't. Jennifer stepped over to me and lay down. As she moved toward me my eyes left hers. Her body was more beautiful than any dream I had ever had about her. She didn't put her hands over her breasts, try to cover up in any way, but lay next to me naked, staring at the gray, cracked plaster ceiling. She had a far-off look on her face. She was breathing a little faster than usual.

She turned to me and smiled.

"Your turn, laddie."

I stood up next to the bed, pulled off my T-shirt, and slipped down my swimming trunks. I wasn't able to hold her eyes with mine. I looked away as I took off my clothes.

I stood naked. Jennifer did not pretend not to stare. I, in turn, looked at her naked body stretched out in front of me, at her pubic hair, a mere shadow between her legs, at her white breasts, at the delicate tracery of lavender veins around her shell-pink nipples.

Jennifer moved over to make room for me. At first I did not dare to do more than kiss her, but Jennifer had made up her mind. She resolutely pulled me over on my side and moved her body under mine.

Jennifer opened her legs and I caressed her. It was a lot different than the time out on the rock when I wedged my hand under her bathing suit. There were more layers, more folds. It was softer.

Jennifer reached down. I felt her cool hand wrap around my penis and direct it. I knew this was the moment.

Jennifer gave a gasp. I looked into her startled blue eyes. They had opened very wide. She whispered, "Go on, laddie."

I pushed a little harder and her eyes opened wider. I saw them fill with tears. "Is it hurting?" I whispered.

"Yes, but go on. Slowly!"

I pushed again. And then, all at once, I felt as if I had plunged deep into warm water.

Jennifer gasped as I moved in and out, only once or twice; it happened so fast Jennifer didn't notice when I finished. She kept pushing against me for another minute or two. Then we lay still, panting; exhausted. I kissed her and couldn't think what to do, or say, until Jennifer blurted out, "Are you going to lie on me all day like some bloody great ox?"

I rocked back on my knees. I saw her glance down. I looked. I had blood on me.

She laughed. "Poor boy, you look so surprised! Didn't anyone tell you that girls bleed?"

"You mean you're 'off the roof'?"

"Off the *what?*"

"You know, once a month."

"No! You silly twit, not like that at all!"

"I don't understand."

"Oh, you poor gormless twit! When a girl loses her virginity she bleeds because some great oaf's gone and stuck his whacking, great stick into her oven! Things give way, bleed! But not the next time, or so I was told by a friend of mine."

"Is that why it hurt you?"

"Bloody well right!"

I couldn't think what else to say except "Thank you."

Jennifer quit teasing me, sat up on the bed, took my face gently in her hands, kissed me, and whispered, "I love you, Calvin."

"I love you, too, Jennifer."

"I expect we'd better get dressed."

Jennifer stood up and pulled on her bathing suit.

"Jennifer, I think we should wash off the blood in the laundry on the way out."

Jennifer laughed and gave me a shove. "I thought I'd just leave it smeared down my legs so as to arouse the curiosity of casual passersby!"

Chapter 25

WHEN I CRAWLED OUT FROM UNDER THE HEDGE I discovered that our last four young people had left. Mom told me that they had packed, walked up the back road, then hurried into Dick and Jane's chalet.

Mom said that Dad watched them go from the balcony. He did not try to stop them. All he did was whisper, "So it has come to this," over and over again. Mom told me not to mention the young people's treachery in front of Dad since it might send him "right over the edge."

Dad had waited until they were all inside the Keegans' chalet. Then he stepped back into his room, closed the shutters, and locked his door. He refused to answer when Rachael tried to bring him his lunchtime sandwiches. There was no opera that afternoon. When, at about four P.M., Mom knocked on his door to ask him if he wanted some tea, there was no answer. So we were surprised when Dad came down to dinner. He was more cheerful than we had seen him for days. He had even taken a bath, shaved, and changed his clothes.

After we ate, and had after-dinner devotions—the daily passage from *Daily Light*—Dad wiped his mouth slowly on his napkin, smiled, then in a low, gentle voice said, "Tomorrow we are going on the offensive for Christ."

None of us replied. No one wanted to seem as if they were questioning anything Dad said. Mom put her teacup down on its saucer as gently as possible. We waited for Dad to explain. He nodded several times, then slowly stood up.

"Tomorrow at dawn we will march on Babylon to reclaim the vessels of the temple for the Lord."

None of us answered him. We sat staring at our plates, at the scraps of meat loaf, rice, and gravy that were left from dinner.

"Enough is enough!" said Dad, his voice rising in volume. "The time has come to take back what belongs to the Lord! We can no longer sit and idly watch as the Gospel is squandered! *Tomorrow we cross the Red Sea!*"

Mom delicately cleared her throat. "Ralph, what do you mean, darling?"

"I *mean* that we're going to march over to that nest of vipers and turn them out! That's what I *mean*, Elsa! I *mean* that I'm going to throw that false teacher out with my own hands! That's what I *mean*! I *mean* that I'm going to say to the young people over there, 'Choose ye this day whom ye will serve!' That's what I *mean*! I *mean* that by nightfall tomorrow, by God's Grace, we will have reclaimed the Keegans' chalet for the Lord!"

Mom bit her lower lip. She looked pale.

"I have a map!"

"Yes, Ralph?"

Dad reached behind him to the sideboard, picked up a roll of brown paper, carefully unrolled it, picked up four thumbtacks, and stuck the "map" on the pine paneled wall between the sideboard and the grandfather clock.

We gaped at it.

"Give me your full attention!"

Dad began to point out various items with his dessert fork. "Here's our house. Here's the front road and here's the back road. Got it?" Dad made little rows of holes wherever he poked.

"Here's the Keegans' front door. Back door. Side door. Here's the entrance into their basement through the coal shed at the side. Got it?"

We nodded.

"Good! Now, Elsa, at 0400 hours, that's four A.M. to you, you will go up to the front door and ring the bell! You'll wait until the Keegans come to the door. You'll say that the Lord has led you to be reconciled and could they please come out and talk and pray with you. You will *make sure* that *both* Dick *and* Jane come to the front door! This is phase one."

Mom made a little choking noise.

"Yes?"

"Nothing, dear."

"Well, pay attention! I'm going to ask you all to repeat the plan back to me and woe betide you if you fail in the *least* detail!"

We nodded. I felt the edge of the chair cutting into my leg. I wanted to shift my weight but I decided I had better sit still.

"Calvin."

"Yes, Dad?"

"Your mission is essential."

"Yes, Dad."

"As soon as the front door opens, here"—Dad stabbed the map— "you are to enter the backyard of the Keegans' chalet, run to the coal shed, and get into the basement. There's no lock on that door, and unless they have barred it, you should be able to gain entrance. Got it?"

"Yes, Dad."

"Now as soon as you hear voices—that will be Mom talking to them at the front door—you are to quietly exit the basement and go up the back stairs, to the Evangelism Resource Room, and unlock it. Got it?"

"Yes, Dad."

"Good! I will be hiding behind the red currant bushes along with Rachael and Janet. When you gain the Evangelism Resource Room, wave the Summer Bible School banner from the window. That will be our signal. We will then enter the door you will have unlocked. At that time we will proceed as follows." Dad carefully unpinned his map, turned it over, and pinned it back up again. "Now, as you can see this is a diagram of the *interior* of the Keegan stronghold. By the time we're all inside, the Keegans will, Lord willing, still be in conversation with Elsa, who will hold them there talking about the Lord's leading. Now, Elsa, it's *vital* that you stay *outside the door!* That way Dick and Jane will be standing *in the doorway!* That way when we tiptoe down the hall they will be close enough to the *open door* so that with a *good shove* from me and the girls, we *should* be able, Lord willing, to push them outside. You are then to *jump* in across the threshold and we will *bolt the door!*

"At that point phase two will be complete. Then we'll proceed to phase three.

"Calvin, you will race back to the side door to make sure it's locked. You will then go to the basement and jam that door shut with the wooden wedge that you will carry on your mission. I will supply the wedge. I have it ready upstairs.

"At the same time the girls, Mom, and I will go up to the door on the third-floor landing that separates the Keegans' quarters from the young people's dormitories. We will lock that door so that the young people will not be able to effect an escape, or to aid the Keegans in reentering their lair.

"This should not be difficult. I anticipate that up until then the young people will not have woken up. I imagine that the Keegans will be in some confusion, particularly because we will, by God's Grace, have just roused them from sleep. In addition to this, they will be in bare feet and thus unable to run on the sharp gravel of the path around to the side of the chalet where the young people's rooms have windows.

"Do you understand?"

None of us said anything at all. Mom was biting her lower lip so furiously it looked like she was chewing gum. Rachael and Janet were staring straight down at their plates, pushing around bits of rice and gray, congealed gravy with their fingers.

"Now, as to phase four, this is where strategy gives way to action! I will go to the Keegans' room and take all their personal belongings, clothes, etcetera. I will throw these out of their window. Having cleansed the premises, I will then go up to the young people's quarters and address them through the locked door. At that time I would ask that you all pray that the Lord will give me the words to speak. I have prepared a sermon on the text 'As for me and my house, we will serve the Lord.' It seems appropriate. I believe that the young people, when they understand the gravity and depth of Dick's apostasy, will come around to our side, after which we can march in a body to deal with The Ladies and liberate their spastics. Any questions?"

Dad turned around, took down his chart, rolled it up, tucked it neatly under his arm, sat down, and smiled.

That's when Rachael and Janet burst into tears. Mom didn't cry. She fainted and slipped under the table with a gentle sigh.

Chapter 26

ALL I COULD SEE WAS RICE AND GRAVY. A crash made me look up. Dad hit the table so hard that all the dishes at his end bounced off onto the floor and smashed. Rachael and Janet leapt to their feet and shrieked. Mom was still under the table.

"I am surrounded by weaklings!" Dad screamed.

Janet and Rachael started to sob.

"Will you shut up?"

They tried. Rachael wiped her eyes.

"But, D-Dad . . . I don't think it's even l-l-legal to do . . . do this . . . what . . . will . . . h-h-happen?"

"Will you shut up! Listen to me!"

Rachael began to hiccup violently.

"We are to obey the law of God rather than Caesar! The law of man is beside the point! We're talking about reclaiming the *Lord's work!*"

"Ralph! I won't let you involve the children in this scheme."

While Dad had been yelling Mom came to and quietly crawled out from under the table. She was standing clutching the tablecloth. She was pale, angry, and covered with gravy, but determined looking in spite of the tea bag stuck in her hair.

"Elsa, if you and the children turn against me, then it's good-bye. *Forever!*"

"Ralph. Your mother's right. You *have* gone out of your mind! How can you possibly think that we can succeed with your ludicrous plan? Do you think we'll be allowed to stay over there? They'll call the police. We'll get *arrested!*"

For a moment Dad stood silent, head bowed. The only sound in the room came from Rachael's loud hiccuping and the ticking of the grandfather clock. I thought that maybe what Mom had said was sinking in. I thought Dad was cooling down, reconsidering his plan.

Dad looked up, smiled, gripped the table, and upended it. The dishes, gravy boat, water pitcher, bread basket, teapot, cream pitcher, sugar bowl, flowers, *Daily Light*—everything slid to the floor with a long, rattling, splintering crash. Dad slowly turned from the wreckage and casually pushed over the grandfather clock.

As the clock teetered, then gently toppled to the floor, Dad whispered, "You should not have cast my mother in my teeth."

A moment after the clock hit, while the bells were still clanging, Grandma yelled from upstairs, *"What in tarnation's goin' on? Dammit, will somebody tell me what the hell's happenin'!"*

The clock was our most valuable possession, an antique. Mom once said that people with our "sacrificial income" could never hope to buy such a priceless object. It had come with the house. It was an unlooked-for, "special blessing."

Our special blessing was lying on its side, the glass panel in front of the pendulum shattered, the enamel face hopelessly chipped. Bits of splintered wood lay mixed with glass, enamel, meat loaf, and gravy. The wreckage was liberally scattered across the yellow linoleum of our dining-room floor.

Dad spoke in a calm voice. "Very well, I will go alone."

"*No,* you will not, Ralph! No, you won't do this thing! You'll go right up to your room, take four aspirin, and read your Bible! In the morning we'll pack up and leave. We're going back home! This has gone far *enough!*"

Rachael, Janet, and I stared at Mom. I had never seen or heard her stand up to Dad this way. Even though she was ankle-deep in the broken dishes, there was no shake or quiver in her voice. Rachael's hiccuping went up in volume. It sounded like a Ping-Pong game.

"Elsa, this is the end. This is the abandonment of your marriage vow to obey me. After I gave into my doubts in Zermatt I obeyed your prophetic call. Now you must obey me! You are leading my own children in open rebellion against their father. Moreover, you are doing this over an issue of the *Lord's clear leading*. I have forgiven you your constant nagging, your spiritual pride. I have forgiven your snobbery regarding my humble beginnings, but *I will not forgive this*! You are siding with Mother and Dick against me! You are now as an unbeliever to me. Go! Join the ranks of the apostate! Go to Dick and Jane!"

Dad turned to Janet, Rachael, and me.

"Children, think very carefully. The decision you make now is the most important of your life. It is forever, for eternity. I am asking you whether you will follow the Lord or your mother? Will you be cast out of this house with Elsa or remain here with me, faithful to the Lord's calling, obedient to your father and doing the Lord's work?"

"*Oh, Ralph! How can you!*"

"*Let them answer!*"

Rachael and Janet looked from Mom to Dad and back again. Rachael was hiccuping so violently she was turning blue. Janet was speechless.

"And you," said Dad, suddenly looking at me. "How will you choose, my son, my only begotten son?"

I didn't have time to think. Maybe I was confused by Rachael's hail of hiccups. Anyway, I just blurted out the first thing that came into my head.

"I'll stick with you, Dad!"

"*Calvin!*" shrieked Mom.

Dad nodded grimly. "I'll never forget this, boy!" A tear trickled down his cheek. He crunched through the broken glass, walked around the table, and shook my hand. Dad turned to face the women.

"This is your last chance, girls."

Rachael and Janet didn't say anything for a moment. Then they sobbed out *"Mother!"* and leapt to where she stood. The women grabbed each other, hugged, kissed, and cried.

"There is a gulf fixed between us now. Leave the house and go where you will, even unto Dick, the enemy of the Lord!"

"Daddy!" wailed Janet.

"In future, if we ever meet again, you will call me Reverend Becker. I am no longer your father. Get out!"

"No!" screamed Mom.

"What the hell is goin' on? Will one of ya goddamned lunatics come up here? Jesus!"

No one paid any attention to Grandmother. We were all frozen, staring at Dad. He was reaching down into the mess on the floor. He grabbed the carving knife Mom had used to slice the meat loaf. He took a threatening step toward Mom and the girls. For one terrible second they hesitated, then Mom turned and bolted. The girls followed her. Dad walked ponderously after them. Before he even got to the hallway, the front door opened, then slammed.

The last thing I heard was a despairing wail followed by a machine-gun fire of hiccups. Then there was nothing but silence.

I peeked into the hall. The women were gone. Dad was alone in the dark.

"Lock the doors." Dad's voice was flat. He dropped the knife onto the linoleum and walked up the hall to the stairs. The knife stuck by the point and gently swayed back and forth.

"Lock *all* the doors." Dad began to climb the stairs slowly.

I stood alone in the hallway and listened to Dad walk down the upstairs hall, open his door, then close it behind him.

"What's goin' on? Will somebody tell me what's goin' on? Where's everybody? What's 'at fool doin' now? Goddammit, talk to me!"

I wondered whose side Grandmother would be on. Then I wondered about whose side I was really on. What had I done staying with my father? What was I supposed to do now? I didn't dare go up to

Dad's room. And I didn't want to try and explain things to Grand-mother.

Then it hit me: Jean-Pierre. I would sneak over to Chalet Beau Rivage and find him. We could make some sort of a plan.

I tiptoed down to the basement, crept to the side door, and unlocked it. Once I was out in the yard I dashed across the garden, ducked under the "No Trespassing" string, then crept to where I could peek into Chalet Beau Rivage's windows.

The spastics were sitting around their big, oval, pale blue Formica dining table, oblivious to the storm brewing around them. The Ladies were feeding some of them with spoons. I could see Jean-Pierre eating something off his green plastic plate. His back was to me. The air was thick with the smell of carrots and pot roast.

They had on a record of hymns sung by George Beverly Shea. It was easy to get into the chalet without being heard above the rich, warbling baritone. I walked right in at the front door and up the stairs to the middle floor. I slid under Jean-Pierre's bed.

The Ladies weren't very good at housekeeping. There was a lot of dust. If Dick had been hiding with me he would have sneezed until his nose hemorrhaged. I pushed a dirty sock away and settled my head on my arms.

George Beverly Shea's deep voice, accompanied by hundreds of violins, floated up from the dining room. I could just catch the words of "How Great Thou Art." I absentmindedly began to hum along. Then I turned over and stared at the bedsprings a few inches above my face. I closed my eyes.

Jennifer and I washed ourselves standing in the stone laundry tub, in the Hotel Nazionale's laundry room. Then we stepped out into the alley and ran all the way back to where our rowboat was tied to the barge.

The first boatload of tourists had just arrived from Santa Margherita. People were beginning to mill around the square.

Tourists were fanning out across the quay taking pictures of each other with the yachts in the background, exclaiming about the expensive prices in the windows of the boutiques, and pausing to look at the more affordable contents of the souvenir carts.

I stepped from the edge of the barge while Jennifer untied the rope, jumped into our rowboat, and cast us off. I began to row out of the bay, being careful to keep glancing back to avoid the speedboats and yachts that were moving in and out of the harbor mouth. Jennifer lay on the paint-spattered decking at the bottom of the boat, her long narrow feet up on the seat facing me. She sunbathed as I rowed. We traveled in silence, broken only by the lapping of the water on the wooden hull.

As I rowed I glanced around at the surrounding hills, the villas and port. But mostly I watched Jennifer. Her hair was loose, a golden halo around her face. The old boards framed her slender figure, throwing it into sharp relief. With her eyes closed, one languid arm above her head, the other resting across her stomach, she looked completely at peace. I tried to row as silently as possible.

I studied Jennifer and thought about the years we had been friends, about all the things we had done, about the fact that she was the only person I not only loved but liked completely. I could see the scar on the bottom of her right foot; a cold, white welt. It vividly recalled to mind the day she stepped on the broken wine bottle; how brave she was.

Jennifer fell into a deeper sleep. She smiled as she slept. Her soft lips parted slightly. We drifted into the Paraggi bay with Jennifer dreaming and me rowing as quietly as I could.

I stopped about one hundred yards from the shore. I didn't want Jennifer to wake up. We sat gently drifting, the sound of laughing children, the clink of glasses, and shouts of parents floating across the water, washing over us in a mixture of friendly, familiar summer sounds.

Jennifer must have felt the change in the boat's motion. She moved, opened her eyes, and lay looking up at the pale, cloudless sky. I stepped forward, knelt, and kissed her. She reached up and pulled me down and kissed me back. Her face and lips were hot from the sun. She tasted sweet.

She kissed me long and tenderly before she pushed me away, smiled, and peered over the edge of the boat. Jennifer spotted the Banini on the beach, waved, stood up, and dived over the prow. A moment later I heard her exhale behind me where she resurfaced, having doubled back under the hull. She reached up, held on to the back, and kicked up a storm of foam as I rowed to the beach. When the water was shallow enough, Jennifer walked on the rippled, sandy bottom and pushed us the rest of the way in.

Jennifer strode out of the water and started to run toward her parents. Halfway she stopped, turned, marched back to me, took my hand in hers, and led me down the beach. She didn't drop my hand, even as we got closer and closer to her parents.

I darted a quick sideways glance at Jennifer, to see if she really wanted to hold hands in front of her mother and father. She didn't return my look. She just kept marching, her chin jutting out.

When we walked up to Mr. and Mrs. Bazlinton I expected that Jennifer would let go of my hand, but she held on hard enough so that if I had wanted to let go, I would have had to wrench my hand from hers.

"Hello, Mum."

Mrs. Bazlinton glanced down at our clasped hands.

"Hello, pet."

"Morning, dear," said Mr. Bazlinton.

"We had a lovely row."

"How splendid," said Mrs. Bazlinton.

"Where did you go?" asked Mr. Bazlinton.

"To the lighthouse, then to Portofino, where we got married and had ice creams. I had pistachio and Calvin had . . ."

Mrs. Bazlinton frowned.

"What was the other bit, darling?"

"We got married in the church."

"I don't quite follow you, dear," said Mr. Bazlinton.

"It's quite simple really. We went into the church and exchanged our vows in front of the altar, then sprinkled ourselves with holy water. Of course we shall still need rings and a proper priest to make it legal, but that can wait. I wish you'd been there!"

Mr. and Mrs. Bazlinton opened their mouths as if to say something, then shut them again.

"It *was* rather a spur-of-the-moment idea, though of course Calvin and I have loved each other for ages and ages, and in a way, I knew I would marry him someday but had no idea it would be so soon! But then, as you always say, Mum, life *is* full of surprises!"

Jennifer had done many things that took my breath away but never anything on this scale. She stood smiling at her parents, then turned and kissed me gently on the cheek.

Mr. Bazlinton cleared his throat and looked at Mrs. Bazlinton, who had turned a brighter pink than her enormous, floppy sun hat. Mr. Bazlinton coughed again and started to say something but stopped, petered out. I looked at Jennifer but she still wouldn't look at me, so I stared at my feet and began to dig a hole in the sand with my big toe.

Mrs. Bazlinton said, in a voice that sounded a lot higher than usual, "How *lovely*, darling!"

"*That's* all right, then! I *knew* you'd be pleased, especially since Calvin's *not* a religious lunatic like the rest of his balmy tribe! Are you, Calvin?"

Jennifer looked at me expectantly.

"No, I'm not."

"There, you *see!* Sane as a brain surgeon and twice as handsome!"

I prayed the beach would swallow me before Mr. Bazlinton turned any redder or exploded into fragments.

Mrs. Bazlinton looked up at the pale blue sky.

"It's a lovely day. So mild, yet not too hot!"

"We will, of course, finish our schooling before we begin to cohabit," said Jennifer.

Mr. Bazlinton seemed to choke.

"Well, my dears, will you join us for lunch?" asked Mrs. Bazlinton.

Jennifer clapped me on the shoulder.

"Splendid! That would be super, wouldn't it, Calvin!"

At lunch the only person who talked much was Jennifer. She rattled on about our plans, or at least her plans, about how she expected we might live in England, but then again, since I was an American, even though I lived in Switzerland, how we might eventually move to the United States. She said she had heard that some parts of it—Boston, for instance—were fairly civilized, not really as bad as everyone said.

I spent a lot of the time studying my food. We had gnocchi with ricotta cream-cheese sauce, followed by a grilled pork chop, dressed with porcini mushrooms, and rucola salad with radicchio.

As Jennifer talked, and Mr. and Mrs. Bazlinton exchanged furtive glances, I began to realize how clever Jennifer was. If we had kept our marriage a secret we would have had to sneak around for years pretending we were just friends, not man and wife. This way, even though it was terribly embarrassing, Jennifer was getting it over with all at once. How could her parents stop us from living together now that they knew we were married?

One thing about Jennifer, once she decided to do something, she did it right! When Lucrezia came to take our orders for drinks, Jennifer gave her a radiant smile. *"Lucrezia, per favore una bottiglia di champagne francese."*

When Lucrezia brought the bottle of champagne Jennifer said to her father, "You can propose the toast!" Lucrezia popped the cork and all the other diners craned their necks to see what occasion was being celebrated. Only Jennifer smiled at them.

Mr. Bazlinton didn't look like someone who wanted to propose a toast to anything right then. But I guess he had learned a long time before that his only child was pretty obstinate. He poured out a glass of champagne for each of us.

Jennifer said his toast was lovely, even though all he did was stare into his glass and mumble, "Here's to our young friends."

Mr. Bazlinton drank his champagne down in one gulp, refused Jennifer's offer of a second glass, and gazed out at the sparkling sea, a muscle twitching in his brick-red jaw.

Chapter 27

LATER RACHAEL TOLD ME WHAT HAPPENED. After Dad kicked her out, Mom panicked and got Dick, and all the young people, to go with her back to our chalet. Mom stood in the moonlight on the flagstones, in front of the living room, and shouted at the third-floor bedroom window until, after about half an hour, Dad finally answered her.

Mom challenged Dad to let me go. He yelled that he didn't know where I was, then he threw a pot of geraniums at Mom. The pot hit Trudi on the head. It could have killed her, Rachael said, but fortunately it only knocked her out. That's when Mom ran back to the Keegans' chalet and called the police.

Mom accused Dad of kidnapping me, of having gone nuts and maybe even of having killed me with the carving knife. The police searched our house. They didn't find anybody except Grandmother, holding anyone who came near her at bay with her scissors and demanding to be sent home on the next plane.

I didn't wake up until one of The Ladies, Mary Lou, found me the next morning. She spotted my foot sticking out from under Jean-Pierre's bed. Mary Lou screamed. That's when I woke up. As soon as I stuck my head out and Mary Lou recognized me, she stopped screaming, grabbed my ankle, and dragged me into the middle of the room.

"Do you know what you've done?"

"I'm sorry, I was just, ah . . . playing a game. I wanted to visit Jean-Pierre."

"A game! They've arrested your father because of you! He's down at the *police station* in Monthey being *questioned!* Your dear mother's beside herself!"

"I don't understand," I said as Mary Lou pulled me to my feet, by my ear, pulled so hard I heard a cracking noise. Then she dragged me downstairs and out the door. She held on to my ear the whole way. I had to walk practically doubled over. Mary Lou was only about four feet, six inches tall.

"I've found him! Here he is!" Mary Lou kept shouting as she led me through Chalet Beau Rivage's yard, ducked under the string, and marched me up to my chalet.

Rachael was in the yard standing with her arm around Trudi's shoulders. Trudi's head was swathed in bandages. Beside Rachael and Trudi, a small group of young people were gathered in a circle praying. Rachael looked up, gave a shriek, then ran over to me and hugged me. That's when Mary Lou finally let go of my ear.

"Where did he have you hidden? Did he tie you up? Are you all right?" Rachael kissed and hugged me as the young people, some with tear-streaked faces, gathered around saying things like, "Danke you, Lord!" and "Praise Jesus!"

Mary Lou interrupted them. "He wasn't kidnapped or anything like that! He was just up to his usual tricks! He *hid himself* under Jean-Pierre's bed just to scare us all half to death, to get his dear father in trouble!"

Everyone looked at me, dumbfounded and horrified.

"Schweinhund!" shouted Trudi.

"Oh, you wicked boy!" screamed Rachael.

"Oh Calvin! How could you!" said Mom, after Mary Lou, Trudi, and Rachael dragged me into our chalet.

"Jean-Pierre was in it with him. We will punish him severely," said Mary Lou.

"No, he wasn't. He didn't even know I was under his bed. I hid there when he was down eating supper. I guess that's when I fell asleep."

"I don't believe you. I'll get the truth out of him! I know what you two were really doing! I happen to know something about you two, but we'll discuss that another time!" Mary Lou marched grimly out of the front hall of our chalet and slammed the door behind her.

Mom grabbed me by the shoulders and shook me severely.

"Calvin, do you realize what you've done? *Do you realize what your awful prank has resulted in?*"

"Do you?" screamed Janet as she ran down the stairs. *"Do you?"* she screamed again as she slapped me on the back of my head while Mom shook me.

Trudi tugged angrily at her bandages. *"I have been gravely wounded unt mein head!"*

Rachael shrieked, *"You're wicked!"* Then she started to hiccup and cry at the same time. Trudi burst into tears and fled from the hall, clutching her bandages and yelling things in German.

Grandmother's door was open. She must have heard all the commotion. She yelled from upstairs, *"Leave the boy alone, dammit!"* No one answered her.

Janet pulled my hair and Mom kept shaking me until finally Mom said, "That's enough, girls." Janet reluctantly let go.

"I don't understand why you're all so mad at me!" I yelled, finally able to get a word in edgewise.

"Maybe this'll help you understand." Janet gave me another slap. The sound ricocheted like a gunshot.

"Goddammit!" shouted Grandmother. *"I said leave him be!"*

Mom pulled Janet away from me.

"Janet, that's *enough*! Oh, Calvin, because of your silly trick—and why you should choose a moment of family crisis to try and fool us is *beyond me,* your *dear, dear father* has been *arrested* and falsely accused by the Swiss authorities of abducting you or worse. He's in the Monthey *jail*."

"How could I know?"

Janet gave me a shove.

"If I were in your shoes I wouldn't answer back!"

"Keep him here," said Mom as she ran to the phone.

Mom sent me to my room to wait for Dad. About two hours later Dad was brought back by taxi. After he had been home for ten minutes or so, he opened my door. He looked bad. Dad had a black eye and swollen lip.

"Dad, I didn't mean it!" I blurted out as fast as I could.

When he answered he sounded more like his old self, almost normal. "It's all right, son, the whole thing's my fault. We know you didn't mean any harm. I'm the one that was led astray. I don't know why anyone would blame you."

"Oh, Dad!" I was flooded with a sense of relief. I hugged Dad and he hugged me while Mom stood in the doorway wiping tears from her eyes.

That afternoon Mom and Dad called a special prayer meeting. Everyone in our community crowded into our living room. Even Grandmother was carried in under protest.

"We have been gathered together," said Dad, "so that we might be restored one to another. I have been tragically led astray."

Dick choked back a sob. "I have, too."

"Bunch a no-good morons," muttered Grandmother. No one looked at her.

Then Mom spoke. "The Lord has used Calvin, however unwittingly, to bring healing to our community in answer to my prayers! It's now clear that the unfortunate incidents of last night were the result of yet another demonic attack upon Ralph. The split is healed!

The time of testing past! It's now evident we stand on the threshold of a marvelous new chapter in the Lord's work!"

Dad and Dick hugged and all the young people applauded and burst into tears. Then, except for Grandmother, who was lying on the couch staring morosely at the ceiling, sliding her lowers in and out with her tongue, everyone sang "A Mighty Fortress Is Our God."

When the singing was done Dad turned and faced us. "Dick and I have had a chance to discuss what we thought was our difference of opinion. It turns out we were deluded by Satan. Dick never abandoned his belief in Unconditional Depravity or the sovereignty of God. Satan has sown division amongst us, but the Lord has reunited us!"

"Praise the Lord!" shouted Dick. He sneezed and his nose began to bleed.

Grandmother cackled with laughter, but no one paid any attention as we surged forward, even Jean-Pierre and I. We all hugged. The spastics bellowed and thrashed with joy. Mom held me close and whispered, "Let this be a lesson to you! See, God *is* in charge of our lives!"

Janet embraced me. "I'm sorry I doubted your word and hit you so hard. I didn't know at the time that what you did was part of God's plan. Are you okay?"

"I'm fine."

Only Trudi still looked angry. She stood to one side whispering things in German under her breath and touching her bandages with the tips of her thick, trembling fingers. Dick stuffed two wads of Kleenex up his nose. Then we all went outside, except for Grandmother, who refused to be moved to a lawn chair, and Trudi, who stalked out of the yard and down the road toward the village.

Dad and Dick marched around the garden taking down the "No Trespassing" signs. The young people cheered each time Dad or Dick cut a piece of string or pulled down a sign. Then Dad burned the signs, one at a time, in the hot-dog pit. We sang "Just As I Am," accompanied by Jane Keegan on her old accordion.

The "No Trespassing" signs smoked, flared, and finally fell away into curls of hot white ash. A gentle breeze wafted the ashes up and out into the void, where they hovered over the Rhône Valley. While I watched the ashes disintegrate I wondered, for the hundredth time, about when to ask if we would go to Italy, now that the crisis was over. I decided to wait for the right moment.

Chapter 28

I NEVER GOT THE CHANCE TO INQUIRE if our vacation could be reinstated. A week after the "Day of Deliverence," as Mom called the day Dad and Dick were reconciled, a registered letter arrived. It was from the Swiss authorities. All our residency permits had been canceled. We had one month to close our ministry and leave Switzerland!

Farmer Ruchet told me that the villagers had complained to the Commune de Monthey, the local government. They said that we were a cult. It was rumored that the leader of our cult, Dad, had gone mad, was a dangerous lunatic. Farmer Ruchet said that he and his wife were the only people in the village who had not signed the petition, circulated by the post lady, asking for our expulsion. The sight of Trudi, parading around the village, her head swathed in bandages (Mom called it a shameless example of Germanic exhibitionism), had done nothing to help our cause.

Dad placed an emergency long-distance call to the P.C.C.C.C.U.S.A. mission headquarters in St. Louis, Missouri. When the call came through, Mom, Janet, Rachael, and I were gathered in the hall around Dad as he told the chairman that we had been kicked out. He asked him to appeal on our behalf to the U.S. State Department, to get them to ask the American embassy in Bern to intervene with the local Swiss authorities. Dad told the chairman that the split in our work had been healed by God, that he and Dick now had a new brotherly understanding, that the Lord's hand was clearly in all this.

The chairman answered that the Lord's hand was beside the point.

It was too late. Dad had left the P.C.C.C.C.U.S.A; he had written letters denouncing the P.C.C.C.C.U.S.A.; he had tried to get other pastors and missionaries to join with him in his open rebellion against the church.

After Dad hung up the phone he stood silent, head bowed, for several minutes. Janet, Rachael, Mom, and I took a few precautionary backward steps, expecting an outburst. But when Dad spoke it was in an icy, calm tone.

"We are suffering persecution for the Lord. Those whom we might have expected would support us in the hour of need have, like Judas, abandoned us."

"Oh Ralph, what shall we do?"

"The board's being very clever and deceitful. Since we've been kicked out by the Roman Catholics, because of our godly Reformational stand, the P.C.C.C.C.U.S.A. can now seize our property, claim it's theirs, and sell it, maybe even install a new mission over which *they* can have complete control."

"Oh darling, did he say that?"

"Of course not, but I can read between the lines!"

We were frantically busy during the days that followed. We worked around the clock, under Dad's command, sending out an avalanche of letters. Mom and Dad composed them together. Dad paced up and down the floor of their bedroom dictating in a loud voice. Mom added her suggestions and typed. For once they worked in perfect harmony. Rachael said that Dad had risen to the occasion, was taking command "like a great general." She said it was inspiring, that it was his finest hour. Janet said that she could see the dark hand of communism lurking behind the attack on our ministry, that we should not be surprised if Dad was assassinated.

Every morning Dick, Jane, Rachael, Janet, or I had to take the tram to Monthey to mail boxes full of letters. Dad said it wasn't safe to mail them from our local Trois-Torrents post office, that the villagers, including the post lady, were involved in the Roman Catholic plot.

Janet had the job of retyping the letters onto special wax stencil sheets. Rachael and I poured purple ink that smelled like a combination of nail polish and wood alcohol into the mimeograph barrel, fastened the stencil in place, and started to crank out copies. Janet said that now she knew how the French Resistance fighters must have felt as they stood up against tyranny. Dad said not to put our return address on the envelopes so that the Roman Catholic Swiss postal workers wouldn't intercept our correspondence and pass it on to the Vatican.

Grandmother said we all had shit for brains, that if we didn't put her on the first plane back to Philadelphia, she'd sue. No one had time to pay attention to her.

Chapter 29

RALPH AND ELSA BECKER
L'ARCHE
CHALET LES TULIPES
TROIS-TORRENTS-SUR-MONTHEY
VALAIS
SWITZERLAND

June 24, 1967

Dear Praying Family,

The Roman Catholic Church has taken off the velvet glove of apostasy and revealed the steel fist of papacy hidden beneath! We are in the heat of *spiritual warfare!* The Swiss authorities have been swayed by the worldwide power of the Roman Church. They have arrayed themselves against us like the bands of Midian who went up against the armies of Israel. But *who* can be against us if *the Lord be for us?* We sense that God is about to do a mighty work!

(We thank You Lord that He who is *in us* is greater than he who is *in the world!* Amen!)

Please *pray* that the Lord will do the following by moving the hearts of you Precious Ones in our Praying Family to:

1) Write to the State Department asking that they intervene with the Swiss authorities on our behalf, that they might speedily restore our suspended residency permits.

2) Send us funds to use in this *emergency* to relocate L'Arche, *if necessary,* that the Lord might still have a faithful witness in Europe.

3) Write to the Mission Board of the P.C.C.C.C.U.S.A. (Attention Reverend Bahre, Ph.D.) in godly rebuke of the fact that the board has withdrawn financial support from L'Arche *in the heat* of spiritual *battle!* Demand an immediate retraction of the *false accusations* by the board blaming Ralph for our tribulations. Tell them to tell the *truth! We are being persecuted* by seen and unseen powers for the *sake of the Gospel!!!* The sake of the Reformation!!! The sake of the truth of Calvinism and *Reformed theology!!!* All other rumors are *false,* dear brothers and sisters!

4) Pray! Pray! Pray! *Intercede* before the throne of God night and day, seek His face, that this thorn in the flesh might be speedily *removed from us.*

We are reincorporating in the state of Maryland. Elsa's brother, dear Reverend George, Th.D., D.D. (C.I.M. retired), is our new treasurer. We will be able to give *our own tax-deductible receipts.* Those the Lord moves to make love offerings may send them to:

> The Ralph and Elsa Becker Defense Fund
> c/o Reverend George Coswell
> 103 Parker Lane
> Silver Springs, Maryland

PS. Our *beloved* brother and sister and colaborers in the Vineyard, Dick and Jane, send you Christian greeting in the Lord. What a joy it is to us that they are standing *shoulder* to *shoulder* with us as we, like Nehemiah, defend and rebuild the wall of Jerusalem! "*Come, Lord Jesus come quickly.*" But *until* He comes, may He keep you Who is able!!!

Love in Christ Our Lord, by Whose
Grace *alone* we are saved . . . In the
Lamb, Rev. Ralph and Elsa Becker

Uncle George called us long-distance to say that the response to
Dad's letter was "overwhelming." Mom proclaimed that because of
our uncompromising stand for truth, God had opened the windows
of heaven to bless us. Support was pouring in.

Uncle George said that he was making a wire transfer of funds to
cover our immediate expenses, that he was investing the rest of the
love offerings in a high-yield certificate of deposit at the First
National Bank of Maryland. Uncle George also said that his sources
had informed him that the P.C.C.C.C.U.S.A. board was getting it in
the neck because of Dad's letter, and that we might expect the board
to relent soon, given the flood of irate calls they were receiving.

Sure enough, only ten days after Dad sent his urgent letter to our
praying family, we received an official document from the board by
express mail. Dad immediately called a special meeting of prayer and
thanksgiving. He read the letter in a loud voice quivering with triumph.

P.C.C.C.C.U.S.A. MISSION HEADQUARTERS
1 LAFAYETTE RD.
ST. LOUIS, MISSOURI
U.S.A.

REV. RALPH AND ELSA BECKER
L'ARCHE
CHALET LES TULIPES
TROIS-TORRENTS-SUR-MONTHEY
VALAIS
SWITZERLAND

July 1, 1967

Dear Brother Becker, Brother Keegan, and our Sisters in the Lord, Elsa and Jane, and Dear Ladies of Chalet Beau Rivage,

Greetings in the name of our Lord Jesus Christ! We have wrestled in prayer before the Lord concerning the sad rift that has been opened between us by the Evil One.

Satan has indeed been active in attacking the faithful servants of God! After prayerful consideration we feel that perhaps we were too hasty in our decision to sever relations with you, our dear brothers and sisters in Christ.

Therefore what we would like to propose is that, like Joseph who wept on the necks of his brothers when they were restored to him, even so we pray the Lord will bind our mutual wounds, restore the years the locusts have eaten, and bring to our midst sweet peace, joy, and love so that the peace that passeth understanding may indwell each of us so that we might, together once more, go forth in His mighty Name to do battle for the Kingdom together!

We are awaiting your reply, dear brothers and sisters, and look forward to doing all we can to move our government to prevail upon "the King that arose who knew not Joseph," that his heart might be moved to let you find favor in his sight, that the sweet Name of Jesus might be proclaimed to all nations and your residency permits speedily restored to you.

> With prayer and in the heartfelt love of *our* Master—warmest Christian Greetings of the Chosen to the Elect!

> Reverend Bahre, Ph.D.

(For the P.C.C.C.C.U.S.A. Mission Board General Synod— Reformed Calvinist Missionary Alliance in association with the Presbyterian World Mission Alliance of the Reformed Faith)

Dad worked most of the night. I lay awake listening to him dictate, redictate, pray over, edit, and perfect his reply.

RALPH AND ELSA BECKER
L'ARCHE
CHALET TULIPES
TROIS-TORRENTS-SUR-MONTHEY
VALAIS
SWITZERLAND

REVEREND BAHRE, PH.D., D.D., M.DIV., CHAIRMAN
P.C.C.C.U.S.A. MISSION HEADQUARTERS
1 LAFAYETTE RD.
ST. LOUIS, MISSOURI
U.S.A.

July 4, 1967

Dear Reverend Bahre,

After prayerful consideration of your letter, it gives Elsa and I, as well as our dear colaborers in the Vineyard, Dick and Jane and the dear Ladies of Chalet Beau Rivage, great Christian joy to reply to you that the Lord has led us to be reunited to you in Christian love.

However, the above notwithstanding, I would be remiss if I did not mention that during the past days of sad division amongst us (the result of the tragic misunderstanding that Satan sowed between us) we were led of the Lord to set up a separate fund so that the needs of the Lord's work might be met in an orderly New Testament fashion. God has blessed this fund and we see, in the outpouring of love offerings, His blessing and promise. His gentle hand is surely leading us. So we are sure you will understand that we now desire to heed His call and keep this covenant fund separate from the general funds raised to support L'Arche that normally come through the P.C.C.C.C.U.S.A. headquarters from which tax-deductible receipts were formerly sent to our Praying Family.

We will gladly rejoin the mission, therefore, with the provision that we be allowed to obey the Lord's clear calling to us as He has spoken to our hearts and told us to keep these covenant funds in a separate account that will be wholly under our supervision and administered by Elsa's dear brother, Reverend George, in Maryland.

We also sense the Lord laying it upon our hearts that the board of the P.C.C.C.C.U.S.A. should no longer deduct the usual 25 percent overhead ministry charge as before from designated funds sent for the support of L'Arche. In this manner we will be able to dedicate, as the Lord leads us, these funds that have been provided by God for the express purpose of combating the persecution we have suffered at the hands of Rome.

In the Name of the One who *is* able!

Greetings in the Name of the Lamb!

Reverend Becker, Elsa, Dick and Jane, and the

Ladies of the Chalet Beau Rivage

The answer to Dad's letter arrived on July 11 by special delivery, registered, express airmail. Dad read it at an emergency prayer meeting he called to ask God for guidance as to how to deal with the P.C.C.C.C.U.S.A. board's tragically worldly response.

P.C.C.C.C.U.S.A. MISSION HEADQUARTERS

1 LAFAYETTE RD.

ST. LOUIS, MISSOURI

U.S.A.

Rev. Ralph and Elsa Becker
L'Arche
Chalet les Tulipes
Trois-Torrents-sur-Monthey
Valais
Switzerland

July 7, 1967

Dear Reverend Becker and colaborers in the Vineyard,

It grieves us that there has arisen a gulf between us. You apparently wish to enjoy the fruits of fraternal godly association without shouldering the burden of apostolic trust!

The Lord's leading in this matter is *clear.* He has laid it on our hearts to tell you that we *cannot* in good conscience allow you, under our charter of accountability to the P.C.C.C.C.U.S.A. General Synod, any separate "covenant funds" to be maintained outside of the general support budget. The Lord has laid it on our hearts that we cannot forgo the stewardship tithe of 25 percent of the funds deposited in our accounts designated for L'Arche.

It is therefore with godly concern for your spiritual welfare that we ask you to place yourself under God's authority in this matter and be guided by God in placing your "Ralph and Elsa Becker Defense Fund" back into the accounting structure of the P.C.C.C.C.U.S.A. Mission Fund as the Lord has made clear to us you should do.

Please inform us at your earliest convenience of your prayerful decision regarding this matter of godly stewardship.

With Christian Greetings and in the hope that God
will lead you in His perfect will,

Reverend Bahre, Ph.D.

(For the P.C.C.C.C.U.S.A. Mission Board General Synod—
Reformed Calvinist Missionary Alliance in association with the Presbyterian World Mission Alliance of the Reformed Faith)

Chapter 30

AFTER THE SPECIAL EMERGENCY PRAYER MEETING, during which he called the P.C.C.C.C.U.S.A.'s board a bunch of crummy thieves, and Reverend Bahre, Ph.D., a Judas Iscariot, Dad said that God had led him not to answer the board's last letter. He said it was time to take our cause to the whole membership of the P.C.C.C.C.U.S.A.

Mom agreed that this was the Lord's will in the matter. She had prayed about it and God laid a special verse on her heart, "Let them grow into a multitude in the midst of the earth" (Genesis 48:16). She said as how this verse spoke to our immediate need. She said that it meant we should step out boldly by faith and grow into a multitude without the P.C.C.C.C.U.S.A. Dick and Jane agreed that the Lord had spoken to Mom, and so did The Ladies.

Uncle George had a cousin, a retired missionary from India, who worked at the world headquarters of the P.C.C.C.C.U.S.A. in St. Louis. Mom said this cousin was a True Woman of Prayer. When the True Woman of Prayer heard about our troubles, she was moved by God, when no one was looking, to make a copy of the P.C.C.C.C.U.S.A.'s General Donor Mailing List and to send it to Uncle George by express mail. Uncle George forwarded all 2,321 names to us, by special delivery, airmail, registered post, express.

Even though Uncle George, and his cousin, the True Woman of Prayer, were the "human agents" in getting us the General Donor Mailing List, Dad said, we could clearly see the Lord's hand at work. Mom, Dick, Jane, and The Ladies agreed.

RALPH AND ELSA BECKER
L'ARCHE
CHALET TULIPES
TROIS-TORRENTS-SUR-MONTHEY
VALAIS
SWITZERLAND

July 12, 1967

Dearest Prayer Partner and Friend of L'Arche,

It is with *deep sorrow* that we must *lay before you* the matter at hand. As you know the *Lord called Elsa and me into His service many years ago. We have* remained *loyal* to the P.C.C.C.C.U.S.A. and were amongst *the founding members* of the P.C.C.C.C.U.S.A. When it split off from the P.C.C.C.C.U.S.A. (when that denomination was infiltrated by a spirit of liberal apostasy and allowed some pastors to teach their version of *Conditional* Depravity rather then the true *Reformed* view of *Unconditional* Depravity), *we* remained *faithful* to the cause of Christ!

Since the days of those battles for the Kingdom, *the Lord has blessed* the P.C.C.C.C.U.S.A. *and our work here at L'Arche.* But *sadly* this is not where our story ends!

As you know a rift developed between our ministry and the home office when the Roman Catholic Swiss authorities canceled all of our residency permits in this field of the Vineyard. They did this because of *pressure from the Roman Church* which is acting to extinguish *the light of Calvinism* from Calvin's own country, Switzerland! (What a terrible judgment against the Swiss who knew Him not! Rejecting not only Calvin, but us and Jesus!!!)

Now the P.C.C.C.C.U.S.A. board has heard from many of its faithful supporting members, who the Lord has spoken to and who let the board know of their disapproval of its lack of support and the *false rumors* it was spreading as to the cause of the persecution of L'Arche during our time of severe testing.

The P.C.C.C.C.U.S.A. board, under the so-called "leadership" of Reverend Bahre, then proffered the hand of *false friendship* as a result of the righteous protests of godly men and women like you!

We all desire peace and I am afraid that the *human* side of us wanted to go along with their request for the sake of the love of Jesus. But *the Lord has spoken to our hearts* and told us that it is *better to lose the whole world,* including the favor of the P.C.C.C.C.U.S.A. board, and *gain the Lord's blessing,* even if we lose *everything* by the world's impoverished standard!!!

Will you stand with us, dearly beloved? The fields are white with harvest! We labor in the heat of the day! We ask no more than your *prayer support!* And (if God so leads), we ask that you send your tax deductible love offering to:

THE RALPH AND ELSA BECKER DEFENSE FUND

C/O REVEREND GEORGE COSWELL

103 PARKER LANE, SILVER SPRINGS, MARYLAND.

(Please use the enclosed envelope.)

With warm greetings in the Lord from our colaborers Dick and Jane and the Ladies of Chalet Beau-Rivage and all the dear little handicapped ones dependent on you, In the Precious Name of *The One*, our Reformed Lamb,

Reverend Ralph and Elsa Becker
Dick and Jane Keegan

Chapter 31

It only took seven days before "the wall of Jericho fell." When it did there was great rejoicing.

"Praise the Lord and all his marvelous works!" said Mom.

"This is the day the Lord has made!" exclaimed Dad.

"Oh, Lord Jesus! We just thank Thee!" squealed Rachael.

"He has gone before us like a cloud of fire," said Janet.

"Thank You, Lord Jesus, my sweet Lord!" whispered Jane.

"Oh, Jesus Christ, we just fall down before Thee in worship and adoration!" sobbed Dick.

"I've got goose bumps. I feel like I'm standing at the Garden Tomb on Easter morning!" said Mary Lou.

"The inmates are runnin' the goddamned asylum!" muttered Grandmother. No one looked at her. They all stared expectantly at me, so I said, "Dear Heavenly Father, we just thank You for smiting our enemies like You did for, uh . . . Gideon."

Everyone but Grandmother said, "Amen."

This was the greatest day in our ministry, ever. That morning, a dazzling mid-July morning when the air was so clear that every boulder on the Dents du Midi was visible and the smell of fresh-cut hay wafted on a gentle breeze into every room of our chalet, we had received three letters. Any one of them would have counted as a miracle. But taken together, they were one of those "once-in-a-lifetime events when you can actually see God directing your life as clearly as Moses saw the burning bush," Mom said.

Dad said God was visibly "reaching down and shaping history

with His sovereign hand before our very eyes and that at last I am certain I have been forgiven for my time of doubt during our terrible time of testng in Zermatt." The fact that all three letters had arrived the same day could be no coincidence. Even a "Jewish atheist from New York would have to admit that," Mom said.

The first letter was from Uncle George. He wrote to say that almost thirty-one thousand dollars had come in as a response to the letter Dad sent to the P.C.C.C.C.U.S.A.'s General Donor Mailing List.

The second letter was from the Chairman of the mission board, Reverend Bahre, Ph.D. The board was asking Dad to become a board member. They had waived all conditions. We could keep the funds the Lord sent us for our special battle. All they asked us to do was to send out another letter to the General Donor Mailing List to ask people to prayerfully start supporting the P.C.C.C.C.U.S.A. mission fund again, and to tell them that we were all restored one to another in loving fellowship.

The third document was the most amazing, miraculous, and marvelous of all. It was from the Commune de Monthey, Police des Étrangers. They had rescinded their orders! New permits to live and work in Switzerland were to be issued to us.

Dad explained that the hand of God had moved the hard hearts of the authorities, and that all the mail the State Department had received from Reformed Presbyterians, from all over the world, probably hadn't hurt any since they must have let the Swiss authorities know about it.

"And I thought, for once the big cretin upstairs had answered *my* prayer and shut ya all down so I could go home again!" Grandmother growled. No one looked at her.

At the end of the Day of Miracles, as Mom called it, she came to my room to say good night. Mom sat down on the edge of my bed.

"Calvin, you know sometimes we all begin to doubt God as your father did. But today we had a real demonstration of His sovereignty."

"Yes, Mom."

"You know God really *does* have a wonderful plan for each of our lives. He really *is* watching over us!"

"I know, Mom."

"Well, it's good to remember that. It helps us to do the right things."

"I know, Mom."

Mom reached over and began to run her fingers through my hair, to smooth it back the way she used to when I was little and couldn't sleep.

"Calvin, are you always truthful with me?"

"Of course, Mom."

"Well, darling, I don't want to embarrass you, but you know a mother always knows."

"About what, Mom?"

"Calvin, when the Precious Seeds dry they leave a slight discoloration on your sheets. I'm afraid I've been finding unmistakable signs."

"Mom, I haven't been—"

"Don't lie, Calvin, especially on the Day of Miracles when we've seen the hand of God especially not after what you did in Zermatt with Eva."

"But, Mom, God's been answering my prayers, sending me wet dreams."

"Three times a week?"

"I don't keep count."

"You're not touching yourself?"

"No."

"Oh, how I wish Ralph was an easier person to confide in. With two daughters and having had no brothers . . ." Mom sighed. "If only Ralph would guide me, but he positively refuses to discuss these matters with me. I just don't know what to believe about the stains."

"Good night, Mom."

"Calvin, remember God's real. He sees. Remember the demonstration of His awesome power we were privileged to witness this very day."

"I will, Mom. Good night."

"It's just that I've never had experience in these . . . boys' matters before."

"Don't worry, Mom. I never do it."

"I pray that's so. Good night, Calvin."

"Good night, Mom."

Mom bent over and kissed me. She held me close. She felt heavy. Her breasts pressed on my chest for a long time. Before Mom stood up to leave she gave me an extra-tight squeeze and whispered into my ear, "Please, please, do not touch your Little Thing! I beg you!"

I did not argue back, didn't say that I still had bad dreams about our Zermatt disaster and what Dad had done. And of course I didn't tell Mom that when she presses against me she reminded me of Eva, the maid at our winter vacation hotel that none of us ever dared mention.

When Mom was gone I lay still for a while, eyes open, until the smell of her perfume faded. Then I closed my eyes. Jennifer stood and, looking straight at me the whole time, slipped off her shorts, unbuttoned her blouse, then pushed the straps of her bathing suit off her shoulders, not slow or fast but normally, as if she had been undressing alone. She pulled down the top of her bathing suit past her sharp clear tan line, past her soft white breasts, and then over her flat stomach, narrow waist and hips, until her bathing suit fell to the linoleum floor.

Chapter 32

EVERY YEAR ON JULY 19 a famous bicycle race, Le Tour de Suisse, whizzed past our chalet. On that particular leg the cyclists sped down our hill, freewheeling to the Rhône valley. We always stood on the front steps and cheered as the racers flew by, their bicycle wheels stirring up a rush of wind powerful enough to make Mom's summer dress flap high around her shapely legs.

The racers were preceded by police on motorcycles. Then some race officials' cars went by. These were followed by the contestants, first the leaders, then the pack—several hundred cyclists sailing down the steep incline in a body, wheel to wheel, knee to knee.

The long stretch of mountain road directly in front of our chalet was the ideal place to watch from. The cyclists got going terrifically fast before they had to brake for the sharp hairpin bend, just above our village. It was very dramatic.

It seemed especially fine to see Le Tour de Suisse the very day after the Day of Miracles. Everyone was in a festive mood. We all lined up to watch, even Dad.

After the race, Mom, Dad, Dick, Jane, Janet, Rachael, and the young people returned to their various tasks. The Ladies went back into Chalet Beau Rivage with the worst cases, the two spastics who were unable even to lift their heads, who lay all day knotted up. They left the rest of the spastics out on the lawn above the driveway with Jean-Pierre and me to attend to them.

It was a glorious day. The hot sun was punctuated by a cool breeze, fragrant with the field flowers. The mountains wreathed in heat haze seemed to float above the valley, light as air.

The game we were supposed to be playing was to bounce a big red, white, and blue beach ball. When the ball dropped to the ground, Jean-Pierre or I would pick it up and start it bouncing again.

None of us liked bouncing the ball, even though it was supposed to improve the spastics' coordination. Once I was sure The Ladies weren't going to come out and check on us for a while, we began to play the spastics' favorite game: Nazi Killers.

Jean-Pierre was the Jew, tied up with my belt. The spastics circled around him in their wheelchairs and yelled insults. The ones who didn't know any German just shouted *Heil Hitler!* over and over again.

After we made Jean-Pierre beg for mercy, it was time to take him to the firing squad. Some of the spastics couldn't move their arms well enough to pretend they were holding rifles, so they got to be Lutheran chaplains, to read him his last rites, or to be SS commanders and scream, *Fire!*

Jean-Pierre writhed. He died well. After Jean-Pierre was dead, he helped me liberate Auschwitz. We rounded up the spastic Nazis, who had run the camp, then played Nuremberg.

After we finished with the trials and executions, that's when I got my inspiration, my idea for a new game. The spastics agreed with my plan for Le Tour de Spastics enthusiastically.

Before I moved the spastics from the lawn to the road, I explained very carefully about how they must use their brakes to slow down well before the curve, how they must not get carried away, how they'd never make it around the hairpin bend if they took the curve too fast.

I tried out the course myself in a borrowed wheelchair. It was perfect. Even though the front wheels shimmied a lot, I had no trouble controlling the chair by a judicious use of the hand brakes. But with the spastics, things didn't work out so well.

They froze, except for one of the girls. She only mostly froze, just enough so that she pulled the left-hand brake handle early in the race. That's why she didn't get as hurt as the rest. She veered and tumbled over the edge of the road before she picked up much speed. The pack got going fast. That's when they started to panic, squeal, and bellow.

I was standing on the finish line I had chalked across the asphalt. I saw a lot of flailing arms and legs and wheelchairs flying toward me down the road. I yelled, *"Slow down!"* But no one was using their brakes. The more I yelled the more they panicked.

It was at that moment that I made a big mistake. I got distracted. The reason I got distracted was because a couple of weeks before our troubles with Dick Keegan and the P.C.C.C.C.U.S.A. started, I had been sitting up in Mom and Dad's bedroom, idly looking at Dad's *Illustrated Bible Atlas of the Holy Land.* For some reason, after I put the book down I absentmindedly tried the latch of the door on Dad's bedside table.

Dad was sitting across from me working on a sermon. He heard the latch rattle and looked up and shouted, *"What do you think you're doing?"*

"I just want to see what you keep here. Why's it locked, Dad?"

Dad took a deep breath, as if he were about to shout. Then he let it out, in a long, soft sigh. He smiled. "I keep important papers there, things we can't afford to lose, like birth certificates."

The way he answered me was too polite. I decided right then and there that I wanted to look in that cupboard no matter what.

I got my chance the next day when Mom and Dad took the train to Zurich to teach the men's and women's Reformed Bible classes. When I walked into the bedroom it was very quiet. Sunlight fell through the small panes of the windows in big slanting rays that made the dust in the air twinkle. I stood contemplating Dad's nightstand. I tried to figure out a way of opening the locked door. First I tried to pick the lock, but I only bent a couple of Mom's hairpins. Luckily I had thrown the hairpins into the wastepaper basket before the door unexpectedly opened and a young woman barged in. She was the pretty daughter of some French missionaries stationed in Gabon, Africa. She had dark red hair and pale skin. She wore a white dress.

"Oh sorry, I theenked eet ees empty. I come to wash *les fenêtres pour Madame,* your *maman.*"

"I'm just looking for Dad's hymnal. I want to choose hymns to sing in church this Sunday. Dad told me to pick them out so Rachael can type them up on a stencil and mimeograph them."

"I lof to seenging!"

The girl started to wash the windows. I sat on the edge of the bed and studied the problem of the night table while she worked. When she stood on a stool to reach the little windowpanes at the top of the balcony door, the sunlight illuminated her in such a way as to outline her figure under her light cotton dress. It was as if she was naked. It made me think of Jennifer.

After the French girl finished the windows, I waited until I heard her footsteps recede before I hurriedly turned to the bedside table. While I was staring at the curves of the girl's slim body, silhouetted against the light, I had had an idea of how to get into the cupboard.

I pulled out the drawer. It had Dad's alarm clock, some paper clips, a pair of cuff links and a box of Moody Bible Institute Bible memorization cards, in a plastic loaf-shaped box with the words THE BREAD OF LIFE stamped on the lid in gold letters.

I put the drawer down on the bed and reached through the space where the drawer had been into the cupboard below. I touched something. I slowly withdrew my arm. In my hand I held a magazine, with writing on it in some language I didn't recognize. I could tell it wasn't English or French; the letters had dots over them in strange places.

On the cover was a picture of what appeared to be a family on a beach. A man, a wife, a son, and a young daughter. They were no ordinary family. *They were stark naked!*

My heart started to thump in my chest as I began to turn the pages slowly. I felt a tingling in my Little Thing. There were lots of pictures of naked people on beaches and in fields. Some were standing around a huge pool; others were lying nude while people who looked like nurses rubbed mud on them and massaged them.

A few months before I found the magazine, a German young person had given her testimony at Wednesday-night prayer meeting, about how she got born again. She described her worldly life before she was saved. She said as how she had grown up in a "nominal Lutheran family," who were so far from the Lord that they not only smoked and drank alcohol, but even went to a special beach each summer where they took off all their clothes.

The night the girl had given her testimony (it was the best one I ever heard), Mom came into my room to say good night. She explained about nudist colonies in Germany, how it was depraved of people to uncover their bodies in such an immodest way, how she didn't believe people got naked for health reasons at all, but for "other reasons." The magazine pictures seemed to be of someplace like those German nudist colonies. And judging by what some of the people were doing to each other, they had plenty of other reasons for taking their clothes off besides sunbathing.

In the Bible it says the sins of the fathers will be visited on the children. This was certainly true in my case. On the day of Le Tour de Spastics, Dad's magazine was the source of my fatal distraction and thus my destruction.

I was watching a tall sixteen-year-old spastic girl with short black hair hurtle toward me. The wind velocity pushed her dress up. I could see her panties. That's when I got distracted. I was wondering if the shape of her pubic hair was the same as a girl with short black hair I had seen in Dad's magazine who had looked so much like Eva the day I had seen her naked in the Hotel Zippelberg on our last vacation in Zermatt. I stared at the pretty spastic's panties far too long. My pubic speculation was why I didn't notice Gustave, the most obese spastic in Chalet Beau Rivage, veer toward me at forty miles an hour.

Chapter 33

I SAT STARING AT MY FRIEND GINO as he fumbled for a glass. We were sitting in his outdoor studio. The air was soft. It smelled of paint, whiskey, and pasta sauce. It was dusk.

"Ah! Dee love!"

Gino poured us drinks, stood up unsteadily, and toasted my marriage. He raised his glass with a lot more gusto than Mr. Bazlinton had.

"To youa wives and youa 'appiness! *Salute!*"

We drank our whiskey.

"Gino, do you think we'll be able to work things out so that Jennifer and I can live together?"

"No, you must suffer first. You must suffering deeply. Thees is youa fate!"

"How can you know that?"

"Because it is dee way. It is dee one theeng that never change!"

"I could follow her to England."

"And who is youa friend in Eengland? Who ees allow you to sleep on his couch and to giving you *i soldi?*"

"Well maybe next year. Then I'll be old enough to get a job."

"You must finish *la scuola.*"

"I can work and study."

"Yes, if you were at 'ome but not when you are alone. It costa too much—leeve, study, eat, love, work. Not posseeble."

"Other people get married young."

"Sure, but they 'ave parents to 'elp them or they suffer. I told you no one 'elps young lovers. *No one!*"

"You're helping me. You're letting me live here."

"Yes, but for 'ow long? Jennifer, she leave soon."

"I'm going to follow her. I might even ride on their train and hide in the toilet."

"To Dover? On the boat to Eengland? From Dover to London? In their taxi to their 'ome? In dee *toletta* of Jennifer?"

"Gino, you're not being serious!"

"Yes, I am, but not as you wish."

"*Please,* Gino, help me to stay with her."

"There is nussing I cana do. Thees is nota the olda day when bambino married. It was better in the twelve century. People know then, young lovers musta make love, so they 'elp them. Girl, she marry when she is fifteena, sixteena, like Jennifer. Boy, when 'ee is sixteena, seventeena. Then they living with mama and people 'elp them. Now is all change. Parents say, no 'ave sexual, and no 'ave married! No one remember 'ow it ees at fifteena or sixteena, only say, '*No, no, e NO!*'"

"I want to be with her, I don't care what other people say."

Gino sat back in his deck chair and stared at his glass. A tear splashed into his whiskey.

"Calvino, I 'ave somesing to say."

"Yes?"

Gino drew in a deep, shuddering breath. "Calvino, you must forgive me, I 'ave betray you."

"What do you mean?"

"Today the manager of the Nazionale, 'ee calla me. 'Ee say you papa, 'ee call to ask if they seeing you. 'Ee say no. Then you fasser ask 'eem eef 'ee 'ave my telefono number to ask maybe I know. The manager say 'ee will asking. 'Ee call me and I tella 'eem the truth."

I sprang to my feet. "*Gino!*"

"What cana I say? 'Ow am I going to lying? Then I become reeseponseeble, and if I say, 'No, 'ee ees not 'ere,' and they find out, then I will be accuse of 'iding a child and because, likea I explain you, everyone say, 'Ah, 'ee 'ide dee boy, why?' I cannot go to preeson even for you, Calvino. Even for you, *mia* friend!"

"Gino, why didn't you tell me to leave? Then you could have said I wasn't here!"

"I'm a tell you now!"

Gino stood up, tried to steady himself as best he could. He laid his hand on my shoulder. "I'ma sorry, Calvino, I'ma very sorry. If you wish I weel speaka to youa papa. I will tella 'eem that per'aps you could stay weeth me until the *scuola* start. Maybe 'ee let you. Shall I trying?"

"Gino, if I get taken back I'll run again, but I won't run here because I can't trust you! You lied to me!"

"*No, I deed not!* I did not lying to *anyone!* I never say to you I weel lying to youa fasser. *You* lie to me!"

"I never lied to you!"

"You lie *now!* You lying saying I lie! That's 'ow you lying!"

Gino tried to march around, but he was more drunk than angry. He crashed into one of his easels and knocked a half-finished canvas to the ground. It fell face forward onto the littered floor. Gino knelt, picked the canvas up, and studied it. A cigarette butt was stuck to the fresh smeared paint.

"Now you are destroying my lifea work! Now you calla me a liar and you destroy *il mio lavoro!*"

"*I didn't knock over your painting! You did because you drink Johnnie Walker Red Label all day!*"

"*Keela me! Go on, keela me! You 'ate me so keela me! 'Ere,*" Gino shouted, picking up a fallen palette knife. He held the palette knife toward me. "You 'ave broke my 'art, so now stabba mia with this knife! Go on! *Do eet!*"

"*Don't be ridiculous. I don't hate you or want to kill you!*"

"Yes, you do! You 'ate me! Like everyone else you 'ate me!"

"Everyone likes you, Gino! Everyone does!"

"They only pretend. In their 'arts they 'ate me like you do!"

"Gino, put down the knife! C'mon and sit down!"

"*Morte!*" Gino stabbed at his chest.

The blunt triangular blade was crusted with thick, dry oil paint. It couldn't have killed Gino even if his chest had been bare. Gino was wearing a baggy, paint-spattered, cotton knit sweater. The palette knife did no damage at all. I was scared nevertheless.

"Gino! You'll hurt yourself!"

"*Morte!*"

"Gino, *stop!*" I jumped forward, reached down, and grabbed at the knife. Gino lunged at me. I didn't pull back quickly enough. His wild, drunken stroke caught me across my shin.

I looked down. There was a long shallow scratch across my bare leg.

"Gino, you cut me!"

Gino dropped the palette knife in horror and struggled to his feet.

"Calvino. I'ma sorry! I didn't mean to 'urt you! Ah *misericordia!* 'Ow is it *possibile?* It is an olda knife, I only use it to meex the color!"

"I guess the tip poked through the dried paint."

"Calvino, I 'ave betray you and now I 'ave tried to keela you, forgeevea mia!"

Gino staggered toward his chair, collapsed into it, and began to sob. Between sobs he said, "Go to the *ospedale.*"

"Gino, it's only a scratch. Look." I stuck out my leg.

Gino peered at my shin. "I'ma so sorry," he kept repeating.

"Don't cry, Gino. I'm fine. They would've found out where I am anyway. Lucrezia, the Banini, the Bazlintons—everyone's seen me. Sooner or later they would've found me. Have a drink."

Gino wiped his eyes.

"Calvino, youa are a beauteeful boy, *bello bellissimo!* You 'ave a big 'art."

I poured Gino a half glass of whiskey. Then I poured out a little for myself.

"Gino, shall I put on a movie?"

"Put ona number twelve. It is the one thata 'as peectures of Jennifer getting off the bus when she was a child."

I threaded Gino's old eight-millimeter projector. One of Gino's white, unpainted canvases, propped up on the easel, was our screen. We sat watching the familiar flickering black-and-white images of Gino's home movies.

By the time the movie finished, Gino was asleep. I unplugged the projector, put the reel of film back in its battered can, and went out for a walk.

At the bar below Gino's studio, women with dark tans, framed by low-cut, formfitting black dresses, sat opposite men in loose white sweaters, gray flannel trousers, and expensive-looking loafers worn with no socks.

In the piazza, people ambled arm in arm, laughing and talking, the noise of their conversations mixing chaotically with the music drifting from the dining terraces of half a dozen restaurants. I glanced at the late diners on the terrace of the Hotel Nazionale, where our family always sat. Then I walked to the church.

I had never gone into the church at night. The air felt warm. The smell of musty plaster, candle wax, and incense was pleasantly familiar. The only illumination came from a solitary red oil lamp burning dimly in front of the altar.

I walked slowly up the aisle, slipped behind a pew, and knelt down. High above me there was a gentle rustle of feathers as a dove, nestling somewhere in the dome, stirred in its sleep.

There was nothing to do about the fact that my father knew where I was. What I had to decide was whether to wait for him to show up or to run again. My leg began to sting where Gino had cut it.

My leg was hurting worse than ever. A nun loomed into view. She smiled. *"On a bien dormi?"* I wasn't thinking about sleeping well, but about the fact I couldn't remember the words, in French, for *I'm going to throw up*.

I did. The nun seemed to be expecting it. She slipped a pan under my chin. As I bent over I wondered what would happen to Dad, what his chastisement would be. I had only looked at his magazine once and was run over by a fat spastic.

It felt like my leg had turned to stone, stone with nerves. My heavy cast was warm and damp. They said I fractured my ankle. I had a big lump on the back of my head, and the back of my hand was scraped.

The hospital room was a sickly pale green. There was an ominous stain on the ceiling above me, a strange brown splash. I wondered if it was blood. My bed was next to three others. They were empty. I couldn't see the mountains, just the wall of a gray building.

My room had a medium-sized crucifix on the wall, a lot bigger than the one in Farmer Ruchet's kitchen, but a lot smaller than the cross in the Portofino church. The cross was wooden. Jesus was carved in ivory. His blood drops were sculpted, not painted. You could only see his wounds clearly when the late-afternoon sun slanted in at an angle and threw Jesus' blood into sharp relief.

My room had an alcove with a statue of Mary in it. There were a bunch of yellow and pink plastic flowers set in a brass ring at Mary's feet. She had dusty prayer beads laced through her delicate plaster fingers. Her eyes were turned heavenward. The alcove was painted blue with gold stars.

I was asleep when visiting hour started and Mom, Janet, and Rachael trooped into my ward. Mom woke me with a long, warm kiss. She brought her Bible to read out loud to me. Janet presented me with a box of Frigor chocolates, my favorites, brittle dark chocolate on the outside, soft creamy milk chocolate, lightly flavored with almond, within. Rachael gave me a large sketch pad and a new box of Caran d'Aché colored pencils. They were arranged in precise order; black at one end, through the whole spectrum of the rainbow, to white at the other. The box had a drawing of Château Chillon on the lid. When I opened it the aroma of cedar filled the ward and temporarily drove the antiseptic smell away.

"How do you feel?"

"My leg hurts a lot, Mom."

Janet shook her head in disgust.

"Why, oh *why*, were you so dumb?"

"Janet!" exclaimed Mom. "We have *already* discussed this. He might have acted more wisely but he has suffered the consequences."

"Really, Mother! They all could have been killed!"

"Janet!"

The icy way Mom spoke made Janet shut up for a while.

"Mom," I asked, "are they . . ."

"They're fine, darling. Only cuts and bruises."

Mom reached out and began to run her cool fingers through my hair. Her nails felt good on my scalp.

"They say if you lie still and behave you can be home in two or three days, darling."

"You'll probably never walk again."

Mom gave Janet a furious look. "Janet, that's a terrible thing to say! And it's certainly not true. The doctor says it's only a tiny crack, a very minor fracture!"

"Janet, sometimes you're as bad as Grandmother—so unpleasant, so critical," said Rachael.

"I'm afraid I agree with Rachael, Janet. You really do seem to have inherited some of your grandmother's attitude problem. I would think that the Day of Miracles would have been enough to inspire you to change your attitude!"

Janet stood up.

"Mom, if I'm not wanted, I'll go! I'll wait in the entrance hall."

Mom frowned as she watched Janet walk out. Then she turned and spotted the crucifix on my wall. She shuddered.

"It's no wonder Janet's on edge in this awful place. Dr. Zwingli should have warned us! He really . . ."

A nun walked in. She brought a wheelchair. I was to be taken down to X ray. Mom and Rachael helped the nun get me into the chair, then followed her as she pushed me into the hall.

The day before, when I had been admitted, I went straight to the emergency room. I hadn't noticed my surroundings much. Now I had a chance to look around. Nuns, wearing long black robes and big silver crosses with very realistic dying Jesuses on them, were everywhere. They had huge, white-winged hats. The nuns' heads looked as if giant seagulls were perched on them, that flapped their wings when the nuns walked.

Mom glanced unhappily up at a church-size crucifix hanging above the door in the entrance hall. Rachael glared at Jesus, then shook her head in despair.

In X ray they had another crucifix over the door.

"It's so Catholic!" wailed Mom in a loud whisper. "If only I had known! What was Dr. Zwingli thinking of! He knows our views. How could he have sent you here of all places?"

Mom wouldn't call the nuns soeur, only mademoiselle. Mom and Dad never called nuns sister or priests father. Mom said she would rather die than bow to such papist pretensions.

When we got back to my room, Mom and Rachael kept giving the statue of Mary dirty looks. As visiting hour was about to end, Mom glanced at the statue one last time, shuddered, and said, "Let's pray together before I leave.

"Dear Heavenly Father, we just come before Thee and ask that the power of darkness in this sad place be broken. We claim Thy promises and ask that You protect Calvin, just as You delivered us on the Day of Miracles so marvelously. We just ask that Calvin may be protected from the spirit of idolatry present here and we claim Thy blood to protect him from the false and demonic influences that are represented in this room by these terrible man-made gods, these statues of wood and clay that, like Dagon, Thou hast cast down. In thanksgiving for the Reformation and in Jesus' precious, wondrous Name. Amen."

After Mom left, I lay back and gazed at Mary holding her beads. Then I looked at the wound in Jesus' side, at his blood carved in little rivulets. I crossed myself slowly and said, *"Ave Maria,"* like a real Catholic. It was nearly as good as being back in Italy. I could almost smell the cool damp plaster, the incense and candles.

I was glad Dr. Zwingli had been so "insensitive," had mistakenly told the ambulance driver to take me to the Monthey hospital, in the Roman Catholic canton of Valais, instead of the Aigle Hospital, across the Rhône River, in the Protestant canton of Vaud.

I closed my eyes. I began to get my picture of Jennifer. But before I could get the story started, I opened them and glanced at the statue of Mary. She seemed to be watching me.

I was glad Mary intervened. A second later a nun gently opened my door. If I had kept my eyes closed she would have caught me.

My picture of Jennifer slipping off her bathing suit dissolved at the sight of the nun's flapping hat, wrinkled, parchment-pale skin, and thick glasses. She reminded me a little of Grandmother.

I jerked my hands out from under the sheet and asked, "Sister, do you have a chapel?"

"Mais oui, on a la messe à six heures."

"May I go to mass?"

She smiled sweetly and made the sign of the cross and answered, *"Mais certainement, mon petit."*

The Monthey hospital chapel was not as nice as my church in Portofino, but there was still a good-sized Mary, and a larger-than-life crucifix with plenty of lash marks. Best of all the incense smelled the same. There was also a fine, life-sized St. Sebastian standing in a corner. He was shot full of long, bloody arrows, his serene eyes absentmindedly turned heavenward, as if he had not yet noticed that he had been pierced with twenty barbed shafts.

In a whisper a nun asked me if I had been to confession. I nodded. She wheeled me up to receive the body of Christ, like the Catholics believe communion is.

While I was being wheeled to the altar rail I crossed myself and murmured, *"Ave Maria, Ave Maria . . ."* over and over again so I would look as if I was fervently repeating a Catholic prayer my mother had taught me, which of course Mom hadn't.

I was wheeled back to my place while the wafer slowly melted in my mouth. It reminded me of the sugar cones that the *gelateria* lady in Portofino served her ice cream in, only not as sweet. I sniffed the incense, closed my eyes, and tried to feel holy. Suddenly I laughed out loud as a vision of the spastics crashing through the pine hedge came unbidden to mind.

Jean-Pierre never got to wave the blue-and-white-checkered dish towel that I had given him. The spastics had sailed off the road before they got to the finish line. Gustave kept going straight down the bank after he clipped me, over a bumpy field toward the forest. The bank below the road was almost vertical. Gustave's wheels only touched a couple of times before he flew into the trees, six or seven feet above the ground.

Once the spastics started to bellow I could tell they were going to keep it up for a long time. I knew from experience that even if I begged them to shut up, asked them to pretend they were all right, it would have been no use. They were thoroughly out of control. Anyway, I couldn't move. My leg hurt. I lay on my back watching the sky go dark.

Before I lost consciousness, I saw The Ladies running down the road as fast as middle-aged Presbyterian women from Lynchburg, Virginia, who love to eat, can sprint. They were screaming louder than their spastics.

The Ladies ignored me, leapt over the steep embankment, and slid and tumbled down to their bruised, groaning patients. Mary Lou cartwheeled at least thirty feet in a shower of pebbles and dust, her skirt pushed up over her head. The last thing I remembered seeing was her fat, white thighs shining in the brilliant late-afternoon sun.

Chapter 34

"I ALWAYS SAID YA WAS DUMB to take up playin' with them retards."

"They're not 'retards,' Grandmother."

"When Ralph were a boy I never let him play with no cripples. Ya can catch bad luck, I says!"

I rolled my wheelchair back a few feet from Grandmother's bed. "Dad's told me how you ruined his life. You must've been the worst mother in the world!"

Grandmother took a swing but missed.

"If I could get up I'd kick your broken leg for sayin' that!"

"If *I* was at the end of my days, I'd be nicer to everybody."

"More fool you!"

"Mom says the reason you're so terrible is because you don't know the Lord."

"I know everybody I want to and plenty I don't!"

"Well, I'd be nicer."

Grandmother started to cough. She picked up her handkerchief and spit into it.

"There's spit on your chin."

"If ya don't like it then go back ta the hospital or your room or some damn place afore I spit on *you!*"

"And your manners are deplorable."

" 'Deplorable.' *Pshaw!* Your highfalutin mom sure has *you* trained."

"What do you mean 'trained'?"

"Mean? I mean what I said, or is your ears broke, too?"

"I'm not 'trained.' "

"Then tell me you'd drop your pants in church."

I tried not to laugh. "That's a *terrible* thing to say!"

"Well, you tell me one thing that I don't know 'bout you. Tell me anythin' where you're different than 'em other religious nuts wandering around this loopy joint, talking 'bout their 'Day a Miracles.' Pshaw! Sing me one song 'at whining bitch didn't teach ya!"

"*Grandmother!* How can you say such things?"

" 'How can you say such things?' " Grandmother mimicked me in a high cracked voice. "Who taught ya ta talk like that? 'How can you say such things!' What did they do ta ya in that stinkin' hospital? Ya talk more like Rachael all the time! You're just as bad as any of 'em with your shit-eatin' grin!"

"If you weren't so old, I'd . . ."

Grandmother licked her lips and grinned. "You'd come over here where I could get a good swing at ya and break ya other leg!"

"You know if Dad knew you talked this way to me he'd put you in a—"

"Bullshit he would! Talk, talk, talk, they're too cheap for anythin'. Them homes cost a bundle, and another thing, your mother likes it."

"Likes when you talk bad?"

"Yup, she does, how else can Miss Sunday School feel like she 'saved' your pop like she says? How else can Miss Goody Two-shoes feel so goddamned pleased with herself all the time? If it weren't for me how could she say she were takin' up her cross and followin' Jesus? Ain't I the best goddamned cross ya ever seen?"

Grandmother laughed so hard it sounded as if she was barking. I started to laugh, too.

"How do you know Mom likes it that you're bad?"

Grandmother gave me a sly sideways glance. "I know lots of things ya never even dreamed of."

"Like what?"

"Lots, that's what. I know that afore ya broke your leg ya used ta sneak in here and change my clock, ya li'l brat."

"Grandma!"

"Don't ya *Grandma* me! Ya can't lie ta me, ya pie-faced goof! I ain't no stupid, god-awful, 'ain't Jesus grand,' shit-for-brains, born-again moron! So don't even try it! *Ya hear!* I know what I know. Ya know why I put up with it?"

I shook my head.

" 'Cause I'd rather sleep in this nuthouse than see all of ya anyways! Ya know what else?"

I shook my head.

"I know ya killed my goldfish! Now don't go denyin' it, ya li'l brat!"

After a moment of awkward silence I glanced up and caught Grandmother's eye. She winked.

I nodded.

Grandmother cackled with laughter. "So! Ya admit it! How'd ya do it? 'Lectricity? What?"

"I put bleach in the water."

"Figures you'd use poison, ya sneakin' li'l bastard! Now, if your grandfather had wanted ta kill somethin' he'da grabbed it an' smashed its head in, not sneaked around puttin' poison in the water. *Coward!* Ya afraid of a little blood?"

"I chop off the chickens' heads."

"Don't signify, you're supposed to be doin' that. You're just a crappy li'l coward. You'll make a good missionary!"

"What's that supposed to mean?"

"I told ya before, bein' a missionary ain't no real job. This missionary stuff, it's all sneakin' around, tellin' lies like your mom does, pretendin' she's coming up to visit me, but I see she's brung her lousy Bible with her. She ain't visitin' *me.* She don't even *like me!* She's just sneakin' around trying to con me into sayin' I'll love Jesus so she can feel good 'bout herself 'cause misery loves company."

Grandmother started to cough again. She went on hacking for a long time. When she was done she spit into her handkerchief and waved me away.

"I'm gonna sleep."

She looked so old and tired. I suddenly felt kind of remorseful, so I said, "Sorry about the fish."

"Aw, shaddup!"

Chapter 35

ON THE FIRST SUNDAY MORNING I was home from the hospital, Mom came up to my room to wake me for church.

"Mom?"

"Yes, darling?"

"Now that things are better in the Lord's work and all, are we going on vacation?"

"I'm afraid not, darling. We need to stay right here to rebuild the work. Anyway, darling, you have a broken leg."

"But, Mom, it'll be better by the time we go. The doctor said I'd only need a cast for two more weeks."

"That's right, dear, but your father feels that we need to be on hand regardless. I know it's hard, but you'll have to be patient and wait till next year. I've canceled our reservations, so that's that."

"But, Mom?"

"Yes, dear?"

"Isn't there any way that I could go alone, or with Rachael or something?"

"I'm afraid not, dear. At the most, maybe we can have a nice long day off down by the lake."

After church I sat up on the balcony in front of my room. I was thinking about Italy, about canceled reservations. I felt depressed. The slate-gray sky was convulsed with huge, summer rain clouds. They seemed to fit my mood. The tops of the peaks were obscured, cut off by the towering banks of vapor.

I had just whispered "Jennifer" for the hundredth time or so when

Dr. Zwingli's car pulled up. Dr. Zwingli usually visited on Mondays to check Grandmother's hip, so I thought he had come to see me. I wheeled to the top of the stairs to wait.

Dr. Zwingli walked up the stairs with Mom. When she saw me she said, "The doctor's come to see Grandmother, dear. She's not well."

I followed Mom and the doctor down the hall in my wheelchair. Dr. Zwingli listened to Grandmother's chest, then started tapping all over it with his fingers. When he was done he pulled her covers up to her chin and snapped his bag shut. Then he nodded to Mom and they both stepped into the hall.

Dr. Zwingli stood, stroking his goatee thoughtfully. "May I speak with you, Mrs. Becker?"

Mom glanced at me. "Run along to your room, darling."

Mom led the doctor across the hall to Grandmother's empty sitting room and shut the door. By the time I had my ear pressed to the wood panel, they were already talking.

While Dr. Zwingli was examining Grandmother it had started to rain. The torrential downpour beat a loud tattoo on the roof. I had to keep my ear pressed tightly to the door to hear the conversation.

"Is the pneumonia in both lungs?"

"Yes, and quite severe. Now that she's broken her hip again, it was only a matter of time. Lack of mobility, you see."

There was a loud crack of thunder overhead. As the echo died away Mom said, "Dr. Zwingli, would you mind if we took this matter to our Heavenly Father?"

Mom often said the most effective evangelistic tool was prayer. That fervent, sincere prayer created a longing in people for the Things of The Lord. I guess Mom thought that this was a perfect opportunity.

"Dear Heavenly Father, we just bring dear Grandmother before You and ask that Thou wilt give us wisdom in how best to treat her. That Thou wilt reach out to Dr. Zwingli and that Thou, the Great

Physician, wilt give Dr. Zwingli great wisdom and skill that cometh only from Thee. We thank Thee that Thou hast sent Thine only begotten Son to die for our sins that whosoever believeth in Him shall not perish. I thank Thee for Dr. Zwingli and I pray Thou wilt draw near unto him. In Jesus' precious Name, amen."

"Thank you, Mrs. Becker."

There was another earsplitting crack of thunder. There must have been an open window somewhere in the house. I could smell wet earth, tangy and moist, heavy with the scent of mud, field flowers, and damp hay.

"Dr. Zwingli, what would you do?"

"She's eighty-one years old, she has rebroken her hip and will simply develop one set of complications after another. This case of pneumonia will be followed by other respiratory problems. With aggressive treatment she might linger, but at a certain moment . . ."

"I hope she won't be in pain."

"Oh no, with proper hydration and care, none at all."

"When you say 'aggressive' . . . ?"

"Antibiotics, feeding by tube . . ."

"And, ah . . . less aggressive?"

"Hydration, liquid by mouth, and if necessary by intravenous drip, sedation, and plenty of the wonderful love you have in your heart, Mrs. Becker."

"Thank you, Dr. Zwingli, but the love that we have is not ours but comes from our Heavenly Father."

"You are a wonderful person. I would like to be like you, Mrs. Becker."

"Dr. Zwingli, if you want to share that joy, then you need to come to the precious fountain and be washed in the Savior's blood."

"Mrs. Becker, I need a little time to, ah, think these things over. Perhaps you could recommend what passages in the Bible I might study. . . ."

"Wouldn't you like to pray with me right now and invite the Savior into your heart?"

"Perhaps another day when I have, um . . . studied more, ah, profoundly."

Mom sounded disappointed. "I think you should read the Gospel of John, then come back and talk to me about it. But you know we should not let opportunities, times when the Lord is speaking to us, slip away."

"I shall read the book of John with great interest."

I knew Mom was thinking that Dr. Zwingli might get away, but what more could she do? She couldn't very well tell Dr. Zwingli she didn't want him to read the Bible.

"Mrs. Becker, shall I guide you in this physical matter as you have guided me in your spiritual wisdom?"

Mom didn't answer.

"Let me keep her comfortable. You pray that God does as He sees fit. I will keep her comfortable."

There was a distant rumble of thunder. The storm was receding over the mountains.

After a pause Mom said, "I'm sure that this is what the Lord has ordained in His sovereign will."

Chapter 36

THE WEATHER TURNED HOT after the storm. Grandmother was lying under a single sheet plastered to her narrow, bony chest with her own sweat. Her window and balcony door were open, but the air was unusually humid, breathlessly still.

With Grandmother dying, Mom called a special prayer meeting to intercede with God on her behalf, that before Grandmother passed away the Lord might do a work in her heart. Mom, Rachael, Janet, Dick, Jane Keegan, and The Ladies took turns sitting and reading the Bible to Grandmother. Every time Grandmother seemed to be even a little bit alert, they would talk to her about her urgent need to accept Jesus. It was a marathon of round-the-clock witnessing. Time was running out. They even made Jean-Pierre come over to help. But they sent him home when Grandmother woke up and yelled, "Get that damned retard outta here!"

I was supposed to be working on Grandmother, too. When Mom or Janet got tired of reading the Bible to her, they came to my room, nodded solemnly, and wheeled me over to take the next shift.

Since I couldn't read well enough to witness through the Word, Mom said I should just talk to Grandmother about the Lord, or sing a simple hymn to touch her heart. But I felt silly sitting next to her in my wheelchair, singing, "The B-I-B-L-E, Yes, That's the Book for Me!" "Jesus Loves Me," or "Wide, Wide as the Ocean," all by myself while Grandmother dozed or muttered, "Shut up, ya li'l shit. The heat's bad enough without you carryin' on!" or "You're as bad as the rest of your crummy family. Anyways, ya can't carry a tune. Shut up, dammit!" So instead of witnessing, I asked her questions. Sometimes she woke up enough to answer me.

"Grandmother, when you were a little girl, where did you live?"

"What's it to ya?"

"People are supposed to know about their families."

"Sez who?"

"Look at the genealogies in the Bible."

"Don't ya start with that crap!" Grandmother coughed and shifted restlessly. "Germantown, there was still *Germans* in Germantown in them days, no niggers at all."

"I thought you were English."

"My poor Limey mother married a goddamned Kraut!"

"Didn't you like your dad?"

"What's to like? Never saw the poor bastard, he worked all day, died when I was fourteen, run over by a train some Spick retard were drivin'."

"Were you upset?"

Grandmother peered angrily at me.

"Ya're dumber than ya look, ain't ya?"

"I was just asking."

"What do ya think? I had to quit high school and go to work. I wanted to be a teacher, not do piecework in some stinkin' shoe factory!"

Grandma kicked feebly at her sheet.

"Pull this goddamned rag offa me, will ya?"

I folded the limp, damp, yellowing sheet halfway down to Grandmother's waist. She had on a blue cotton nightgown. It was stuck to her withered body tight as paint.

"Fan me with that paper, will ya? And don't stare at my goddamned tits!"

I hurriedly looked away from Grandmother's chest, picked up an unread *Philadelphia Inquirer,* and began to fan her face.

"I bet you would've made a nice teacher!"

"Don't get smart with me, ya li'l shit!"

"For one thing, teachers don't swear."

"How would you know, ya never been ta school! Besides, they do if they're bein' yacked to death by fools an' parasites! Anyways, saying *shit* ain't swearin'."

"How can I be a parasite? I'm only fifteen."

"Parasite-in-trainin'!" Grandmother laughed, which made her cough. She coughed so hard she had trouble breathing. After that she dozed for a while. I kept fanning her until she fell into a deeper sleep.

Two days later Janet, Rachael, and Mom were standing in the hall outside my room.

"She's beginning to slip away," Mom whispered.

Rachael sniffed. "I don't think her heart has begun to warm up at all."

"Well," said Janet, "you never know what she's hearing or thinking. She might make a decision without us knowing."

"That's right," said Mom. "We'll keep trying right up to the very end."

An hour later Dr. Zwingli visited. He started Grandma on an intravenous drip. He said the liquid would keep her comfortably hydrated since she couldn't swallow.

I sat next to Grandmother most of that afternoon. It had finally turned cool. The air was crystal clear. Grandmother now had a plain, brown wool blanket pulled up to her shriveled chin.

I sat in silence, slumped down in my wheelchair next to Grandmother's bed. I was thinking about not going to Italy, about not seeing Jennifer. I dug at the cotton in the top of my cast, trying to scratch my smothered skin. It had been irritated by the hot spell. I listlessly watched the birds in the larch trees pecking seeds out of the tiny new cones. I stared at the saline solution trickling down the clear plastic tube into Grandmother's arm. I watched her translucent eyelids flicker. She seemed to be dreaming.

Grandmother never had her teeth in now. She looked sunken. The infection, Dr. Zwingli explained, was causing Grandmother's lungs to fill up with fluid. She gasped and whistled with each breath. I could hear the liquid bubble.

I missed Grandmother's ranting.

I sat next to Grandmother and watched her try to breathe. I kept thinking she had died. Sometimes a lot of time went by between each breath. Then she would take a shallow, short gasp, silent and wispy.

I followed each IV drop down the tube as it trickled into her arm. I imagined it getting into her bloodstream and pumping around through her hard, blue veins into her infected lungs, another drop of liquid slowly choking her. I wished she would act up, even swear at me, not lie there getting smaller. It didn't look like anyone was in the bed. Just a small, wrinkled face above the sheet was all that seemed to be left of Grandmother.

It was too late for Grandmother just like it had been for Farmer Ruchet's pig. Grandmother was drowning. All Dr. Zwingli was giving her was more water.

It was thinking of the pig that did it.

I wheeled to the head of the stairs and called for Rachael. When she finally came upstairs and asked what I wanted, I had to work hard to keep a tremble out of my voice. "I want to go to the living room and look through the Sunday-school flannel graph stories and pick out one to do for Grandmother."

Rachael smiled. "That's a precious idea!"

As Janet and Rachael carried me downstairs Janet gave me a suspicious look.

"Grandmother's practically unconscious. Even if she *can* still hear us, what's the use of setting up the flannel graph board?"

"That's not kind," said Rachael. "You said yourself we can never know what she's hearing."

As soon as Rachael and Janet went back upstairs, I pushed aside the box of flannel graph characters, then quickly hopped to the door of our living room and across the hall to the furnace room. I tried to scramble up on the side of the stone tub.

I slipped a couple of times and almost cracked my cast. In the end I had to knock the box of *pénicilline vétérinaire* off the shelf with a garden rake.

The box tumbled into the stone tub. As I leaned over to get it I fell in. My leg hurt so much I got tears in my eyes. I tasted blood. I had bitten through my lower lip to stop from yelling.

As soon as I stopped crying I retrieved the box and emptied all the packets of penicillin out, stuffed them into my underpants, and hopped back to the living room. When I finally managed to get there I picked up the flannel graph materials and sorted out the Bible characters. My leg was beginning to throb. I had difficulty holding on to David. My hands were shaking.

Rachael and Janet helped me back upstairs. I involuntarily yelled out in pain when my cast tapped the doorjamb of the living room.

"Now what's the matter?" Janet asked.

"My leg hurts."

"How can it? It hasn't hurt you for days."

"Well, it does now."

"You just want sympathy!"

Rachael looked reprovingly at Janet. "That's not very kind."

"He's so spoiled!"

Janet and Rachael set up the flannel graph on its easel at the foot of Grandmother's bed and rolled my wheelchair to where I could stick the characters on the board. Then they left, but not before Janet looked from Grandmother to me and back again, tapped the side of her head, and rolled her eyes. Grandmother was sound asleep.

Chapter 37

THE IV BOTTLE WAS LIKE A GLASS JAR hung upside down by a wire.

It had a hole in the lid from which a tube ran down to Grandmother's arm. If you turned the IV bottle right side up you could unscrew the top like a jam jar. I did this as I held it between my knees. I knew opening the bottle would render it unsterile, but that couldn't be helped.

I decided to go for ten times the dosage of *pénicilline vétérinaire* I had used for the chicken, about what I saw Farmer Ruchet inject his sow with, a week before he gave up treating her and cut her throat.

I should have dissolved the penicillin first, then added it to the saline solution. The antibiotic powder floated in a lump on the top of the liquid. I rubbed the lump between my thumb and forefinger until it melted away. I screwed the lid back on, turned the jar upside down, gave it a shake, took the wire hanger, hooked it onto the IV stand, and pushed up the pole to its full height. I tightened the wing nut. To my horror I saw the tube was full of air.

All I could think to do was to pull the tube out of the top of the needle stuck into the back of Grandmother's hand, which was taped to a board, and suck to get the liquid flowing. I had a lot of trouble maneuvering my wheelchair around the other side of the bed. When I pulled the tube off the needle some blood squirted out. I thought this might happen. I was ready and put my finger on the top of the needle. Holding one finger over the aperture I held the tube in my other hand and sucked.

At first nothing happened. Then, suddenly, salty bitter liquid shot into my mouth. I spit, let some run out onto the floor, then stuck the tube back onto the needle.

I opened the regulator wide and watched the veterinary penicillin pour into Grandmother. I was panting and sweating. It took a minute to regain my composure. My hands shook. I was in pain, but I was satisfied. The IV jar was emptying quickly.

When I looked down I saw blood on the back of Grandmother's wrist. I took the damp facecloth Mom kept in a dish by Grandmother's bed to give her sponge baths with, and wiped up the blood. The face-cloth was dark purple. To my relief, I couldn't see blood on it.

Next to Grandmother's bed was a big cardboard box with five more full IV jars. Dr. Zwingli said that the visiting nurse would come every morning to hook up a new one. The only way I could be sure Grandmother would get the antibiotics was to open the jars and put some powder into each one. To prevent the liquid getting milky the dosage had to be less than the amount I used in the first jar. I figured four packets in each would only make the solution slightly opaque. I had to work fast. I unscrewed the lids, poured some penicillin into each, stirred the liquid up with Grandmother's scissors, and put the lids back on just as I heard footsteps on the hall landing.

Thankfully I remembered to stuff the empty penicillin packets back into my underpants. By the time the door opened I had put the box of IV jars down and was sitting on my hands to stop them from shaking. Janet walked in, looked at me then at the flannel graph board. "You haven't even started!" she exclaimed.

I glanced at the board. I had forgotten to exchange the pictures at the beginning of the story, David coming up to the camp of King Saul, for the last scene, David triumphantly holding up Goliath's head.

"I thought she enjoyed it so much that I was just about to start over again."

Janet stared at me, then nodded meaningfully toward Grandmother, who was still fast asleep.

"There's something wrong with your mind. I'll wheel you back to your room. You're just wasting my time."

I lay down on my bed. My leg was throbbing so hard I could hardly stand it. I felt dizzy. The room seemed to be spinning. I closed my eyes.

A thin, charcoal-gray cat gave me a furtive look, lashing its pencil-thin tail from side to side. The cat ran a little way up the alley, stopped, turned, then watched me suspiciously as I silently opened the laundry door and stepped into the sweet-smelling, damp interior.

It was pitch-black in Jennifer's and my room. But it wasn't stuffy like it had been when we first went in. I felt a cool draft of night air playing about my bare legs. I stood in the dark getting my bearings. The window Jennifer opened was the source of the fresh air.

I lay down on our bed. I tried to remember each moment of our wedding day. All I could conjure up in my mind's eye was Jennifer waiting on the Santa Margherita station platform, a train arriving, Jennifer getting on board, the train leaving, with me left standing on the platform. I was waving good-bye.

I imagined myself crying, feeling how sad I was going to be. I lay in the dark with tears trickling down my cheeks, running into my ears. I didn't move or brush them away. My nose got stuffed up until I could no longer smell the gardenias that were blooming in terracotta pots in the courtyard below.

"Jennifer, oh Jennifer, how can this be? How can you leave? How will I live?" My words merged with the clickety-clack of the train wheels taking Jennifer away.

I began to doze as the picture of Jennifer, waving from the train window, replayed endlessly in my head. Sleep engulfed me.

"How you doing?" I asked.

"I'll live. I been thinkin'."

"What about?"

"Dreams."

"Did you dream while you were sick?"

"I did have a kind a dream. You was in it."

"I was?"

"Yup. You was foolin' around in here doin' all sorts of stuff with them bottle things, comin' in an' out all the time."

"That's a strange dream."

"Ain't so sure it was a dream, ya li'l brat."

"I did visit you a lot."

"Well, at least ya wasn't bleachin' me like you done ta my fish!" Grandmother laughed. "You're not such a bad li'l shit after all. Maybe you'll come to somethin' yet."

"Thanks. I want to be a doctor."

"Calvino! Che fai?" The maid who always had cleaned our rooms at the Nazionale was standing over me. Sunlight was pouring in dusty narrow beams through the slats of the junk-room shutters. The maid, sixty years old, tiny, angry, and dark-skinned, her hair in a tight, gray bun, stood looking down at me severely. She held a dustpan and brush. She prodded me with her dustpan.

"Buon giorno," I said.

"Calvino, perché sei in questa camera? Che fai?"

I couldn't think what to tell her. I was still confused by my dream about Grandmother, so I sat up and shrugged.

As I walked out of the room the maid called after me, *"Calvino! Vieni qua!"* I ignored her, turned the corner, and ran down the back stairs.

Judging by the activity in the square, it looked as if it was mid-morning. I didn't stop at Gino's studio. I half trotted, half ran around the edge of the harbor, to the steps that led to the Paraggi path.

Jennifer was sitting at the beach snack bar having a cup of cappuccino. Her upper lip was flecked with foamy milk. It tasted sweet when I kissed her.

"Calvin, you look dreadful."

"I missed you awfully last night."

"When was the last time you had a bath or slept in a proper bed?"

"I slept in a bed last night, or on it anyway."

"Mum and Dad have gone to Santa Margherita to do their last day shopping. Come to my room and have a bath. I'll order a second breakfast. Lucrezia will bring it up."

I thought about taking off my swimming trunks and T-shirt in front of Jennifer. But at the last second I changed my mind and walked into her bathroom and closed the door. Jennifer said through the door, "Put your things in the sink. They look a bit grotty, darling. I'll wash them when you've finished."

"Thanks."

"Use my shampoo and razor if you like."

"Thanks."

I turned the hot tap all the way but only got a trickle of lukewarm water. I washed my hair and soaped up, then shaved my upper lip as best I could with no mirror. When my face felt smooth, I turned off the limpid dribble.

"Jennifer, have you got the towel?"

I waited for Jennifer to open the door a crack and hand a towel around the corner. Instead she flung the door wide. I froze. Jennifer laughed.

"That's not very nice!"

"Silly boy, we're married!"

"C'mon, Jennifer!"

"One more teeny look!"

I took this as a sort of a dare. I spun around in the doorway stark naked. That's when Lucrezia walked in carrying a breakfast tray with a silver pot of hot chocolate, two breakfast rolls, two pats of butter, one miniature jar of Yugoslavian apricot jam, and two lumps of sugar, wrapped in paper that had a picture of the pope on them.

"Dio mio!" shrieked Lucrezia. Jennifer tossed me a towel. I caught it, dived back into the shower, and pulled the curtain behind me. Jennifer hurriedly closed the bathroom door. I could hear her laughing and telling Lucrezia she could go.

I stood with my heart pounding. Jennifer opened the door a moment later. "Oh, you did look silly! How simply priceless!" she said, then laughed until she collapsed on her bed.

If it had been any day except her last one with me, I would have yelled at her about how I didn't think what she did was funny. But that day I didn't want to waste any of my precious time fighting with her.

As I ate my rolls, sitting wrapped in Jennifer's towel, I watched her standing in the bathroom washing out my T-shirt and swimming trunks. The white lace curtains flickered in the hot morning breeze. Wisps of Jennifer's hair danced around her face in the warm draft. She opened the window to hang my clothes up on the shutters. The whole time she worked I studied her. I wanted to memorize Jennifer, to remember the way her long legs and narrow hips moved, the way her golden ponytail swished when she tossed her head, the delicate, crescent-shaped dimples on either side of her lips.

She turned and caught me gazing at her. Jennifer walked over to the bed and sat down next to me and put her arm around my shoulders.

"Calvin, do you know what day this is?"

"Your last day with me!"

"I didn't mean that. I meant the date."

"No."

"It's your birthday, silly! *Happy Birthday!* If I hadn't already given you my ten pounds, I'd have bought you a gift!"

"You could stay here with me. That's what I want."

"Dear Calvin, I shall miss you, too, you know."

"Jennifer, I really don't know how I'll live without you. I really don't!"

"You won't have to. We'll only be apart a little while . . . then we can be together. But first we need to get older. Soon we shall do as we please. Sixteen, seventeen, eighteen—it won't be long and we'll be twenty-one!"

"Gino says we have to suffer because no one helps young lovers."

"Gino's been to too many operas, I expect."

"He said I had broken his heart. He tried to stab himself with a palette knife."

"There you are! That should put his dire predictions in perspective!"

"But *I am* suffering! I'm suffering *right now!*"

"Steady on, old chap, we can't go throwing ourselves on the ground, wailing, gnashing our teeth, that sort of rubbish. Men go off to war and come back again. The women wait, and then they're reunited in a tearful embrace and all's well!"

"Jennifer, I'm serious!"

"So am I! Would you prefer that I shriek and tear my hair?"

"No, but I don't know what I'll do!"

"You'll bear up, old chap! You'll stop feeling sorry for yourself and start feeling jolly well lucky that you've got a girl like me that loves you and will wait for you to grow up! *That's what you'll do!*"

Jennifer gave me a shake. She shouted, *"That's what you'll do!"* again. I'm sure people on the beach heard her.

Jennifer's eyes were a dark blue green. Her chin was quivering. I guess she saw me glance at her chin. "Never mind, you twit! If you make me cry I shall scratch you!"

That's when the door opened and Dad walked in. I leapt up. Jennifer's towel fell off me. My breakfast tray crashed to the floor and the dishes broke. A small river of creamy, dark brown hot chocolate swirled around my father's feet.

Dad stared at me but said nothing.

Jennifer, who had also leapt to her feet, stood rooted to the spot. Then she calmly said, "Good morning, Reverend Becker, how lovely to see you."

Chapter 38

I COULDN'T IMAGINE how Jennifer could be so calm about everything. I was about to ask her when I woke up. Mom said it was three A.M. Mom telephoned Dr. Zwingli after she saw the sausages that used to be my toes sticking out of my cast. My leg was horribly swollen.

An hour later I was on the way back to the Monthey hospital in Dr. Zwingli's car. On the drive down the mountain I lay with my head cradled in Mom's lap.

As Dr. Zwingli slowly maneuvered down the steep, dark road, Mom asked me what I had done.

I took a deep breath.

"Mom, I did a dumb thing," I whispered.

"What?"

"I took a couple of steps on my broken leg."

"Oh Calvin, why on earth did you do a thing like that?"

"Well, you see I was doing the flannel graph Bible story for Grandmother and David's slingshot fell off the board. It went under her bed. I took a couple of steps and bent down to get the slingshot picture, and that's when it happened."

"What? What happened?"

"That's when I slipped and banged the cast hard on the side of her bed."

"Oh, Calvin!"

Mom gently stroked my hair in the dark. We swayed around a curve. The breeze from Dr. Zwingli's open car window felt good on my hot face. I could just make out the shapes of trees flickering past us in the moonlight.

"Calvin, what you did was thoughtless in one way, but I'm proud of you nevertheless. It was in a good cause. What a shame we have to go back to the Roman Catholic hospital, but I expect Dr. Zwingli's right. We'd best keep the same orthopedic specialist."

"Calvin, you broke something again, rebroke it—now they have to reset it."

"Respirez normalement, un, deux, trios . . ." A nun leaned over me. She put a hard, black rubber mask over my face. The taste of the ether made me gag. Her headdress was flapping wildly.

"Respirez—un—deux . . ."

I tried to hold my breath and closed my eyes. Jennifer turned to me and picked up my fallen towel.

"Calvin, perhaps you'd like to slip into the bathroom and get dressed."

A guest at the *pensione* walked by Jennifer's open door and glanced in. That's when I grabbed the towel from Jennifer's hand, wrapped it around me, walked to her window, reached out, retrieved my T-shirt and swimming trunks, walked into her bathroom, and closed the door. My hands were shaking so violently I had difficulty latching the door.

All the while Dad watched me in silence. As I closed the door I saw him move his feet out of the spreading lake of hot chocolate. I noticed that his khaki pants were splattered.

It only took me a couple of seconds to slip on my T-shirt and swimming trunks. Distraught as I was, I got pleasure from feeling the warm, damp clothes on my skin, from smelling the Pears soap Jennifer had washed them in, from thinking that she washed them for me, that she ordered breakfast and remembered my birthday like a real wife.

I was about to open the door but I hesitated. I couldn't imagine what I was going to say to Dad, or worse, what he'd say. Then it occurred to me that Jennifer would know exactly how long it took to put on a T-shirt and shorts. She would know I was procrastinating, and if there was one thing Jennifer hated, it was a coward. I opened the door and stepped out as boldly as I could.

My boldness was wasted. Jennifer and Dad were nowhere to be seen. The broken breakfast dishes were the only evidence Dad had been there.

I paused. I didn't know what to do. It would be strange if I went looking for my father when I was running away from him. On the other hand Dad must still be with Jennifer someplace. Dad showing up wasn't her problem but mine. I knew Jennifer would get furious with me if I bolted down the hall, ran out the back door, across the road, up into the hills above the beach, and hid in the olive groves next to the Roman road at the top of the ridge. I was tempted to do this, but I could imagine what Jennifer would say about me being a feeble, pitiful, wet coward, a poor imbecile, a demented simple-minded child who should really be put in a home.

I tried to arrange my face into a defiant expression, squared my shoulders, lifted my chin, stepped over the puddle, and followed Dad's milk-chocolate footprints along the gray marble floor until they petered out at the top of the stairs.

I heard a voice coming up the stairwell from the lobby. It was Jennifer's. By tiptoeing down to the first landing I got close enough to hear what she was saying.

". . . You've made him very unhappy. Calvin's a sensitive boy."

"Jennifer"—Dad's voice was tight and hoarse—"I don't know what business this is of yours!"

"Reverend Becker, it's my business because I love him and I shan't stand by while he's tortured."

"How dare you stand there talking to me like that?"

"I'd rather say you're the one who should answer that! Do you know that you've lost his trust? It's you he ran from! You're the one who has to explain yourself!"

After a long pause I heard Dad answer quietly, "You're right, Jennifer. How can I get him to see that I love him?"

Jennifer sounded angry. "For starters you can apologize to him, begin to treat him like a young man with a mind of his own, buck up, and take some responsibility for him! You might even ask him if he jolly well wants to live in a religious lunatic asylum!"

"Well, he's not going to have to be in the Lord's work anymore."

"Good show!"

"Jennifer, will you talk to him for me?"

"Not unless you solemnly swear that you will be kind to him. Not unless I understand *exactly* what it is you intend to do to him about his running away. Not unless you promise to bloody well be a better father to him than you've been!"

Dad flared up. "Jennifer, I don't know what right you have to talk to me like this!"

"I'm his wife!"

There was a long silence. Finally Dad murmured plaintively, "I don't understand."

When Jennifer answered, she was matter-of-fact. "We went to the church in Portofino and took our vows."

"Jennifer, what are you talking about? No one would marry two fifteen-year-olds!"

"It's Calvin's birthday. He's sixteen today."

"Oh, Jennifer . . ." It sounded as if Dad was on the verge of tears.

"Besides," said Jennifer, "no one married us. We married ourselves."

"Like a game?"

"No! We love each other. We did it in front of Christ, so it's rather awfully official, you know. It's frightfully bad form to promise things and then break your promise."

There was a long silence. Then Dad answered in a low voice I could barely hear, "I know. That's what I've done, but I've paid. Elsa and the girls left me. They discovered my sin."

"Reverend Becker, I don't understand what you're talking about and it's really not any of my business, but I expect whatever's happened, Calvin will forgive you."

"I hope so. I know I don't deserve it."

The way Dad said this, so quiet, so sad, so beaten down, made me yell out, *"I do, Dad, I do forgive you!"*

I tore down the marble staircase, around the landing, and into the lobby.

Dad's face was white. I ran over, flung my arms around his neck, and hugged him. Dad blurted out in a rush, "I'm sorry, Calvin, will you forgive me?"

"Yes."

"Oh, Calvin! Happy birthday, boy!"

Dad burst into tears and so did Jennifer, but I wasn't able to cry. I felt like someone watching other people, not like I was the one this was happening to. It was as if I had become two people, one that things were happening to, the other a mere observer who felt nothing more than a mild curiosity at the events unfolding around him. One part of me hugged Dad while he cried, but the other part crossed the lobby and stood, arms folded, head to one side, and watched.

Dad cried louder and louder and clutched harder and harder at the boy. I saw Jennifer stop crying and step back to watch. She began to look dismayed on behalf of the boy who was stuck in his father's weeping embrace. I saw the boy try to pull away. But Dad hung on grimly and kept saying, "I'm sorry." The boy stopped saying, "It's all right, Dad," and began to wrestle to get free.

Then the detached part of me sat down on the gray leather lobby armchair to watch the father and son sway back and forth, as if locked in combat. It seemed like they'd be at it a long time, so I put my feet up on the chrome-and-glass coffee table. My mind began to wander. I started to think about where my sisters and mother were, what they had done with Grandmother; if my plan to save her was working. Someone took my hand and held it. Her hand was dry and cool. I took a deep breath. There seemed to be a faint smell of gardenia. She tightened her grip. I opened my eyes.

I was looking into a beautiful face. At first I thought it was Jennifer in disguise. Then the face smiled. It belonged to a nun.

It was not nearly so bad as after I woke up when they set my leg the first time. This time I didn't vomit.

The nun smiled. I squeezed her hand. She squeezed back. We sat quietly for a moment.

I spoke the first thought that floated into my head.

"I deserved to break it again."

She stroked my hair.

"Tell me about it, *mon enfant.*"

"I deserved it because of my sin."

"Oui?"

"I was thinking about a naked woman."

"Yes?"

"That's when I broke my leg the first time. It was nakedness that did it. I guess it happened again because I still had some punishment coming to me, hadn't suffered enough or something."

The nun kept stroking my hair.

"My child, God does not punish us. We punish ourselves. God loves us."

"Like the verse 'All things work together for the good of those who love Him'?"

"Ah, you know *votre Bible. Très bien!*"

"God used a wheelchair as the instrument of his wrath."

The nun smiled and slowly shook her head.

"Who has filled your head with such folly?" I tried to remember who had. It took a moment.

"Dad. He's a minister."

"He is only human. No one can understand God. We are too small."

"But he's sovereign."

She smiled. "Who? *Votre papa?*"

"No, God."

"*Mais oui, mon petit,* he is sovereign but he is also love." The nun paused, seemed to be thinking. Then she asked me a question. "How can he be both things at once?"

"Both what?"

"Both sovereign and *amour*—love."

"I don't know."

"Ah, and nor do I, your papa, or any other priests know this. Not even the pope knows this."

The nun bent over, kissed my forehead, got up, and walked to the door. She turned. "If your leg is painful, press *le bouton.* I will come . . . even though you say you deserved to break it!"

When she shut the door I heard her laugh in the hall.

Chapter 39

FOUR DAYS AFTER THE PIN WAS PUT IN, the nuns woke me by wheeling in two new patients. One was an old peasant with a red face, a friendly, toothless smile, and both arms bandaged. He reminded me of Farmer Ruchet. The other was a boy, I think. He lay perfectly still. A tube came out of his bandages in the place where his nose was. Tubes snaked out from under his covers and fed into jars under the chipped, white enamel bed frame. I called him the Mystery Boy.

By the time visiting hour arrived, the Mystery Boy had woken up. I could hear muffled groaning coming from him as he shifted his feet. I don't think he could understand what the nun, who came in about every half hour to check on him, said. I called her the Swiss Nun as opposed to the one I called the Nice Nun, who had held my hand and who I never saw again after she sat with me when I came out of the ether.

The Swiss Nun said that when the bandages came off, the Mystery Boy's father wouldn't recognize him. It would be a lesson to him, serve him right for drinking a liter of wine with his lunch, then driving.

The Swiss Nun bossed the peasant, too. She said he was lazy. How else could he explain the fact that he had dozed and fallen under his threshing machine while he was fixing it? What sort of fool would do that? His injuries served him right. She hoped he had learned his lesson. Next time he came to the hospital, if he had done some foolish thing, some *bêtise*, he could expect no help from her.

When the peasant's fat, smelly wife visited him, she and the Swiss Nun berated him together. The farmer's wife agreed with everything the Swiss Nun said. "Listen to Sister," she admonished the peasant, "it will do you some good." Sister was right, why couldn't he leave the homemade apple vodka out of his morning coffee? How many times had she told him to leave it out?

"How many?"

"Many times," the squirming peasant mumbled.

"There! You see!" The peasant's wife nodded. Her double chins quivered with satisfaction at how right she was, how respectable, how Swiss, how correct in every way.

"*Pomme?*" exclaimed the Swiss Nun. "You mean he was drinking *pomme* in the *morning?*"

The peasant shifted uneasily. "Only with the coffee, to make me a little warmer."

The peasant's wife shook her finger. "I'll make you warmer!"

"What sort of an idiot runs a threshing machine when he's fixing it?"

"*This* sort of idiot!" The peasant's wife gave her cowering husband a hard poke in his striped pajama chest with her short red finger. "The kind of old fool who forgets to mend the machine in the spring and leaves it in everyone's way in the hay barn so he's got to move it in the middle of summer!"

"I said it was laziness that caused his accident!" said the Swiss Nun. "I said it all along!"

"Laziness *and* drunkenness!"

The Swiss Nun and the peasant's wife stood at the foot of the farmer's bed, arms folded, their bosoms heaving in a concert of righteous indignation. The peasant shrugged and glanced at me for support.

"Don't bother looking at that young fool!" said the Swiss Nun. "He's as big an idiot as you. Worse! He rebroke his leg, made us do our work all over again!"

When the Swiss Nun and peasant's wife left, I went back to worrying. Each day I got more preoccupied with my problem. I was useless, stuck in the hospital. How could I find out if Mom and Dr. Zwingli were even feeding Grandmother, let alone if the IVs were being administered, without letting Mom know that I knew they had decided not to treat Grandmother's pneumonia? I couldn't think of any way to contact Jean-Pierre, and of course I couldn't trust Rachael, let alone Janet, with my secret. The more I brooded, the more I realized I had to get home.

"Mom?"

"Yes, dear?"

"Is it true that Jesus was just a good man?"

"Calvin! Did the nuns say *that*?"

"I didn't know scientists had found explanations for all of Jesus' miracles, and discovered that they were just tricks. Mom, is it right that when the children of Israel crossed the Red Sea it was at a natural low point in the water, it wasn't really a miracle at all?"

Mom sprang to her feet and marched out of my ward.

A moment later I heard shouting. There were a lot of footsteps, then my door burst open. Mom, the Swiss Nun, and a doctor all came trooping in.

The Swiss Nun's face was red. Mom was pale. The doctor appeared agitated. The peasant turned his face to the wall and pretended to be asleep during the whole argument. The Mystery Boy groaned from time to time.

Mom's command of French was not very good. It got worse when she was excited. Mom was so upset she was vibrating.

"I will *not* allow my son to be deceived by Jesuits!"

"Elle est complètement folle." The Swiss Nun's winged hat flapped wildly as she spoke.

Mom turned to the doctor.

"What did that woman say?"

"La soeur she saying you not right in your minds."

"She has nerve after what she's done! I may be a fool for Christ but at least I have the honesty to openly proclaim my faith! She, *she pretends* she's a nurse, albeit dressed in that ridiculous hat, but all the while she's scheming to come between me and my child!"

The doctor wrung his hands. "*Mais, madame,* we do not know of wheech you speakings!"

"*C'est insupportable!*" muttered the Swiss Nun.

"What's that woman saying?"

"She says that it is insupportable to have false accusation made of her honoring."

Mom drew herself up.

"That poor, deluded woman in her silly hat can say what she wants, but you tell her that there are plenty of good and sufficient reasons to believe that the children of Israel *literally* crossed the Red Sea, and *not* where it was shallow! Besides, if it was so shallow how is it that the Egyptian army was swallowed up afterward when Moses stretched out his arms over the waters like God told him to? Tell her and her precious pope to explain *that!*"

The doctor tried to translate. Halfway through his hopelessly tangled explanation, the Swiss Nun smiled bitterly, tapped the side of her head, turned, and marched out of the ward. The wings on her hat flapped furiously. She slammed the heavy door behind her. The Mystery Boy groaned and the peasant shifted uneasily.

"You are insulting the staff with not true sayings, not true at all."

"She left because she has no answers for the plain facts, for the *biblical evidence!* She may be able to cast the shadow of papal superstition over some innocent child's mind but she has no answers for the *truth!* That's what!"

"Mom," I whispered, "she said that the pope and Jesus are equal. That tradition is more important than the Bible."

"*That's it!* He doesn't spend another night in this Roman slough!"

"*Mais, madame,* be reasonable, eet ees not posseeble 'ee should leaving. . . . What ees *slough?*"

"Read *Pilgrim's Progress!*"

"Comment?"

"If you force me to keep him here I shall call the American con-
sulate in Geneva! *We have religious freedom in America!"*

"Mais, madame! Ce n'est pas a question of religion but of *médica-
ments,* of medications. *Nom de Dieu!"*

"The Lord can effect a healing if he so chooses."

"C'est vraiment intolérable!"

The doctor squeezed his chin as if he expected that to solve his
problem. He was distraught. It seemed to be a stalemate. No one
spoke for a moment. I saw Mom beginning to look a little uncertain,
to chew her lip. I thought I'd better do something to make her
harden her godly resolve.

"Mom, it's not so bad, one of the nice nuns prays with me at night.
Last night she prayed to Mary that my leg would get better. It made me
feel full of unspeakable joy when she prayed. I think Mary heard us."

Mom rounded furiously on the doctor. *"He's coming home with me
tomorrow and that's final!"*

The Mystery Boy groaned loudly. The doctor stared at Mom, then
at me, gave his chin a last desperate squeeze, spread out his hands,
and shrugged. "Very well, you are a foolish woman, but if you een-
sisting, then very well. I will discharging 'eem een *le matin,* you must
be arranging of your own transportings. It is entirely your own
responsibility, *Madame.* I take no responsibility any longer for hees
feet! I will notify the proper autorities of your negligence. I am
washing my fingers of you—"

"Hands, you mean you are washing your hands of me."

"Exactement! I fling you my 'ands!"

"Just like Pontius Pilate!"

The doctor slammed the door. Mom quivered for a moment, then
turned to me. "You did the right thing," she said. Then she burst into
tears.

Chapter 40

AFTER MOM LEFT, the nuns wouldn't look at me. No one did. I seemed to embarrass them. I can't say I blamed them for being mad at me after all the lies I told.

That night I lay awake, worrying about my problem, mulling over the events of the day, making plans. I needed more medication for Grandmother. I had mixed every bit of penicillin into the saline solution. Farmer Ruchet usually gave his pigs a ten-day course of *pénicilline vétérinaire*. Grandmother had only had four or five, as best as I could figure it.

On the bedside table between me and the peasant, the nuns kept his medications in a stainless-steel box. I had heard the doctor explain to him that his arms had become infected. The peasant was taking a big dose of antibiotics, in pill form, at each meal.

I checked the peasant's breathing. It was slow and rhythmic. I quietly reached out and opened the lid of the metal box on the night stand. I made sure not to knock over the farmer's urine bottle. He had used it just before falling asleep. I could not see it, but I could tell by the smell it was full.

I opened the lid of the box and groped inside. I put my hand right on a heavy glass bottle. I lifted the bottle out, making sure not to bang the side of the box. I carefully emptied the pills onto the sheet covering my chest. I counted out twenty-five and put the rest back.

I knew if I stole them all, let alone the whole bottle, the nuns would notice right away. By only taking some, I hoped that I had a chance of getting the pills home before anyone would find out they were missing.

When they dressed me in the morning I'd be stripped of my hospital gown. The nuns would notice if I had twenty-five pills clutched in my hands. If I put them with my things in the nightstand drawer, Mom would see them when she packed my bag in the morning. I couldn't think of a good place to hide them. I tried my colored-pencil box but there was no room. If I left the pencils out, Mom would put them away and discover the pills.

I looked at the statue of Mary glimmering in the moonlight. "Hail Mary, full of grace, please help me to save Grandma."

Mary answered right away. Not that I heard a voice but I definitely got a clear idea.

I pulled a little damp cotton from around my sweaty leg and wedged the pills into the space between my thigh and the plaster cast. I looked up at the statue and whispered, "Thank you." Then I closed my eyes.

Chapter 41

I WAS IN HIGH SPIRITS and laden with penicillin. Everyone seemed happy to see me. The sky was cloudless, the sun hot, the air cool. The mountains loomed clear and beautiful. Every bird in the forest was singing.

Rachael and Janet made a big "Welcome Home, Calvin" banner and hung it over the rail of the top balcony. Mom, Dad, The Ladies, Jean-Pierre, Dick and Jane Keegan, Janet, Rachael, and some of the young people trooped out to help the taxi driver carry me to my bedroom. I could smell fresh-baked cake. Mom said that I had won a great spiritual victory against the Roman hospital.

After I ate a piece of cake and drank a glass of milk, I asked Mom if I could visit Grandmother.

"Why dear, that's awfully sweet of you but I think you'd better rest."

"Mom, I've been praying for her. How is she?"

"Well, it's strange, darling, but she seems to be making a remarkable recovery. Dr. Zwingli says he's never seen such a thing."

"I'd like to see her to, ah, tell her how God answered my prayers for her. She might be more open to the Things of The Lord—it might be an opportunity to witness to her."

Mom smiled. "I think our accident has been a source of spiritual growth!"

Grandmother's breathing sounded clearer. She was sleeping when Mom wheeled me into her room. Mom whispered, "I'll just leave you here. When she wakes up you can share the burden God has laid on your heart for her." Mom tiptoed out.

I lifted myself up in my wheelchair and peered over the bed to see if there were any full IV bottles left in the box sitting below Grandmother's bedside table. They were all empty but one. I sighed with relief. It looked like Grandmother had had a good dose.

Grandmother turned and opened her eyes. She reached out to her bedside table and fumbled for her glasses. Her giant eyes blinked behind the thick lenses.

"Just as I'm startin' to feel better they bring *you* back. Ya sure are a moron! Ya get run over by a retard, an' then ya go on an' bust it again all by yourself! You're the one that oughta be in a goddamned home!"

"Hi, Grandma."

"I thought ya was suppose ta be in the hospital?"

"I was, but I came home to see how you are."

"I bet ya did!"

"How are you?"

"I was doin' good till I woke up to see your dumb little kisser starin' at me. What d'ya want anyhow?"

"I told you I just wanted to know how you're feeling."

"Well, I'm talkin', ain't I?"

"That's good. When did they stop giving you intravenous fluids?"

"None of ya goddamned business!"

"I need to know."

"Oh, now the little shit thinks he can boss me around. Well, I got news for you, I ain't gonna answer none of your goddamned questions!"

Grandmother turned her head away. I sat quietly pondering the situation, staring out of Grandmother's window at the huge black ravens circling high above our mountainside. I counted the ravens. There were twenty. Something must have died in the forest. The far-off sound of cowbells made me feel sleepy. I think I dozed a little. An idea jerked me wide awake.

"Grandmother, has the food been as bad as usual?"

"Ya got 'at right. Your mom shoulda spent more time learnin' to cook an' less time prayin'."

"What's she been feeding you?"

"All her fancy-schmancy stuff. Last night I said I'd like a nice piece a meat loaf with some stewed tomatoes. She made some goddamned sauce an' spread it all over it. I made 'em scrape it afore I'd take a bite. I could still taste it, though. Phooey!"

That night Grandmother and I were sitting side by side in her room. She was propped up in bed. I was next to her in my wheelchair. Mom said it was nice that "both of our invalids can eat together." We had trays on our laps. The pungent smell of liquid manure poured through the open window. The farmer who owned the field below the road must have finished the first hay cutting. He always fertilized to boost the growth of the second crop.

Grandmother spit her spinach out.

"Tastes like *shit!*"

"It's the smell of liquid manure."

"No, it ain't. I can smell that shit okay but I'm not talking 'bout that shit, I'm talking 'bout this here goddamned *shit!*"

Grandmother jabbed her fork into a mound of gooey creamed spinach.

I decided I'd sprinkle less antibiotic on the next course.

"Mine's okay."

"Then you eat it, ya brat."

When Janet brought up the second course I had more pills ready. I had crushed them to powder between two spoons and the powder was in my hand. When Janet passed me Grandmother's plate I opened my hand and sprinkled the powder over her corned-beef hash and poached egg.

"Even *your* mom can't screw up hash," said Grandmother. She took a bite and made a sour face. "I'll be damned, I guess she can."

"Why?"

" 'Cause it's bitter! How'd she do it? I wonder. She sure is stupid! Ya know that?"

"Looks fine to me."

"Well, it ain't!"

Grandma must have been hungry. Bitter tasting or not, she ate most of the hash, even though she kept muttering insults about Mom's cooking between mouthfuls.

When she finished she started yawning. "Reach over an' pull one of them pillows out, will ya? I'm real tired."

Grandmother lay back and went fast asleep without another word. I sat awhile, but she only settled into a deeper sleep, so I left her room and wheeled myself to the top of the stairs to call for Rachael to come and get the dishes.

After Rachael tiptoed out of Grandmother's room with the tray, she paused in the hall outside my bedroom door. "Calvin, how come you wanted to be with her all day?"

"What do you mean?"

"Oh, come on, you know. You've been hanging around all day since you came back. What's going on?"

"What's so strange about that? I'm up here alone, stuck in my wheelchair. Why shouldn't I want to visit her?"

"You know why. No one in their right mind would choose to visit Grandmother. What are you up to?"

"I want to witness to her."

"Oh, come off it."

"You sound like Janet."

"Janet's pretty smart."

"She's mean."

"She knows enough to know you're not telling the truth. So do I."

"So *she's* the one who's putting un-Christ-like doubts in your mind!" I tried to laugh, to make it sound like a joke. Rachael didn't smile.

"Neither one of us believe you want to witness to her. In fact we know you don't."

"How?"

"We took turns and stood outside the door practically all afternoon listening. You hardly said a word to her. *That's how!*"

"It's not very nice to spy. She was resting."

"So why did you sit there?"

"I told you. Anyway, when I'm not sharing the Gospel, I'm praying."

"Why lie to me? What are you up to?"

I lowered my voice.

"Rachael, can you keep a secret?"

"You know I can."

"Please don't tell Mom."

"If it's not something disgusting, dangerous, or degenerate, I won't."

"Rachael, I'm waiting for Grandmother to die."

Rachael's voice went up an octave. "What on earth do you *mean?*"

"I want to watch, to see if her soul's visible as it comes out of her body, if I can see anything, you know, supernatural."

"*Calvin!* That's *horrible!*"

"I just want to know."

"But it's *too awful,* it's *so morbid!*"

"Well, you asked, and you promised not to tell. It's not dangerous or sinful, plus I did witness to her a little, anyway."

Rachael stood looking at me for a full minute.

"Calvin?"

"Yes?"

"There's something wrong with you.'

"I know. Will you pray for me?"

"Oh, shut up!"

Chapter 42

THE WEATHER TURNED COOL. The morning was gray. A light drizzle was falling. The smell of liquid manure had faded in the night.

I was worried Grandmother would relapse. So far I had only been able to give her one pill successfully. The peasant in the hospital took two doses with each meal. So I put six ground-up pills into Grandmother's breakfast coffee. She took it black.

Grandma sipped her coffee and never said a word. I felt triumphant. I had finally found the means to medicate her properly now that she was conscious and off the IV. The coffee masked the flavor perfectly.

As soon as Grandmother finished slurping down her scalding coffee, she dozed. She hadn't eaten any of her Cream of Wheat. This worried me. She couldn't live on coffee and penicillin alone; she needed to build up her strength. I leaned forward in my wheelchair and poked her in the ribs with my spoon.

"*Wake up!* Eat your breakfast!"

Grandmother lay breathing deeply, her mouth open, her lowers sliding rhythmically in and out, a single thread of saliva trembling between her parted lips.

"Grandmother! You can't be *that* tired, you just woke up!"

I shook her shoulder. Grandmother eased down a little further in her bed. The strand of saliva broke. Her tray began to tip over. Milk trickled out of her bowl and soaked into her blanket.

"*Grandmother!* Sit up, you're spilling your Cream of Wheat!"

I got scared. It looked as if Grandmother had taken a sudden turn for the worse. I set my tray on the foot of her bed and wheeled down the hall.

Dad's opera—*Tosca*, I think—was up full blast. I had to wheel myself all the way into his room and shout before I was able to get his attention.

"Dad! Something's wrong with Grandmother! She's asleep!"

Dad looked up from the Bible he was copying references out of. *"Sleep's good for her! Let her be!"*

"Dad! It's not like that, I can't wake her, she fell asleep in the middle of breakfast!"

Dad slowly walked over to his dresser and turned off his record player. "I better come see."

Grandma didn't stir.

Dad turned to me. "You stay here. I'm going to get Elsa."

Mom was all the way down in the living room giving the young women her talk on how to have a Christ-centered marriage. No boys were allowed to attend Mom's talk for girls. That way, Mom said, the boys wouldn't be tempted by hearing about things meant only for the ears of chaste young women, and the girls would open up and not be afraid to share their hearts, their doubts and fears concerning marriage and the Physical Things.

Mom loved giving this particular talk. That's probably why it took Dad so long to pry her loose and get her to come upstairs. Finally I heard footsteps, then voices. Mom sounded annoyed.

"Really, it's *too bad*. I wish she'd make up her mind!" Mom marched past me down the hall and into Grandmother's room.

A moment later she came back out and said, "I think this is it." She walked down the stairs and dialed Dr. Zwingli.

Grandmother was dying again. Mom said it was the right thing for all of us to gather around her bed. Janet whispered, "I guess *you're* pleased! Now you'll see it happen!"

I didn't look at Rachael to give her the dirty look she deserved for telling on me. I wanted to be sure to pick up any signs between Dr. Zwingli and Mom about what they planned to do, or not do, with Grandmother. I could always yell at Rachael later. The doctor listened to Grandmother's chest. No one seemed to mind that I was watching as he pushed up her nightgown and exposed her breasts. She was so withered that you couldn't tell whether she was a man or a woman.

"I do not understand it," said Dr. Zwingli as he readjusted Grandmother's nightgown. "She seems to have gone into some sort of coma." He looked in Grandmother's eyes with a flashlight. "I can only say she has probably had a stroke. It's not the pneumonia—her lungs are clear."

"What shall we do?" Mom queried.

"Well, if she were younger I might suggest she be moved to the hospital for observation. As it is . . ."

Mom stepped forward.

"I think she'll be more comfortable here—what do you think, Ralph?"

"Well, I don't think there's any point moving her. After all, we thought we had lost her last week, now this. No, I think we should just let her rest."

While the doctor was putting away his things Mom asked, "Dr. Zwingli, how should we proceed with her, ah, care . . . at this . . . ah, point?"

"We will resume our prior method of treatment. It's a question of hydration and comfort. I will call the visiting nurse with instructions to keep her hydrated as before." Dr. Zwingli shook his head. "What a bewildering case."

Chapter 43

NEW IV BOTTLES ARRIVED with the visiting nurse the next morning. She slammed the door when she arrived. She was annoyed at being called out on August 1, the Swiss national holiday. Usually I would have been down in the village listening to the band practicing for the parade, or up on the slope behind the village watching the school-teacher and some of the farmers stack piles of brushwood into an enormous pile for that night's bonfire. When darkness fell, it and thousands of other beacons would be lit all over Switzerland, as they had been hundreds of years before to warn of invaders. But on August 1, 1967, I had weightier matters to concern me than bonfires and Swiss democracy. Besides, I still couldn't walk.

The nurse hooked Grandmother up to a new IV bottle. It took her six tries to find a vein. When she was gone, I took the five bottles still in the box and wheeled into the bathroom. I pulled the remaining pills out of the top of my cast and put them into a water glass. The water went gray.

I knew what a stroke was. Rachael had read *Medicine for Young Minds* to me several times. I knew antibiotics wouldn't do any good in mending a burst blood vessel in Grandmother's brain. But I also knew they wouldn't do any harm. Grandmother was still immobilized, subject to recurrent respiratory infections. Maybe more penicillin would at least prevent complications.

I opened the bathroom cupboard, where Mom kept her bottle of Shackley Vitamin Supplements. I hooked the vitamins off the shelf with the toilet-bowl brush. I took out about a dozen pills. I added these to the antibiotics and stirred them up with the handle of Dad's toothbrush, until they dissolved into a smelly yellow-gray mess. I knew it was unsterile. The answer to the germs was in Dad's toilet bag.

Dad had a travel toilet bag packed with a razor, shampoo, aspirin, aftershave lotion, toothbrush, cream for his athlete's foot, and other necessities. He kept his bag on the lower shelf of the cupboard. His regular toilet articles were in the medicine cabinet over the sink. Dad prided himself on how fast he could pack. Mom took a lot longer. She used so many toilet articles it was out of the question that she should keep a separate travel set. Her toiletries took up two whole shelves in the cupboard and most of the medicine cabinet.

In addition to Mom's makeup, creams, brushes, combs, and ribbons littering the shelves, there were big plastic bags of sanitary napkins. They filled the bottom of the bathroom cupboard. Mom and my sisters had a good supply laid in.

When I was little, about seven or eight, I used to pull the napkins out and play with them. Janet came into the bathroom one day and found me lining them up on the floor, end to end, to make a pink, fluffy train. She ran out yelling for Mom to do something. Mom made me put them all back in the bag. Afterward she took me to my room and explained about God's wonderful plan for women, how the Precious Eggs get washed out every month until God, in his sovereignty, chooses one to be a baby.

On the shelf above where Mom kept the pads, Dad stored his permanently packed traveling toilet bag. The bag contained the item I planned to use to sterilize Grandmother's vitamin-antibiotic medication.

Mom gave Dad this thing at Christmas. It was a metal coil, about the size of a dinner spoon. It had a red plastic handle attached to an electric cord. When you plugged it in, the coil heated.

Using this water heater, Dad could make himself tea, even instant

Knorr soup, in hotel rooms, for free. When he was traveling, he hung the device into a glass or mug and boiled water. Then he would take the thing out, unplug it, and mix in his soup, a tea bag, or instant coffee. Dad said it was a real money saver.

That's why I didn't worry about the bacteria from my cast. I hooked the money saver over the edge of Dad's toothbrush glass, then plugged it in and waited. Through the open window I could hear the village band in the distance, as discordant as ever, striking up the national anthem. The music petered out, then began again. I could picture farmer Ruchet gasping for breath as he played his huge dented tuba, face red, cheeks distended.

Tiny bubbles began to form on the coil. The plastic handle started to get warm. After another minute or two I set the glass on the edge of the sink. It was too hot to hold. The water boiled so hard some splashed out. I let it boil a good five minutes.

I took out the coil, rinsed it off, and put it back in Dad's travel toilet bag. I added some of the mixture to each jar.

I was about to unlock the door when someone tried the handle.

"Who's in there?" asked Janet.

"It's me."

"What are you doing?"

"What do you think?"

"Don't get smart with me. Hurry up!"

I couldn't very well wheel out with the box of Grandmother's IV bottles on my lap. I decided to hide them on the bottom shelf of the bathroom cupboard, under the bags of sanitary napkins.

Before I put the jars under the napkins I glanced into the wastepaper basket below the bathroom sink. I needed to check and see if there were any little packages in it.

I remember exactly when I found out all about what Mom and my sisters did with their Secret Helpers. It was when I was nine years old. We had just returned from our vacation in Portofino. I was unpacking my snorkel and mask when Rachael burst into tears outside of my room. It turned out she had tried to flush a sanitary napkin down the toilet. It was the first time she had been off the roof. It blocked the pipe.

When the toilet overflowed, Dad demanded to know what fool had blocked the pipe. Rachael denied she had done it, even though she had just come out of the bathroom. Dad yelled, "Well then, let's find out *who else* is off the roof and stupid enough to do such a tom-fool thing!"

Since Janet and Mom were not off the roof and since the girl young people had their female problems in the downstairs bathroom, Rachael finally admitted her guilt. That's when she ran down the hall and burst into tears.

I stuck my head out of my bedroom door in time to see Mom put her arm around Rachael's shoulders and say, "It's all part of growing up, dear. *Anyone* can make that mistake! What I always do is wrap my soiled little Secret Helpers in toilet tissue and place them in the wastepaper basket."

That was why, before I put the IV jars down on the napkin shelf, I checked the wastepaper basket. If Janet, Rachael, or Mom were off the roof, the first thing they would do was open up the cupboard and get out a Secret Helper. Then they would see the IV bottles.

The wastepaper basket only had some used Kleenex in it and a matted ball of hair from the bathtub drain. I rolled back over to the cupboard, opened the door, placed the jars on the shelf, and put the two big economy-size bags of napkins on them, one on top and one in front. Janet banged on the door.

"Have you died in there or what?"

"No, I'm just coming out."

After Janet used the bathroom, I wheeled back and retrieved the box. Grandmother never stirred as I replaced the almost empty IV jar with a new one, adjusted the regulator, tightened the wing nut, and wheeled back down the hall.

In the distance there were sounds of muffled explosions. Some of the village boys must have been letting off a round of firecrackers in anticipation of that night's festivities.

As the sound of the fireworks died away my door opened. Dad barged in. He looked angry. Mom was standing behind him, chewing her handkerchief.

"Calvin, I want you to tell us the truth."

"About what, Dad?"

"About this." Dad held out a letter.

"I'm sure it's just that awful nun trying to get back at—"

Dad interrupted my mother. "Calvin, yesterday a letter came from the administration of the Monthey hospital. I thought it was a bill, so I only just opened it now."

"I don't understand what you want me to tell the truth about?"

"The people at the hospital say after you were discharged, the nun in your ward found a large quantity of sleeping pills missing."

"I'm sure—"

"*Elsa, please!*"

I took a deep breath. "Dad, I didn't take any pills. Why would I?"

"Exactly, Ralph! It's ridiculous!"

I took another deep breath. "Dad, are you sure they said *sleeping pills?*"

Dad looked at the letter. "They say that in a box of medications for the patient next to you, there were two bottles, one with antibiotics, and one containing *des narcotiques puissant,* highly narcotic sleeping pills, powerful drugs, very dangerous. They need to know what happened to them."

"Dad, I *promise,* I have no idea."

Dad looked hard at me. I met his gaze steadily. At last he said, "I believe you, boy. I can always tell when you're speaking the truth. Well, it's a mystery. I can hardly believe a nun, no matter how depraved, would deliberately do something like this."

Mom looked horrified. "I wonder what those awful Jesuits did with them?"

"Elsa, call Dr. Zwingli and ask his advice on how to respond."

Mom and Dad left the room, but not before Mom held me close, kissed me, and whispered, "You're a good boy!"

Chapter 44

ALL THAT DAY I TRIED TO GET INTO GRANDMOTHER'S ROOM, to undo the damage. But each time I wheeled up the hall, someone was there. Janet, Mom, or Rachael kept asking me what I wanted. After the seventh time or so that I answered I was just checking on Grandmother, Rachael said, "Look, we'll call you if she starts dying! Okay?"

The first of August was a terrible day. By late afternoon I was beginning to think God had predestined Grandmother to die after all, that the idea Mary gave me was a kind of mean practical joke. When Mom poked her head around my door to say good night, Janet was still sitting with Grandmother. It was the *one and only day* she was attentive to Grandmother in all the time she was sick! I tried to stay awake, to get into Grandmother's room after everyone was asleep, but Mom and Dad stayed up for what seemed like half the night.

The next morning I woke up with a terrific jolt. Smoke lingered in the still dawn air from the holiday bonfire. But I was uninterested in the fact that I had missed the festivities of the night before. I had a terrible sinking feeling in my stomach. At first I couldn't remember why I had woken up feeling so awful. Then it hit me. I struggled into my wheelchair.

Everyone was asleep. Grandmother's door was wide open. Mercifully, she was alone. Her face was tinged with the pink glow from the sun rising over the Dents du Midi. She looked younger than usual, but she also looked dead. I thought the worst had happened. She seemed not to be breathing. It seemed as if Dr. Zwingli and Mom had won. Then she took a small breath.

I hurriedly wheeled my chair around to the side of her bed, shut the drip regulator, and lowered the IV pole. I took off the jar and tipped it right side up, unscrewed the top, pulled back Grandmother's sheet, and poured the liquid, about a quarter of a jar full, between Grandmother's legs, onto the square, green foam rubber pad that was supposed to soak up her little accidents, as Mom called them.

I screwed the top back on the jar and put it back so it would look like it had emptied naturally. I took the box containing the remaining IV jars, put it on my lap, wheeled myself out of Grandmother's room and into the bathroom.

I locked the door behind me, unscrewed each jar and poured the vitamin-sleeping pill mixture down the sink. When the jars were empty I filled them with tap water and screwed the lids back on. Then I put them back. I returned to my room and lay down on my bed. I closed my eyes.

The time passed so slowly I was tempted to go out and wait in the hall, even to creep up the stairs to the dining terrace, to see if Jennifer and her parents had finished eating. I decided not to for fear Lucrezia might see me. She'd shout *"Calvino!"* and hug me. Her mother would come out of the *pensione* kitchen, wiping off her plump hands on her apron, and make a fuss. Jennifer and her parents would hear the commotion. My surprise would be ruined. Besides they'd all ask where the rest of the family was.

Someone was bouncing a ball in the alley below Jennifer's window. I heard shouts and squeals from the beach. The bus pulled up, then pulled out again. I could tell it was heading toward Portofino because the driver sounded the horn. (The first big curve came up right away.) A speedboat revved its engine as it accelerated out of the bay. I wondered if a water-skier was being pulled behind it.

Then the door opened and Jennifer walked in from the bright sunlit hall. She closed the door behind her.

Before her eyes adjusted to the shade of her room, I said, "Hi, Jennifer."

Chapter 45

GOD CHANGED HIS MIND, or maybe this was how he had planned it all along; maybe I outwitted him or perhaps Mary helped me after all. In any case, Dr. Zwingli said that he had never seen a stroke victim make such a sudden, complete, dramatic recovery. Mom told him there was a reason: God. Dr. Zwingli said he believed it but hurriedly added, "I still have not finished reading John's gospel."

That night, Mom told everyone at prayer meeting how the Lord had healed Grandmother in answer to her prayers, in order that Grandmother might yet have time to repent.

Chapter 46

MASTER CALVIN BECKER

L'ARCHE

CHALET TULIPS

TROIS-TORRENTS-SUR-MONTHEY

VALAIS

SWITZERLAND

JENNIFER BAZLINTON

1 HARROW COURT

LONDON W1

ENGLAND

August 14, 1967

Dear Twit,

Counting the days. *Buon Viaggio!*

Love, J.

A few weeks after Grandmother recovered, I received a postcard. It had a picture of a horse on it. Mom read the card to me when she brought my lunch. I didn't even have the heart to dictate an answer. There was no point telling Jennifer we weren't going to Italy.

August 20 was fast approaching. Every evidence of midsummer made me sad. The beech trees at the edge of the forest were a mass of fluttering gray-green leaves. They made me feel like crying. I could hear birds singing as they hopped from branch to branch. I hated them. The mountains seemed to grow, become larger as the last of the snow melted, leaving nothing but gray rock jutting into pale blue sky. I wanted to blow them up. In two days, August 20, Jennifer would arrive at Paraggi as she had each year since I could remember.

Mom handed me the card and smiled sympathetically. "Oh dear," she said.

"But now that my cast's off I can walk."

"I know this is hard for you but there's nothing to be done."

"Couldn't I go alone for a few days?"

"Don't be ridiculous, darling!"

"But we've *never* missed our vacation!"

Mom bent over, kissed me, then left the room.

"Grandma?"

"Huh?"

Grandma peered at her paper, scissors poised, then asked, "What's an MG?"

"It's a kind of English car." I hooked my cane over the end of her bed and sat down.

"Says here they hit a hearse. Had a drum set in the backseat. His head were sliced right off by a flyin' cymbal! She were killed by a snare drum. I ask ya! He were always one to fool with 'em Limey cars an' drums. I warned 'em!"

"When you're done cutting out those names I want to tell you something."

"Uh-huh. Never thought I'd be around when Cathie and Danny were gone. A drum set, what a nutcase!"

I adjusted the cushion under my leg. It ached a little.

"Grandma?"

"Yup."

"You're not a believer."

"Don't go startin' all that!"

"I'm not going to witness to you."

"Thank you, Jesus!"

"The reason I mentioned it is because I want to tell you a secret and I want you to swear on something that you'll never tell, no matter what. How can you swear on something if you don't believe in anything?"

Grandmother peered at me over the top of her glasses and smiled. "Why, you tricky li'l shit!"

"I'm serious. If you tell I'll probably get killed or something."

"What did ya do now? Cut off another kid's dick?"

"First you have to swear on something you believe in."

Grandmother tapped her yellow fingernails lightly on the obituary page. "I swear on these here names from the *Philadelphia Inquirer.*"

I sat a minute getting up my courage. I took a deep breath.

"Grandma?"

"Yup."

"I'm not telling you this so you'll thank me, but because you have to take care of yourself. I can't think how to arrange it except to tell you the truth so you can take precautions. That way they won't let you die. At least you'll have a chance."

Grandmother grinned. "I told ya not to memorize all them god-damned Bible verses. Now ya ain't right in your head!"

"I'm smart enough for you. I saved your life."

"It don't figure. Ya still seem pretty regular but your brains is melted to shit, boy. Ya musta caught spastic polio germs from next door. I warned ya!"

Grandmother shook her head in mock sympathy.

"Remember how you were asleep?"

"I remember wakin' up."

"I put sleeping pills in your IV bottles because I was saving your life with antibiotics since they were letting you die." Grandma's expression changed. She stared at me through her thick, smudged lenses. She slowly laid her paper and scissors aside.

"Pshaw, boy, ya *are* crazy."

"No, I'm not, Grandma. I'm not crazy. I *did* save you with chicken medicine, *pénicilline vétérinaire;* it worked on your pneumonia, just like it does with chickens and pigs. They were letting you die, just keeping you comfortable."

Grandmother's eyes bulged.

"What the hell are ya sayin'?" she yelled.

"*Shhhh!* I'm saying that I've got to leave but I've got a plan to keep you alive in case you get sick while I'm gone. I may never come back."

Grandmother stared at me. Her pale eyes blinked slowly, her mouth worked. Her uppers and lowers slid in and out. For once she was at a loss for words.

"I put medication into your IV bottles. That's when you got better."

"Why ya—" Grandmother started to speak, but I held up my hand.

"Dr. Zwingli and Mom decided not to treat your pneumonia, just make you comfortable. I wanted you to live, so I used the veterinary medicine we keep for the chickens—antibiotics. It worked, that's why you're sitting here talking."

Grandmother blinked, shook her head slowly, and whistled under her breath.

"Why are ya sayin' alla this?"

"Because like I said, I'm leaving and I can't think what else to do to keep you alive except tell you the truth."

Grandmother sat silent a long while. She sighed.

"I sure don't blame ya for goin'. I wish I could walk. I'd go with ya! You're takin' after your grandpop. Did ya know he run away ta sea when he were twelve?"

I shook my head.

"Well, he did!" There was another silence. Then she seemed to explode. "I ain't surprised. 'Em two-faced lyin' *parasites!* 'Em *bastards!* 'Em no-good sneakin' missionary *insects!* After all the goddamned money I give 'em for the household expenses an' they wouldn't even buy me some *stinkin' pills!*"

Grandmother's lower lip and chin started to tremble. I reached out and took her hand. It felt as dry as a chicken's claw. I had never held it before. I squeezed. She squeezed back.

"You won't tell on me, will you?"

Grandmother rounded on me furiously. "What do ya think, ya li'l shit? What do ya take me for? I swore on the goddamned paper, didn't I?"

Grandma yanked her hand away, wiped her tears, grabbed me by the hair, tugged me down, and gave me a hard kiss on the mouth. I had no idea what to do. I had never seen Grandmother touch anybody, let alone kiss them. Grandmother pushed me back.

"*Shit!*" she said, turning away.

"I've got to tell you the plan, Grandma."

"Buncha assholes!"

"Will you listen to me?"

"No, I gotta train to catch! What else can I do, ya li'l shit?"

"You've got to get saved, Grandma. You've got to accept Jesus and tell Mom you've wasted your life and you want her to come up and give you Bible studies, and all, to catch up. Say you want her to help you to restore the years the locusts have eaten, say you know it's late in the day, but like the thief on the cross, you hope it's not too late for you."

"*Bullshit!*"

"If you want to live you'll follow my plan."

"Jesus Christ!"

"Yes, but not like that. Say you want her to disciple you in the little time you have left, and that the reason you want to know Jesus is because of how you've seen him shining out in her life, how you've seen her face glow when she talks about the Lord, how all those years you've been bad and were persecuting her and all, you've secretly admired her faith, how you want to be like her, and how you want her to teach you so you can live a life pleasing to the Lord and have a marvelous new chapter of your life unfold and be a thread in Mom and God's tapestry!"

"I'd rather die!" Grandmother shuddered and started to gasp for breath.

"Grandma, it only takes about half an hour a day to be a Christian! If you quit swearing at the young people and tell everyone who comes by how you've accepted Jesus, because of Mom's witness, Mom'll make Dr. Zwingli keep you alive *forever!* You want to live, don't you?"

Grandma shook her head slowly from side to side, trying to get her breath.

"Not that bad, I don't!"

"Well, I want you to live!"

After I said that I kind of surprised myself because I started to cry. Grandmother reached out and took my hand until I stopped. Then we sat and stared out the open window for a while. The birds twittered in the larch tree. Fleecy white clouds drifted across the sky, driven by the warm summer breeze blowing over the Dents du Midi.

Suddenly Grandmother grinned. *"You got fuckin' nerve!"*

It was her way of saying thanks.

I smiled back. The way she said it was a real compliment, like we were old friends.

"C'mon, Grandma, practice, repeat after me: 'Elsa, I want to ask Jesus into my heart.' C'mon, Grandma."

"I don't want no Jew livin' in my chest!"

"Grandmother!"

"Aw right, aw right."

"C'mon, say it."

Grandma slid her lowers all the way out a couple of times then sucked them in. "Elsa, I want to ask Jesus into my heart . . . ya bitch!"

"Grandmother! This is *not* a game!"

"Aw right! Aw right! Elsa, I want to ask Jesus into my heart!"

"Now we're cooking! Praise Jesus!"

"Go to hell!"

Chapter 47

I HADN'T BEEN ABLE TO HELP JEAN-PIERRE relieve his animal desires while I had my cast on. He was desperate. But we needed a new place to hide. The day after I explained my plan to Grandmother, I walked downstairs for the first time without my cane and discovered that Dick had given the hedge its end-of-summer clipping. You could look through the branches into the tunnel between the trunks.

Once, years before, while looking for an escaped hamster, I had climbed under our basement staircase and discovered a secret room formed by the crawl space below the landing. That's where I took Jean-Pierre when he ran up to me and begged me to help him.

I opened the broom closet. We crawled under the water tank. It was hard to get Jean-Pierre into the secret room. He crawled with sudden, jerky movements. I had to inch along next to him, keeping one hand on the top of his head. When he convulsed, my hand acted like a helmet; got between his skull and the underside of the metal water tank.

I brought a candle stub and stuck it on the steel beam that supported the far end of the tank. Before I lit the candle I crawled back and shut the door. My leg ached a little.

When I tried to strike a light I found that the matchbox was damp. I had carelessly set it down on the beam, next to the underside of the water tank. While I'd helped Jean-Pierre pull his pants down the matches had soaked up a lot of moisture from the condensation that puddled on the beam.

When I tried to light the candle the match head smeared. As I opened the box to get another I heard the wooden matches scatter on the floor. I knelt down to pick them up and I struck my forehead on the end of the I beam. The blow didn't hurt much, but when I reached up and touched my forehead my hand got wet. I could feel blood running down my face.

"Why you not lighting *la bougie*? 'Urry up, Calvin!"

"Shut up, I've cut my head open."

" 'Ow 'ave you doing thees?"

"I don't know, I just have."

"Lighting *la bougie,* then we shall seeing."

"I've dropped the matches."

"Imbécile!"

"*Imbécile* yourself."

"Picking them up!"

"You pick them up! Anyway, they're wet."

"Go to opening *la porte* and we shall going out."

"I have to get something done about my head. I feel blood all over my face."

"We weell going out first!"

"No, you stay here. I'll come back after I get a Band-Aid."

"Non! Non! Ne me quitte pas!"

"I can't help it. There's blood all over me. I've got to go!"

Jean-Pierre began to panic. I guess the idea of being left in the dark, stuck under the back stairs, unable to crawl out by himself, made him anxious. He started to snort and bellow. I had to reach out and put my bloody hand over his mouth to calm him down. He thrashed but I held on and pinched his nose until he stopped kicking.

"Listen," I hissed, "you *must* be still! If they hear you, we'll get in trouble. I'm sure they won't like it that I've brought you under here and all. You *have* to be still! I'll come right back. *Tu comprends?"*

"Oui, je comprends," Jean-Pierre said sulkily, after I slowly took my hand off his mouth.

"Calvin Dort Becker!" shrieked my mother. "What *have* you done?"

The cut on my forehead was deep and bleeding profusely. Because of the sticky blood on my shirt and pants, the dust and cobwebs had stuck all over me.

"I guess I bumped my head."

"Bumped your head! I'll say you bumped your head! Quick, press this against the cut!"

Mom soaked a dishcloth in cold water and handed it to me. "Sit on this stool while I call Dr. Zwingli and ask him what to do. I think you need stitches."

"Can I just have a Band-Aid, Mom?'

"Don't be ridiculous!"

After Mom made an appointment to see Dr. Zwingli, she marched me up to our bathroom, sat me on the edge of the tub, stripped off all my clothes, except my underpants, and washed me off. All the while she had me hold a dishcloth filled with ice on the cut. Mom dropped my clothes into a sink filled with cold water to soak the blood out. She wrapped a big bandage around my head, put a clean shirt on me, and handed me a fresh pair of pants.

"Now, you tell me *exactly* what you did."

"I was in the chicken shed, cleaning it, you know, catching up with my chores, and I slipped and fell. I caught my head on a nail that was sticking out. That's how I did it. I'm sorry."

"I do wish you'd be more careful! Why, oh why do you *keep* having so many accidents?"

"I don't know, Mom, maybe it's just the marvelous changes in my body that are making me clumsy."

"You're probably right, darling, but I wish you'd stop getting into trouble!"

"Mom, before we take the tram, can I just run down to the living room to get a book to look at in the waiting room?"

"*No!* You'd probably fall and break an arm or something! *Really!* Besides, you're not supposed to be on that leg too much."

"But, Mom, I'd like to bring a book I was looking at."

"Honestly, don't you think you've caused enough trouble?"

Mom took me firmly by the arm and helped me out of the bathroom, down the hall, down the stairs, and out into the road.

All the while I was wondering how long Jean-Pierre would wait under the stairs; whether he would be stupid enough to try and touch himself. I hoped he wouldn't. I knew he'd bellow.

Chapter 48

WHEN WE ARRIVED AT THE DOCTOR'S OFFICE, there were two tired-looking young mothers with babies ahead of us. I sat and waited nervously, thumbing through old copies of *Elle* and *Paris-Match*. Finally the nurse stepped into the waiting area and asked us to come to the examining room.

Dr. Zwingli was washing his hands. He turned around, wiped them off, stroked his goatee, and said, "Let's take a look at our patient."

He cut the bandage off. My head started to bleed.

"Oh, we have been in the wars today. My, my, this does not seem to be your summer!" Dr. Zwingli smiled.

"I guess not. How long will this take?"

"Are we in a rush today?"

"Oh no, I was just curious."

It turned out I didn't need stitches after all. Dr. Zwingli said it was a deep puncture wound. He cleaned it and taped a big pad of gauze over it. After he had tended my head he said, "Let's take a look at your leg."

Dr. Zwingli gingerly felt the small scar on my ankle. "Any trouble walking?"

"No, it's fine now."

"Well, you're a fast healer! Excellent!"

Janet was waiting at the tram stop. She looked grimly delighted. My heart sank.

Mom got off the tram first. I walked right into Janet's clutches.

Without saying a word, she marched me across the road, pushing me ahead of her. Mom caught up with us.

"What on earth do you think you're doing, Janet?"

"Calvin's in a lot of trouble. Dad sent me down to meet the tram. I met the last one too."

"It was an accident. He didn't mean to cut his head. Let go of his arm!"

"Dad said I was to bring Calvin right up to him."

Janet dug her fingernails into my wrist.

"Ow!"

"Janet, let go!"

Janet obeyed, but she still stayed close behind me, giving me helpful shoves every few steps until we got inside.

Janet knocked on Mom and Dad's bedroom door.

"I don't understand," Mom murmured as we stepped into the room. Dad stood up. "Don't understand what?"

"Why Calvin's in trouble . . . Oh, hello, Mary Lou."

Mary Lou was sitting on the edge of the couch drinking tea.

"Hello, Elsa," Mary Lou answered in a mournful, quiet voice. She didn't look at me.

"Calvin, you come in. Janet, that's all. You can go now," said Dad.

Janet looked disappointed to be sent away before hearing what was going to happen to me. Dad motioned me to sit on the edge of the bed. He stood for a while, arms folded, looking at his feet. Then he looked at me.

"This is the most serious moment of your life. Your perversity casts doubt upon your election. It would seem that you are one of the hopelessly unregenerate, a Vessel of Wrath. It is clear that as of now you have not yet been called. It's clear that your profession of faith has been a sham."

Dad had said a lot of things to me, on a lot of occasions, but never that I was doomed, a Vessel of Wrath chosen from before the foundation of the world to be damned.

Mom was shocked.

"Oh, Ralph! How can you say that?"

Dad spun around furiously. "Elsa, you don't know the facts! *It's worse than you can possibly imagine!*"

Mary Lou put down her teacup and began to cry. "I'm afraid we have some very bad . . . bad news, Elsa. He has . . . has masturbated with Jean-Pierre and performed other . . . other acts. There is a witness and Jean-Pierre has *confessed!* This is even worse than what he did in Zermatt with Eva. And this time he does not have my time of doubt as an excuse."

When Mary Lou said the word *masturbated,* Mom screamed *"Oh no!"* and fell on the floor.

Dad looked steadily at me. "This is only the first fruits."

Dad and Mary Lou helped Mom up and stretched her out on the couch. She lay moaning, "Oh no, oh no, oh no, I begged him not to, I really did. Oh, Calvin, Calvin . . ."

Dad gave my shoulder a shake. "What do you have to say?"

Before I could think of anything, Mary Lou began to talk. She said that one of the spastic girls saw Jean-Pierre and me sneak under the hedge, months ago, before I broke my leg. The girl peeked through the branches and told Mary Lou what she had seen. The Ladies decided to wait, not to tell anyone but to catch us "in the act" instead, since, Mary Lou said, "We needed definite proof before we could bring a charge of gross immorality against one of our own."

As I feared he might, Jean-Pierre *had* tried to relieve his animal needs under the staircase. He bellowed and was discovered, panicked and thrashing in the dark with his pants down. Dad called Mary Lou, who then accused Jean-Pierre of committing unspeakable acts. He had burst into tears and admitted it!

From what Mary Lou said, it sounded like Jean-Pierre claimed that I took him under the stairs and *made him* touch himself. Mary Lou asked him if I did other things to him. Jean-Pierre admitted to everything Mary Lou accused me of or suggested. Mary Lou suggested a lot.

If the spastic girl hadn't seen me helping Jean-Pierre, I would have staunchly denied the whole thing. The problem was, like Mary Lou said, "How could a guileless handicapped eight-year-old girl have made such an awful thing up? Why, she didn't even know the name for it!" There was no getting around that.

When Mary Lou was done speaking, Mom groaned, "Oh, Calvin, why did you touch it!? Didn't I warn you? Didn't I beg you to leave it alone?"

"But, Mom, I—"

Dad gave me a hard shake. "Shut up, Calvin!"

I tried to hold on to Dad, to bury my face in his chest. He shoved me away. "You'd better tell the whole truth!"

I took several deep breaths.

"Dad, I did touch myself with Jean-Pierre under the hedge. Because he's spastic I had to help him keep quiet. But the rest is a lie."

Dad slapped me, hard. "I said tell the truth! We know what you've done!"

"Don't hit his bandage!" screamed Mom.

"He's going to have more to worry about than a cut on his head!"

Dad hit me again so hard I fell on the floor.

Mary Lou jumped up and stood over me. "In the name of Jesus I adjure you to tell the *truth!*" she shrieked.

Mom fell on her knees next to me and sobbed, "Oh, Calvin! In the name of God, *confess!*"

"I am!" I shouted. "We only touched ourselves! That's all we did!"

Dad grabbed my shirt, hoisted me to my feet and slapped me again. This time he hit me on the mouth. I tasted blood when I licked my stinging lips.

"You are a liar and a homosexual! You are hopelessly unregenerate and utterly depraved! You are not my son!"

I guess Dad read in the Bible about how the Jews tore their clothes when really bad things happened. When he said I wasn't his son anymore, he tried to tear his blue plaid flannel shirt. He only managed to pop the buttons off and pull his undershirt out of his pants.

Mom was still on the floor, her head in her hands, rocking back and forth, moaning, "The stains, I should have done something when I found the stains . . . oh . . . God forgive me, I knew there were too many stains. . . ."

Mary Lou began to yell uncontrollably.

"There's no way you can give Jean-Pierre back his life! He has been destroyed, violated, ruined! An innocent handicapped child entrusted to our c-c-c-care! Sodomized! Raped! Fondled!"

"This is the saddest day of my life," said Dad. "I'm sickened by your behavior."

My front tooth was loose. I guess that's what did it; that's when I snapped. When I felt it wiggle, that's when I jumped up onto the middle of Mom and Dad's bed and screamed, *"You're the liars! You're the Vessels of Wrath! Dad, you're the one that has the magazine of naked people in your bedside table!"*

Dad stood frozen, gaping at me. I jumped off the other side of the bed, wrenched the drawer out of the bedside table, yanked out the plastic loaf, scattering the Bible-verse memorization cards all over the bed and floor. Then I reached down into the locked cupboard below. Dad made a dive for me across the bed. He dove too late.

The first time I discovered Dad kept pictures of naked people in his locked bedside table, he only had one magazine. Now there were three. The first magazine had been mostly in black-and-white. These were in color. I tossed them at Dad as he tried to grab me. One of them bounced off his chest and fell open on the bed, to a fold-out picture of a naked, fat, white woman bending over. A thin black man was having sexual relations with her from behind.

Before Mom, Dad, or Mary Lou could do anything, while they were still staring openmouthed, gaping at the picture of the man with his penis stuck into the fat woman, I jumped up on the bed, took two steps across it, leapt for the door, and in one bound was out of the room.

Janet sprang up from where she had been bending over looking through the keyhole. Her mouth was wide open. She made a grab for me at the same time as Grandma yelled, *"What in God's name are you doin' to that miserable boy, you sons-of-a-bitches!"*

I hit Janet in the face. She didn't say a word, just sank to her knees, with her hands held up to her nose.

I didn't hear her first scream until I was almost all the way down the stairs.

I thought about how if we had no free will, how they could blame God if they didn't like that I had broken Janet's nose. I thought about this as I locked the basement door behind me, ran down the steps, and yanked open Mom's filing cabinet. I grabbed the mailing lists, carried them to the hot-water furnace, and dumped them into the silent blue flames.

As I raced back to Mom's office, and reached into the vacation-money box, I heard footsteps and pounding fists on the basement door. I grabbed all of our passports in one hand and stuffed a handful of money into my pocket with the other. My hands were shaking but I managed to open the first passport. I saw a picture of Rachael. Next I found mine and jammed it into my shirt, then took the others to the furnace.

When I tossed in the passports I had to jump back. A roaring orange tongue of fire leapt out of the furnace as oxygen hit the smoldering stack of mailing lists.

I heard more pounding, calling, and shouting from upstairs. Doors were opening and closing. I dashed for the side door.

I had been planning to run away as soon as I had the chance to pack and hide my suitcase in the forest. Events overtook my plans. Suitcase or no suitcase, it was time to go.

Chapter 49

I FELT LIGHT. Below me were the steep cow pastures crisscrossed by farm tracks and stands of trees. Beyond these the forest grew thick and unbroken. After the forest, the vineyards ran down to the Rhône valley floor, spread out flat and green, a geometric pattern of fields and orchards. It was a stunningly beautiful day.

I glanced up. Across the Rhône valley the peaks of the Dents du Midi were hazy, light gray against the pale summer sky.

I held out my arms. I felt like I was flying.

When I came to a single-strand, electric cattle fence, I jumped it. Because I was running so fast, and the slope of the hill was so steep, the leap carried me twelve, even fifteen, feet further down the mountainside.

Moments later the golden sunlight was extinguished as I hit a wall of cool, damp air that hung motionless between the straight, gray pine trunks of the forest. I slowed and began to walk. I was careful not to slip. I knew that I was approaching the top of a cliff that was about five hundred feet high. I could imagine what would happen if I slipped; the roll to the edge, the futile effort to hang on, then the screaming plunge to the vineyards below, the crunch of being impaled on one of the metal stakes, to which the vines were tied in neat rows, the trickle of my blood soaking into the sandy gravel.

When I got to the top of the cliff I didn't approach the edge but stayed a couple of rows of trees back. I carefully picked my way along until I came to what I was looking for, a huge metal pipe about four feet in diameter.

The pipe ran all the way from Trois-Torrents to the hydroelectric plant in Monthey. A stream had been diverted into it. If you put your ear to the cold, sweating, gray metal you could hear the rush of water.

The massive pipe emerged from the ground just before the cliff. It snaked over the precipice, hugging the rock face. By the time the water fell to the bottom it had gathered so much velocity it drove six turbines, and still had energy enough to spurt from under the hydroplant with a deafening roar.

Alongside the pipe was a steep staircase. At the cliff face the stairs ended and a steel ladder began. Maintenance crews painted the pipe once a year, and replaced bolts if they rusted. That was what the ladder was for. The ladder was the key to my escape.

I cautiously peered over the precipice. My stomach turned over. I didn't like heights. I knew no one would think I had been stupid enough to go this way. They might search the road but they would never think of the pipe.

The descent was terrifying. The worst moment was at the top when I had to swing myself around the locked, spiked metal barrier that had a danger sign on it warning people not to approach. I had enough sense not to look down, but that hardly helped.

My toe loosened a rock from the soft limestone cliff. I heard it bounce off the ladder far below. A long time later there was a quiet thud as the rock hit the gravel soil. My only comfort was that every time my shaking, sweating hands slid down a rung, I was closer to the ground.

A half hour later, when I had almost reached the bottom, I got a shock. The ladder ended twelve feet or so above the vineyard. It just stopped. I could see the missing section padlocked to a concrete block below me. I guess the people at the electric company didn't want children to climb up the ladder. That's why the last section was down.

I stopped and looked up. Overhead the rungs stretched to a vertical point, where they disappeared into the golden, late-afternoon sky. My leg was hurting. There was no way I could go back. I looked down again. Twelve feet was a long way to fall, especially since the ground below sloped away steeply. I knew I would roll and slide when I hit.

I jammed my passport more firmly into my shirt, pushed the money further down into my pocket, climbed to the lowest rung, hung until my fingers went white, then I dropped.

I shut my eyes as I rolled between the rows of vines. I came to a stop when my foot snagged between two vine roots. My leg ached.

I lay for a moment on the warm, dry gravel, then stood up and felt for my passport and money. My leg still hurt, but otherwise seemed to be all right. I took a deep breath. The smell of bruised vine leaves and copper sulfate reminded me of Italy. I took it as a sign.

Chapter 50

I HAD THE SENSE TO HITCHHIKE UP THE VALLEY from Monthey to St. Maurice. I knew Mom and Dad might call the Monthey or Aigle stations to inquire if I had been seen, had gotten off the tram, bought a ticket, or said where I was going. I felt safer catching the train further south.

I bought my ticket and waited. The cash I found in Mom's drawer only amounted to thirty-three Swiss francs. This was enough for a one-way second-class ticket to Milano, but not enough for the fare to Santa Margherita. I planned to hide in the toilet of the Milano to Santa Margherita train and avoid the conductor.

When I bought my ticket the stationmaster glanced at my bandage and dirty clothes and asked how old I was. I pretended I couldn't speak French and held out my passport, as if I thought that's what he wanted. As soon as he saw I was a foreigner, an American, he lost interest in me.

I stood in the hall, up by the toilet compartment. I didn't want to ride in the train car. I might have sat across from some officious Swiss who would study my face, remember me, report me to the police if they put out a description.

An hour later, we passed Brig, the last station in Switzerland, without incident. Then the train roared into the mouth of the Simplon tunnel.

We descended deep beneath the mountain, hurtled toward the plains of Italy, losing altitude the whole way. My ears popped. The air was so heavy with dank humidity that the windows began to stream with beads of condensation.

The Milano station was very different from when my family changed trains there in the day. Electric lights suspended high above the platform made everything look colorless. During the day the noise of people coming and going, the squeal of trains braking, the clanking of couplings, the hiss of compressed air brakes and shouts of platform vendors formed a vast roar against which you had to shout to be heard. Now even the slightest sound made you look to see what was disturbing the lonely silence.

Far up the track a man shouted and languidly waved a greasy, torn red flag as he directed an engine to a row of waiting cars. As the engine backed into the cars I could see the jolt move down the line. A split second later I heard the sound of the heavy steel couplings as they clanked together in rapid-fire succession. The slate-gray, grimy glass-and-steel roof vault acted as a sounding board, amplifying the noise in a long roll of thunder.

A short blast from the horn of an arriving train made me look toward the gaping mouth of the station. Beyond the vast opening it was pitch-black. Emerging from the velvet darkness was a long, brown, bottle-nosed *Rapido*. The express train's diesel engines roared in a high-pitched whine as it braked to a stop. A few tired travelers straggled off. A mother with three young children climbed unsteadily down the steep steps to the platform. One child was in her mother's arms. The other two followed her. They were hardly awake.

Once the mother collected herself, she slowly walked up the length of the train, her children trailing behind. She approached the middle car and stopped, handed the sleeping baby to her eldest daughter, then reached up to where the window above her had just opened. Her husband began to hand out their luggage.

It looked as if this family was moving. They had six huge cardboard suitcases, as well as numerous bundles tied up in brown paper and string. Once everything was piled on the platform, the father put up the window and momentarily reappeared at the door. He got off and sauntered toward his family, who were sitting on the various suitcases.

The mother sliced up some fruit for the children and passed a bottle of mineral water around. Then she pulled up her white blouse, uncovered, and began to feed her baby. Even from where I was sitting I could see her large brown nipple, stretched across a startlingly full, white breast.

I decided to walk over to the Motta coffee bar. I didn't want to go to sleep for fear I would miss my train. Halfway to the bar I remembered that all I had in my pocket were a few Swiss francs, the change from my ticket. I didn't have any Italian lire.

The *cambio* kiosk was closed. Its pale blue steel shutters, rusted at the base from countless dogs relieving themselves against them, were up and locked.

I walked over to the barman. *"Cambio?"* I asked. I held out a one-franc coin. The barman put down the glass he was drying, wiped his hands on his apron, took the coin, and looked at it.

"Svizzera?"

*"Si, Svizzera, cambio—*change*—lire?"*

He shook his head and handed the coin back.

"Non faccio cambio." He shook his head.

I stood staring at the rows of exotically shaped bottles of liquor sitting on the glass shelves that lined the mirrored wall behind the bar. Next to the liquor bottles was the espresso-cappuccino machine with the usual big upside-down, cone-shaped glass container full of black, shiny coffee beans. Rows and rows of miniature espresso cups were stacked on a rack above the machine.

In the daytime customers stood leaning on the bar, drinking down their scalding espressos in one or two quick gulps. The heavy miniature cups would be wet all day. They never had time to dry between customers but were rinsed, placed on the wooden drain board, then handed to the next man who stepped up to the bar, put down his copy of *La Stampa* and a fifty-lire coin, and said, *"Un caffè."*

The barman finished drying a glass. He walked to the espresso machine, flipped the switch that made the coffee beans tumble into the grinder, then hit another switch and ground the coffee. Then he wrenched the handle of the coffee container hard to the left, banged it out on a wooden block, filled it with fresh ground coffee, tamped it down with a wooden paddle, and twisted the container into position.

A couple of seconds later the machine began to bubble and hiss. A dribble of pungent black liquid, streaked with light brown foam, trickled into the cup. When one cup was half-full he pushed it deftly aside with the second. He knew exactly when to make the switch. Both cups ended up with exactly the same amount of espresso in them.

The barman reached up, got down two saucers, and with a flourish, pulled out two tiny spoons from a bin under the bar, slammed the saucers and spoons on the counter in front of me, then slid the glass sugar jar, with its fold-back, stainless-steel top, toward me. He put the cups of espresso on the saucers, took two heaping spoonfuls of sugar, stirred them into his coffee, and drank it down in one hot, long slurping gulp.

I hadn't touched mine. I said, *"Cambio?"* and held out the Swiss franc again. The barman laughed, spooned two helpings of sugar into my cup, and stirred. He pushed my coin away, then picked up the espresso cup and held it toward me.

Chapter 51

AT ABOUT THREE A.M. the cars for the Santa Margherita train were pushed into position. The only light inside the compartment was pale, artificial twilight that filtered through the grimy window. I sat on a drab velvet seat, pushed up the armrest, and lay down with my face against the upholstery.

When my family had traveled to Italy I always loved the exotic smell of the Italian trains, in contrast to the odorless Swiss ones. Now, as I breathed in, the same vacation feeling came flooding back, only it was better. When Mom, Dad, and my sisters were along they kept doing things that got in the way. For instance, we would be about to eat a plate of chicken, roasted with fresh rosemary, and Dad would complain that he sure missed good American cooking, how he didn't understand why they put "stuff" on his chicken, and didn't just "fry it up."

Mom always had family prayers at the table on the hotel dining terrace. While other guests sat sipping espresso or brandy, Mom passed out songbooks and made us sing hymns. The other guests stared at us.

I spent a lot of time arranging my vacation days so that I would be as far away from my family as possible. I had two vacations, one where I spent my time trying to be invisible, the other when I would swim and snorkel with Jennifer, spend hours with Gino, my artist friend, or wander around the byways of Portofino while Mom and my sisters went shopping in Santa Margherita and Dad sat in his hotel room reading his theological journals.

I adjusted the armrest and noticed how the velvet in the crease was a fresh green in contrast to the colorless, faded gray of the seat. I took another sniff of old velvet, lint, ferrous oxide, diesel residue, and splashes of red wine. I sighed and closed my eyes. The big green ashtray acted like a prism, made the sparkling sunlight shimmer on the whitewashed ceiling of the *pensione* lobby. It came to me that the boy, being clutched by his weeping father, didn't really matter anymore.

What did matter was the rainbow made by the sunlight, as it refracted through the ashtray. It mattered because it reminded me that the morning was beautiful, that children were playing by the water's edge, that I loved Jennifer, that the first batch of pizza was about to come out of the snack bar's oven, that on the shady side of the bay the octopus would be under the rocks, that the old lady in the church was lighting a candle to the Virgin, and that the mother on the beach was pregnant again.

I stood and walked out of the door of the *pensione,* across the beach, to the end of the pier. I looked out over the turquoise Mediterranean and took a deep breath. The smell of gardenia was drifting on a warm breeze from someplace over the water.

Bright sunlight flickered on my eyelids. Across from me a short, fat priest with a round, flat face was sitting reading a newspaper. It rustled loudly as he turned a page. That's what woke me. I sat up quickly. The priest looked over the top of his paper, smiled, and said, *"Buon giorno."*

"Buon giorno," I answered. Then I remembered I had no ticket, that my plan called for me to hide in the toilet until we got to Santa Margherita.

I got up as casually as I could, slid open the compartment door, and made my way down the gently rocking passage, past dark-skinned men in shiny suits and white shirts, smoking strange-smelling cigarettes. I stepped into the toilet, closed and locked the narrow, metal door behind me. Then I realized I had no idea what part of the line we were on. Had we already gone through Genoa?

The toilet window was made of thick frosted glass. Only a narrow vent opened at the bottom. When I peered out all I could see was the flash of railroad ties. I unlocked the door, stepped back into the hall, crossed the passage, and studied the scenery framed through the round window of the car's door.

It was a beautiful view, but it was the *wrong view.*

An unfamiliar fishing village flashed past. I saw white-and-red rowboats pulled up on a cobblestone wharf in front of pink-and-white houses. Then there were rocks with pines growing out of them at crazy angles, hanging precariously over shimmering water.

Prickly pear clinging to a sandy bank flickered by in a dusty blur. A young dark-haired girl, standing next to a donkey loaded with sticks, waved as we flew through a crossing. Her black dress whipped around her brown legs. I heard the crossing bell change tone. We went into a tunnel. The roar of the train engulfed the car. Soon we were back out in the clear, fierce sunlight.

I had slept right through the two-hour train ride from Milano to Genoa, through the stop at Genoa. I must have been asleep when the train pulled into Santa Margherita. I had no idea where I was. For all I knew we had gone past Rapallo and La Spezia and were halfway to Rome!

I made my way back up the hall of the car until I found the compartment I had been asleep in. The priest was where I left him. He had pulled out the fold-down tray under the window, set a sheet of brown paper down, then laid out *focaccia,* an apple, and a thick, creamy wedge of Bel Paese cheese. The priest picked up his Swiss army knife and sliced the green apple in half, quartered it, looked up, and motioned me to sit.

"*Vuoi mangiare,*" he asked.

"*Si, grazie.*"

He handed me a piece of apple and made the sign of the cross over it. It tasted delicious. I was very hungry. He cut off a wedge of *focaccia* and handed it across the table.

As I chewed the *focaccia* I breathed the smell of the olive oil that glistened in green puddles on the bread's salty surface. I felt happy. I almost forgot that I should find out where the train was and make a plan.

When we finished eating, the priest got out a bottle of San Pellegrino mineral water and, after he took a sip, passed it to me. I had picked up enough Italian over the years while vacationing in Portofino to understand pretty well what people were talking about and to say a few words back. But many Italians spoke English, so I usually tried that first.

"*Americano.* I'm American. Do you speak English?"

"*Si,* aleetle."

"Where are we?"

"*Come?*"

"The train." I pointed to the exterior. "Where is it? Where are we? What station, *stazione,* are we coming to?"

"*Ah, si, si.*" He smiled. "*La Spezia,* ees our nextastop."

"*Grazie.*"

"*E tu?* You to *Roma?*"

"No, *La Spezia.*"

"*Bene, bene,* I go to *Roma. Al Vaticano per una conferenza di teologia.*"

"I see. Well, thank you for the food. *Molto buono!*"

He shrugged. "*Di nulla.*"

The train began to slow. We emerged from a short tunnel and were instantly surrounded by buildings, mainly the backs of the big apartment buildings that made up the downtown area of La Spezia. The wind from our train whipped hundreds of sheets, hung in dingy courtyards, into a snapping storm.

I got up to leave.

"*Grazie e arrivederci.*"

"*Buon viaggio!*"

The priest smiled.

At La Spezia I looked up at the clock. It was nine-thirty A.M. I could feel the heat radiating off the stained, rust-colored surface of the station platform. The dry weeds growing in the middle of the track rustled in a light breeze. Scraps of paper eddied in a gust of hot air, then settled on the stones between the rail ties. There weren't many people on the platform.

I crossed the track, not underneath, like you do in Switzerland, but right across, and walked up to a bulletin board. It took me a while to decipher the schedule. Eventually, with a little help from a porter, I discovered that the next train to Santa Margherita would arrive at five past ten.

The train was only a little late. As soon as I got on I went right to the toilet cubicle, locked myself in, and waited. The cramped toilet smelled strongly of well-aged urine. It reminded me of the farmer in the Monthey hospital. Once the train picked up speed, it wasn't so bad. I opened the vent and stood next to the stainless-steel sink, my back to the wall, so that a draft of fresh air flowed directly in my face. I looked in the mirror. I noticed the bandage on my head was a filthy, dark gray.

The faded yellow Santa Margherita station house, with its false, intricately painted "windows" decorating a blind wall, was the same as ever. So was the irregular silvery tinkling of the station bell. Even the lizards, sunning themselves on the gigantic granite blocks which lined the edge of the platform, were identical to the ones I had tried to catch every year since I was three years old.

I strolled over to the *cambio* kiosk. This one was open.

After changing my remaining francs into lire, I left the station and walked to the bus stop. I stood waiting for the Rapallo–Santa Margherita–Portofino bus. I was glad I had saved the last of my money for the bus ride. My leg felt heavy. It would have been a long walk to Portofino.

Chapter 52

THE BUS WAS FULL. I stood jammed with other passengers against the rear window. At each corner the driver sounded the horn, a deafening, warbling klaxon, then negotiated the bend in the narrow, single-lane, coastal road. All oncoming traffic, a host of Vespas, mopeds, and Fiats, stopped or backed up to let us pass. Our bus seemed in danger of tumbling into the sea at every turn. The back end would swing out over a thirty-foot drop to jagged rocks and water, then swing back to safety as we laboriously rounded each bend.

As we turned the hairpin bend along the Paraggi bay, we passed the rocky point on which the villa we called the "castle" stood. Below the castle were tumbled heaps of rock leading down to the water. I knew every nook and cranny of that cove. The shape of each pine, hanging over the water, was familiar. If one had been cut, if a boulder had been moved, I would have noticed.

The neat rows of red-and-white deck chairs, the blue Cinzano umbrellas, the Pensione Biea, and the sunbathing deck, were all where they had always been. I studied every brown body lying on the beach and scanned the people lounging at the snack bar. The bus stopped. I almost disembarked but I resisted the temptation. I decided I'd better go to Portofino first, look up Gino, find a place to stay, then walk back to the beach and search for Jennifer.

I remained on the bus. As we slowly meandered up the far side of the cove, I pushed my way through the crowd so I could continue to peer out the left-hand windows, keep scanning the beach for a glimpse of a golden pony tail.

After three more sweeping turns we drove into a long, dim, echoing corridor formed by the backs of the houses that lined Portofino's bay. We maneuvered into the communal parking lot. Except for early-morning deliveries, no motor vehicles of any kind were ever allowed into the narrow alleys and town square.

The bus stopped. The doors opened with a hiss of compressed air. I stepped down to the broiling surface of the parking lot. I fingered the few lire in my pocket and thought about the fact that the people I knew in Portofino were really only vacation friends. It wasn't as if they would ever expect me to turn up without my parents, stroll in, and ask for a place to stay.

I had anticipated how wonderful it would be to arrive in Portofino, but until that moment I hadn't thought about whether my friends would be pleased to see me when I told them I was alone, had no money to pay for a room in the Hotel Nazionale, no money even to buy food.

I stood staring at the heat haze shimmering above the rows of parked cars. As the bus emptied of its last passengers the driver strolled toward the umbrellas and chairs of the cafe on the corner of the parking lot. I was trying to collect my thoughts. Meanwhile the driver reached the bar, took off his cap, and mopped his bald head with a big blue handkerchief while the barman made him an espresso.

I had half a mind to give up. I contemplated buying a bus ticket with my remaining lire and leaving. I could hide in toilets on the trains all the way back to Switzerland. Then I remembered how Jennifer looked as she peered over the water, her eyes sparkling, how her wet ponytail cast an arc of silver droplets high into the air when she resurfaced from a deep dive and tossed her head.

I walked away from the parking lot and plunged into the shade and noise of the street that ran down to the harbor square. I passed familiar grocery stores, fragrant crates of huge, ripe, misshapen red and yellow peppers and tomatoes stacked in front of their doors, shoe shops, and souvenir stands. Then I turned the last corner and saw the glittering bay in front of me. Gentle summer swells moved the yachts up and down in a lazy rhythm. I took a deep breath and sighed.

I cut across the cobbled square, past boutiques, past people gawking at the yachts, past old ladies sitting in the shade of their doorways making lace, past a fisherman spreading out his nets to mend, and walked up the staircase, to Gino's summer studio.

I stepped over a scrawny cat, chewing on a fly-swarmed fish head, and ran up the stairs to the gate at the top. The gate was ajar. I pushed it open and walked in. Gino stood at his easel with his back to me. He was working on a large canvas of a nude woman walking down a railway line with a porpoise on a leash. Her hair was on fire.

As usual Gino was surrounded by a clutter of easels, beer cases, boxes of spinach, and other restaurant supplies jumbled together with his art materials. He puffed a filterless Gitane cigarette. An acrid cloud of smoke drifted toward me, enveloped me, and made me cough.

Chapter 53

GINO GLANCED OVER HIS SHOULDER, motioned me with his chin to sit, then turned back to his work. I gingerly perched on the edge of a crateful of cans of tuna fish and waited. I waited for Gino to get to a stage in his painting where he would lay down his brushes, light a new cigarette, and talk to me.

As Gino painted I glanced around. Above me were the familiar strings of dusty, colored lights, left over from when the restaurant he rented his studio from used to have tables in the courtyard, before they built their new roof terrace. To one side was the gray-brown bedrock, on the other, an ocher stucco wall with a solitary window blocked by a big fan, from which steam, and the smell of cooking, poured incessantly. Next to the fan was the door that led to the kitchen. The bottom, right-hand panel was deeply scratched, evidence of generations of scrawny cats begging for scraps.

For most of the day the building and rock face prevented the sun from shining into Gino's courtyard. Only at noon would a patchwork of sunlight fall through the vine leaves that hung, tired and withered, on the dilapidated trellis.

Gino painted without glancing at me. He stood in his sandals, khaki trousers hanging loosely about his long legs. He wore a paint-stained apron. His hair was swept back in greasy, streaked locks. His eyes were set in a permanent squint, produced by hours of standing with a lit cigarette between his lips.

On the edge of Gino's pallet was an ashtray, long ago abandoned to clotted paints. I moved from the crate and settled myself in Gino's paint-smeared deck chair. I leaned back, stuck my feet out, and relaxed. I had spent hours like this, watching Gino paint, step back, look at his work, step forward, paint some more, mix colors, rub out mistakes, paint again, smoke, cough, drink, and squint. It felt good to not have to worry about being caught visiting him. Mom had never liked Gino. She called him "that awful alcoholic" and said I was never to visit him unless it was to give him a tract.

"*Bene,*" muttered Gino. He put down his brush, wiped off his hands, lit a fresh cigarette, and turned to me. " 'Ow are you?"

"Very well, thank you."

"I meessed you. I thought you were not 'aving youa 'olleeday this year!"

"We weren't able to come last week."

"But you all 'ave coming now? *Bene, bene.*" Gino walked over and patted my cheek. "What you did to youa 'ead?"

"I banged it. It's nothing really.'

" 'Ow? 'Ow you do it?"

"It's a long story."

"Good! You tella mia!"

"Gino."

"*Si?*"

"Gino, I have something to ask you."

Gino poured out a quarter of a glass of Johnnie Walker Red Label and lowered himself heavily into a deck chair.

"Sit 'ere!" Gino patted the edge of a lettuce crate. I moved over, sat down next to him, and absentmindedly pulled out a leaf of rucola and chewed it.

"Gino, something happened. I'm here alone."

"Weetha you *sorellas*?"

"No, all alone, just me."

"By youaself in the Nazionale!"

"No. I just got here this morning. I'm not settled anywhere yet."

"I do not understanda you. Calvino, where is youa *famiglia?*"

"They're home. I came without them."

"I do not think you fasser wasa so wise to sending you alone. He is a strange man!"

"Yes, he's strange. That's one reason why I came alone, but he didn't send me. Gino, I ran away."

"Madonna!"

"Yes."

"They knowing you are 'eer?"

"No."

"Misericordia!"

"I left in a hurry. I don't even have any clothes with me. I don't have any money either, just a few lire."

"Calvino! *Why* you doing thees?"

"There was a big fight in our ministry between Dad and another person, then Dad and Mom had a fight with the mission board— that's the people who Dad works for. That's why we were going to miss our vacation. Dad accused me of being a homosexual. It was all lies, so I left as soon as I saved my Grandmother's life and my leg got better, after I broke it again. Besides I wanted to see Jennifer. And you, of course."

I thought Gino would ask me lots of questions about what the different things I had told him meant, for details and all. Usually he questioned me closely about my family's doings. But he just sat staring at me, smoking and sipping his drink. He sat silent so long I got nervous and kept talking.

"Gino, I've decided that I don't believe in predestination anymore."

"You are atheist now?"

"No, not an atheist—I just don't believe that God arranges everything."

Gino said nothing.

"Gino, you believe in free will, don't you?"

Gino looked at me, took a deep drag on his cigarette, so deep the tobacco crackled, and smiled. "Calvino, you are an interesting boy! Why did youa father call you a 'omosexual?"

"It wasn't true. A girl saw me and my friend from the home next door together. She told The Ladies and they told Dad. I cut my head under the stairs and had to leave my friend, Jean-Pierre, stuck in the dark, and when they found him, while I saw the doctor, they questioned him and made him tell a bunch of lies. I had to help him because he bellows when he touches himself."

Gino shook his head, perplexed.

"You know, ah, masturbates . . . Anyway, he would bellow like I said. I only touch myself once in a while. Actually quite a lot. That doesn't make me a homosexual, does it?"

"No. It is normal. But froma my point of view, it is a shame you are not really a 'omosexual! To *theenk!* A nice younga boy all alone with *mia!*" Gino threw back his head and laughed.

I must have looked dismayed because he patted my hand and said, "Calvino, don'ta worry, I'm only joke."

"I don't mind."

Gino took a gulp of whiskey, swallowed, and smiled. "Jennifer, she come to look for you when you were not on *la spiagia* . . . the beach."

I jumped up.

"She did?"

"Yes. She ask me if I 'ave see you."

"When?"

"Lastaweek."

"Great!"

"Not 'great.' Where you go? What you do? Where you sleep?"

"I don't know. That's why I came to you. I thought you could help me."

"Ah Calvino, you know what they weel say if they finda you 'eer?"

"I just need a place to sleep and a little food once in a while, not that you'd have to feed me all the time. The barman down by the dock always gives me the last pizza slice, plus I can get leftover breakfast rolls from outside people's doors, off the breakfast trays in the mornings. I know a back way into the Nazionale."

Gino laughed.

"Look, I need to go see if I can find Jennifer. I'll come back later." I took a step toward the gate.

"Calvino, Calvino! Wait! You are mad, so crazy, so young. Once I ran away. I 'ad to go 'ome after onea day because my cousin tell my uncle I was 'iding in their barn outside Modena. They tooka mia back to my mama and she beat me. I remember! Aie-ya-yai. *Mama mia!*"

He rubbed his thighs.

"Well, I hope no one sends me back. If they do I won't go!"

"I am not you uncle or the police. But I cannot 'ave you in my apartemento. You are too younga. People know what I am. They calling the police and alla will be lost."

"I'd tell them the truth."

"They might believe you but even so you would be sent 'ome."

"What can I do?"

"Why you no go 'ome?"

"I can't. I burned the other passports and all. Besides I think I broke my sister's nose."

"Calvino! What it is you are doing?"

"I told you."

Gino took a few more swallows of whiskey before he said anything. Then he looked at me and winked. "Come, I makea you an offer. You must promise me to keep you part of the bargain. I offer to let you sleep 'eer in my studio and I will 'avea food for you 'eer every day on *one condeetion,* that you write a postcard to you mama saying you safe and well and will come 'ome soon."

"No!"

I jumped toward the gate.

"Then I weel not 'elp you! I weel not 'elp to killing youa mama with sorrowing!"

"They're the ones who started it. I'll never go back!"

"Dee postacard, why not at least writing a card? You must letting them knowing you not *morto*."

"They'll know where I am. They'll come and get me if I write. My dad hates me."

"You musta theenk carefully. Sit down!"

Gino pointed to the crate. I sat. Gino's cigarette burned down to a soggy stump between his lips and went out. Flies buzzed around the battered garbage can by the kitchen door. Sounds of shouting and laughter drifted up Gino's staircase from the harbor. I could hardly stand to sit there, all the while knowing Jennifer was in Paraggi.

Gino looked at me. I wouldn't meet his eyes. Instead I stared at the naked woman in his painting. A cat let out a long, angry growl.

Gino sighed.

"Calvino, I will 'elp you but we *musta* send a card. I will send the card in an envelope to my brosser een Modena and aska 'eem to mail it from there. Then they won'ta know where you are. We will using a plain postcard. No peecture of Portofino. They will knowing you are in Italia but nussing more. In the end they weel looking for you 'eer anyway. In the end it is better that they do not 'ate you for worrying too much."

"If I do this, can I stay here?"

"*Si.*"

Chapter 54

I WROTE THE CARD. I had never told Gino I couldn't spell well before. When I did he said nothing about it, didn't even look surprised, just checked the card for me and nodded.

> Mom,
>> I am in Italy and fine. Do not worry.
>>> Calvin

"Gino, I'm going now, but before I do I need to ask you something. How old do you have to be to get married in Italy?"

"What you saying?" Gino poured more whiskey into his glass, sipped, and squinted at me.

"I want to marry Jennifer. How old do I have to be?"

"Thirty-seex, I think." Gino laughed

"No, I really want to know! How old, Gino?"

"Olda than you."

"I'll wait but I want to know how long I have to wait."

"How olda you now?"

"Almost sixteen. My birthday's next week."

"Fifteena! *Dio mio!* You wanta to get married at fifteena!"

"I said it's my birthday next week!"

Gino laughed so hard he spilled his whiskey.

"I love Jennifer!"

"Ah! *Amore!* It is beauteeful!"

When Gino finished laughing he started to cry. I suppose it was because he had been drinking. In between sobs he kept repeating, "Beauteeful, eet ees beauteeful!"

"Gino! *Please!* What's the legal age?'

Gino wiped his eyes. "With or weethouta you parents permeesion?"

"Without."

"I don'ta know, maybe sixteena weethouta their permeesion and eighteena with."

"You mean sixteen with and eighteen without."

"Yes, likea I say, twenty-one yearsa old!"

Gino began to cry even harder than before. I ignored him.

"Could I fake my father's permission? Or could you say you were my dad?"

Gino finally collected himself enough to answer. "Calvino, whata about Jennifer? What about 'er mama? You theenk they gonna to let you marry 'er when she is a child? Calvino, why you no love 'er and that'sa all?"

"Gino, I only get to see her in the summer. It's not enough!"

"Calvino, where youa gonna to leeve?'

"We can live here in Portofino."

"Where?"

"With you until I can get a job. Maybe the Banini will pay me to work with him on the beach or something."

"But youa *Americano.* 'Ow you work in *Italia*?"

"Everyone knows me around here. Who would stop me?"

Gino began to sniff deeply. A tear trickled down his cheek.

"Eet ees beauteeful but eet ees eempossible!"

"Why? She loves me."

"You say so. You 'ope so. I 'ope so, too!"

"I know she does. Last year she almost let me touch her breasts!"

Gino's sob ended in an explosion of laughter. His drink started to slosh all over him. The more he spilled the more he laughed until his glass was empty and the stink of whiskey filled the air.

"Gino! Don't you believe me?"

Gino laughed so hard his glass slipped out of his hand and broke. Finally he calmed down, wiped his eyes, stood up unsteadily, got another glass out of the crate he kept his drinks and paintbrushes in, poured more Red Label, sat back down, and looked at me.

"Ah, Calvino! I 'ave almosta touch dee breasts and I 'ave not married them!"

"I touched one of the maid's breasts once, at the Hotel Riffelberg in Zermatt and liked it. But that didn't mean anything, except for all the trouble later, but this is different. Jennifer isn't just some girl. She's my best friend."

"Yes, that is deefferent like you say. Maybe you *weel* marry 'er someday. But you cannot be sure that 'er mama will give permeession for 'er to marry you when she ees fifteena!"

"Almost sixteen."

"Ora seexteena."

"I can't live without her."

"Don'ta you go to school in Eengland?"

"I did once but nowhere near her."

"Ah, yes, *mi ricordo.* Wella, you can writing 'er letter."

"You know I don't write well enough . . ."

"*Ah, si, si! Scusa!* Senda 'er flower."

"Gino! I want to be *with* her!"

"*Mio Dio!* What cana I do?"

"Gino, if Jennifer stays here with me, runs away like I have, can we live here in your studio?"

"Ah no! no, no, *e* no, theese ees *not possible!*"

Gino reached out an unsteady paint-spattered hand and laid it gently on my arm.

"Calvino, I theenka you are going to 'ave youa 'art broke. I 'ave 'ad my 'art broke. Eet ees going to 'urt you very much. I ama sorry for you."

He looked at me; big tears began to run down his cheeks again. They dripped on his grimy shirtfront and into his whiskey glass.

"Gino, you don't know Jennifer, she'll stick with me!"

"Calvino. I know 'ow things work. Jennifer weel go 'ome and een the end you weel also. Then time will passa and you will see 'er somea place and eet will not be dee same."

"I'll *always* love her!'

"Yes, you weel, and she weel always lovea you. But no one 'elps young lovers. That is why you 'art weel break. No one 'elps!"

Gino was now crying so hard he had to pass his drink to me so he could bury his face in his hands and sob. Between sobs he looked up at me and repeated, "No one 'elps!"

After a while he calmed down, sniffed a couple of times, wiped his eyes on the back of his hands, reached out to get his glass back, took a few sips, and fumbled around until he managed to get out a cigarette. I lit it for him.

"Calvino, you know why 'arts break? I tella you why. Because no one 'elps young lovers, because no one takes their love serious."

"Gino, I think I should get going. I want to see her now."

"But eet *ees* serious and eet *ees* never dee same after. *Never!* But you know why youa 'art break? I tella you why."

"Gino, I'm going to walk over now."

"Because one person ees always more in love than the other person. And *you* are dee person who is more een love!"

"How do you know that?"

"Because I looking in you 'ot eyes! You are dee one with dee 'ot blood! You run away, you smash the nose, you masturbatings with you friend, you scream you *papa* and *mamma*. Calvino, I know youa since you leetle, you 'ave dee 'ot blood. Jennifer, she 'ave dee Eengleesh blood. Eet is youa 'art weel break, Calvino, because it ees you who lovea dee more. I know eet!"

"I'm going to ask her anyway."

I took a step toward the gate.

"Calvino, weel you making me a *promessa?*"

"What?"

"Calvino, when you 'art break, weel you promessa me to come 'ere and to cry weeth me? *Prometti mi* you won't go run after 'er. *Prometti mi* you no go chase 'er in *il treno* and ride een *toletta* and be catch and then Jennifer parents 'ear about eet and laugh or are angry at you and youa go and keela youself for a leetle girl because you are a boy weeth 'ot blood. *Prometti mi* you come 'ere!"

"But Jennifer won't break my heart."

"*Prometti mi* eef she do, you will comea to mia first before anything else!"

"If you want me to. But I've got to go now."

"Do you *prometti mi,* Calvino?"

"Yes."

I stepped through the gate. Gino called after me.

"Good! We will crying together. 'Ave some whiskey."

"No!"

"Eef you no 'ave a drink I noa let you staying!"

"Gino!" I stepped back into the courtyard. "But you said . . ."

Gino poured a few drops into a filthy glass and added a splash of water. He staggered to me and proffered the glass. I took a sip.

" 'Ow much *soldi* you 'ave?"

"About one thousand lire."

"What are you think of! Ees not enough for one egg!"

"I spent most of what I took on the train ticket. With a place to stay, why do I need any money? I can get all the food I want. I don't need anything else. I'm going now."

I held out the empty glass but he wouldn't take it.

"You needa clothes and you weel needa osser thing."

"I'll be fine."

"If you steal things, you weel be caught. No one weel 'elp you and you will be sent back to *Svizzera.*"

"I won't steal anything."

Gino winked laboriously. "Not even a bathing suit to sweem?"

"I might borrow one from the clothesline behind the changing cabins at the beach. I'll put it back."

"Ah! You see! What do I say! You are going to *thief!*"

"No, I won't!"

"I weel lending you *i soldi.*"

"You don't have to."

I took a step toward the gate. Gino grabbed my arm.

"Gino! I have to go! Now!"

" 'Eer is three thousand lire. You go to buy a bathing suit. A pair of sandal and summer shirt." Gino plucked at his paint-stained T-shirt.

"I'm fine."

"I eenseest!"

Gino opened his wallet, pulled out three very worn, paint-stained one-thousand-lire bills, one of them torn and Scotch-taped back together. "If you go the market behind the parking lot, you cana buy a pair of sandal likea thees"—he held out one rubber-thong sandal-clad foot—"for three 'undred lire. They also 'ave reasonable summer shirt. Go! *Via!*"

He handed me the money and pushed me through the gate.

Chapter 55

THE PATH OVER THE HILL FROM PORTOFINO to Paraggi had always been my favorite walk. It began with a long flight of wide, tiled stairs. The grade was so gentle you never got tired. At the top the path wound around the crest of the hill that separated the two bays. Broken tile, flagstones, ferns, wild rucola, thyme, and oregano gave the narrow lane the look and sweet smell of an ancient, abandoned greenhouse.

About halfway to Paraggi I reached into an old, disheveled tree to pick a huge purple fig. I heard a low buzzing sound above me. High in the tree and there were thousands of wasps, lured to the figs by the languid, pungent scent of fermentation that filled the balmy air. I could tell the fig was ripe by the fragrant pink slit in its side.

As I ran on, my new sandals slapped on the flagstones. A low stone wall bordered the path. Ferns grew from cracks into which lizards of all shapes and sizes scampered. Below the wall, the hill fell steeply in a tangle of prickly pear, figs, and blackberry brambles to the lapping turquoise water.

After ten minutes of intermittent fast walking and running I reached the end of the footpath. I was out of breath.

I stepped onto the narrow road, crossed to the side that bordered the sea, and began to trot toward the cluster of buildings and the small crescent of sand that was the beach of Paraggi.

Children were jumping off the low pier that ran out into the shallow bay. Pontoon rowboats, which you could rent by the half hour, were aimlessly bobbing on gentle waves. The smell of pizza, mingled with Bain de Soleil suntan lotion, wafted across the water.

Except for the size of the women's bathing suits, which got smaller every year, each summer was the same as the last. The Banini had been raking the sand, arranging deck chairs, renting rowboats, ever since I could remember. The fat, elderly couple who ran the snack bar, the owners of the Pensione Biea, their pale daughter Lucrezia, and most of the Italian, German, English, and French families were the same from year to year.

As I rounded the bend in the road I could hear the chink of cutlery and glass coming from the tables under the umbrellas at the snack bar. I didn't have to look to know that people were eating pizzas and mozzarella and tomato salads. The faded lunch menu, painted on the side of the snack bar, never changed. Only the prices were adjusted upward from year to year.

"Jennifer, darling, come up for lunch!"

I looked wildly around until I spotted Mrs. Bazlinton walking down the pier, calling for her daughter. Then I saw an arc of shining water tossed from a golden ponytail. My chest constricted.

Jennifer swam a few deft strokes to the ladder hanging over the end of the pier. She climbed, smoothed her hair, and ran down the wet planks to her mother. She ran like a boy, straight and firm with no side to side motion or waving arms. She had on a plain, black, one-piece bathing suit.

Jennifer got to the middle of the dock, stopped, collected her towel, then raced up the beach to where her father was picking up his newspaper. Mrs. Bazlinton walked back to her deck chair, slipped on a white robe, and adjusted her huge straw hat.

The Bazlintons took their lunch in the *pensione*. When Jennifer had been a little girl she had a nap after lunch while I got to stay on the beach because our family, too poor to afford daily lunches at the *pensione*, ate picnics. I made fun of her for having to take naps. She teased me because my mother said such long prayers before and after dinner.

I knew exactly what the Bazlinton lunchtime routine was. They would shower in the *pensione's* tepid water. Jennifer would put on some flowery print dress or a pair of shorts and a T-shirt. With her ash-blond, sun-bleached hair pulled tight into a ponytail, wet and glossy from her shower, she would stroll out onto the dining terrace of the *pensione* and sit, sipping mineral water and nibbling bread sticks, her long, brown legs splayed awkwardly under the table.

I had often crept up the backstairs to sit, hidden in the dark hallway, watching Jennifer. Once, years before, she looked up and spotted me. I leapt to my feet and pretended that I had only come up to the dining terrace to ask her something. I don't think she believed me.

I decided I would stay out of sight until I was sure the Bazlintons were at lunch. Then I'd go to Jennifer's room and wait for her there. No one locked their doors at the *pensione.*

When I stepped out of the sunny hall into the cool, dark bedroom, I knew right away that Jennifer was staying in this room as usual. I knew before my eyes adjusted to the dim light filtering through the louvered shutters. I knew by the fresh scent of Pears soap and talcum powder.

I could see Jennifer's few belongings neatly arranged on top of the plain pine dresser that stood against the whitewashed, plaster wall. Jennifer's blue-and-gray plaid skirt hung over the back of a chair. Her hairbrush and comb were on top of the dresser. Next to them something glinted in the gloom, something silver. It was a photograph about the size of a postcard. I gingerly picked it up and took it over to a solitary sliver of sunlight that cut between the shutter slats. I turned the picture right way up. I felt a tingling rush of surprise race from the pit of my stomach, through my chest, and into my head. It was a picture of me standing next to the pier in my swimsuit. Jennifer's dad must have taken it the year before without me knowing.

My heart was thumping. I could hardly stand still. I was tempted to go out and wait in the hall, even to creep up the stairs to the dining terrace, to see if Jennifer had finished eating. I decided not to. Lucrezia might see me.

I slowly set the picture back on the dresser. Again and again I paced from the photograph to the door and back. Each time I stared at my picture I thought about how Jennifer prided herself on never packing anything unnecessary. She made fun of my family, especially my mother, for all the luggage we brought, what Jennifer called "all that useless rubbish."

No one besides me was in the photograph. It was the kind of memento married people keep of their spouses, not a tattered snapshot used as a bookmark or something, but framed in silver. It had been brought all the way from England to Italy by a person who only carried one change of clothes, two books, no makeup, and one pair of sandals.

Someone was bouncing a ball in the alley below the window. I heard shouts from the beach. The bus pulled up, then pulled out again. I could tell it was heading toward Portofino because the driver sounded the horn.

Then the door opened and Jennifer walked in from the bright sunlit hall. I held my breath. She closed the door behind her.

Before her eyes adjusted to the shade, I said, "Hi, Jennifer."

She gave a start. *"You bloody swine!"* she shouted.

"Sorry, did I make you jump?"

"Yes, you did!"

"Are you glad to see me?"

"Not particularly."

"How long have you been here?"

"About ten seconds, I should say."

"You know what I mean."

"We arrived last week."

What was so strange was how our meeting turned out exactly like my story. I had rehearsed each word. I had repeated our conversation many times under the hedge, in my bed, up in the forest, even walking to Farmer Ruchet's. Then I spoiled it all. I burst into tears and threw my arms around Jennifer's neck.

I cried harder than I ever had, except for when Dad had gone crazy and whipped himself to "take my punishment" after I got caught with Eva the maid at Hotel Riffelberg.

At first Jennifer stood still. Then she slowly put her arms around me. Her bare arms were warm.

When I stopped sobbing Jennifer took a step back and cocked her head slightly to one side. She smiled. "Well, I must say that I thought you'd be *pleased* to see me. If the very sight of me produces a flood of tears, I expect this holiday will be rather tedious!"

I wiped my eyes. I was only a little embarrassed. After all, Jennifer had seen me cry when we were little. I had seen her cry just a few years before when she cut her foot.

Jennifer reached out and took my hand. "Calvin, has something dreadful happened?"

I was about to answer but changed my mind. I decided I'd try to get the story back on track. I pulled her toward me by her shoulders and kissed her. She lifted her face to mine and kissed me back. Then she surprised me, or rather didn't, because it was the way it was supposed to be, the way I had imagined it. She pushed me back onto her bed. I fell on the plain gray blanket and Jennifer fell on top of me and pressed her long slender body down on mine. I breathed her in and she kissed me and I put my arms around her as she pushed against me.

We lay kissing and rubbing our bodies against each other through our clothes, and instead of Jennifer ending it, when my hands found her breasts, she arched her back so I could touch her.

Jennifer was breathing as hard as I was. The straps of her dress were slipping. Only one button separated me from the fulfillment of my prophesy. I undid the button. The top of her white-and-blue flower print dress opened. It was predestined. I felt like I was drowning.

I fainted, died, exploded, and Jennifer did, too. I heard her gasp.

Afterward Jennifer didn't jump off of me the way she always did in my story. Instead she lay on me, held me. Then she slowly sat up, turned, and said, "There! I expect you're feeling better now." She smiled.

I lay quietly. I was trying to make up my mind whether or not to start explaining everything. Jennifer must have known what I was thinking.

"Calvin, there's no need. Your father called the *pensione* late last night and asked for Daddy. He told Daddy you'd done a bunk, might be on your way here, said if you turned up that Daddy should ring him. Daddy says your father was weeping like a child, that he was quite out of control." Jennifer squeezed my hand and stood. "Daddy says your father told him to tell you that he's sorry, wants to be forgiven or something, or that he forgives you. I'm not sure which." Jennifer gave my knee a gentle pat. "Seems that the Becker tribe's in a bit of a palaver, eh?"

I nodded but didn't know what to say. So I stared at the light reflected off the water as it shimmered on the cracked plaster ceiling. Then I noticed how wet and clammy my new swimming trunks were. I sat up and glanced down at the spreading stain. Jennifer laughed.

"Are we having little troubles?"

I avoided her look and walked to the shower, took off my T-shirt, stepped in with my trunks on, turned the hot tap, and let lukewarm water play over me. Jennifer stood in the doorway.

I felt empty, not sad, just used up. Of one thing I was sure. It didn't matter whether Jennifer had Dad's message right or not, whether I was supposed to forgive Dad or he had forgiven me. Either way, I didn't care anymore. What Dad thought, or said, was beside the point. Jennifer was standing next to me. Dad seemed far away.

As I stepped out of the shower Jennifer handed me her towel.

"Calvin, I missed you."

I smiled and glanced through the bathroom door at my photograph.

"I know."

Jennifer followed my glance. When she looked back at me her face was flushed. She was blushing. She was so beautiful I forgot to use my towel. All I could do was to stand, dripping wet, and stare at her.

"Oh, do stop gaping at me and asking questions like some gormless twit!" Jennifer said.

"I didn't ask you anything!"

"Well, I jolly well want to ask *you* some things! For starters, what's that filthy, great sticky plaster doing all over your face?"

"It's a long story." I sighed.

"You can tell me all about it in a bit."

Jennifer spun on her heel, took three strides across her room, and flung open the door to the hall. On the threshold she turned, hand on hip. "Well? Are you coming or not?"

I nodded and hurriedly used the towel. Jennifer marched down the passage to the top of the stairs that led to the lobby. I dropped the towel and ran to catch up.

As we stepped out of the *pensione* Jennifer grasped my hand and led me along the path to the beach. We passed a small orange tree in a huge terra-cotta pot, turned the corner, walked around the row of changing cabins, and stepped onto the hot sand.

"About the bandage . . ." I began.

Jennifer gave my hand an impatient tug. "Not now, laddie. We've got bags of time. Tell me all about it while we're swimming to the point."